SILVER GAMES SERIES

RECKONINGS

JESS STEVENS

Reckonings (Silver Games Book 2) — 1st Ed.

The characters and events portrayed in this book are fictitious. Any similarity to real persons, living or dead, is coincidental and not intended by the author.

Book cover and design by Mayhem Cover Creations

Developmental Edits by The Blue Couch Edits

Line and Copy Edits by Editing4Indies

Additional edits by Lauren Joskowitz

ISBN: 979-8-9922688-3-6

AUTHOR'S NOTE & CONTENT WARNINGS

Well, hello, little Queens.

Before diving into *Reckonings*, I want to share a few things so we're all on the same page about the type of book you're currently holding.

Reckonings is a dark dystopian romantasy. Book one in the series, *Remnants*, was inspired by *The Princess Bride*, and you'll see threads of that theme continuing in book two, though *Reckonings* is a different type of dark book.

This book contains content that may be triggering for some readers and explores morally complex characters, relationships, and choices. If dark romance isn't for you, that's okay.

If you prefer to go in blind, skip ahead to Chapter One.

If you'd like to review content warnings, please read below.

Content warnings for *Reckonings* include:

- violence and murder
- torture and captivity
- drugging, needles, and addiction
- death
- sexually explicit content
- coercion and power imbalance
- morally gray relationships
- strong language

Now, if all that sounds good to you... turn the page.

CONTENTS

PART III
THE MATCH

To Megan, who was brave enough to
burn her world.

PART I

THE HAND

1

Lissa

Two years ago.

Dia threw open the door of my room, and I scrambled to stand, nearly falling from the velvet chair where I'd been curled reading. It was late in the night. I'd been about to go to sleep.

Why did everything bad always happen in the middle of the night?

Kenji met my gaze from where he stood guard at my door. He looked like he was trying to hold himself back from saying something. I gave an imperceptible headshake. It would only be worse if he got involved. Dia outranked him. He couldn't stop the snake-eyed man from entering. He couldn't object to anything that would happen next without severe consequences.

"What do you want?" I demanded, my silver sparking at my fingertips. It did that when my emotions were high. It always happened around Dia. He was the second-in-command at this compound. Stark against his skin, the bloodred King of Diamonds tattoo denoted his rank. While Gideon, the Ace and leader of this compound, was brutal in his stoicism, Dia was the storm. He was volatile and unpredictable in his brutality.

He eyed the electricity in my hands, but it didn't stop him from gripping my upper arm tightly. "You're being summoned."

That was all he said as he marched me down the hallway toward Gideon's wing of the mansion.

His calloused fingers dug into my bicep until I winced from the pain, and I fought to keep my silver contained. I'd always hated Dia the most out of the kings. His eyes were cruel. His face was hard. And his fists, more often than not, were bloody.

He'd dragged me from my rooms like this a few times before, and it always meant trouble. Gideon only bothered with me when he needed a personal blood bank, which was the last thing I wanted to be. His high assholeness could rot for all I cared.

Which was exactly what it seemed like he was doing when Dia marched me into Gideon's primary room. He practically dragged me past the white walls and contemporary furniture and into the ornate bathroom.

Gideon was slumped inside the expansive walk-in shower, framed only by panes of glass. A crimson streak swiped across one glass panel of the otherwise pristine space. He clenched his hand in a bloody fist by his side, eyes pressed closed, and jaw tight in a grimace. The dark blood pooled around the drain by his hip.

I tensed at the sight. It wasn't the first time I'd seen blood like this. Gideon and the Cards tended to find trouble or, rather, create the trouble. It always made my stomach roil. How many people had Gideon killed tonight?

Karadin, the only doctor on staff, knelt next to him, working with some pliers over the large, bloody wound in his shoulder. His black button-down was torn open, and intricate tattoos covered the impressive planes of his torso from what I could see through the gore. I'd seen hints of the designs beneath his tailored shirts, but to see the swirls of tribal ink scrawled across his broad chest, it was difficult not to get lost in the designs. They were like mazes meant to be traced with light fingers over his perfect body. Gideon was a sight to behold;

there was no denying that. He was the most attractive and the most terrifying man I'd ever seen.

Tonight, it wasn't the sight of his perfect features that made me gasp.

No, it was the bloody horror in front of me. Red blood. Lots of it. Gideon cracked an eye open at my intake. The glimmer of his depthless blue eyes met mine and held. I wanted to look away, told myself to look away, but I was caught. The tattoos and his perfect fucking chest forgotten. My breaths felt heavy and loud in my ears. It was as if I'd walked out to sea and allowed the waves to swallow me whole. I was drowning in his presence.

He had that effect, and it only made me hate him more.

Gideon hadn't become the leader of the most powerful gang in the city without a certain charisma. Yes, he was an arrogant asshole who would sooner push a Card from the cliffs than give anyone in his ranks a second chance. But there wasn't a Card in this compound who wouldn't kill to be him. And the women would kill for a piece of him.

I would rather see him dead.

He'd kidnapped me, dragged me against my will to this compound, and held me prisoner for the past three years. He'd left my best friend to die in the streets of the city. And he'd hoarded my silver blood for himself. In this city, silver meant power. Our blood was the currency with its medicinal properties and ability to grant strength and energy to those who drank it.

The plink of something hitting the shower tile snapped me back to the moment.

Karadin wiped her hands on the towel, staring down at the hunk of bloodied metal she'd pulled from his shoulder. A bullet.

"Well"—she stood—"you'll live to lead another day, Ace. The wound is superficial."

"It won't be a wound for long," Dia said, drawing attention to where we stood.

Gideon grinned lazily at his second. "Dia brought me a pretty little drink."

My lips curled in disgust. "I am not your fucking blood bag."

As soon as the words escaped my mouth, I realized my mistake. Dia grabbed me roughly by the collar of my dress. His fist curled. "Watch your mouth—"

Gideon held up a hand.

Dia practically spat with anger at my outburst, but he stopped his fist from swinging at the Ace's silent command. I swallowed down the obstinance and fear raging in me, curling my fingers against the silver sparking in my palms. My gaze snagged on a wide-eyed Karadin, who looked just as concerned by my sharp tongue. Gideon had men tied to the posts and whipped for less.

I could destroy this man with my silver, but I couldn't control it. I was just as likely to kill everyone in this room as I was to hurt Dia. I could never unleash myself like that. My life, instead, was a constant fight for control.

Despite his pain and the obvious bloodlust, Gideon was deadly calm as he told me, "You're whatever I want you to be, little Queen, and tonight it's my blood bag."

My teeth clenched as the silver continued sparking at my fingers.

"Leave us." Gideon sighed.

Dia looked at him like maybe he'd lost too much blood.

"Everyone out." Gideon's voice had more strength this time, and he pressed himself up, using the glass wall of the shower as leverage. His wound seeped more blood. "The little Queen stays."

Karadin looked like she might object—not for Gideon's protection, but for mine. Gideon spoke before she had the chance. "You too, Karadin. Preferably before I bleed out on this bathroom floor."

She looked from Gideon back to me, her nostrils flaring delicately. But she tilted her head in a small acquiescence and followed Dia from the room.

As soon as they were gone, Gideon slid back down to the shower floor. He cursed under his breath as he palmed at the wound with a towel, applying weak pressure.

I crossed my arms and stood my ground in the doorway of the bathroom. If he was going to hurt me, then at least I wouldn't be a willing victim. I would fight him in whatever small way I could, and I was fairly certain I would win in his current state.

"You can get my blood from the clinic. Karadin has plenty of vials stored."

Gideon tipped his head against the shower, giving me a bemused, dark look. His blue eyes sparked with a heat I was only just beginning to understand. "Your blood is far from the only thing I want, Lissa."

My pulse spiked. That statement shouldn't have been surprising, not with the way he'd been singling me out over the past few months. Still, to hear him voice his desire so blatantly had me retreating a step even as something dark wound deep in my belly.

Could I run?

In his current state, could I fight him and win?

My mouth had gone dry, and I realized I'd been panting for shallow breaths as I contemplated my next move. I swallowed, my lips pinching as my jaw hardened.

No, there was no running.

Dia and Gideon's guards would be just on the other side of the door.

Instead, I schooled my shoulders and faced him, covering the shock with the anger I'd worn like a mask for three years. "I think you've lost more blood than you realize."

"Come here," he said again. "I won't punish you for your mouth if you obey. Unless you'd like me to, that is."

Even slumped in the shower, Gideon was an imposing sight. I wasn't an idiot. He was a threat.

"Would you do that?" I dared ask. "Force yourself on me without permission?"

"I don't need to ask permission to take what is already mine. Now do as you're told."

"No."

I didn't know what gave me the strength to challenge him, to utter that word. Maybe it was all the blood leaking around him. Or perhaps it was a reckless part of me that craved the challenge. The rage I'd kept bottled for so long rose to the surface as if sensing the impending fight and demanding it. My skin tingled as if coming alive for the first time in years. And even in the fear of standing before the Ace, I felt a sudden thrill at that awakening. It urged me on.

So I took another step back. "No."

The smile he gave me was feral as his expression turned dark. "I was hoping you'd say that."

That fast, he was on me, yanking me into the shower and pressing my body flush against the tile. His body pinned me, his panting breaths hot as he dragged me to the floor. The blood from his shoulder smeared against my skin as he pressed into me, erasing any hint of space between our bodies. I cried out as he held me with his good arm.

My skin burned hot with my silver, but instead of letting me go, Gideon smiled down at me through the burn.

"The only way you'll ever have me is like this," I snarled, struggling against his hold. "I'll never stop fighting you."

The bullet hole in his arm must hurt like hell, and my silver was effectively singeing his skin, but still, his body pinned me, his hand curled lazily around my throat.

"Yield," he ordered, his voice full of dark amusement.

I fought him harder, gripping him until I could see the smoke from his skin.

His hand only tightened, cutting off my air.

I glared into his dark stare, struggling against his hold, wondering if he would wait until I was unconscious, then take my blood while I was passed out on the floor.

But no, Gideon liked the fight.

Without taking his gaze from mine or his grip from my neck, he withdrew a small knife from his back pocket and flicked it open. His thumb kneaded along my pulse, following the vein that raced with my frantic heartbeat. Even as I struggled to breathe, my pulse only kicked up harder at his touch.

My fight dulled as my vision blurred. Somehow, he remained focused on my gaze as he drew the knife along the side of my arm where I clutched his wrist. Was my silver still burning him? I couldn't tell amid the haze that had overtaken my senses. I didn't even feel the slice of his knife as he drew a line across my flesh.

But I felt it when his mouth touched my skin.

White-hot heat like the static of my own silver traveled through my veins, starting at the point where his mouth met my wrist. My back arched as he finally, finally released my neck to hold my arm against his mouth, and I sucked in the oxygen my body so desperately needed. The rush, paired with the way he licked along the cut, taking my silver, made my body sing with adrenaline.

Gideon groaned as the wound on his shoulder and the burns I'd given him began to knit themselves closed. His eyes flashed black as he looked up at me from where he was hunched over my arm, silently telling me he had no intention of letting me go.

Asshole.

Finally free from his grip around my neck, I did the only thing I could think to do. With my free hand, I dug my fingers into his shoulder, where I knew the bullet wound would still be tender.

He broke free of my wrist with a gasp.

His chest heaved. His eyes caught mine and held as we both struggled to catch our breath. I scrambled back against the wall, glaring daggers at him even as I felt the bruises along my throat beginning to heal, thanks to the silver in my veins.

I resisted the urge to touch the spot where his thumb had pressed harder and harder against my pulse. I didn't dare break eye contact to look at the door.

I was caged with the beast within the glass of the shower. My every sense was keenly aware of the danger. If anything, now that he was high on my silver with his wounds healing, it was only heightened. Would he drain me dry? Would he lose control and do something worse?

Gideon ran his tongue across his bottom lip, savoring the taste of my blood. I could see the rush of it glinting in his dark gaze.

His grin was feral.

And then he launched himself at me.

"More." Before I could register what he meant, his lips were moving against my mouth.

I cried out in shock, but he only pressed closer, his tongue sweeping into my mouth in rough strokes, just like he'd lapped at the cut on my wrist. He gripped the sides of my face, and I could feel the blood from his fingers smearing across my cheeks.

The gasp I tried to take as he melded against me turned into a strangled noise in my throat, and he swallowed it. He devoured me as if my kiss was just as addictive as my blood. Even as I scrambled to grip his fingers and pry his grasp from my face, he claimed me until I wasn't sure if I was pushing him away or trying to find purchase on anything that would keep me from sinking into this frenzy.

He was the enemy.

But wrapped in his grasp on the bathroom floor, as our mouths locked and our tongues battled, the hardened exterior I'd worked so hard to build and keep over the past three years faltered. There was a release in this physicality with him, one my body desperately craved. I would lose myself to him, which felt like an even more terrifying option than the moments before when I thought he might drain me dry.

So I did the only thing I could do.

I bit him.

Hard.

His blood coated my teeth. Iron filled my mouth. And finally, *finally* he released me.

As I gasped to catch my breath and wiped at the red blood streaked across my mouth, his deep and reverberating laughter echoed around the tiled room.

Gideon's body took up so much space, with one hand resting on the tile, his smile wicked, and his breath heaving.

"Bastard." I spat on the ground, the pink tinge of his blood mixing with my saliva. I didn't want to swallow it. Silvers didn't react the same to ingesting outside silver blood. It nullified our abilities instead of heightening them. It would make me sick if I wasn't careful.

Gideon continued to chuckle darkly, the cut along his lip already healing.

"You kissed me back." He grinned, licking at the blood on his lip in a suggestive gesture that had my scowl deepening as I glanced to the bathroom exit.

"Only to get my teeth into you." I felt feral as I sneered, my teeth and mouth still coated with his blood.

Could I make a run for it now before he caught me? Could I be that quick?

He rolled out his shoulder. The wound was stitching itself closed. "I need to shower."

I glanced from him to the door, then back again as he rose to his full height in front of me. My gaze settled on the unmistakable bulge that was now squarely at eye level. I pressed myself farther against the white tile even as my thighs clenched. My breath rattled in my chest as the air around us grew thick, almost as if he'd turned on the water and the steam was hot in my lungs.

He reached above where I was crouched and grabbed for the shower handle. But he didn't turn on the water.

Instead, he leaned his forehead against the wall, his other hand reaching down to twine into my hair, applying just enough pressure to force my head back, my gaze tracking up his large frame to meet his blue-black eyes.

"You'd let me, wouldn't you?" he asked.

Words evaporated from my brain, and his wicked smile told me he loved watching it happen.

He groaned, and the hand on the faucet became a fist, his hips drawing tight just inches from my chin.

"Get out, Lissa." His words were clipped with barely held restraint.

The beast lurked just beneath, and I watched his irises bleed to black.

I scrambled from his hold, crawled from beneath his grip, tripping as I hurried to right myself and run from the room.

And then I sprinted out of the bathroom and through his

bedroom to his door, which was just in front of me. My fingers splayed toward the handle. My guards would be just on the other side. Kenji and Laykin would be waiting for me, and I could forget this mad night ever happened.

I hated him. I hated Gideon now more than ever. It was worse than the way he'd kissed me by force. It was the fact that he'd forced his way into my mind, too. He'd twisted my hate into something fiery and raw that itched to escape from beneath my skin.

I had to get out of this room.

But a hand fisted into my hair, pulling me back into a hard chest as a sharp cry broke from my throat just as an arm came around to press against my windpipe.

Gideon inhaled along the side of my throat. His masculine heat aligned along every curve of my body as he breathed me in.

"I lied." His voice was a low purr in my ear.

"When— when you told me to get out?" My breath stuttered as adrenaline coursed through my veins. Yet my silver was quiet. It wasn't fear or anger I felt, but something primal that quieted my emotions and took control of my body.

"No." Gideon trailed his nose into my hair, his grip tightening. "No, I was lying to myself when I thought I could let you leave. Because you're mine. And even if you walk out that door, I'll still own every piece of you. And what good would it do to deny it? I'm not a man who denies himself, Lissa. I'm a man who takes. It's instinct. You run, and I'll catch you."

"I know," I breathed, wetness beginning to coat my thighs at his feral words.

As if sensing it, his hand slipped from my neck and down the length of my body. I shuddered as he reached the waistband of my pants, his hand slipping underneath the fabric, pushing aside my panties.

I'd never been touched like this.

My eyes flew open.

I hadn't even realized they'd closed.

I opened my mouth to object, to stop this. Gideon was the last person I should be allowing to touch me. Gideon was my enemy. Gideon's father had my mother killed. Gideon forced me to be at this compound. Gideon—

His fingers slipped inside me, and I groaned. My head pitched forward as he kept me tightly in his grasp. My hips jerked at the feel of him sinking deeper. First one finger, then two. My soaked core easily adjusted to him claiming me.

His thumb ran along my clit, holding pressure at just the right angle until I was choking on air, gasping and writhing in his grasp. His other hand had a tight hold of my hair, which kept me upright as his fingers traced from my clit to my entrance, dipping inside me.

I'd touched myself. Of course I had. I was a twenty-one-year-old woman. I'd explored my body and given myself orgasms. I'd imagined what it would feel like to have a man sliding inside me.

But I never imagined this. I never imagined I'd feel so consumed, so owned, and so cherished all while his fingers worked deeply inside me, stroking and curving in a way that had my hips writhing of their own accord.

"Gideon—" As soon as my mouth opened on his name, the fingers of his other hand slipped into my mouth, hooking on my bottom lip as I cried out and rode against his hand.

"Suck," he ordered into my ear.

And I did. I hollowed my cheeks and licked at his fingers as he once again drew his thumb along my clit, applying circular pressure that had me unraveling around him.

I screamed, the sound muffled by his fingers in my mouth, as the orgasm ripped through me. It felt like my body splintered into a thousand tiny pieces, as if my silver would erupt and burn the world. And it felt so good that I didn't care.

Gideon kept me like that, draining every bit of pleasure from my body until I sagged in his grasp, two fingers still buried inside my core with two more hooked around my bottom lip.

The fog lifted.

I turned my head from his grasp, still trying to catch my breath.

The guilt settled in my belly now that the pleasure had been sated.

"Let me go," I breathed.

To my surprise, he did.

I stumbled away from him, feeling off balance, and braced myself against the door.

But nothing had been burned by my silver.

Gideon himself hadn't been burned, either. The only tear in his shirt was the one from the now-healed bullet wound.

I felt disappointed to find him unscathed when I was unraveling beneath him. I wanted to hurt him for making me feel this way, for confusing what I knew to be true in my heart.

Gideon was my enemy.

My enemy.

He brought his fingers—the ones that had just been buried inside me—to his mouth, licking them clean.

"You taste just as delicious as your blood." He grinned.

"I'm leaving," I said, surprised I kept the tremor from my voice.

His smile grew. "You should, little Queen. Because now that I've had a taste, I think you've made me an addict. And I love the thrill of the hunt."

2

Lissa

The day after the shower incident, Gideon hardly spared me a glance as he marched around the mansion in his black boots. Dia was at his heels, and the other Kings were close behind. They made a formidable bunch, the five of them. They looked like warrior pirates with their black ensembles, open shirts, and guns holstered at their waists or across their backs. I was loath to admit that it did strange things to my insides, reminded me of the way he'd claimed me the night before.

"Gideon," Enver cooed, calling to him from across the hall. "It's market day. Do you need anything, Ace?"

I rolled my eyes and slunk down in my seat.

Fucking Enver.

Ooh, it's market day.

I remembered the smell of Madam Cartenoth's chamomile tea, and a shot of longing stabbed me deep within my belly. I'd only been allowed out once in the three years I'd been here. Only once to go back to the loft Tayna and I had called home. Once to rescue the books and the stuffed turtle from their dusty grave. Because that was what the space had become. A tomb of memories with no life left to give.

Tayna was gone.

"You gonna eat that?" Kenji eyed the bacon on my plate.

I shoved it forward, standing from the table as my chair screeched back. "No." I marched toward the hallway, suddenly needing some air. I needed to breathe.

Judging by the sound of the chairs screeching behind me, Laykin and Kenji had dashed to follow. They were new to guarding me. Just a few weeks earlier, some douchebag had gotten handsy with me in the yard. My guards had failed to stop him. They'd laughed, actually, as the guy handled my ass and jeered, "It might be worth it to be singed by you."

While my guards had laughed, I'd turned and shoved the guy before I'd even realized silver was sparking at my fingers. He'd grabbed me hard enough to leave a red mark in the shape of his fingers on my behind. It had faded after only a few minutes thanks to my silver. The burn marks I'd left on his chest? Well, those had scarred even after the help of silver. I'd seen the marks as Gideon had him stripped, beaten, and thrown out of the compound.

Gideon had watched me while Dia did the dirty work.

I'd flinched but hadn't objected.

Maybe that made me a bad person for not asking for mercy on his behalf. Gideon was not a man of mercy, and my begging meant nothing to him. Really, the man was lucky Gideon hadn't just thrown him from the cliffs.

The man hadn't screamed or begged, either, and the waves had swallowed the sounds of Dia's fists hitting his flesh again and again.

But the waves were a quiet lull today as I made my way outside. I needed some air. I needed to release this pent-up silver. I needed to forget about the mind-altering orgasm Gideon gave me in his bedroom.

So I headed to the edge of the cliffs behind the clinic, where a break in the rocks led to a pathway down to the sea.

"Stay here," I told Laykin and Kenji before beginning the descent.

"Lissa." My name was a low objection from Laykin. He was the stonier of the two, the rule follower.

"I'm allowed to go by myself." I didn't slow my steps. "I need to release some of my silver. Otherwise, it gets too pent up and volatile, so it's okay for me to go to the cove alone. Ask Gideon if you don't believe me, but don't come down unless you want to feel my silver for yourself."

That had him pausing, though his nostrils flared, and he looked over his shoulder back at the mansion like he just might go looking for Gideon.

Kenji held an arm across Laykin's chest, stopping him from taking another step. "Just be careful walking down the rocks. Those slippers you're wearing aren't exactly made for hiking."

No, they were made for pampered prisoners.

But I kept that snipe to myself as I made my way down to the ocean.

It was a beautiful space with cliffs on either side and dark sand. The waves stretched out against the morning to caress along the beach.

I left my shoes and my Queen's cloak near the rocks and sank my feet into the earth. The cool sand cocooned around my toes.

The waves in front of me weren't blue like the oceans I'd read about in my books. No, here, the ocean was a slate gray, and it glittered against the sun like the silver at my fingertips. I sank to my knees at the place where the water met the sand, not caring that the bottom of my dress would be soaked. I relished the cold. It helped dull the fire in my veins as I let go of the hold on my silver.

It flowed from my fingers into the sea. My silver was a fissure through the water, cutting in tendrils until it finally dissipated in the depths beyond.

I stayed like that for minutes, maybe longer. This release was my silent meditation. It was one of the only moments of peace I found in this place. The silver trailed from my fingers, and the waves lapped at my knees, lulling me deeper and deeper into the sand.

I stayed like that until the sun was hot on my face, and my skin felt rough from the salty wind. Only then did I finally pull myself to stand.

It wasn't until I turned around that I realized I wasn't alone in the cove.

"What are you doing?" I snapped, my words clipped but mostly from shock and my peace being so abruptly interrupted.

Gideon pressed up from where he'd been leaning against the rocks, watching me. He was a dark god, his nearly black hair swept across his face, and his midnight-blue gaze met mine. "You and I have some unfinished business, don't you think?"

And maybe that was exactly what I expected him to say. Hadn't this always been where his dark looks, crude words, and rough touches had been leading? I forced away the memories of his fingers buried deep inside me as I shook with pleasure and instead looked over my shoulder to the rocks behind me.

When my gaze met Gideon's again, his eyes lit with the game. "I told you I love the chase."

I stared back, running my tongue along the back of my teeth. There was a challenge in his words, a dare. He wanted me to run. He expected it.

He let me have the moment. His arms crossed over his broad chest as he watched me in a way that told me he liked the thoughts flickering over my face. And that desire in his eyes had my body suddenly warming. This time, it was decidedly not from the sun.

"Fuck you," I spat.

And I ran.

My sprint toward the rocks was an invitation, not an objection. We both knew it. Gideon was a tyrant, but he still operated within his own fucked-up moral code. He liked the game. And he liked it best when I was playing.

It was hard to keep telling myself that I didn't like playing, too.

But I wasn't doing this because I wanted Gideon to fuck me. Well, not entirely at least. I was doing it because in these moments, when my adrenaline spiked, my heartbeat pounded, and my breath came erratically, I felt alive for the first time in nearly three years.

I made it to the rocks, climbing over the first few before he caught me around the waist. My hands slid against the slick surface of the smooth boulder.

"That wasn't hard at all," he mused against my ear, his hips pressing into my backside to pin me flush with the surface.

I struggled against him, letting out a feral cry of frustration as he held me, feet braced in the sand as I flailed.

My silver was weak and depleted, my reserves floating away on the ocean waves, but I still singed his skin as my fingers worked to pry free from his grasp. He just laughed, his chest rumbling against my back as he pinched my nipple until my frustrated protests turned into a sudden exhale of heat.

Did it have to feel so damn good when he touched me?

My head fell back against his shoulder as he continued his kneading and pinching until my hips were rolling, not to get away but needing more of him. I could feel him hard against my backside before he was pressing me away, just enough to fish for the hem of my dress.

It was enough space to clear my head.

Fuck, this was happening.

The panic replaced the lust.

The urge to get away spurred in my gut.

And I kneed him, squarely in the balls.

His back rounded with the pain, and he braced himself against the rock as I scrambled from his hold and sprinted to the trail leading back up to the compound.

His words carried over the waves. "That was a mistake, little Queen."

But I was running, leaving my shoes and my Queen's cloak behind on the rock cliffs. My feet cut against the stone as I began to climb the steps, but I didn't stop. They would heal. And I relished the pain. It made me see more clearly and remember why this was a bad idea.

Gideon could have any woman at this compound he wanted. Hell, I was sure he'd had plenty of them before. The way Enver fell all over him, she would absolutely suck him off whenever he asked. And so many of the Queens were the same. So many were willing. Gideon could have them. He could have them, but he couldn't have me. Even if we had sex, even if he claimed my body, he would never have my heart. My heart belonged to Tayna and to my mother and to the Silvers, who were kept prisoner by the gangs without a choice and without options.

The physical thing happening between Gideon and me was just that. It was a release, but that was all it would ever be. He was my enemy. Sex wouldn't keep him from being my enemy. I hated him. And no matter how many ecstasy-filled orgasms he gave my body, my heart would never be his.

By the time I reached the top of the cliff, I was panting heavily. My chest burned from the exertion, and my feet were smeared with my chrome blood from nicks and scrapes along the rocks. They itched as they stitched themselves closed once I reached the grass.

It was the second wind I so desperately needed. Because, while Gideon hadn't caught me yet, he was close on my heels. I didn't dare look over my shoulder. I wouldn't do anything that could slow me down. But I could feel him at my back.

I didn't spare so much as a glance at Kenji and Laykin as I sprinted past them, heading around the clinic.

I wasn't sure where, exactly, I would run. I couldn't run inside the mansion. That would be like asking to get caught. There were too many people, too many obstacles to give myself the head start I needed to hide.

But maybe I could find a place on the grounds. Behind the mansion, past the pool, was a small clearing of trees. Maybe I could make it to those. Maybe I could—

Thick arms closed around my torso, and the next thing I knew, I was rolling, tucked tightly against a sturdy, large frame. We skidded to a halt in the dirt. And when I finally opened my eyes, all I could see was the cliff's edge.

We had stopped just before the drop.

I screamed.

But Gideon only held me tighter.

"Stop struggling, or you'll send us over the edge, little Queen. And I'd like to fuck you before I meet my maker."

That had me freezing, but only long enough for him to pull me to my feet and walk me a few paces away from the cliffs. Then I pushed at him, my silver making the blows sting and burn. But he held me tight. This time, his grip didn't waver as he hauled me into his arms and threw me over one of his shoulders.

"You're a fighter." He chuckled. "I knew you would be." I screeched at being handled so rudely and pounded mercilessly against his backside. "But now it's time for me to claim my prize."

3

Lissa

Gideon carried me like that to his rooms, kicking and screaming the entire way, even as half the compound watched me raging. I didn't care. Let them see. Let them see their hero of an Ace manhandling me. Not that he seemed inclined to care, either. He just ordered his guards not to disturb us before slamming the door behind him.

But instead of throwing me on the bed and ripping off my dress, he took me into the bathroom, setting me on the sink before stripping out of his shirt and running the water. My mouth went dry at the planes of his tanned skin and broad shoulders, the tattoos stretched across his chest and back. He was a haunted masterpiece made man. There was no trace of the injuries from last night, just the dark god who'd come to claim me.

"What are you doing?" I asked tentatively, watching him stalk from the shower to the rack, pulling down towels and laying them out.

"Would you rather I fucked you dirty and bloody?" he asked. His expression was dark from the chase, but a glimmer of blue in his eyes told me I hadn't lost him entirely to the feral darkness. Not yet.

He tested the water's temperature and, seeming satisfied, turned back to me. "Come here."

I thought about refusing, but he quirked a brow as if to remind me the dirty and bloody fucking option was still on the table, so I slid from the countertop and found myself suddenly shy as I approached him.

I considered running again, but well, I'd seen how well that worked last night. And all thoughts of escaping slipped from my mind as he caught my chin with his hand, tilting it up to study me. Instead, I had the urge to trace my fingers along the stubble of his jaw. I could do that. And then sink my teeth into his shoulder.

It would serve him right.

But his hands fisted the material of my dress at my waist, sliding it up and up and up until I lifted my arms, and the steam of the shower wafted around my bare skin.

I froze then.

Gideon growled at the sight of me bare in front of him. It was the first time a man had seen me like this, entirely exposed for his feasting eyes. It was overwhelming and thrilling and somehow satisfied the need deep in my belly to still make him pay. There was a control in the way he watched me that felt good.

He kept his gaze on my face as he hooked his fingers around my underwear and slid them down until he kneeled in front of me. The cotton panties pooled around my ankles, and his face was at eye level with my belly button... and much more intimate parts of me.

"Step out of them and open your legs," he said, breathing me in as if intoxicated.

I swallowed, hesitating.

"Do it, Lissa," he said, his voice edged with something darker.

His words spurred me to obey, first one foot and then the other.

Gideon tossed the panties aside before spreading my folds with his fingers, sliding along the wetness he found waiting for him.

"Did our game turn you on too, then?" he asked.

My cheeks flamed with my obvious need, and I moved to push him away. Before I could, he grabbed my thighs, pressing his tongue against my very center. The hand that I'd laced into his hair to push him away ended up twisting in the thick strands for purchase as he sucked hard.

"You are mine," he said, low and gruff, between strokes of his tongue. "Your blood. Your body. Your pussy. It's mine."

I noticed he didn't insist on my heart too, so I let go. I gave in to the pleasure and the sensations and the moment as he devoured me until I unraveled, bucking against his mouth as he licked at every bit of pleasure pulsing from my core.

He didn't bother to wipe his mouth as he stood and pulled me into the shower. His face was slick with my wetness, and his eyes shone blue.

As soon as we were under the spray of the shower, he was on me, kissing me. His tongue delved deep into my mouth as his hands ran over the length of my torso. I didn't have much experience with kissing. The kiss with Tayna in our loft had been sweet and tender. This, this was something entirely different. This was primal and insatiable. My back pressed into the cool tile, and I groaned as the hot and cold sensations peppered goose bumps across my skin.

It felt *so* good. Too good to object. My brain screamed at me to object, but not because I didn't want this. And I forgot at that moment why I didn't want this. Gideon wasn't responsible for my mother's death. That was his father's doing. And Gideon wasn't responsible for Tayna's death. That day in the market street was on me.

I faltered in the kiss, turning my head as I choked on my sudden grief.

Gideon caught my chin, his hips pinning me against the shower wall as the water cascaded between our bodies, sliding over my chest to where my body met his. I could feel his thick length growing against my belly even though he'd worn his pants under the spray.

"Give it all to me, little Queen," he said against my lips. "Give it to me. I'll take your anger and your pain and your grief and that beautiful sadness in your silver eyes. I'll take it all. And then I'll take your pleasure, too."

"I'll never stop hating you," I said earnestly, my voice echoing against the walls of the expansive shower.

"It's mine," he breathed. "Your hate is mine."

I swallowed.

"Let me have it, Lissa." His tone was a demand, but his blue irises were earnest. His hand came up to fist next to my head as he held a tight leash on his desire. "Give in to me. I've waited long enough."

And so I did, my mouth crashing into his in a clashing that was as much a duel as it was desire. Fuck him for making me want him so desperately. He groaned as I bit his lip the way he'd bitten mine last night. The anger felt just as good as the desire.

"That's right, baby," he said, rolling his hips into my bare, exposed heat.

I scrambled to pull his belt free from his waist. I needed to feel his skin against me.

And I was choosing this. This was my retribution. This was my restitution. This was my revenge. If he wanted my hate, he could have it in spades.

My silver flickered at my fingers as I fumbled with the buttons of his jeans, and he cursed.

"Watch—" He grabbed my wrists in one hand, and I glared up at him. "Those fingers."

"Oh, suddenly you can't handle my heat?"

He laughed, pinning my wrists above my head as he took care of the rest of the buttons himself.

"I'll gladly burn for you," he growled. "But not before I've been buried inside you."

And with that, he pulled me from the shower, not even bothering to grab towels before he led me into the bedroom.

It occurred to me then that this was truly happening as Gideon stripped off his soaking pants and stood to his full height in all of his naked glory. His thick cock was so hard it nearly hit his belly button.

I'd seen a cock before. Sure. I mean, I had, right?

I could remember nothing but the sight of the man in front of me.

Maybe I'd seen a naked man before, but I'd never seen anyone with a body like Gideon. He was a prowling predator of the night made flesh. His tanned skin was corded with muscle, and black tattoos traced his skin, with a peppering of hair down his perfectly sculpted chest. I traced the V-shape of his hips before lingering on the length of him, unable to hide my interest in every magnificent part of him.

And he was mine.

For tonight, as much as I was his, he was mine.

And so I stepped into him. I let my breasts caress his ribs as I fisted a handful of his cock between my fingers. He lurched in surprise as a groan slipped from his lips.

I was wet from way more than just the shower, and I stood on my tiptoes, wrapping my arms around his neck. I dragged his cock from my belly button down to my center, rubbing myself against him. The friction was delicious against my swollen clit, and he greedily found the rhythm set by my hips, sliding his length along my folds until I was gripping him to stay upright.

His back arched. "I'm trying to take my time with you."

"Don't take your time." I was surprised to find my voice didn't sound like my own. It was a breathy, desperate thing as my hips jerked greedily against him.

"Fuck, Lissa." He shoved me then, and the sudden free fall had me reeling.

But I hit the mattress.

"You asshole." I scrambled to sit up on my elbows, but Gideon pounced on top of me, his mouth claiming mine.

"Are you ready?" he asked between kisses.

"I—"

He positioned himself at my entrance, and my head kicked back at the sensation of him settling between my legs. Even that felt incredible. Everything was heightened and too sensitive. He would make me come again. I knew it.

"Do it," I said.

He didn't pause any longer.

Gideon pressed inside me, slow inch by slow inch. His mouth

captured mine, swallowing my choked cries, tasting them with his tongue as he worked his sizable cock into me.

The feel of him pressing into the deepest part of me burned into my belly. I almost asked him to stop. Was it supposed to hurt like this? I'd heard the Queens whispering about sex. I'd heard them talk about how good it was, how the pain only made the pleasure that much sweeter. And I understood. As much as it hurt, I wanted this pain.

He broke the kiss, rocking his forehead against mine, my hairline already slick with sweat as I panted around the stretch, the utter fullness of him.

"Fuck." It was a low moan as he rocked himself even deeper into me. "It's hard to take you slowly, little Queen."

"I don't want slow." I gritted out the words, reaching around our connected bodies to drive my nails into his lower back, forcing him closer.

His body jerked and, with it, his cock inside me. I arched against the sting, but the pain was acceptable. The pain made it okay that there was also so, *so* much pleasure.

My movement was his undoing.

His hips slammed into mine, breaking through the barrier of my virginity, his cock driving to the hilt. My back arched as I scrambled to grip his neck, to keep hold of myself. The sensation was overwhelming. The pain was sharp in a way that had tears leaking from my eyes. But I wasn't just crying from the sting of losing my innocence. There was a deeper loss, too. This was supposed to be Tayna. Tayna should have been my first.

But he was gone.

He was dead.

And the pain that hit my heart at that moment was not the pain I craved, but Gideon trailed soft kisses along my cheeks, smearing the tears on my face.

I tried to push him away. I didn't want him gentle. I wanted him to distract me from my grief and my anger. I wanted him to make me forget, and when he was gentle, I couldn't bear it. The grief was the worst pain I knew, and I needed Gideon to take it away with that delicious kind of pain that edged with pleasure. I needed him to force me to forget in the way only he could.

He held himself unmoving inside me, his hips pinning mine to the bed.

"Fuck me," I demanded.

His answering chuckle was deep and low, rumbling against where my hardened nipples were pressed into his chest. He snaked one of his large hands around my neck, not enough to cut off my air but enough that I felt the pressure as he lifted his head.

His thumb caressed along the line of my jaw as his midnight-blue eyes found mine.

I looked away, unable to turn my head with his grip on my neck, but I shifted my eyes to the window. The waves crashed in the distance. The sea spray misted against the oncoming light of the morning.

His grip on my neck tightened and, when I looked back at him, his gaze had darkened.

"You're with me," he said, rolling his hips just enough that I gasped. It was no longer from pain. I found myself searching for that push and pull. Like the waves outside, my body ached for the swell.

"Gideon—" His name was a hoarse plea against the grip on my neck.

"That's right, baby." He rolled his hips again. "You're mine. However I want you." He did it again, the pleasure of it making me shudder against him with need. "And right now, it's deep and slow. I'm going to stay this deep inside you until you are wild beneath me, begging for release like one of those silver addicts on the streets. My little silver whore. Then, and only then, will I truly fuck you."

Silver sparked at my fingers, and I moved to slap him, but he moved quicker, releasing my neck to pin my arms above my head.

I gasped at the rush of oxygen filling my lungs so much so that the world blurred out of focus for a moment. The only thing I knew was the feel of his body, his thick cock pistoning inside me in small movements that weren't enough.

I needed more.

"There she is," Gideon said, watching me as I writhed beneath him. He allowed me to rub myself along his length, the press of his hips against my clit while he was thrust to the hilt had my body spasming with need.

"Please fuck me." I gasped as his mouth claimed mine again. His tongue pressed past my lips, sweeping in to taste me. He consumed me, body and soul. He sank his teeth into my lower lip, drawing blood, licking the wound as he continued his slow, torturous rhythm. I tasted my silver, sharp and metallic as he sucked until the wound healed.

"Gideon!"

I felt his lips turn up in a grin against where he was kissing my mouth.

"You want it rough, little Queen?" His breath caressed along my cheek.

I nodded, swallowing against the torturous pleasure of his body. I was closer to the edge than I wanted to admit, his body driving me mad with delicious pleasure. The pain was gone, replaced with wet heat and unbearable need.

"Get on your hands and knees," he ordered. I scrambled to comply, feeling a hollow emptiness in the pit of my stomach as he withdrew from me and flipped me onto my stomach. Ass in the air, I groaned as he sank back into me. The new angle had me squirming my hips.

But then he did as I asked.

He fucked me.

He drove his hips in and out of my soaked core. The slapping of our bodies echoed around the room, and I screamed into the mattress.

"You can take it," Gideon said, fisting my hair and pulling me to my knees. My hands found purchase on the wall in front of me as he continued a quick rhythm in and out of my body.

"Oh god," I moaned as he slid a hand to my clit and began working me in time with the strokes of his hips.

My body was pulsing and sweating. I felt out of control as the pleasure built and built until I was falling, my orgasm crashing into me in wave after wave. And as I rode the pleasure, Gideon sank his teeth into the side of my neck.

I screamed in surprise, my body jerking with another wave. He laughed against my neck as he licked at the wound he'd created. My neck was sticky with my blood. His cock jerked inside me as his tongue lapped at me. His strokes slowed until the wound closed.

He whispered, "Again."

And delivered.

By the time we'd finished the second round, I was boneless and surprised when Gideon pressed up from the bed.

He walked naked to the door that connected his room to his office, and I had the sudden realization I was being dismissed. He'd gotten what he wanted. He had me in his bed. And now I was worthless to him.

Humiliation washed over me as I scrambled to sit up, unable to move for a moment as the waves of shock left me feeling like the biggest fool. Of course Gideon wasn't interested in a relationship with me. He'd even said he liked the chase. Now that he'd caught me, the thrill had dulled.

It was better this way. I was a fool for agreeing to be in his bed in the first place. There was no denying I was attracted to the man. Even if I were blind, he exuded a dark sexuality that made my body respond. It was in the way my body seemed to heighten when he was around, in the way he spoke with that low lilt, and in the way he touched me with those confident fingers. All of it had dragged me under some intoxicating spell that was now breaking as he left the room.

I scrambled from the bed, pulling the sheet with me to shield my body, not wasting time to find my dress somewhere in the room. My cheeks flamed at the idea of going back to my room in just this sheet. I wouldn't be able to look Kenji and Laykin in the eyes, knowing I'd been so thoroughly played. But, well, better than staying here and making even more of a fool of myself.

As I was about halfway across the room, with the sheet hugged tightly to my chest, I felt it.

I felt *him*.

His larger-than-life presence invaded the room, making the hair on my neck stand on end.

"Leaving like that?" His voice was dangerous, more a growl than a sentence.

I whirled to find him in the doorway. He held a box in his hand. It was a rectangular shape with rounded edges, covered in navy velvet that glimmered in the room's white light.

He leaned back against the doorframe, still naked and fucking glorious.

Yes, if I were blind, I'd still be attracted to Gideon. But the sight of him? Damn if it wasn't enough to make my body feel boneless and wanting.

I needed to get a hold of myself.

"You left first," I snapped.

His dark eyes glimmered as I saw the rings of blue that matched the navy of the box. If they refracted the light in just the right way, they were like glittering stones of sapphire.

"I was just going to my office, little Queen. I have something for you." He lifted the box just slightly in offering.

"You—" I was confused. Something for me?

I took a step back, my gut telling me I probably wouldn't like it all that much.

"Were you running from me again?" His eyes tracked over my body to the white sheet I had clutched to my chest. And then he was approaching me, his hand coming around to pull at the bedding draped around my frame. "There's nowhere you can run," he said near my lips. "I thought we already sorted that matter. But if you want to run again..."

I shook my head. "No more running. I think I'll burn you with my silver instead."

The threat was more a reminder for me, a reminder that I couldn't trust anything about this man. This had been about sex. I'd let him catch me for the sake of the release. This wasn't meant to be intimate, and it certainly wasn't supposed to turn into him giving me presents.

I realized, maybe, as much as it hurt, that the reality where he stalked into his office and left me alone to deal with the rejection might have ultimately been the kinder option.

Now, with Gideon standing in front of me, I felt confused. The pull of my body toward his warred with the signals from my brain, reminding me that this man was my enemy. This man had kidnapped me and kept me captive for three years. This man forced me to give him my silver. He was a tyrant who ruled this city while others suffered.

He tugged at the sheet, but I held fast.

"You thought I was leaving you here?" He kept the box in his hand but traced his knuckles along my jaw, curling over my bottom lip in a gentle caress as he guided my mouth closer to his until our breaths danced.

He tugged at the sheet again.

I swallowed roughly as I fought the urge to lean into him.

"Let go," he murmured.

"No," I breathed back.

"Yes." This time, he pulled roughly enough that I gasped at the force of the fabric jerking from my fingers, and then the sheet was pooling at my feet. Every inch of my skin was exposed to Gideon's lingering gaze as he leaned back to take me in.

"You're perfect." He turned me to face the full-length mirror in the corner of the room, and I took in the body of the woman I had become. The smooth, supple lines of my curves admittedly looked good framed against his broad, tattooed chest. He ran a hand along my shoulder, trailing light kisses along my neck, making goose bumps rise along my skin. "But something's missing."

Again, I felt my defenses snap up. "Fu—"

But he popped open the box, and a moment later, he draped a silver chain across my neck. As he swept my hair to the side to snap the clasp in place, I realized it wasn't a silver chain at all, but a row of glittering, pristine diamonds set so closely together that the metal was barely visible.

I'd never seen anything like it.

Jewelry was a rarity in the city. Not many had spare time to craft such fineries. But a necklace like this? I knew it must be old. This many diamonds stacked one after the other until they formed an entire chain must have come from well before the war.

"Do you like it?" he asked, his fingers caressing my skin where the necklace grazed my collarbone. I failed at resisting the impulse to sink into his touch. He felt too good against my bare skin, warm and hard.

But I watched him warily in the reflection of the mirror as I fingered the necklace. "Is this some kind of territorial male bullshit to claim me?"

I liked the necklace. I wouldn't admit it out loud to him, but it was a beautiful, unique piece that made me feel both feminine and strong wearing it. But if this was some power move, then I'd rip it from my neck immediately.

He smirked, and the way he held my stare told me this wasn't another game. He was dead serious as he said, "I don't need to claim you. You were already born to be mine."

PART II

THE SET

4

Lissa

Present

Sometimes the only way to begin anew is to completely burn the old.

And I desperately wanted the burn.

I pressed my palm to the graffiti-covered stucco of the mansion's exterior and allowed my silver abilities to flow from my fingertips until smoke wafted around me and heat licked up the side of my face.

It was only when a hand gripped my elbow that I realized the flames were already dancing up the sides of the building.

"It's done," Laykin said, his voice low as he coaxed me back from the growing flames. He didn't offer me any more comfort than his grip on my elbow, but he remained standing next to me, his broad shoulders tall and his rifle slung across his back. He was always so crisp and composed, his white-blond hair buzzed at the sides, and the longer strands at the top slicked back and styled.

I'd barely managed to braid my mess of hair today, let alone shower. The diamond necklace Gideon had given me hung heavily around my neck. I hadn't been able to bring myself to take it off.

It had been a week, one week since that horrible day on the cliffs. And every day felt even harder than the last. In that week, I'd learned that sometimes time doesn't heal, but only rips the wounds open more deeply, exposing them to the elements. I felt raw and broken and angry.

But I'd made it out of bed that morning so that was... something. There wasn't time for wallowing, after all. Not here. Not in the place I'd destroyed from the inside out.

The farther back I stepped from the flaming wall, the more I saw my former life crumbling before me. Burning thanks to my touch.

My silver.

My decision.

The singeing heat felt good against my face.

I didn't allow my gaze to meet the others, who stood a distance from the mansion in the grass, watching the fire climb, consuming the remains of this once-powerful compound. I especially didn't look at Tayna, though I could feel him watching me. His gaze was burning me, nearly as hot as the flames in front of me.

I turned back to the blaze creeping up the sides of the mansion.

The graffiti art covering the exterior walls was really the only thing I was sad to see go. But there was also beauty in watching the destruction of the spray-painted masterpieces. The crimson lips that had once been curved into a seductive smile drooped and wilted into a frown as they smoldered. The black and white hands clasped together turned as red as the blood that leaked from between their fingers until they were nothing but ash. The rainbow iris set into an all-seeing eye saw no more as it was lifted into wisps of flame.

But maybe most satisfying and heartbreaking of all, the red Ace of Hearts card that covered the entire expanse of one wall, simmered into darkness.

Heartbreaking because the graffiti was ash on the wind while Gideon, the Ace of Hearts—the leader of this once-powerful compound—was dead at the bottom of the ocean. And I had both loved him and been the one to spell his downfall.

Now he was dead, and I was watching the final dregs of his empire crumble.

I wiped at the stray tear on my cheek, surprised to find I had any left.

This mansion was simply a shell of the Cards, who, until last week, was the city's most powerful ruling gang. And though they'd kept me at this compound as a glorified prisoner for five years, there was good here. There were good people here.

My gaze did flick over my shoulder then, only to land where I knew Enver stood. My first female friend, really. And it was hard to believe we had ever been anything but friends at this point.

She was regal with her wind-swept hair, high cheekbones, and upturned silver eyes. The eyes were really the only thing we had in common on the surface. Yet hers were soft where mine were sharp. Even now, her irises glinted not with sorrow but with hope, while mine were dulled with cloudy grief. The meager smile she gave me was a small offering of encouragement as heat swelled from the building and a sharp tang like burnt tar filled the air.

"We should go home."

I sighed at the words, turning back to the flames instead of acknowledging the voice— instead of acknowledging Tayna.

Home.

I wasn't sure I had one.

Nothing had felt like home except for Tayna. Not the man in front of me but the boy I'd known when we lived on the streets all those years ago. Back then, he was my protector. He was my everything.

But it was all a lie.

Tayna wasn't the orphaned street rat he'd pretended to be.

He was Olita Ravidian's only surviving son, heir to the Veiled empire, a gang that had long reigned over this city as the most powerful faction until Gideon had killed Olita's husband and first-born son over a decade ago. Their deaths were retribution because the Veiled, Olita's gang, had killed Gideon's father, Ishmael, first.

That was the way of the gangs. It was always violence. An eye for an eye. The gangs got their power in two ways. One, by being the most ruthless. Or two, by having the most Silvers under their control. Silver blood powered everything in this city. But it most especially powered the violence.

And I was learning all too well that the silver that ran in my veins was an especially unique sort of violence. I nearly smiled at that thought as I watched the flames climb until they licked over the roof of the mansion, reaching into the sky.

Eventually, Tayna and I would need to speak.

But not yet.

My anger was still too raw. The betrayal felt like a live spark of silver stabbing at my heart.

It had only been a week. A week since I'd learned he was the son of one of the most powerful ruling families in this city.

The truth had come from Gideon in those final moments on the cliffs because Gideon, for all his flaws, had always been honest with me.

The flames were growing almost unbearably hot against my face now, and one of the walls began crumbling in on itself.

"Lissa." It was Enver's voice this time, soft but clear against the crackling flames in front of me.

And I realized my silver was sparking at my fingertips.

I balled my hands into fists, extinguishing the electric power that had seeped from my veins into my fingers. Keeping the silver contained was the hardest part of controlling it.

"I'm ready," I said, turning from the house.

After Gideon had jumped from the cliffs, most of the Cards had fled the compound. Only a handful had stayed behind. A handful among thousands.

The rest were likely on their way to defect to rival gangs. And it was a safe bet that the most powerful of the survivors, like Dia, would seize on the change in power dynamics to organize on their own.

Those of us who'd stayed behind spent the week packing up the Humvees with anything valuable from the house. One of the vehicles held the medical supplies from Karadin's clinic. A few held the nonperishable food items from the kitchens. Others held the weapons. We even packed a couple of the trucks full of clothes and jewelry. And, of course. Of course, one of the Humvees held the books. I'd been the one to meticulously comb the rooms until I was sure they'd all been stacked safely within the vehicle.

The only one I'd left behind was Gideon's copy of *In Cold Blood*. That one could burn with this house. Not so much for the book itself but for the time it represented for me within this compound. I'd left it behind in the same way I wished I could so easily leave behind the days he'd kept me locked in his room and tied to his bed, my body his to claim. And I'd let him claim me. I'd let him use me. I'd let him take my silver but give me so much pleasure that I'd started to question if I even wanted it back.

"Lissa!" Enver's voice was more urgent now.

I shook away the memories just as one of the upstairs windows shattered. Glass sprayed toward the cliffs as the ocean waves crested above the edge, as if the ocean sensed the flames and sought to meet its match.

The smoke burned my nostrils.

A cough rattled in my lungs as I finally turned, with Laykin close at my heels.

Enver gripped my elbow, surprisingly tight for someone so willowy. "Are you okay?" I knew the smoke in my lungs was only part of the reason she was asking as she pulled me farther from the flames.

"Fine," I choked out between sputtering. At least the coughing was a good cover for the tears that leaked free from the corners of my eyes.

We had assigned some of the remaining Cards to watch the burn, ensuring it remained under control in the house. The last thing I intended was for the entire cliffside to go up in flames, but we also couldn't leave the mansion standing. Not when Dia and the other Kings were still out there. We couldn't risk the chance that the Cards would simply return and reestablish once we were gone.

We.

Just like that, I'd become a player in this game of gangs.

But it hadn't been just like that. Not really. The desire for more had festered within my heart until I knew in my very bones it was no longer enough to play pretend at this compound. Gideon had named me his Queen of Hearts. He'd given me a pretty cloak. He'd fed me pastries and brought me presents. He'd marked me with the Card tattoos on my shoulder.

But I was so much more than his Silver doll.

I was a Silver, who didn't just have electric power running through her veins. I was the only Silver I'd ever met who could also wield my Silver like a weapon. It crackled beneath my skin, sparked at my fingertips, and lit my skin with energy as I willed it. It was mine to control. But it had taken a lot to harness it. Now that I had, I knew I'd only scratched the surface of my potential.

But was I meant to be a weapon?

The thought twisted in my gut.

With Tayna at the front, Enver still holding my arm, and Laykin just a step behind, we made our way around the house where the Humvees were loaded and waiting. Our small group would caravan back to the farm community run by the Whigs this afternoon. We'd camp for the night, then spend the next day hiking the supplies from the vehicle to the farm.

There was safety in numbers, especially when the power structure of the city had been so severely disrupted with the Cards' fall. The other gangs would see it as an opportunity to stake their own slice of power in this mad game for control. And for the gangs, power meant controlling the Silvers. But that didn't mean they would pass up a Humvee filled with weapons or medical supplies or food.

Karadin came around the side of one of the vehicles, gazing down at a clipboard. Her haphazard ponytail swished behind her with her purposeful strides, and she wiped a bead of sweat from her forehead. Her face was clammy from staying inside this muggy garage for too long on a blossoming summer day.

"Inhaling all that smoke in the air isn't good for a pregnant mother," Karadin said in that calm but commanding way of hers. "We should hit the road."

"I'm fine," Phenola called back, poking her head out from around the corner of one of the Humvees. She had her mountain of dark hair piled on top of her head and a scarf tied to cover her nose and mouth. She pressed one hand into her lower back and another onto her fully round stomach as she leaned against the truck. "Lord knows the baby's survived more than a little smoke in the air at this point."

Her words were matter-of-fact, but I didn't miss the strain in Phenola's neck as she said them. Nor could I ignore the bruising under her eyes. I knew the scarf hid the hollowing of her cheeks. She wasn't sleeping as much as she should. None of us were. But three nights ago, I'd seen Phenola walking along the cliffs late at night, framed only by moonlight. She was taking the path down to the small beach cove, the only access to the ocean from the compound. Something told me she'd been doing that every night.

I understood the impulse.

She'd lost Kenji to those crashing waves. Her love. Her partner. The father of her unborn child.

Kenji had meant so much to me, and my grief was a thrashing, bubbling pit in the very depths of me. Yet Phenola... well, Phenola had been stoic in her grief. She'd screamed when the Cards took Kenji. She'd raged when Gideon had pushed him over the cliffs. But since that moment, her grief had turned into a silent, granite fortress built around her like it was the only protection she had left to offer the tiny life inside her. Her grief was silent tears and stiff shoulders and unshaken words. And nothing I could offer her would make any of it better.

Kenji was gone.

My guard was gone.

My friend was gone.

But Phenola... Phenola's home was gone. So she was slowly building a new one within herself and using her grief to lay it thick, one brick at a time.

My gaze swept to where Tayna stood. Just once. And he watched me back, his eyes shining with a question I wasn't ready to answer.

I felt so disconnected from Tayna, yet my heart ached to be close to him. A different sort of grief existed in the loss of trust. The betrayal I felt at the secrets he'd kept made me feel alone in a world where I'd always had him to anchor me. Even when I'd thought he was dead, he'd been a constant reassurance of hope and stability.

He'd shattered that illusion with his lies.

And when I realized what he'd done—kept things from me, knowing it would hurt me—well, then the anger bubbled hot. And it was a new sort of anger that had my silver sparking like a stab to my gut each time. It made me want to hurt him back. My silence felt like the least he deserved.

And so even as I craved him, I kept my distance. Every time he tried to talk, every time he moved toward me, every time he attempted to connect, I pushed him away. I couldn't risk it. Not now. Not when everything was already so painful. I'd endured too much loss to open myself up to anyone, especially him.

Instead, I walked to Phenola's side, pressing a palm to her shoulder. I wasn't a touchy-feely person. I'd learned to fear contact. Gideon was the only one in the Cards who'd touched me without eyeing my fingertips first. Once my silver had manifested as a live power beneath my skin, touching meant the potential to cause harm, and it terrified me.

But I'd learned to control my silver over the past few months. For the most part. If only I could transfer some of it to Phenola now. If only I could give her strength the way my silver could be used to fortify weapons or fuel cars or light bulbs.

"One breath at a time, ya?" My voice was quiet, meant only for her.

She lowered her head until our foreheads were nearly touching as she said, "For the baby."

I pulled back just enough to say more loudly to the group, "All right, we all know the plan. Karadin, you and Phenola ride together in the medical Humvee. Laykin and Tayna will take the weapons.

Enver, you're on food. And I'll take the books. Tayna will lead, and Laykin will bring up the back."

"Actually..." Tayna had the good sense to look at least a little reluctant as he stepped forward. The scar across his eye pulled against his brow as he narrowed his honeyed eyes at me. "Laykin's recruited a few of the Cards he trusts to take the weapons. We agreed you and Enver shouldn't be alone."

"Excuse me?" I snapped, glaring from Tayna to Laykin. "Since when do you two agree on anything?"

"Books and weapons are important, but not as important as Silver—"

"You'd better not finish that sentence, Tayna," I growled. "I am *not* a commodity."

"Goddammit," Tayna bit back, swallowing as he tried to rein in his frustration. "Of course you're not a commodity."

"I can take care of myself." I crossed my arms. "This is why Laykin spent a week teaching us how to drive. Because we all agreed we could take care of ourselves."

I looked at Enver to back me up, but her eyes fell to the ground.

"Were you in on this too?" I demanded.

"I don't really like driving," she admitted with a small shrug. "The Humvees kinda freak me out. They take up so much of the road."

"Fine." I threw up my hands. "Fine. Enver can go with Laykin. But I'm taking my own car."

"It's a Humvee, so it's—"

"Just shut it, Laykin." I pointed a finger at him. "Not another word."

I knew what this was really about. My friends were going rogue on me because I'd avoided Tayna for a week. This was about forcing us to speak. As if we could just talk it out, and it would make all this churning uncertainty in me suddenly better.

"No," I said again, digging my heels into the concrete of the warehouse.

And when they all just looked at me like I was the problem, I threw up my hands and stalked back outside, only to be confronted with the growing smoke in the air.

Karadin hadn't been joking. It was wafting thick around the opening.

There wasn't time for me to stalk off and take a breath. There wasn't even a place for a breath as the fire grew.

There wasn't time to convince the others that I would talk to Tayna on my own terms, when I was ready.

There wasn't even time to argue about it further.

We needed to leave before the smoke caught the sort of attention we couldn't afford right now.

I begrudgingly turned from the entrance of the warehouse back to my friends, but I glared at Tayna. His arms were crossed over his broad chest. A rifle was slung over his shoulder. The heart tattoo—the one he'd gotten when he'd infiltrated the Cards to find me—was stark against his tanned skin. And he was staring right back at me, determined to have this out.

"Fine," I said between gritted teeth, balling my hands at my sides. "Fine. But I'm driving."

5

Lissa

Tayna didn't even argue about the driving arrangements. He just handed me the keys as we all got into our respective vehicles.

We had silver-charged walkie-talkies to communicate on the road. Enver and I had filled the small battery packs ourselves just that morning. The deep chrome of our blood had sloshed in the small containers that connected to the devices' power. Little silver batteries that fueled electronics that were once powered by other elements of this earth. Those elements had long run dry.

Now, Tayna flipped the power switch and connected the small device to the truck's dashboard. A soft static filled the Humvee's space as he tuned it to the correct channel.

I wished I had insisted he drive in another vehicle. There had to be another option besides sitting with him just a few feet away, my body keenly aware of him with nothing but thoughts of how, even with him this close, we felt a world apart.

The smoke outside the truck had wrapped itself around the cliff-side, giving everything an orange glow as the sun attempted to filter through the smog. Laykin and Enver pulled out first, leading our caravan, followed by the weapons Humvees, then Karadin and Phenola, and finally, the Humvee I now sat in with Tayna. The smell of the books surrounding us was my only comfort.

I kept my eyes on the road. The smoke was so thick that I needed to concentrate as we weaved our way out of the compound and onto the valley roads that would take us down the cliff.

Tayna propped a foot on the dashboard, his knee bent, and I sighed against the seat.

He leaned forward and pressed the walkie-talkie on.

"Enver," he called, "how's it going up there? Roads look good? Over."

Over.

The word had been Laykin's idea to use. Some official nonsense from back in the day to let everyone know they were done speaking. As if we couldn't all just hear the static stop when someone was no longer pushing the button. Ridiculous.

Tayna loved the idea.

I resisted another eye roll.

Instead, I focused on driving.

The field of vision was so thick with smoke, and the roads were so winding that I couldn't see past Karadin and Phenola's truck in front of me. We kept our pace slow, trees revealing themselves as the head-lights cut across their path. The lush greenery of the impending summer was dampened by the gloom I'd caused.

I sent up a silent prayer that the fire would stay contained. Not that I believed in that higher-power nonsense from the olden days, per se. It just felt like the right thing to do in the moment. But we had planned for that. The men who stayed behind would ensure the burn remained contained to the compound.

After a few seconds, there was the crackle of static. "Sorry, sorry," Enver sputtered through the speaker. "I couldn't figure out how to turn it on. We're fine. Laykin's a grumpy driver, though."

"If you'd stop trying to direct me, I wouldn't be grumpy," Laykin grumbled in the background.

"I'm just trying to help you look out. There are rocks in the road!"

"Well, pointing them out with a hand splayed in front of my face doesn't do either of us much good."

Another crackle of static cut into the line. "And here we thought it was going to be Lissa and Tayna bickering on this trip," Karadin deadpanned. "At least mute yourself so we can focus on driving in peace."

There was silence for a few long moments.

And then the crackle of static again. "Over." Enver grumbled the word into the speaker as if she found it just as ludicrous.

This time, I did let out a snort of laughter. And turned to see Tayna smiling the goofy grin that made his dimples pop like they did when we were kids. The smile didn't reach his eyes. Instead, it ran to his shoulders, which scrunched into his ears, as if they were trying to keep secrets.

My smile dropped.

The pain had returned that quickly.

Sharing smiles with Tayna was easy. Laughing with Tayna was easy. Joking with Tayna was easy. But maybe that was because he'd never allowed me to see the tough stuff. He'd held me to his chest on those nights when I'd cried about losing my mother and rocked me gently against his scrawny body until the tears no longer blurred my silver eyes.

Tayna had told me his parents died from an addiction to silver. He'd always said they became so dependent on it that they'd lost their lives to it. It wasn't uncommon. Silver, when used in moderation, was a powerful tool that could enhance a person's strength, help them heal more quickly, and even extend their lifespan. But if used too much, the silver would drain a person dry. Instead of giving energy, the silver would start to demand it in return, forcing the body to function in overdrive until the heart simply gave out.

"Lissa, will you please talk to me?" Tayna's question seemed to take up so much space in this already-cramped vehicle full of books.

It wasn't like I could do anything except stare at the road. It was starting to clear. The path ahead opened to the wide expanse of ocean, leaving the smoke behind on the cliffs where I would never return.

I sighed. "You're the one who insisted we drive together, Tayna. I don't have anything to say."

He sat up straighter in his seat, his large, muscular frame making the space look small. Everything about him felt like too much, from his earthy smell to the way he seemed to consider reaching for me in the space between us.

His hands settled into his lap instead, and I let out the breath of relief I hadn't realized I was holding. I wasn't ready for that. I didn't trust that I wouldn't lean back into him if he touched me.

"I lied to you." His voice was flat, matter-of-fact.

My chest tightened.

"But I don't regret it, Lissa."

"Excuse me?" I shot a look his way until I realized I was drifting on the road as he jerked upright even straighter and braced a hand on the dash.

"Lissa!" he barked. "What the fuck!"

"Me what the fuck? You what the fuck!" I yelled back as I righted the truck. "You don't regret it, Tayna?"

"No!" he shot back. His voice was sharp and still panicked from the swerve.

"Okay." I threw up a hand, perfectly happy to drift back into silence as my anger simmered through the space. He'd lied to me our entire time together, and he didn't regret it. *Noted.*

"Just—" Tayna lifted his hand from the dashboard tentatively as if he was choosing his words carefully lest I jerk the Humvee again. He had every right to be nervous. I was seriously considering slamming on the brakes and running from this truck. My grip on the wheel was so tight that my knuckles turned white. "Just listen."

Between my time with Gideon, the grief that followed, and my own guilt from those moments on the cliffs, this conversation felt like another rock for me to carry, and I didn't know how.

I sighed, my voice shaky as I said slowly, "I'm exhausted, Tayna."

Why couldn't he understand that right now what I needed was space?

He sighed, bracing his elbow on the door and staring out the window. I thought maybe that was it, maybe he was letting it go. But no, letting me go was never in Tayna's nature. He watched as we rounded onto the main road along the ocean as if searching for something out along the waves.

I followed the others south down the stretch of well-worn highway. It crumbled at the edges, like the pieces of asphalt strained to become bits of sand out at sea, as they once must have been, hundreds of thousands of years ago.

"We were both so young when we met." His deep voice cracked through the silence of the interior. He still watched the sea. "Gideon had just killed my brother and my father. And the worst part was, they deserved it."

He laughed, and it was a dark sound. I wondered if that was the first time he'd said those words out loud.

They deserved it.

There was a conviction in those words. He meant them deeply, fully, and I realized at that moment that the piece of Tayna I didn't know may not be a piece he knew himself, either. So I didn't interrupt him. I didn't tell him to stop again. I waited for more words.

Tayna sighed, not feeling bad about the words but not willing to leave them there without an explanation. "My brother... he wasn't well. And my father and mother only stoked his delusions. When they died—fuck—it's a horrible thing to say, but I was relieved."

He looked back at me, and I dared to glance from the road to meet his pained gaze. He meant the words, but they still cut deep. That glance was a brief flash of connection between us. I was listening. For now.

"My mother hardly ever concerned herself with me anyway. But when they died, instead of grieving, she took silver and vowed to get revenge. I was lucky if one of the staff remembered to feed me. Most of the time, I just stole from the kitchens. I got good at hiding and stealing, go figure."

I thought of the time Tayna had stolen those syringes from a traveling nurse so I could draw blood to power our loft. Or when he'd fished a copy of *Treasure Island* from a Forta at the bar where he worked. He was a clever thief. I'd assumed it was something he'd picked up in his time on the streets.

Tayna continued, "I was just a kid, but I still saw it all so clearly. I knew if I didn't get out of there, I would be next. I knew that one day, Gideon would come for me, too, if one of the other gangs didn't get to me first. And I had no desire to be another sacrifice for my mother in her bid for power and revenge. I knew if I didn't go—if I didn't just make the decision—I would end up like the rest of my family. And I told myself I would never be part of the gangs again. That day, I decided I would do whatever it took to be free of them."

"So you built the lie then?" I could see it. It made sense why he'd left it all behind. But understanding didn't stop the ache. I had trusted him with all of myself, and he'd given me only a small fraction in the decade we were together. I'd shared all my broken pieces. I thought he'd done the same.

"No, Lissa," he insisted. "No. When I saw you digging in that trash can, with your long hair all in your face, as if you could hide your eyes. Your silver eyes. When I saw you, I just wanted to shield you from all the fucked-up things in the city. I wanted to protect you from the place I had come from and the people who didn't care unless you offered them something in return. And I knew I would burn this city for you if only I could build some place better so you wouldn't have to be so afraid. So I lied to you. And, Lissa, I would lie to you again and again and again if it meant I got to keep those nights in our loft."

Tayna reached for me then, but I shrank from his touch. I understood. I did. But I still felt so much pain. I wasn't even sure how much of it was because of him and how much of it was because I had been a pawn in everyone else's game. And now? Now, I had no idea what I wanted or who I wanted to be.

"Lissa, I lov—"

The Humvee in front of us swerved.

My foot hit the brake. Our seat belts snapped tight as we jolted forward.

The Humvee in front of us—Phenola and Karadin's Humvee—veered into the dirt.

"Karadin?" Tayna asked into the speaker, pulling the walkie to his mouth from where it was clipped on the dash. Static answered. "Phenola?" His voice rose in panic.

"Everything good?" Laykin cut in.

The smoke drifting along our vehicles was the only movement as the silence hung heavy. I could make out the ocean in front of us, gray against the afternoon light that managed to peek through the haze.

"Fuck this," I said, throwing the Humvee in park and scrambling to take off my seat belt.

Tayna gripped my arm as static crackled through the walkie-talkie.

"She's—" That was Karadin's voice. And then, "Shit."

My heart lurched as violently as the Humvee had jerked to a stop. I yanked my elbow out of Tayna's grip and flung myself from the truck.

The sea breeze whipped at my face. I pushed my hair out of my eyes and ran toward the Humvee in the ditch.

Karadin's door flew open as I sprinted to her.

"What's happening?" I demanded over the crashing waves in the distance.

"Her water broke," Karadin said, barely sparing me a glance. "Phenola's in labor."

6

The Phantom

The hawk screeched from the cloudless sky, circling above my head before swooping low and landing along the sun-faded roof trellis. He was my most loyal messenger, one of the oldest hawks I'd trained. He'd been a stubborn thing in his adolescence. I'd considered snapping his neck and trying again rather than continuing my efforts to break him. He'd pecked wildly whenever I'd attempted to blind him. He'd bucked against the creance. He'd gnawed at the jesses until they'd snapped free from his leg.

I'd been patient. I'd given him food. I'd isolated him to gain his trust.

Nothing had worked.

And one day, I'd grown so frustrated and tired of the beast that I'd clamped his beak shut with zip ties and let him go. I'd thrown open the door and watched him fly away. It was satisfying to know he'd suffer and starve. *Let him learn his lesson*, I'd thought. I relished the idea of finding his dead carcass in the desert one day.

But the young hawk was smart.

After a week, I'd found him sitting on the same roof where I now stood, a collection of newly dead mice piled at his feet as if in offering. I'd taken them away from him, thrown them into the fire, and let him watch them burn before returning him to his dark, isolated cage.

Only after another day did I remove the zip tie from his beak and offer him a single worm.

He'd accepted it.

And had remained loyal ever since.

It was an important lesson in choice. One I hadn't forgotten since.

"What have you brought me?" I asked the bird, my voice strained as it was, especially against the wind. He had a rolled piece of paper tucked into the tie at his ankle, and he lifted it in offering as I approached. His red wings splayed as he balanced against the wind.

After untwining the paper, I turned my back to the bird and toward the rest of my cages, carefully lined with my well-trained messengers. I could hear them shifting in their cages as the afternoon sun waned. I could understand. The air grew stifling beneath my silver mask, too. Itchy beads of sweat gathered at my hairline. But I had grown used to the discomfort over the years.

I read the note.

Then I read it again.

And then I tore it into tiny pieces, scattering it with the wind as I smiled.

Gideon was dead.

And the news was as satisfying as finding my bird returned all those years ago with a pile of mice at its feet in offering.

My patience was being rewarded.

The fact that it was the little Silver Queen who'd been his downfall made the news all the more perfect. What I would have given to see the look on Gideon's perfect fucking face when he realized the woman he thought belonged to him had utterly betrayed him. She'd joined the rebels instead of standing by his side.

Brilliant.

Fucking cosmic perfection.

And now, it was time to make this city break to my will as it was always meant to.

7

Lissa

"It's too early.

"It's too early.

"It's *too* early."

Phenola kept repeating those words in time with her labored breathing. She had one hand clutched to her stomach, the other braced on the center console of the Humvee. A sheen of sweat broke out over her forehead as her back hunched against another wave of contractions.

She stopped her chant only to clench her teeth through the pain.

Karadin dabbed at her forehead with a wet cloth. She'd doused it with some water from one of the canteens, providing the only small relief any of us could offer to Phenola's sweat-soaked skin.

"It's okay," Karadin murmured. "The baby's going to be fine. And you are ready for this."

Or as ready as we could be. Karadin had spent the week we'd been at the compound reading up on whatever she could in her sparse medical books. I'd even read some of the chapters when I'd escaped to the clinic for a few moments of quiet when the grief had gotten to be too much. I found the idea of new life amid so much destruction and death comforting. It had given us all something to look forward to.

But I'd thought when Phenola went into labor, we'd be safe at the Whigs. She'd be surrounded by friends and people who could support her and assist Karadin. We'd have access to fresh food and warm blankets, not stranded on the side of the road, far away from help.

As the contraction passed, Phenola's body uncoiled, her head dipping back against the seat as she tried to catch her breath ahead of the next wave of pain.

"How far away is the farm?" Karadin demanded, looking to Tayna.

He shook his head. "Maybe a thirty-minute drive. But the only way in is to hike up the hill. It's a few miles." He paused, looking around at the road as if looking for a solution to spell itself out in the smoke that was beginning to waft down from the hill. "We could carry her."

"For a few miles while she's in labor? Not an option." Karadin shook her head.

Tayna looked lost, like even he knew it was a terrible idea, but had nothing else to offer.

Enver and Laykin were running toward us.

"Phenola's in labor," I called as they approached the open door of the Humvee. Phenola sat just inside, her breathing evening out in the break from her contractions.

"Not here!" Phenola shook her head. "It's too early. I can't have the baby now. I can't have the baby *here*."

I stepped in to take her hand and gave it a gentle squeeze. The smoke from the compound fire floated into the evening sky above our heads. They'd be able to see it in the city, too. Word would travel faster than the smoke.

Karadin moved to speak to Tayna. "We need to get her somewhere safe. And we can't exactly go back to the Cards' compound. So what are our options?"

Tayna shook his head, running a hand through his tousled hair.

"What are our options?" Karadin repeated. "Otherwise, I need to start unpacking these boxes and setting up some sort of birthing station on the side of this road."

As if in answer to that suggestion, an engine revved in the distance. My gaze snapped up at the sudden noise. Headlights flashed around a corner into view.

A car was on the road. It was a few miles south, closer to the city, but heading our direction from the looks of it.

And then I saw more lights. More cars. I counted four, but who knew if others were following.

Cars didn't usually venture this far north of the city. No one dared. The Cards were ruthless to anyone who even got close to their territory. They—

The Cards were gone.

The threat of traveling this far north was no more.

And the smoke would be like a beacon, welcoming a new age of chaos into the city. The strongest of the gangs had fallen, opening a new opportunity for those who dared take it.

Tayna murmured a curse under his breath.

"We need to move," Laykin said, his voice low with the deadly calm of a soldier as he pulled one of his guns from the straps across his chest, clicking off the safety. "Now." And then he called to the Card soldiers who'd stayed to help us. "Get to your vehicles! And make sure you're armed! We've got company."

"What about an option in the city?" I demanded, suddenly desperate. "Are there other Whigs not at the farm?"

"Shit." Tayna's jaw clenched, the scar across his face drawing tight. "Shit. The Tanks." He looked at me. "We're allies with the Tanks. They're the closest. We'll need to head farther south. We'll need to head past those cars but—"

"How long?"

"Twenty minutes? If we can manage to get around the cars—" Tayna continued to shake his head, watching the lights approach. The headlights grew larger. They were moving fast. Had they already seen us?

Karadin said, "Will the Tanks have a medical center?"

"They'll have something but—" Tayna looked around at the other Humvees. "If anyone sees these supplies, we're sitting ducks. If those cars see all of this, there's no way they'll keep driving. And the Tanks will demand a steep fee for their help. Their captain, Banu, he's an ally, but that doesn't mean he'll pass all this up. Especially not the weapons."

"Then we won't give him that option," Laykin said. "You two go with Phenola and Karadin. Enver and I can make it to the community based on your directions."

"Alaric won't trust you," Tayna snapped. "Even if you could make it to the community on my directions alone, the odds are good you'd be shot on sight and questioned later. Especially since the Whigs know Phenola and Lissa were taken by the Cards."

"Then we'll camp with the guys and keep the supplies safe until you get back."

"It could be days." Tayna was still shaking his head.

But Laykin nodded, resolute. "Then it'll be days. We have a truck full of food. We'll be fine."

"I can drive." Enver gestured toward my Humvee of books.

"We shouldn't split up," I countered, but my attention was snagged back to Phenola as she maintained a death grip on my hand, letting out another pained cry. My fingers began turning purple as she attempted to breathe.

Tayna kept his eyes on the cars in the distance. I could tell by his tight expression he was weighing how much he trusted Laykin.

"You're okay, Phen," I offered, even as I felt breathless at the impending danger. I took a few steadying lungfuls of air with her.

Tayna swiped a hand across his mouth before focusing on the cars and then back to our group, saying, "Okay. Shit. Okay." And then he looked up at Laykin. He was resolute. "Head about another fifteen minutes down this road. You'll see an old sign—"

"We're not splitting up!" I countered.

But he yelled over me, keeping his gaze on Laykin. "You can make out the word 'university.' Take a left. It'll take you back into a bundle of trees."

"Tayna!"

Phenola's wail drowned out my objections. Her teeth clenched as her body bowed.

Fuck.

"Camp about ten miles in from there. Tie a piece of red cloth to a branch near your location and keep your radio on for as much time as you can until I can get back."

I tossed a glare at him. Fine. Fine. If he was getting his way with the plan, then, I started to say, "I'm—"

But Tayna cut me off. "*I'm* driving. You will stay in the back with Phenola and Karadin, and you will keep your head down. If we're going to pass these cars alive, you cannot be seen, Lissa. Do you understand?"

The command in his voice had me clenching my jaw to argue. But the cars in the distance had disappeared behind a bend in the road. It would only be a few more minutes before they were on us. We had to leave. Now.

So I nodded.

Karadin was already moving, squeezing between me and the open passenger door to pat Phenola's forehead again. Phenola was hissing through her teeth. My hand had gone numb against her grip.

"Okay, Phen," Karadin told her. "We're going to move you into the back seat."

Phenola nodded, her brow furrowing against the pain, and she bowed in on herself.

"Ready?" Karadin ran the damp cloth over Phenola's forehead again. "We're right here. Lissa and I will help you. We got you."

Phenola was still nodding as something seemed to release within her. Her forehead smoothed, and she let out a long, full exhale, tipping her head back against the seat.

"Now," she gasped.

It was all I needed to hear before I began lifting, helping her from the passenger seat into the back.

The headlights cast spotlights against the hills. They were so close now I could make out the rusted edges of the doors. They weren't Humvees, but a smaller sort of vehicle.

Phenola was surprisingly steady on her feet. She braced one hand on the Humvee as we moved around it and one hand on her belly. She waddled a bit, but she was strong, and the adrenaline of the moment pushed her forward. One final heave and she collapsed into the back seat. Karadin followed her in.

I moved to take my place in the back seat, but Tayna grabbed my arm.

"I want you to go with Enver." He pulled me close until little space was between our breaths. I was swept into his golden gaze. It was earnest and pleading. "Stay with Laykin and Enver. You can show them the farm."

"Tayna—"

"I already lost you once to the Cards. I just... please don't make me risk you again so soon. *Please*, Lissa."

There was no way I was staying behind. Not now. "Tayna... you told me to pick a side. You wanted me to play the game. I'm on the board now. It's too late to take it back. I'm not going to sit around and wait while you make the moves."

He held my stare. His was firm but, to my surprise, he nodded. The scar across his eye pinched as his brow furrowed and his head bowed, and then he handed me a gun. The weight of it was surprising in my palm.

"I had to try... Just keep your head down. And if anything happens, don't hesitate to pull that trigger, got it?"

I swallowed.

"Got it?" he pressed, and when I pursed my lips and nodded, he finally sighed, taking his position in the driver's seat.

I felt a sudden twist in my heart that I couldn't explain. It was different from the grief I'd been sitting with for a week now. This feeling was one of longing. I wanted his fierce protection to be enough for me. I wanted his words in the Humvee to make it all okay. I wanted everything between us to be like it used to be.

But it wasn't.

And that realization hurt me, too. I couldn't simply go back. Too much had happened on those cliffs for any of us to ever be the same. I wasn't the same. I'd felt it. My silver was different, more volatile. Even with my practiced control, it always seemed to be humming at the surface of my skin, wanting out.

Phenola cried again.

And my gaze snapped to the headlights flashing against the fading rays of the evening sun.

Karadin's panicked voice came from the back. "The cars are getting closer!"

Laykin looked at Tayna and me. "Drive. Drive fast and right past them. If they follow us, we'll take care of them before we get to the turnoff for the Whigs. If they give chase, Enver can drive ahead and wait while we get rid of the tail."

"I don't like this," I admitted. It felt wrong to be splitting up.

"We'll see you in just a few days," Laykin promised, his words hard with the surety. Tayna might have been my protector when we were kids, but Laykin was my guard. He'd been one of my only friends at the compound, and I trusted him with my life. I trusted him with this. He could handle whoever was in those cars if need be.

I pulled Enver in for a hug that was too short. Her delicate arms cocooned me within her warmth. She smelled like jasmine and spring flowers.

"We'll be back as soon as we can," I said against her white-blond hair. "Keep the radios on. As soon as we're in range, we'll call for you."

"Phenola first." She smiled. "I can't wait to hold a baby. I've always wanted to hold a baby." Her voice was wistful. "Go." She pushed me toward the Humvee. "Be safe."

I gave her and Laykin a final glance as I slid into the back seat.

8

Lissa

As soon as I pulled the door closed behind me, Tayna was peeling back onto the road.

His brow was pinched in concentration. His grip was tight on the wheel as our speed climbed and climbed and climbed until we were tearing off into a waning day. The sunset was shaping up to be particularly spectacular, and I couldn't help but wonder if it was from the lingering smoke on the hillside.

I kept Phenola's hand tight in mine. Karadin offered her small sips of water, but she refused.

All eyes were trained on the road ahead, on the cars approaching.

Tayna increased his speed.

My insides screamed for us to stop, to slow down, but I understood what Tayna was doing. He was banking on the fact that the cars wouldn't get in our path. The Humvee was a tank compared to the beat-up cars chugging in our direction. A collision would cause way more damage to their vehicles than to ours. The threat was clear: Don't get in our way, or we'll go through you.

But the cars were moving just as quickly toward us and showed no sign of slowing.

The front car moved left, but my relief was short-lived as the car behind moved into the lane, catching up so the two were side by side, spanning the entirety of the road.

Tayna swerved, centering himself as if he could go through the middle. But no. There wasn't enough room. The Humvee was too wide.

I clamped down on my silver as my panic rose.

We were going to hit them.

I kept one hand on Phenola and the other reached out to grip the door as if that would steady me as we barreled toward the cars. She was quiet, all of us suspended in the scene playing out before the windows. Karadin's lips were pursed in tight dread.

Tayna didn't back down. If anything, I heard the engine rev as he increased his speed.

"Lissa!" he called from the front. "I need you to use your silver!"

Was he insane?

I couldn't.

It didn't work like that!

It came from my fingertips. I couldn't shoot it between cars. That was ridiculous! He knew better he—

"On my cue!" he yelled.

The cars were so close now I could see the driver at the front.

It was a woman, standing up out of a hole in the roof. Our eyes met and she—

"Gun!"

It was all I managed to scream before Tayna swerved to the right. Phenola cried out in pain. The Humvee jerked and bounced as it hit the beach, sand flying around the doors until I couldn't make out anything beyond the haze. But I could hear the bullets pinging off the doors. They ricocheted off the metal, echoing through the cabin. It was all I could do to keep my head from colliding with the window as I braced myself against the rocking of the vehicle.

Tayna jerked the wheel. The Humvee sped into the edges of the water as the bullets continued to ping around us. As the sand settled, I looked back to see that the cars had followed. Tayna outpaced them, but they made a U-turn and had given chase.

"Do you trust me, Lissa?" Tayna asked, turning once to meet my eyes.

Did I?

I faltered.

And he turned back to the road, back to the shallows of the water stretched out before us where he drove just out of reach of the waves that could take us out to sea. I imagined all the times I had sunk my hands into the sand, letting my silver lose into the swells.

And I knew.

I knew what Tayna was asking me to do. I knew why he'd gone into the ocean. I saw the path out of this.

"Yes." I breathed and said more forcefully, "Yes!"

"On my cue!" He didn't look back at me again. Instead, he focused on the road ahead, on the bullets denting the metal of the Humvee.

"Lissa—" Karadin's voice was tinged with fear. She didn't understand what was happening.

But there wasn't time to explain.

And then Tayna was breaking, jerking the wheel to the left away from the water and screaming at me, "Now! Now, Lissa!"

Before the Humvee had even come to a stop, I flung the door open and dropped from the truck into the water. It nearly reached my knees, and it was freezing, even in the warm afternoon.

I left the gun on the back seat. It wouldn't do me any good now. All I needed was the weapon at my fingertips.

My heart beat a furious rhythm that I could feel pulsing like the current through my veins. The fear only fueled me forward. If I died —if the people in these cars reloaded their weapons and opened fire on me—at least I would have saved my friends. At least I would have given Phenola and the baby a fighting chance.

It was the least I owed Kenji.

I dropped into the water as I heard the Humvee peeling off behind me. The cars sped toward me, but the waning sun was at my back, meaning they would be blinking against the rays. I prayed it was enough to obscure their view. I only needed a few seconds. Their bullets were spent, but their engines revved at the prey they'd seen drop from the vehicle.

They would come for me.

They would kill me.

I'd seen it in that woman's eyes.

I counted slowly, three seconds in my head. My hands shook. My silver was primed just under my skin, pulsing and ready.

One...

Two...

Three...

It was all the time I could give Tayna to get out of the water.

I had to trust it was all the time he needed.

And then I unleashed my silver into the waves.

It spidered out like a shock wave of lightning through the current. A thrill pulsed through me. I could see the tendrils of it shoot from my fingertips, fissuring through the depths where it reached the first car in an instant. They hadn't had time to swerve back into the sand. They'd been focused on getting to me, a silver little prize.

They didn't realize I was their nightmare, their retribution for all the people they'd hunted before.

My silver hit the car like a bomb, flipping it from the water where it crashed in circles along the sand, colliding into the second vehicle in an explosion of sparks and metal.

The third and fourth cars barely had time to brake.

When they did, it was too late.

Glass blew as windows shattered and fire erupted from beneath the vehicles as their systems melted.

A door flew open, and a man with a shaved head threw himself from the vehicle into the water, screaming at the burns across his body.

The woman from the front car crawled from the wreckage. The back of her shirt was smoking from where I assumed it had touched the scorching seats.

I stood from the sea, my breath hitching at the damage before me.

Watching the scene in front of me, I remembered all those months ago at the Whigs when I'd told Tayna I didn't want to hurt anyone. I'd thought there was a chance for peace between the gangs. How laughable and naive that seemed now, to assume people would simply see reason.

My silver meant destruction, but it also meant I could protect the people I loved. It felt surprisingly good. The satisfaction was deep in the pit of my belly. For the first time in a week, I felt something beyond guilt and grief. And I relished it.

The woman was near-feral in her rage and pain, her eyes dark and bloodshot. She bared her teeth and screamed as she clawed her way through the sand. She was too weak to reach me.

I considered helping them.

I considered going to the woman and pulling her farther away from her ruined car. I could get her to safety. I could give her my blood.

But no.

These people had made their choices.

I'd made mine.

And I felt no regret as I turned my back on her.

Phenola needed me. And we'd already wasted too much time dealing with the city riffraff.

I realized as I ran back to the Humvee that this violence was only the start. The Cards had fallen. This was a lawless city, and only the strongest would survive. My silver made me strong.

For the first time, I was proud of my abilities. It didn't feel wrong at all to release my silver like I had into those waves.

The water squelched in my shoes as I ran. I was drenched from the ocean, the salt beginning to dry along my neck and hair.

The Humvee waited for me. Tayna had parked it near the road. The sloping hills were orange and pink against the setting sun. Just beyond, a cloud of smoke rose into the air.

Tayna stood near our vehicle. He held his rifle slack at his side, and I knew he'd been aiming it at the cars just in case. Just in case my silver had failed.

He would have come for me. Silver or no, he would have run into that water if I hadn't been able to protect myself.

"Are you hurt?" Tayna met me in the sand. I could feel the particles riding up my calves, beginning to chaff beneath my pants.

"I'm... good," I said, and I meant it.

Tayna looked like he wanted to say more. He looked like he wanted to pull me into his arms.

So I added, "We should keep moving. For Phenola."

He swallowed. His jaw ticked.

And then he clicked on the safety of the rifle and got back into the Humvee.

This time, I sat up front. The last thing Phenola needed was my soaked and sandy skin pressed against her for the remainder of the drive.

But I turned and met her steady gaze as she exhaled deep whooshes of air. Her cheeks puffed, her neck strained. A dark curl clung across her forehead, and sweat beaded down the sides of her cheeks.

Even in her pain, she was radiant. I wished, not for the first time, that Kenji could see her. But now was not the time for my grief. Whatever strength I had left, I owed it to Phenola.

I did what had to be done, and I didn't feel any remorse for the wreckage we were leaving behind on the beach. Not for the ruined vehicles or for the people who had dared to get in our way.

"Are you both okay?" I asked Karadin and Phenola as Tayna peeled back onto the road.

Karadin's jaw was set tight. She had a small cut above her eye. I wasn't sure when or how she'd gotten it. But they otherwise looked unharmed.

The thought crossed my mind that if we didn't have pain pills, then I could at least offer Phenola my silver. It would help with her pain, surely, and strengthen her to get through this labor as we barreled down the road toward a tentative ally who may or may not offer us sanctuary. Especially with word of the Cards' fall spreading across this city.

But was silver safe for a baby? I had no idea. What if, instead of helping, the silver hurt Phenola? The baby? It was a risk I would never take. And so, all I could offer her was my hand. And I kept holding as another wave of contractions rounded her body until she gripped the headrest and my hand as if she was trying to anchor herself somewhere amid the pain.

As her eyes squeezed shut, my gaze landed on Tayna, who was wholly focused on the road. His pupils were blown wide with fear, and I wondered if it was fear for me and what I'd just done, fear for Phenola and the baby, or fear for the place we were now heading.

I knew next to nothing about the Tanks except that they operated in a militaristic style. Where the Cards were sophisticated and run like a corporation, the Tanks operated like a regime. In the streets of the city, I'd always heard them before I saw them. They were a loud bunch, barking orders as boisterously as they downed beers.

And they weren't afraid to push aside or stomp down anyone who got in their way.

Sure, the Tanks might have allied themselves with the Whigs, but that didn't mean they would be any less brutal than the Cards.

Tayna's face reflected the uncertainty I felt. Yet for Phenola and the baby—for Kenji—we were throwing ourselves into a new viper's nest with nothing but hope that we'd all make it out alive.

9

Lissa

The Cards had a compound crafted from an old mansion estate on the cliffs. The Whigs had a community of farmland tucked into the mountainside. And the Tanks... the Tanks had a ship.

Not just any ship. The military vessel filled my entire field of vision as it came into view ahead of the Humvee, as we parked near the docks. The air was briny, just shy of too sharp.

A sliver of sun was left in the sky, blazing red against the backdrop of the ocean. Karadin and Phenola stayed in the truck, Phenola's labored breathing like a steady heartbeat pushing me to hurry, hurry, *hurry*.

We had all agreed it was best they stayed behind while Tayna and I requested entry onto the ship. It would be easier for us to run if things didn't go as planned. It would give us a higher likelihood of keeping Phenola and the baby safe.

I had to ball my fist to keep my silver from spiking in panic as we approached. The last thing I needed was to get us turned away out of fear I might spark at any moment.

The deep bass of a drum rose into the air above our heads. It sounded like they were having some sort of party on the roof. The hum of voices carried on the sea breeze, filtering through as laughter and high-pitched cries of ecstasy kept time with the music.

I kept close to Tayna's shoulder as I took in the vessel. I'd seen it at a distance before, during my trips into the city, but had never dared approach this close. Growing up, my mother had taught me that the gangs were the enemy above all others. The Cards might have been at the top of that list, but that didn't mean the others were safe.

I felt more fear now approaching this ship than at facing those cars in the sea. At least there I'd been free. The vessel stretching before me looked like a giant prison, with its dark metal walls and small, round windows in neat rows. It blocked out the final rays of the sun before it slipped beneath the ocean horizon. It was decidedly larger than Gideon's mansion and definitely taller, with at least five floors of windows I could count above my head.

There wasn't a clear door to access the entrance, but Tayna had obviously been here before and navigated over the old wooden dock with deft steps. Mine were not as sure as I followed, but I kept up well enough, even against the slight sway caused by the waves below.

And suddenly, a spotlight shone on Tayna and me that was so blinding I threw up my arm, blinking against the light, useless in the heavy beam.

A hand grabbed mine.

Tayna. He felt warm and strong and familiar as he twined our fingers, pulling me snugly against his side. My front pressed into his arm, my lips grazing along his shoulder as I instinctively tucked myself against him.

"We're good," he murmured so only I could hear. And then louder, he yelled, "Tanks and tides split the skies."

There was a clipped laugh from above, closer than the pumping music. "Order and thee drown in the sea." The booming voice was raspy, as if it came from the depths of the speaker's chest.

Tayna called back again, almost as if it were a game now, "We're allies, not enemies."

And after a beat of silence, the voice volleyed back, "We're friends, not foes."

It was closer than I would have anticipated, causing me to jump.

Then the booming voice called, "Lower the beams, Samiya." There was a distinct clip to the words, almost as if the man was near-singing them.

The light finally flickered off, still illuminating the area around us, but it was no longer blinding.

As my vision cleared, I found Tayna clasping arms with a proud man, whose pronounced features meant his every expression left nothing to the imagination. And he was delighted to see Tayna, pulling him into an embrace while still clutching his forearm.

"It's good to see you again my friend." He grinned, showing straight white teeth that flashed against the spotlight. He wore a gray jacket that looked like something he'd scrounged from the ship. But intricate, colorful embroidery had been added along the sleeves, turning the garment into a fascinating dichotomy of tailored class and free-spirited mischief. He even had some colorful thread woven into his hair, and a single earring gleamed with gems dangling from his lobe.

"Banu," Tayna said, pulling back, "I wish this was a social visit, but we need your help."

"Yes, *we*." Banu's sharp eyes tracked to mine, and he pulled back from Tayna to run a deft finger up my neck and beneath my chin until my head was tilting up. I allowed him to study my eyes, even as I glared. But he seemed to marvel at the silver he saw reflecting back. "What have you brought?"

I considered showing this man just what Tayna had brought to his ship's door with my silver, but stayed my hand. Not yet. I took a breath, focusing on control, pushing my silver down.

"It's not just her," Tayna said, keeping me tight to his side as if sensing I was close to snapping at him. "I have two other women in the truck. One's in labor. She's having a baby. We need shelter and require medical support, whatever you can offer. The woman with her is a doctor—the best we have. But we don't have much time."

Tayna looked back to the truck as if worried we'd already wasted too much.

But Banu's eyes didn't stray from me. He seemed to have barely heard Tayna, "There've been lots of rumors. Wild tales. Smoke in the hills. Cards in the streets. Dia rallying the riffraff. Lots of tales indeed."

"We will explain all of it. But please, Banu—"

The man held up the hand that wasn't pressed beneath my chin to silence him. His eyes flicked to the Humvee in the distance.

"We are allies, Tayna. I support what your Whigs are trying to do for this city, but that doesn't mean help comes for free. The Tanks have needs, as well. I have to take care of my people."

My eyes narrowed as I finally pulled my chin away. "What do you want?" I demanded.

Banu smiled that too-white smile again. "Five vials of silver, Malkia. From you."

"No—"

"Deal," I said quickly, cutting Tayna off. He might not like it, but I knew this game. I knew how the leaders of these gangs thought and operated. This was about pride and power as much as it was about his people. And then I added, "But not until after the baby's born."

I wasn't sure what "Malkia" meant, but it didn't really matter. The deal was clear enough. And five vials of silver were worth it to keep Phenola and the baby safe.

Banu's smile was near-wicked as he said, "Good. Then get your pregnant friend and your doctor." His steps were swaggering as he moved from Tayna and me to call up, "Samiya! Lower the ramp! We have visitors. And get Ashland from his bunk."

I was already moving, racing back to the truck to get to Phenola.

There wasn't a sound coming from the Humvee, and it made the hair on my neck stand on end.

I couldn't see Karadin or Phenola in the back seat, and the fear caused me to break into a run as soon as I hit the pavement.

My hands were clumsy as I grasped for the handle.

The adrenaline made my chest burn.

But I found the two women grasping each other in silent solidarity. Phenola was still panting and sweating, but she was propped upright against the seat. Karadin clutched her hand as the two breathed in sync.

"They're letting us inside," I said immediately. "Only a few more steps, Phen."

She nodded, letting out a deep breath that turned into a panting wail as she pressed herself up from the seat.

Tayna caught her as she slid from the truck, practically carrying her as he swooped an arm underneath her. I took up the spot on the other side of her, bracing her weight as we began walking.

"You tell us if you need to stop," Tayna said. "We're on your time, Phenola."

Her voice was clipped as she said, "Keep. Going."

Karadin ran ahead to where a large ramp had been rolled down onto the wooden dock, providing a large entry into the bowels of the ship.

She didn't introduce herself. She didn't even spare the emerging Tanks much of a glance as she said, "Don't you people have a wheelchair? Or a stretcher?"

A guy simply put his hands up as if in surrender. A beer hung limply from one. He was young, barely a man, with the same colorful fatigues as Banu. Half of his hair was dyed a flaming red, and his black-rimmed eyes were wide at the wild doctor barreling toward him.

"Fucking useless," she seethed. "Where's your clinic?"

Banu emerged at the entrance, followed closely by a tall, lithe woman whose short hair was pulled back in rows twisted with colorful string along her scalp. Banu took one look from Karadin to Phenola, braced between Tayna and me, and called, "Clear the halls!"

That snapped the watchers into action. They scrambled back into the ship on their captain's orders, though I did notice some of them were swaying slightly. I didn't think it was from the ship but instead from the party that had clearly been going on for a while despite the fact that the sun had only just set.

Banu stalked toward us. "Why didn't you tell me she was this far along?" His commanding tone was heated and directed at Tayna.

"I don't have much experience with... birth," Tayna said between clenched teeth.

Banu raised an eyebrow at that but gentled as he saw Phenola's panting, sweaty face.

"Let's get you inside, Mama." Banu's voice was surprisingly soft as he took my place beside Phenola, bracing one arm under her shoulder and one hand against her swollen belly. He smiled as if he could feel the life within her.

With that, he led her up the ramp and inside with Karadin close at their heels. The interior past the ramp was shadowed against the darkness that had fallen over the ship, and I lost them to the depths.

The woman who'd been at Banu's side now watched me warily from where she leaned against the entrance. Her gaze slipped from my hands to the tattoo exposed on my bare shoulder and finally settled on my eyes. She didn't seem to approve of what she found there, the iridescent tendrils of silver that highlighted my irises.

"You're Gideon's fedha, then?" Her accent matched Banu's but was more pronounced, her words clipped. And, though she was tall and thin, something was dangerous about her as she crossed her arms. She seemed poised to deny me entrance, keeping me from following Tayna and Phenola.

I shook my head, "I—"

"His Silver." She eyed me.

I swallowed, ignoring the stab in my chest, and pushed out the words, "Oh. No." And then, "Gideon's dead."

I didn't add that I had killed him. Well, he jumped from the cliffs. But I'd been the one to force silver down his throat. When silver from different donors was mixed, its benefits were mitigated. And not just mitigated. It caused extreme illness, fatigue, and in my case, loss of abilities for upward of a week. When I'd forced him to swallow a vial of blood, I'd nullified the silver Gideon had previously ingested. He no longer had the upper hand that the blood had given him. Plus, I'd had a gun aimed at his chest.

And I would have pulled the trigger.

If Samiya was surprised by the news of Gideon's death, she didn't show it, but her lips thinned. Her eyes flicked to the mountains behind me where I knew they'd seen the smoke earlier from the compound fire.

She nodded once. "Chaos will be coming. Maybe it's already here." She pushed herself up to stand and dropped her arms.

"Chaos?"

"Mm," Samiya said in response as she turned into the ship.

"I should be with my friend. I need to catch up to them."

"And so you will." She gestured for me to follow. "The woman maybe only has a few hours of labor."

"How do you know—"

"Babies are not uncommon in all places. Only this city." Her voice was growing farther away the deeper she walked into the ship until I lost sight of her among the shadows.

And so I followed the strange woman into the darkness.

10

Lissa

I'd never been claustrophobic. Or at least, I didn't think I was claustrophobic. But following Samiya down endless windowless hallways while Phenola's panting cries echoed off the walls was enough to make my breathing hitch in my chest.

It also made my silver feel volatile, which was... *not* ideal while confined inside a metal ship. I'd just released a ton of silver into the ocean. It should feel more calm, but it was pulsing in my veins. Pressure built behind my eyes from pushing it down, which made my head begin to ache.

The corridors smelled sterile and looked it too—endless gray walls separated by staggered ladders that I could only assume led to still more hallways. It was a strange contradiction to the colorfulness I'd seen so far from the Tanks.

Samiya navigated it all like a mole who'd dug the tunnels herself. Her wide eyes didn't look back at me once to make sure I was keeping pace. I allowed my fingers to trail along the walls, which seemed damp with cold. I knew if something went wrong, if the Tanks turned on us, I would have no hope of navigating out of this place.

Up ahead, blue light filtered from a door that had already been thrown open. Maybe "door" was the wrong word. It wasn't like anything I'd ever seen before, a large metal monstrosity that matched the steel of the walls. It was so heavy that a wheel was attached where the handle would normally go, and I imagined strong arms cranking desperately as the contraption creaked on sturdy hinges.

I glanced behind me once more. The hallways we'd left were dark except for the white lights dotted in the corners near the floor to illuminate our path. They were motion-activated, snuffing out soon after we'd walked past. The corridor behind me was bathed in shadows, and the music from above was a muffled beat reverberating beneath my feet.

With a deep breath and clenched fists, I stepped into the room and found a clinic, already hurried with activity.

This room looked more technical than the clinic at the compound. Where that space had been bright air and views of the ocean beyond the cliffside, this room was full of beeping machines that cast blue light. There were sterile metal counters against one wall and small beds separated by barely opaque curtains. It felt like a place for science experiments more than a place to care for sick people. Yet I couldn't argue with the amount of equipment they seemed to have lining the walls. There was even what looked to be an X-ray machine.

Phenola lay on one of the medical beds, propped with pillows so she was reclined, as if in a large, comfy chair, rather than on the thin medical mattress. A wool blanket was draped around her shoulders, and Karadin held her hand while yelling at people throughout the room.

"Tayna, grab those towels and put them at the table by her feet. You," she pointed at a thin man with thick, round glasses that made his dark eyes appear twice the normal size. He was a stark contrast to Banu, wearing a clean white apron over a buttoned shirt instead of colorful fatigues. "Is there a sink in this room? We'll need plenty of sterile, fresh water. And ice if you have it. Ice chips, specifically."

"I'm—" the man spluttered. "I'm the attending doctor on this vessel."

"It's okay, Ashland," Banu said, with a weary sigh as if he could already tell the two were rearing for an argument. He looked back at Karadin. "The sinks work. The water's fresh and safe for consumption. We can get you ice from the kitchens."

Karadin nodded, taking him at his word. "You can find us some food, too. Phenola will need protein. Cheese or dried meat will work just fine—something more if you have it. Fish maybe? Also, fresh fruit, especially citrus, would be appreciated for the electrolytes. Ideally juice."

Banu eyed her, then looked sideways at Tayna, as if unsure of this spitfire woman who was giving him orders on his own ship but not willing to argue with her when there was a baby on the line.

"Oh," Karadin said, "and a glass of wine would be lovely if you have one to spare."

That did it for Ashland, and he barked out, "Wine!"

"Yes, it'll help her relax," Karadin said, as if this were common knowledge. She may not have delivered a baby before, but Karadin had read enough medical journals to recite the best practices in her sleep.

Banu looked at Samiya, who nodded and slid around me back toward the doors with an, "On it," over her shoulder. "Though I can't guarantee the wine. There might still be some tequila upstairs if the boys haven't gone through it yet."

"What options do you have for pain?" Karadin asked Ashland, who fumbled to clean some contraption that looked like a long pair of tongs. I didn't need to know what that did.

Ashland sputtered at the request. "Well, not an epidural if that's what you were hoping for."

Karadin sighed as if he were an absolute idiot. "Antibiotics?"

Ashland pushed his glasses back up his nose. "Silver works just as well."

Karadin's eyebrows shot up even higher. "No antibiotics? Tayna," she snapped to get his attention. Snapped at him! But Tayna just nodded at attention like a good soldier. "Will you take a look in the Humvee and see what you can find? I think I remember packing amoxicillin in the blue bin."

"On it," he said.

Banu seemed to take that as his chance to leave, too, because he said, "I'll lead you out."

"What can I do?" I asked Karadin when it was only the three of us and Ashland left. I played restlessly with the necklace at my neck. "How're you doin', Phen?"

"Oh," she sighed between a pursed lip exhale. "Just trying to remember to breathe."

"That's all you need to do." Karadin patted her gently. "Especially now that we've gotten rid of the extras in here. Now it's time to get to work." She rolled up her sleeves. "Lissa, you take her hand. We've got a bit of time, but I want to check our progress. Phenola, you just relax as much as you can and keep breathing. Lissa, if a contraction starts, breathe with her. Four counts in, four counts out. Steady breath."

Karadin moved to the back of the room to the sink to wash her hands, and Ashland followed her either to again attempt to take charge or to do the same. I wished I could hear their conversation. Just the thought made me grin.

But the small smile faltered when Phenola said around an exhale, "He should be here."

I brought my other hand up to cocoon her slender fingers within my grasp. Glimmering tears pooled in the corner of her eyes.

"Oh, Phen." I couldn't do anything to take this pain from her. Kenji *should* be here right now. There was nothing right about the fact that he was gone. Dead.

"I don't know how to do this without him." Phenola's voice was reedy as she clenched her teeth around another exhale.

"You're not without him. Not entirely." I leaned in closer to her, resting my elbows on the edge of the bed. "He's here. A piece of him is right there with you within that little one." I gestured to her belly with my chin. "You both did that. Together. And you're not doing this part alone, either. I'm here. And Tayna's here. And Karadin, well, Karadin is so *here* that she's already taken charge of this place."

Phenola snorted a small laugh, the crinkles in her cheeks catching the fallen tears. And then another wave of contractions seized her. Her free hand braced on her stomach as she lifted her back from the bed. "Ah!" She tried to breathe through it. I saw her trying to go slow, but her chest gave way to pants as her eyes shut tightly and her shoulders hunched, seizing all her focus.

Samiya came running into the room with a hastily wrapped parcel of food in one hand and a cup in the other.

"Juice," she announced, bringing it to the side of the bed. "With ice."

I took it from her, pinching the straw between my fingers and carefully bringing the cup close to Phenola's lips.

She took a small sip as she collapsed back onto the mattress. "That was a rough one," she panted.

"Do you want something to eat?" Samiya asked.

Phenola just shook her head, her eyes drifting shut with exhaustion and her breathing heavy as she rubbed her swollen belly.

"More ice would be nice, though." She nodded at the cup, and I obliged, bringing it to her lips.

"Anything else?" I offered as she collapsed her head back into the pillow, letting the liquid trickle down her throat.

"I just need a minute to– Ah!" Phenola clenched again. Another wave. So soon.

"Karadin!" I called, trying to keep my voice steady as I set down the cup of juice and grabbed for Phenola's hand, leashing my silver and pushing it down. She gripped my hand like she was intentionally trying to snap all the bones in my fingers, but I didn't pull away. She could break the bones, and I would happily let her. My silver would heal me quick enough. If that was what she needed to get through it, it was worth the pain.

Karadin dashed back to the bed, her gloved hands raised as she lifted the blanket covering Phenola's legs and settled herself down for a look. It only took her a few moments. When she looked back up, her attention was on Ashland.

"She's dilated," Karadin said. She looked at Phenola. "Okay, Phen, it's time to start pushing."

Phenola nodded, her eyes going wide with trepidation.

"You're almost there." I told her.

Tayna returned then. He clutched a bag of medical supplies but seemed well aware they were no longer needed.

Banu was with him but stayed in the doorway, giving me a slow nod before stepping back into the shadows of the hallway.

Tayna stepped up on the other side of Phenola, and I couldn't help the smile we shared. The moment was overwhelming in its significance. It was a chance encounter on the streets that had led Tayna and me to Tea and Trinkets. It was Madam Cartenoth's strange kindness in offering two street rats a free cup of tea. It was Phenola's curious mind that led her to the Whigs. It was my continued visits to Tea and Trinkets that brought Kenji and Phenola together. And it was Kenji who had pushed us all to dream a little bigger.

It was his dream, inspired by Phenola, of a better world that had connected us all.

We would fight for that dream for this baby.

And this moment somehow felt bigger than all of us for that dream and for this child.

Phenola moved in a way that was so instinctual and primal as she pushed. She was mesmerizing as she fought through the exhaustion and grief and pain and kept going. It was all I could do to wipe her brow, hold her hand, offer her small sips of water, and murmur soft words of continued encouragement.

Even Ashland no longer seemed annoyed but instead fell into the role of willing assistant as Karadin stayed at Phenola's feet, urging her to, "Push! Push again, Phen." All while she was saying, "You've got this. You can do this."

Tayna's eyes were as round as mine felt as he watched the scene playing out, spectacular and entrancing in that it was intrinsically human. And in a world where humanity was so often forgotten, this felt right in a way few things in this city ever did.

And when the first cry of a tiny new life entering this world broke through the already humming space, I knew that I regretted nothing of the decisions I'd made over the course of my life, because it led me here, to this moment.

And I would burn it all again just to know Phenola and Kenji's child would cry into this world.

"It's a girl!" Karadin's voice quaked, her smile trembling. She handed the purplish mess of a perfect newborn up to Phenola, who took the baby onto her bare chest and wept. Her tears were filled with joy and sorrow and all of the unknown things the universe bundled into a tiny, wailing package.

It was worth it.

It was so incredibly hard. But it was worth it.

11

Lissa

The sun was breaking over the horizon by the time I stumbled my exhausted way into the bunk room, where Samiya told me I could sleep. It was a simple space, lined with three steel bunk beds. A small, circular window provided a hint of daybreak, and not much else.

I didn't need anything else. Pausing only long enough to kick off my shoes, I collapsed on one of the bottom bunks. It had been more than twenty-four hours since I'd last slept, after all.

No sooner had my head hit the pillow than it felt like I was stirring awake at a rustling sound coming from the opposite wall.

For a moment, in that hazy place between dreams and reality, I was separate from time and place.

All I remembered was the sweet smell of newborn baby, the shock of dark hair peeking out between a cotton blanket, and a tiny body cradled in my arms that was as light as my hardback copy of *Count of Monte Cristo*. I hadn't wanted to let go of that little bundle, but the exhaustion could no longer be held at bay.

Phenola had named her Calliope in honor of Madam Cartenoth. I hadn't even known the older woman's first name until Phenola had explained. She was always just Madam Cartenoth or Bat, as Phenola had lovingly taken to calling her, thanks to her eccentricities.

Calliope.

It suited the baby. And made me smile—a true smile—as I awoke sleepily in the bunk, stretching up only to smack my wrist on one of the metal beams of the bunk. I groaned.

"Space is tight in here."

I jerked, hitting my forehead on the slats of the bunk overhead.

Pain split behind my eyebrow, and I cursed loudly as the ache settled, then began to tingle as it healed thanks to my silver.

Tayna was over me in a second. "Let me see."

He gripped my chin with strong fingers, tentatively palming the spot. I winced, shaking him off only to crack open an eye and find his shirtless chest taking up nearly my entire field of vision, all hard lines and smooth skin. My stomach thrilled, breath catching as I remembered trailing my fingers over those ridges of muscle that day on the farm. His mouth had been so soft and warm against my skin, the rocks rough beneath my palms as I—

"It's already healing," I exhaled quickly, pushing him away, all too aware of my fingers as they pressed into his hard stomach. His skin was warm beneath my touch, and I sucked in a breath before I could catch myself, inhaling his earthen summer scent. Only to let it out quickly with a, "I didn't know you were in here."

I rubbed at my forehead. The bruise would heal in a few minutes, but that didn't make the sting any less bothersome now. It had started to itch.

"Liss," he sighed, and I wasn't sure if he was disappointed because I'd pushed him away or because I was unsure how to act with him in this room with me. There was a time when we'd spent every night together, curled around each other in the pile of blankets we called a bed. Sometimes it shocked me how much I missed those days. In the midst of the empty bellies and fear, there had been contentment. Now, everything felt as murky as the ocean water beyond the small window in this room.

He stayed hovering over me, his arms caging me in, and his mouth parted just slightly as if he was lost in the memories, too.

The desire was still right there.

"I don't—" I breathed, standing from the bed.

I didn't feel angry with him anymore. Not really. There was a lingering hurt, but I understood. Of course I understood him. Yet I couldn't bring myself to simply go back to the way we'd been before. I felt awkward and unsure of myself as I staggered from the bed.

He nodded, but I could see the rejection lining his face, furrowing his brow. I knew he'd been hopeful after our conversation in the Humvee that things between us would be better... easier. But I hadn't had a moment to think since that conversation.

"I'm going to get some breakfast and see Phenola and the baby."

"I—" He shook his head, stopping whatever words he'd been contemplating, whatever conversations he was considering breaching.

I was honestly grateful.

But as I reached the door, I heard his low words. "What do I have to do, Liss? Just tell me what to do to reach you. I can't take this distance between us."

The pressure was heavy on my chest. I swallowed it down. "I just need time, Tayna."

"I've given you time. I've given you space. You can barely even look at me."

He was right, but I forced myself to turn to him.

He was still my golden champion, who'd stood with me on those cliffs and accepted our fate. Together. For better or worse, Tayna Ravidian was mine.

There was no denying it as I took in the man standing before me. His bronze frame cast in morning light from the small window in the room. His hair fell to frame his face, even as he pushed it back in his exasperation. His muscles flexed, jaw tensing as he forced himself to meet my gaze as if challenging me not to look away first.

He was my mirror, the gold to my silver, and I saw myself reflected in his eyes.

He was supposed to understand me the most, but how could I make him understand this… thing festering inside me? How could I find the words to express the guilt and uncertainty and sadness and anger that twisted my guts until I no longer knew who I was or what I believed? And it wasn't about his lies. Yes, that had been part of it. But more than anything, it was the fact that I couldn't seem to reconcile the tattered pieces inside myself. The woman I'd been was gone. Or maybe I'd always been playing pretend, and the grief had stripped me bare. Since the cliffs, my silver had been different. Yes, I could control it, but I felt more on the edge all the time. How could I possibly tell him that the only relief I'd felt in the past week had been those moments when I'd used my silver to cause destruction? I'd relished burning the Cards' mansion to cinders, just as I'd relished stopping those cars from reaching us on the beach.

I'd done it to protect my friends, but I'd done it for myself, too. And I'd do it again.

What did that make me? A creation I didn't understand with abilities at my fingertips that remained a mystery even as I'd learned to push it down.

So he was right. I didn't know how to open up to him anymore. Because what would the person who knew me best see inside me when I no longer felt like I knew myself? I wasn't ready to know.

Tayna watched the walls rebuilding behind my eyes and sighed. The desire and pain and longing and tension coiled in the room around us like smoke.

I thought of the first time he'd kissed me, the way it had felt like coming home. And god, I wanted that comfort again. I wanted to let it all go and sink into him and let him make it all better. He would do that. I could close the space now, and he would welcome me with those warm, strong arms. Tayna was that man for me. And it would work. For a while. But there was not a world where he swept me back to the farm, and we lived happily ever after. That was not my story. I was no longer that soft and innocent woman.

"I'm leaving." Tayna's words cut through the tension between us.

"Leaving?" The disbelieving words were out of my mouth before I could stop them.

"We slept a good chunk of the morning, and I need to get back to Laykin and Enver. They camped with the supplies all night. I can't leave them out there, especially not with the unrest in the city. There's sure to be more patrols on the roads, and they've got enough supplies in those Humvees to be an ideal prize for any of the gangs. Not to mention, Enver's a Silver."

"Right." I swallowed. The hurt clogged my throat even as I knew this was for the best.

"You could come with me." It was a hesitant offer. Another olive branch extended.

And I responded quickly. "No."

A shadow flickered across his face.

I opened my mouth to search for something more. And then closed it again. Which meant I ended up just sort of blubbering without an actual response before clenching my teeth.

Which seemed to be enough of a response for Tayna, who nodded and grabbed his backpack from the floor. "I'm not going to force you to come back to the Whigs with me, Lissa. You can make your own decisions. You should choose for yourself. If you want some... something else, you can make that choice."

His words had the bite of rejection, and I didn't understand why they hurt so badly. Wasn't my freedom exactly what I wanted? He was affirming my right to make my own decisions. It should have been everything I wanted to hear. But it just felt like the tear between us was splitting more deeply down the center.

It was all I could do to breathe out, "Okay."

"Okay?" He seemed poised to say more, but then just nodded and, finally, shook his head. A lock of chestnut hair fell across his forehead, over his eyebrows, shadowing his already dark expression. "Okay." He nodded again and headed for the door.

I didn't glance up to see if he looked back, and I didn't let the tears fall after he left. I'd cried too many already.

Tayna had made his choices.

And I'd made mine.

My heart ached.

I half expected him to come barreling back into the room. I thought of the first night when he'd kissed me at the farm. The press of our lips had been a fire in my veins. I'd come alive beneath his fingertips. I'd drank in the feel of his skin pressed to every place I could manage when I'd thought I'd never touch him again.

We hadn't had sex, yet those moments with him on the farm had been some of the most intimate of my life.

I braced myself against the cool metal wall, refusing to crumple to the ground, but my silver sparked against the wall. I stumbled back, as I stared at my smoking fingers.

I swallowed down the scream, balling my hands into fists.

The silence of the room pressed in on me.

He wasn't coming back for me. Not this time. And what did I expect? This was what I'd been asking for, right? Space. This would be good. Some time to myself would be good. So why did it feel like I was ripping out my own heart?

I pushed that thought away. There was already too much grief to contend with, too much to swallow down.

With the semblance of control I had left, I threw my hair into a ponytail before braving the maze of hallways.

I would find Phenola and the baby. That would make me feel steadier.

But the hallways all looked the same.

I'd been so tired last night I'd hardly paid attention when Samiya led me to the room.

I needed to eat. My stomach was roiling and tight. I didn't even remember the last time I'd had a decent meal. Two days ago, maybe, with some trail mix in between.

The hallway curved right. Again. And I could have sworn I'd taken enough rights to have gone in a circle at this point.

Had I already passed through this hallway?

I found a door and tried the handle.

Locked.

The gray-painted metal walls suddenly didn't seem wide enough. My eyes scanned for stairs, another path, a way out.

Frustration spiked as I turned only to come face-to-face with another long hallway.

The tears that I'd held back when talking to Tayna threatened because what was I doing? I'd waited years to leave the compound. I'd dreamed of the day when I could make my own decisions. Freedom was all I'd ever wanted. And now that I had it, I couldn't even get myself out of a damn hallway in a ship.

Fucking useless except for the blood in my veins.

I put a palm on the wall to steady myself. The ship vibrated beneath my touch as if it were alive and breathing. It helped, somehow.

"You best not be trying to leave with Tayna this morning."

Boots hit the metal with a reverberating clang as Banu jumped from a hole in the ceiling that must lead to another hallway on the floor above. He landed in a steady crouch before standing to his full height. For someone so large, he was graceful, I'd give him that. He took up nearly the entire length of the hall. His broad frame was just as wide as the gap-toothed grin he flashed me.

"You and I still have a deal to settle, Malkia," he said, striding toward me. The bobbles on his fatigues jangled as he walked.

Right. My silver. I'd agreed to give him five vials in exchange for his help and the sanctuary of his ship.

My silver blood.

The thing people saw first when they looked at me. The weapon.

"I haven't forgotten," I told him, pressing away from the wall and straightening. "But maybe some breakfast first? Unless you want me passing out in your infirmary."

Banu eyed me up and down as if judging my sincerity before he cocked a head down the hallway in the direction I'd come from.

So I was going in circles.

"This way." He grinned as if he knew and had been watching me for some time from his hole in the ceiling.

I finally gave way to the small smile tugging at my lips and sighed. "These hallways are awful."

"I love them." He looked them up and down as if appreciating each detail of craftsmanship. He fell into step beside me, walking with his hands clasped casually behind his back. He sort of swayed when he walked, his body moving like a dance to the drumbeats I'd heard last night. "It used to house thousands of people for months on end in the middle of the ocean."

"For months?" I imagined being stuck within these hallways for endless weeks. I might lose my mind being in the middle of the ocean, yet not be able to experience its peace and serenity.

Banu mused. "With men who were poised to kill if their government demanded it."

"Why would their government demand it?"

Banu shrugged. "Same reason the gangs demand violence. Power. Control. Resources. We humans are simple creatures, really."

"Simple yet we almost destroyed the world." I thought of the silver bombs dropped on top of lands full of innocent people. The death and destruction had been catastrophic.

"Simple creatures are especially dangerous when they are afraid, Malkia."

Banu stopped in front of a door, using his entire body as he bent to pull it open. With an open palm, he gestured me inside like a gentleman about to enter a party with a lady. Only Banu was no gentleman. Not that I knew the captain of the Tanks well, but the Tanks were known for their parties and their riots in the streets. They weren't known for their civility, and I could only imagine their leader set the precedent. Yet Banu had been kind to us. He'd offered us sanctuary on his ship. He somehow seemed larger than life, and he was escorting me now like a guest.

Beyond the doors, I didn't find another hallway, but instead a giant, well-lit room. I exhaled a breath. We were at the end of the ship. The floor-to-ceiling windows showcased the ocean stretching out before us. In the distance, I could make out the city on the shore beyond. Just a day on this ship, and I was already aching to feel the wind on my face. My silver stirred beneath my veins as if spurred by my longing.

The room was quiet. A few people milled about or sat sipping from mugs near the windows. A woman with short spikey hair seated atop one of the tables watched me skeptically, then nodded curtly to Banu. There was no pandering, no shuffling to stand, or respectful bowing. Banu might as well have been just another soldier in their ranks. I could respect the casualness. It made everything feel more at peace, and I needed a little of that right now.

"I guess I missed the breakfast rush then," I mused, content with the quiet of the space.

But Banu snorted. "It hasn't even started yet. We tend to dance until we wake up the sun."

"Every night?"

"Why not? We are the survivors of the end of the world. What else should we be doing if not dancing and drinking and fucking?"

I couldn't hide my blush, even as I shrugged and murmured, "Fair enough."

The Cards had their bonfires, but they were reserved for special occasions, and Gideon still maintained order even among the dancing and the drinking and, well, even the fucking. Gideon would have loved this ship, but he would have hated the lack of decorum. I wondered if he'd ever visited here when he'd left the compound. Would Banu have let him enter?

In front of us, a cafeteria line was set up with a large vat of something steaming. Next to it were simple rolls and jam. It wasn't a fancy spread. Nothing like the Cards offered with their full staff of chefs and bakers and the finest ingredients the city had to offer. The Tanks clearly lived a simpler life. But it looked edible enough, so I grabbed a bowl and spooned some of the mush.

"It's better with sugar," Banu said, gesturing with his chin toward the smaller bowls of brown sugar and honey. I opted for a healthy scoop. If the Tanks encouraged eating sugar in the morning, I would not object. Laykin would have rolled his eyes, and Kenji would have sniffed at the bowl skeptically. I could picture both of them almost as if they were standing next to me right now.

The image stabbed at my heart.

They weren't my guards anymore.

And Kenji wasn't anything anymore.

The bowl of mush slipped in my fingers. Banu caught it with a deft hand, steadying it while watching me. I managed a weak smile and reminded myself of Calliope's sweet sleeping face. I let that image keep me upright as Banu led me to one of the cool metal tables bolted to the floor. He didn't serve himself any of the mushy stuff, which I assumed meant he'd already eaten.

"You don't have to stay with me," I said, shoveling a mouthful of the beige slop into my mouth and realizing it was slightly sticky and a lot goopy. I tossed it between my cheeks for a moment, deciding to swallow instead of spitting it back into the bowl. Thank god Banu had recommended sugar.

"Ah." He waved me off. "And miss the look on your face each time you attempt to swallow? I think not. Plus, I'm making sure you stick to your side of the bargain."

I set down the spoon. "I wouldn't go back on my word."

His dark eyes narrowed on mine in a way that made me want to swallow. And I would have if the remaining mush in my throat hadn't made my tongue feel thick. So I spooned another bite into my mouth and attempted to chew the warm, mushy stuff.

Once I swallowed that down, I asked the question that had been niggling at me. "Why do you need my silver anyway? Don't you have your own Silvers living here?"

Banu rested his elbows on the table. "First thing, Malkia, I don't 'have' any silvers at all. Some choose to call the Tanks their home, and they are welcome here. But they are not forced like your Ace forced you."

I glanced around the room to a corner where a few people chatted. A guy sat on the metal table, his foot braced on a chair and his arm slung across a knee as he leaned into a woman to speak animatedly while she laughed loudly and carelessly. At another table, a woman scribbled notes on a pad of paper, swatting away the attention of a man who was attempting to whisper in her ear. Her brows pinched together as she seemingly scolded him away.

My eyes found Banu's again. "And the second?"

"The second?" He studied me again with a lighthearted gaze that seemed to only barely mask the power of this man. He didn't need silver to have the hairs on the back of my neck rising. He leaned back in his chair, draping an arm over the back of the one next to it. Sprawled and lazy like the pirates I imagined from *Treasure Island*.

"You said 'first thing,'" I prompted. "I'm assuming there are more?"

He blew out a breath, and he was the one to break my stare to look out at the ocean beyond the windows before turning back to me. "Two of the Silvers on this ship went missing last week. They were planning to go to one of the clubs in the city, but they never returned."

The spoon in my hand stilled. "And you're sure they didn't choose to go missing?" I dared to ask.

Banu's answering stare was dark. "I'm sure. They weren't just Silvers. They were my friends."

Were. I didn't miss his choice of words.

And it made sense. They'd most likely found trouble if they'd gone missing. People existed in this city who would kill for silver blood. Actually, most people in this city would kill for silver blood. Whether they were addicts or members of gangs, silver meant power, and if someone saw an opportunity to get some for themselves, well, they wouldn't pass on it.

"Do you think it was Dia?"

"Dia is a jackal trying to be a king. I have a bad feeling this is much, much worse."

I pushed the bowl of mush toward the center of the table.

Banu blinked away his grief, and his aloof mask settled back on his face. The hint of his canines poked out from beneath his top lip as he watched me. "Done then?"

"It's hard to have an appetite when you talk of draining Silvers," I murmured.

"*Missing* Silvers, Malkia," he said and stood, offering me a hand.

I accepted it, allowing him to pull me to my feet. "You keep calling me that." Our faces were close, and I suddenly wondered if Banu was flirting with me. Something told me this was a man who flirted easily. I pulled back just slightly from his towering body. "What does that mean? Malkia?"

He only grinned wider. "It's an old word. It means 'Queen.'"

Now I did jerk back from his grip, but his hand only tightened in mind, not letting me go.

"I'm not a Queen," I hissed. "I haven't been for a while."

"You're still very much a Queen." Banu's voice was low. "And it has nothing to do with that tattoo on your shoulder. The game isn't over, Lissa. It's just getting started."

I shuddered at the words. "What do you mean? What do you know?"

But he shook his head and dropped his hand as if some sort of spell had been lifted. "Things could get ugly now that Gideon is gone. He was a brute, but he gave order to this city." After a pause, he said, "Come on. Ashland will be waiting for us."

I followed the strange, colorful man, feeling vulnerable under his too-long stares, his pet names, and his talk of Silvers going missing. At some point in the cramped metal hallways, I found myself wishing Tayna were still here.

12

Lissa

The upside to being back in the infirmary was getting to see Phenola and Calliope.

Phenola glowed even beneath the soft blue lights. She looked more alive than I'd seen her since the cliffs. She reveled in the new life cradled against her chest. Her eyes only left the small child long enough to pass a sleepy grin at me as I entered the room.

I understood the hope that swelled in her gaze. Calliope's birth had been the first ray of light we'd all had since losing Kenji. I felt it, too. It didn't heal the grief, but cooled it somehow, if only fleetingly.

The longing in my chest didn't subside. The subtle ache lived with me now, like it had joined the pulse of silver within my veins. One heartbeat for grief. One heartbeat for guilt. One for uncertainty. And still another for rage. Each thrum a churn of emotions felt as swirling and endless as the cliffs where I'd lost everything.

It was all I could do to hold it in.

One breath at a time.

I hadn't been lying to Banu. I was not a Queen, and I sure as hell wasn't a Card. But I wasn't a Whig, either. I couldn't claim them as my own, not now. To me, the Whigs were Tayna and Alaric... Alaric. My maybe father—god, I didn't want to go to those thoughts. So where did that leave me?

What am I?

I looked down at the silver veins stretching over my skin as I offered my arm dutifully to Ashland, who wasted no time in drawing the vials Banu had requested. The doctor barely looked at me while he went about his work with the needles, only stared at the vials filling with dark chrome blood. I should have insisted Karadin do this draw. I trusted her. But she was more exhausted than any of us after the delivery. She needed rest more than I needed her.

Banu sprawled himself out in one of the waiting chairs, glancing over his shoulder to watch the sleeping baby. His eyes went sort of gooey as he looked at her.

Despite my better judgment, I liked Banu. The leader of the Tanks was loud and brash and blunt, and maybe that was what appealed to me about the man. He didn't seem to care much what others thought of him, which meant he didn't seem to feel the need to hide anything about himself, especially not from me. But I wouldn't be cowed into submission just because a man was nice to me. And I certainly wouldn't trust him just because he seemed to be telling me the truth.

Ashland sensed my cool appraisal and pursed his lips into a thin line as he drew the fifth and final vial, slipping the needle from my arm with quick movements once it was full.

"Pleasure doing business with you," Banu said, standing to snatch the vials from the table and tuck them into his coat. "The Tanks thank you for your trade, Malkia."

"What you said before—about me still being a Queen—" I rolled down the sleeve of my shirt as I stood. The puncture wound on my arm was already healing. "Why did you say that?"

"Do you know so little about the nature of the Silvers?" Banu asked.

"We were created in a lab by overly ambitious scientists who ended up ruining the world rather than saving it."

Everyone knew the stories of the world destined for self-destruction as overpopulation and toxic technology poisoned the atmosphere and drained the resources of this world until hardly anything was left. The government had decided that if carbon or oil or hydrogen—all elements of this earth—could fuel weapons, why not human blood, too?

They'd created the Silvers, a genetic manipulation that didn't just fuel their weapons but also their armies. And the governments of that world had wasted no time in fighting for control over their new, precious resource. It hadn't taken long before one of those governments was bold enough to drop a silver bomb.

The war was short and deadly, leaving the remnants of a once great nation to pick up the pieces, scavenging for scraps. The inhabitants of this city had been some of the few survivors, and the gangs had picked up the squabbling where the governments left off—albeit, on a smaller scale.

Most Silvers could only be used for their blood. I was different. My silver blood wasn't just a power to be drained from my veins, but a living pulse of electricity that coursed through the very center of me, affording me unique abilities no other Silver had before.

Well, no one except for my mother.

And that meant, maybe there were more like me, too.

"Do you know why I can use my silver then?" I pressed, studying Banu as if I might find the hints of an answer within his cunning hazel eyes.

"You believe in the science," he mused, "but what of faith?"

"Does anyone believe in those myths anymore?" I shrugged, thinking of the thin-paged book I'd found once that spoke of beginnings and love and sin and rebirth. It was a rather sad story.

"Not myths, Malkia." He shook his head. "Destiny. There is a plan for you that is bigger than your Cards and your Whigs."

"And what is that?"

Banu looked up as if gazing through the thick ceilings of the ship and into the sky. When he looked back at me, his eyes glinted with keen amusement. "Maybe you should ask Him yourself sometime."

"Right." I couldn't help the skepticism. "I'll keep that in mind."

"Banu—" Samiya stood in the door. "The trackers are back."

"And?" Banu marched toward her, his steps suddenly hurried.

"They found Kavi's armband on the roads. And farther up, one of her hair clips. It looks like she dropped them as some sort of bread-crumbs. The path led East."

"East—"

"I know," Samiya said quickly, falling into step with Banu as they marched from the room.

"What's East?" I asked.

"The Veiled," Banu said simply before meeting Ashland's gaze. His eyes conveyed some unspoken order that had the doctor stepping in front of me. Bold of the man, knowing my silver was sparking along my fingertips.

I glanced at Phenola, who was feeding Calliope, and balled my fists.

"They're talking about the missing Silvers." I strained to catch anything else from Banu and Samiya's conversation.

"You should stay here while they debrief. Get some rest. You did just have a draw, after all," Ashland said in a way that told me he was only trying to distract me from sprinting after Banu. "Maybe some water?"

"I'm fine." I considered simply removing the man from my path. He wasn't large. A quick zap of my silver would have him crumpling at my feet, incapacitated but otherwise relatively unharmed.

My face must have given me away.

"Do you really want me passed out on the floor, unable to look after your friend and her newborn baby?"

"Karadin's around here somewhere," I grumbled, giving in to the fact that Banu's voice had faded, and my chance to chase them down in this labyrinth of a ship was gone anyway. "What does this have to do with the Veiled?"

"My guess is that's what they're discussing." Ashland looked afraid. His wide-eyes held a hallowness.

He knew the missing silvers then. My chest twisted. I understood that feeling of loss only too well. But if two Silvers had gone missing, the odds weren't high they were still alive. If they'd found themselves in trouble, it was likely the kind that would end with their drained bodies being found on the side of some crumbling road.

"Who were the missing Silvers?" I asked.

Ashland didn't miss my choice of the word "were" and flinched.

"Kavi," Ashland sighed. "And... Valenia." It was the way he swallowed as he said her name, his voice breaking at the center of the syllables, that told me Valenia meant more to him than a shipmate.

"Why did they leave?"

"We don't police our members. Not like your Cards. Tanks are free to come and go as they please. We'd all go stir-crazy if we only ever stayed within these steel corridors day in and day out. Valenia loved... loves... going to dance. She's a regular at one of the central clubs."

His voice once again cracked on the word "loves." Right. He wasn't deluding himself either.

I thought of Gideon and the way I'd run from him on the night of the bonfire. I thought of burying my hands in the sand and screaming at the world as the silver trailed from my fingers. There had been such betrayal in my heart then. I thought I'd experienced the true measure of grief. It had been enough for me, in those fleeting moments, to decide to leave the Cards.

But now... now, I pictured myself rising from that sand and returning to him. I imagined him cocooning me in his strong arms and telling me he would protect me from all of it, even my own rage and heartbreak.

Of course, that was the fantasy.

All illusions of Gideon as my protector were dead. They'd died even before he'd jumped from the cliffs. I absentmindedly brushed my fingers along my neck where he'd pressed his weight against my windpipe as I struggled in the sand on that last day. I'd known for a long time before that moment that he was a monster. But I hadn't known until that moment, among the dust and fighting, that the monster would come for me, too.

The blue of Gideon's eyes haunted me as much as the black. One, a promise of what could have been. The other reconciliations of what truly was.

Acceptance was the hardest step of all.

Across the clinic, Phenola watched me as Calliope fell asleep against her chest. Her grief reflected in mine.

I put a hand on Ashland's arm, surprising even myself. But he was only just beginning this journey of pain. I felt like a well-trodden soldier at this point, welcoming him into battle. The least I could do was let him know, in some small way, that he wasn't alone.

He flinched, and I pulled my hand back. Right. My touch caused more fear than comfort.

I gave him my words instead. "I'll stay here. Phenola will keep me company. Promise. You should go see what they found."

He glanced at me and then at the door.

"You have my word. Or I'll give you another five vials." I forced a smile that I didn't feel.

He didn't need more encouragement. He simply nodded and thanked me as he left.

I sighed, rolling my shoulders back and swallowing my grief.

"You're really going to stay here?" Phenola eyed me.

"For now."

I moved to where she lay in the small hospital bed, and she pulled the covers down, scooting over to the edge. It was just enough room that I could curl in next to her, and I accepted the gesture.

The warmth and new-baby smell cascaded over me as I crawled into the bed, running a delicate finger over Calliope's plump arm.

"Are you okay?" Phenola asked me.

"Am I okay?" My laugh was incredulous, even as I felt the tug on my chest. But I couldn't share my grief with her. Not when she was lying in a hospital bed with her hours-old daughter cradled in her arms. "You're the one who just had a baby. Shouldn't I be asking you that question?"

"Back at the ocean…" Phenola's words were tentative. "The way you burned those cars."

I shook my head, realizing she was asking me about those people on the beach. "I'm fine."

"But Lissa—"

I squeezed her hand, forcing myself to meet her gaze, forcing it to be true. "Promise. It was an easy decision."

"That—that can't have been easy. Your silver. It's a gift, but it's also a burden to be the one who can burn. I've seen how you've always tried to keep it contained, to not hurt people."

"I—" How could I tell her it *was* easy? The hard part was pretending I was normal. Fighting to keep my silver contained was always the struggle. Unleashing it had felt freeing. "I did what I had to do."

That response felt ridiculously flat on my tongue.

Phenola seemed to sense the same, weighing my reply with a tight expression before dropping her gaze to Calliope sleeping in her arms. "I see him when I look at her." She gently tucked the corner of the blanket under the infant's chin. "She has his nose."

I looked at her, too, reminding myself again that yes, yes, she was the reason I'd so confidently burned those cars. She was the reason I didn't feel guilty about hurting those people.

Or at least… part of the reason.

It had been thrilling.

I shook off that reminder but pulled my fingers from Phenola's grasp.

"I think it's the lips," I offered. "You know he had that kinda pucker most women would kill for."

Phenola let out a small sigh that sounded almost like a laugh. "He really did."

My throat dried out as I felt a fresh wave of grief wash through me, but it felt wrong to cry when Phenola was being so strong.

She shimmied herself in the bed to face me more fully. "You didn't leave with Tayna."

I shook my head. Maybe I should have gone with him. I wasn't sure. When he was here, there was an ache. When he was gone, it was worse. Maybe it was time to accept that even in my grief and confusion, I needed him.

I already missed him.

She shoved me with her shoulder.

"I didn't want to leave you," I finally said.

"Karadin's here." Phenola nodded her head in the direction of the room next door, where I assumed she'd gone to rest. "And I have Calliope now." Her smile was soft. "I wouldn't have been alone. Plus, the Tanks don't seem that bad. Banu's rough around the edges, but I actually think I'm more afraid of that sister of his."

I thought of Samiya with her barely disguised resentment at our presence on this ship and found myself almost smiling. "I don't think she likes us very much."

"She doesn't seem like the type who likes anyone much."

"What do you make of the missing Silvers?"

Phenola sighed. "The honest truth of it? If they went out by themselves without any weapons or protection... then it's no surprise danger caught up with them eventually, is it? This city isn't safe, but for your kind most of all. Let's hope whoever found them just drained them and moved on."

Nausea roiled in my belly. I could feel the mush I'd forced myself to eat for breakfast. Phenola was right. Gideon never sent out the Queens without a heavily armed escort of guards for a reason.

Yet something told me this wasn't a simple case of Silvers finding themselves in the wrong place. At breakfast, Banu had insisted they were missing. And based on what Samiya had shared, one of the Silvers had seemingly left clues for the Tanks to follow her path. That meant they'd been taken alive. And conscious. Which meant whoever was taking them wasn't draining them, not immediately, at least.

"Can I sleep in here tonight?" I asked .

"The bed is miserable," Phenola warned. "And Calliope is almost certain to wake you at least twice." Something in my expression must have made her reconsider saying anything else. A crease formed between her eyebrows as she studied me. "Of course you can stay in here with us."

And I knew what she'd seen in my eyes. It was fear. Fear that we'd gotten rid of one monster when we'd destroyed the Cards only for something worse to creep from the shadows and venture into the city.

13

Lissa

"Calliope isn't getting enough milk." Karadin declared over the screaming infant, who was purple in the face from her crying. She'd kept us all up the past two nights, and Karadin, Phenola, and I stared down at the infant with bruised eyes and helpless grimaces.

"Has anyone ever tried giving an infant silver?" I asked, unsure whether I had managed to keep the desperation out of my words. Calliope hadn't even napped yet today, and though I couldn't see the sun in this isolated room at the bowels of the ship, I was fairly certain it was afternoon by this point. Of course, my sleep had also been erratic and unpredictable. Turned out, humans needed the sun to keep their own sleep schedules consistent. Plus, the Tanks kept decidedly odd hours for their rooftop parties, which carried on until the sun rose. The thumping bass had been my only cue that the sun had even set last night.

More than anything, I'd felt restless because Tayna had yet to return.

Phenola looked at me with wide eyes at my suggestion. "We are not experimenting with my child."

"Only if it's safe!" I insisted, looking at Karadin, who just threw up her hands in a shrug.

"The Cards may have acted like big babies sometimes," she said, "but I don't actually have any experience treating babies."

Karadin had spent last night hunched over a medical book she kept with her. Some old text with only one chapter on pregnancy even though the entire book was supposed to be about human anatomy. Apparently, the old world hadn't cared much to study or understand female reproduction.

Ashland hadn't been much help on the subject, either, and had promptly excused himself this morning after Calliope had leaked through her cloth diaper and onto his shirt. He hadn't returned.

Karadin had mumbled something about him being a doctor but not being able to handle a little poop.

The truth of it was that we were all out of our element with an infant.

What we really needed was to get back to the farm. The Whigs weren't just a rebel gang. They were a family. They'd raised an entire community of children, and they supported one another. They would know what to do. I tried to picture what Grant would say. Something just told me he would sweep this baby into his arms, spin her around the kitchen, and have her cooing in a matter of seconds.

My lungs constricted.

Tayna should be back by now.

He hadn't been far from my mind in the days we'd been apart. Part of me had wished I'd gone with him. Phenola had been right that I wasn't much use on this ship. And I was restless.

The dread grew in my stomach with every hour he wasn't here.

He needed to come back, and we needed to get off this ship.

Fuck.

Unease pricked my chest.

Silver sputtered at my fingers.

I was too tired and too erratic to do this.

Calliope's screams created an echo chamber in the medical ward, and I closed my eyes against the pounding in my heart that settled into a pounding at the base of my skull.

A strong hand gripped my shoulder.

Karadin.

"Take a break," she said in a low voice.

"I'm fine." I shook off the thoughts with a long exhale.

"You haven't left this room in two days. Go find someone who can help us get some nutrient-dense foods for Phenola. Ideally, they'll have some nuts or fresh spinach. At the very least, get her some of that oatmeal."

"I want to stay."

"Lissa—"

"No!" My voice was louder than I'd intended. Silver sparked at my hands.

And I realized with a deep-seated fear that my silver was as volatile as my emotions right now. Phenola had Calliope clutched tightly, the infant's wails only growing louder.

My breaths shook. "I'm sorry." I pressed my fingers against my eyes. "I'll-I'll find..."

I didn't even bother finishing my words as I darted from the room.

I'd worked so hard over the past six months to gain control of my silver, but since the cliffs, it felt like something unpredictable living beneath my skin. I couldn't lose control. I couldn't fall apart. I couldn't allow myself to get to the edge like this. Because it didn't just mean destruction for me. It meant destruction for every single person I loved. And I would jump from this ship before I ever allowed myself to hurt that child.

I didn't know my way around this ship. I only knew up.

So I climbed.

I took each ladder.

I pushed open each ceiling latch.

Even as my lungs burned from the effort, I kept moving. I was exhausted. My muscles protested from the movement after being stagnant for so many days.

Up.

And up.

Until I heaved open a hatch and felt the sea breeze caress my fingers.

Only then did I truly exhale, pulling myself onto the roof. My palms met the cool, damp metal. On hands and knees, I caught my breath. My lungs burned from the exertion. I'd never really been one for exercise, not until Alaric had forced me to begin training. Even then, I was barely able to keep up on the hikes to and from the farm.

I gave myself a few steady breaths before I looked up, pushing to stand as the wind whipped my hair around my face.

This was the place where the Tanks held their nightly parties, and it looked it, too. It was unkempt. The chipped and marred edges of a watchtower jutted out from the center. There was a greenhouse at the far end, where I could see plants in giant buckets lined up in haphazard rows. It was a makeshift garden that was not well attended. Tables and chairs were scattered about. A few empty bottles clattered against the railing as the wind brushed over the space, creating a tickling melody in time with the ocean waves. The deck was sticky and stained beneath my feet.

At this hour, early in the afternoon, the space was quiet. Everyone was still passed out down below or completing their daily chores. I'd learned well enough that the Tanks were the work hard to party even harder types. At night, when the music echoed through the ship, the traces of the beats vibrated along the medical room. I hadn't felt like joining. I'd never felt comfortable in crowds and couldn't imagine forcing myself to dance or celebrate right now. Although maybe some liquid courage would do me well. But my silver was already feeling volatile enough, and I wouldn't risk it by adding alcohol into the mix.

I didn't even dare release my silver in the open air. Not when I stood on top of a metal ship housing thousands of people below. Instead, I pushed it down and forced it away as I walked toward the railing and used deep inhales of the clean air to steady my nerves. The trembling in my hands calmed with my breath.

It had only been a few days, yet, it already felt like I needed a release again.

I shoved it back.

It was an overcast day. It rarely rained in the city, but the summer months brought in the murky marine layer, especially in the mornings. Still, I could see through the fog enough to make out the eroding roadway beyond the docks.

Past that, the city stretched out before me in a crumbling mass of buildings that had, once upon a time, been a grand sight to behold. Now it was like time was laughing at these feats of architecture. Humans thought they were so clever building their attractions near the ocean. I could imagine the elegance of this place, rebuilding the pieces in my mind, as if the sun would break through the clouds and the city would be reborn anew.

Could that be possible for this city?

Maybe what I was really asking was if it could be possible for me, too. Could there still be hope in a place that had shattered my heart into as many crumbling pieces as the buildings beyond the coast?

I let myself pretend.

And as I daydreamed, I let the wisps of wind at my back turn into the caress of fingers, brushing aside the strands of my hair to reveal my skin. It was calming, so I didn't resist and just let the tendrils turn to touches.

I could almost feel a warmth at my back, though I didn't dare press into the towering frame, even as goose bumps from the chilly air crept along my arms.

Lips traced across the skin at the back of my neck, and the wind whispered, *"Mine."* The deep male timbre made me shudder.

"You would have killed me." I murmured the words.

"Do you really believe that?" the daydream asked at my back, a hint of laughter in the words.

"I stopped being yours when you killed Kenji."

The daydream did chuckle then. The sound brushed against the shell of my ear in a sensual caress. *"You never had a choice, little Queen."*

I swallowed against the tightness in my throat. "I took my choice back when I leveled that gun at your chest."

"But you never would have pulled the trigger."

"You're wrong." Even as the anger tightened my chest, a tear slipped free, and I let it trail down my face. More blurred my vision. Gideon had known I would pull the trigger. I think that was why he'd jumped from the cliffs. He'd known he'd lost. He'd known I'd reached my limit. He'd known the game was over between us. It was a mercy, sparing me from the act of ending him myself. Because I would have done it. I would have killed him. A breath more, and I would have pulled the trigger.

"I would have taken the bullet," the daydream whispered.

"I hate you," I breathed, choking on my tears. "I hate you for taking my friend. I hate you for taking my silver. I hate you for not letting me go. I hate you for marking me. I hate you for making me play this game. But I hate you most of all for making me hate you. It hurts too much."

Silence was my answer.

What had I expected when confronting the wind?

For a moment, I cried. I allowed the grief to consume me, gripping the railing to hold myself up as I let the wind have my tears.

It was a too-brief moment before the breeze settled at my back.

Unnaturally this time.

I spun, suddenly coming face-to-face with Banu, who watched me curiously as if I were a creature he was discovering for the first time. "I don't think you'll find food up here."

I wiped at the streaks on my face as if I could hide my tears at this point. "Food?"

For Phenola.

I hadn't even been thinking about the baby or my poor friends suffering through her wails as I'd found my way to the roof. "I can get it now. Are they—"

"I had some warmed and sent to the hospital ward already." Banu's eyes glittered with that knowing wisdom as he watched me. "Take a break, Malkia."

"Why does everyone keep saying that to me?" I could handle this. There was no choice but to handle it. We were all grieving. That wasn't stopping the others from doing what needed to be done. I didn't want to be the volatile one.

"Your silver is sparking." Banu gestured with his chin to my hands, and I gulped in a lungful of the salty air, pressing it down, down, down.

"You keep doing that, and you'll blow."

"What do you know about my silver?" I snapped, sparks of it lighting again at my fingers.

"Silver? Not so much. But that rage you're pushing down. I know a lot about that and about what happens when you try to pretend it isn't just underneath the surface of your skin."

"I'm fine."

"That is for you, not for me."

"I don't know what that means."

"You loved the Ace?" Banu's question had my silver spiking again.

I gritted my teeth against the tears pricking at my eyes and the grief squeezing around my windpipe. "I hated him."

Banu shrugged. "So I heard." He paused as if weighing the worth of his words before he said, "Both can be true."

That statement hung between us.

It was chilly in the damp morning air. I wished I had my Queen's cloak to wrap around my shoulders, which was a silly thought. But it was a decadence I no longer had. Now I barely had a change of clothes. I didn't miss the finery of the Cards. I'd never liked the dresses and the flimsy shoes. But I did like the baths. And the pastries. And, yes, my Queen's cloak.

I opened my mouth to say something to Banu. What, I wasn't sure.

But then I heard the screeching of tires behind me.

Something was happening on the roads.

Fear skittered through me, propelling me to turn and run back toward the hull of the ship, gripping the railing and gazing through the fog as a Humvee slid to a stop in the parking lot.

Tayna?

I felt such sudden relief that a small sob escaped my mouth on my exhale. But the relief was quickly followed by concern. Something wasn't right.

Was he being chased by more cars?

The door flew open.

He was running from the Humvee.

He was hard to make out from the distance above, but I'd know his form anywhere. I couldn't see anyone following him. I didn't hear any other cars on the dock.

But by the way he was running, I knew something was very wrong.

14

Lissa

Tayna sprinted down the docks, and I didn't wait to see more. I should have gone with him. I never should have left him alone. Was he hurt? Had something happened to him?

I ran to the hatch, determined to get to him as quickly as possible.

Banu was at my heels, also sensing trouble. Once we hit the first landing of the ship, he took the lead, gesturing for me to follow. "There's a shortcut to the entrance," he said over his shoulder.

We pushed past a couple walking in the halls. They were a gray flash of the faded fatigues they wore. I didn't even register their faces as Banu pulled open another hatch and directed me to follow him down the ladder.

Samiya met us from where she was running down a corridor. "The guards just alerted me on the radios," she said.

"Tell them to lower the gangway." Banu didn't break a step as Samiya fell behind us.

The radio crackled as she gave the directive. A few others in the halls pressed to the sides out of our way.

I balled my fists, pressing the silver down, holding it back, even as my anxiety spiked and the blood pounded in my ears.

Something was wrong.

Something was very wrong.

The air was thick with its tension. The panic had swallowed my grief, but between the sleepless nights with Calliope, the heartache straining my soul, the distance between Tayna and me, and now this, I didn't know how much more my system could take. My hands were shaking, and my feet were unsteady as I kept pace with Banu.

And then we were turning a corner, walking into the foggy light, which was stark against the dark of the hallways.

I blinked to adjust but didn't stop moving. Tayna's form became clear in front of me, and then he grasped my shoulders.

"Are you okay?" I breathed into him, gripping his face to quell my panic. "Are you okay?"

"They didn't make it." Tayna's clothing was dirty. It was the same outfit he'd worn the day he'd left, I realized. He smelled like sweat and damp earth. But still I clung to him, my hands tracing down his face to his chest. He was sturdy beneath my touch. My fingers buried in his shirt. "Enver and Laykin didn't make it to the meeting point. They're gone."

"Gone?"

I thought of Kenji falling from the cliffs.

"The Humvees. The Cards with them. The supplies. None of it was there."

"Where—where are they?" I couldn't catch my breath.

"I don't know, Liss." He gripped me tightly. "I don't know. I hiked back to the community to see if they'd made it to the Whigs somehow. Alaric, Grant, everyone was there safe and sound. But I couldn't find Laykin and Enver. There wasn't a trace of them."

His scar was taut as his brow furrowed. His hair hung limply over his forehead, and days of sweat and dirt clung to his broad frame. His once-white shirt was now the color of the clay that surrounded the farm.

"No, no, no." I felt panicked and disbelieving. This had to be a mistake. There had to be an explanation. "They have to be—Maybe they—"

He must have just missed them. They must have misunderstood his instructions. They must be camping somewhere just waiting for us to find them. They were probably waiting for us, and this was all just a mistake. "The radios—" I gestured behind me. We'd kept the radio charged and in the medical ward, but there'd been no activity on it. The signal was just a low static drowned out by Calliope's wails.

"I couldn't get anyone to answer me on the radio. There wasn't anyone there. I thought at first we must be out of range, but there was nothing, Liss."

"These friends of yours," Banu cut in, and I suddenly remembered he and Samiya were with us. "Were they Silvers?"

"One." Tayna nodded. "Enver was another one of Gideon's Queens."

Banu looked at Samiya, and they exchanged a wordless, knowing conversation.

"Missing Silvers..." Samiya said, almost to herself.

My stomach lurched, and my nails dug into Tayna's arms as I struggled to remain upright. I was going to be sick.

"She's burning you!" Samiya said, her voice rising in alarm.

"Don't—" Tayna put out a hand to keep them at bay, but I gasped, quickly yanking away from him and inspecting the red welts that rose in the shape of my hands along his biceps.

"Malkia, you need to burn off some of that silver before you return to my ship," Banu warned.

"It's okay." Tayna gripped me again. And for a moment, I let myself be okay with the fact that he was exactly what I needed at this moment. He was the safety I craved. He was the warmth that seeped into my veins. As the world crumbled around me once again, he was the rock that would keep me from drifting out to sea.

"We have to find them." I pressed my hands together like I'd heard people did when praying to the old god. Only I wasn't praying. I was trying desperately to spool the silver back inside. It was vibrating under my skin, buzzing for release. My neck strained as I tilted my head to the sky, willing it to go away. I just needed a break. But I was breaking. The energy was spooling from my skin, and I couldn't... I couldn't stop it anymore.

"Go back inside," Tayna yelled. "I've got her. I've got her."

I was burning.

"Tayna!" I yelled in warning when Tayna reached for me again.

"You won't hurt me," he insisted, forcing his arms around my body, wrapping me in a tight embrace. "I've got you."

The fabric of his shirt began to sizzle as he pulled me close, and I pressed it down, down, down. I wouldn't hurt Tayna. Not again. I'd hurt him enough. We'd wounded each other. Two broken things in the land of lost souls.

He lifted me easily into his arms, and I felt small curled against his chest.

I should push against him. I should make him set me down, but instead I clung to him. Pressed against him, the storm in my mind calmed.

I thought back to the moment when we'd reunited in the barn at the Whigs. We'd clutched each other like this until the sun had set and my muscles had cramped, and still, I hadn't moved from his embrace.

Safe.

With him, I felt safe.

But I wasn't safe. I was close to burning. I was dangerous.

He shouldn't be touching me like this.

Yet I couldn't bring myself to pull away. I craved having him close. It was selfish.

Even dirty and musky, I breathed him in. My nose traced along his collarbone, taking in the sunshine and his fresh-cut grass smell. The way our bodies fell together was infinitely familiar as he walked me down to the beach.

"We have to find them," I murmured, my silver calmed for the moment.

"We will." His fingers brushed against my hair, curling into the strands to keep my head cradled against his tanned chest.

My lips traced across his bare skin, velvety smooth over hardened muscles.

I reared back then, causing his hand to inadvertently yank at my strands of hair. The momentum sent us sprawling in the sand, next to each other. My hair cascaded into my face as I pushed it aside, taking in the smooth skin.

"Your skin," I balked, sitting back on my heels in the sand. "I burned you, but you're not—"

His shirt hung in tatters, barely clinging to his torso. His unmarred, unburned, perfectly sculpted torso.

"I told you, you wouldn't hurt me," he said, lifting onto his knees. Reaching for me again, he grasped my chin as he whispered over me. "I don't want you to ever pull away from me like that again, Liss."

"Tayna—"

He was taking silver.

The boy who had refused it all his life, who'd avoided it at all costs, who'd told me his parents had died from a silver addiction, was now taking silver to be close to me.

"You don't have to do that." I shook my head. "I don't want you to do that."

We hadn't yet discussed the fact that I'd forced it on him again when I'd bit my lip and kissed him on the cliffs, saving his life after Gideon shot him in the stomach.

"I'm just taking enough to protect myself," he explained, his hand still gripping my chin and his eyes still on my mouth.

"From me?" I balked, even as my silver sparked at my fingers.

"From stray bullets," he deadpanned.

"You never needed it before."

"I think I've had enough near-death experiences at this point to justify it, don't you?"

I thought of the rage I'd seen in Gideon's gaze, of the darkness that had clouded his features. The silver had turned his blue eyes dark, letting the monster within him out to play.

"This is how it starts, Tayna. You take a little, and next thing you know, you can't go a day without it."

"It's not like that."

But I shook my head. It *was* like that.

Just as I thought it was beginning to mend, the fissure splintered between us. The space between our bodies suddenly felt like the steep chasm of an unbreachable canyon as my silver sizzled in my palms.

"Lissa—" He reached for me.

I stood abruptly, smelling the electricity radiating off my skin in the air. It had been wrong to fall into him only when I needed support. I couldn't expect him to carry me. I had to carry myself. "I need to go into the water. I need to release some silver." I took a few steps back. "You should go back to the ship."

"Lissa, you're not going alone. You heard Samiya. Silvers are going missing."

"Let whatever bastards are out there try." I threw up my hands, silver flaring as I kicked off my shoes. Banu was right. My silver was too volatile to risk getting on his ship right now. Even I could recognize it. I was emotional. Angry. *Unstable*.

I padded out to the edge of the waves until the water was catching along my feet.

Just as I'd suspected, the cloud coverage was starting to break, revealing tendrils of sunlight in the distance. The breeze whipped my hair from its braid, curling around my cheeks.

It wasn't warm.

But I wasn't looking for warm.

I was looking for release.

So I waded into the water, my steps sloshing before I fell completely into the waves, splaying my fingers and allowing the silver to cascade from my palms. I shuddered at the sheer relief as I let go, allowing the waves to take me where they willed.

Only, the water was still around me. The electric current combated the waves and, even, it seemed, the gravitational pull of the moon. A large circle of stillness rippled out around me. Even a hundred or so feet from the boat, I watched the trajectory of my silver to ensure it wouldn't make it that far.

The water was so cold, it stole my breath, but I relished the burn and the icy barbs trailing along my body. My skin prickled from the silver and from the frigid tendrils skating over my skin.

I wasn't worried about sharks or jellyfish or any other creatures in the murky depths beneath me. The silver would act like an electrical current, warning them away. It was a shield spanning around me. No creature would dare get close, human or otherwise.

Even as the cold crept into my lungs, I forced my breaths to steady inhales and exhales, counting the measures.

Enver was missing.

Laykin was missing.

The silver streamed from my fingers.

More of my friends were gone.

If Gideon were still alive, he would send the Cards out into the city to kill for any bits of information about his missing Queen. He would send out his spies to weasel out any information and rumors from the streets. He would declare war on anyone who dared to touch one of his Queens.

But Gideon wasn't alive.

He was gone because of me.

And maybe that was exactly why someone now saw an opportunity to start snatching Silvers in broad daylight. The gangs wouldn't sit idly by as the strongest among them fell. There were spoils to be had, and the most valuable of them all was not the Humvees filled with weapons or the medical supplies. No, it was the Card Silvers, now prime targets without any protection. The promise of war with the Cards if a person messed with the silver supply had burned away right along with the compound. Guilt twisted through me, replacing the silver under my skin.

It could be any number of gangs in the city who'd decided to be bold. I thought of the cars that had confronted us on our drive here, and the woman crawling from her burning vehicle. Had they been in a gang? The Fortas had been reportedly getting more vocal. I'd heard one of the Tanks talking about it at mealtime. I remembered Gideon complaining about their brash behavior, too. It could be the Slips, though I wasn't sure they were organized enough for a coordinated kidnapping.

And then there was the Veiled.

Based on the snippets of conversation I'd overheard between Samiya and Banu, it seemed they believed the Veiled was the most likely gang behind the kidnappings.

Olita Ravidian surely had the strength and numbers to waste no time claiming the city for herself. The Veiled was a mystery to me. Only rumors swirled of their brutality and thirst for Silver blood. But what was the move if they were responsible for these kidnappings? Olita had about as many Silvers as the Cards, if gossip was to be believed. Maybe more.

There was only one way to be truly certain if the Veiled was responsible for these kidnappings. And if Olita had Enver and Laykin, well, then I would threaten to burn down her compound just like I'd burned the Cards if she wouldn't give me back my friends.

Olita may have her isolation, her masked Phantoms, and all the silver blood she could possibly want, but she didn't have a Silver like me.

I didn't want to be a weapon, used by whichever side had my loyalty. I wanted to be more.

And maybe I could make a difference by being a player in this game.

15

Lissa

Alaric waited for me at the water's edge when I finally lifted my head from the waves. I should have known he'd come with Tayna. Of course, he hadn't let Tayna come back alone, not with everything happening in the city. It was really a miracle he hadn't found us sooner, hadn't stormed into the Cards compound with a group of rebels.

Tayna had warned him off, though. And Alaric, for as brutish as he was, was not stupid enough to think he could take on the Cards with fists and barely silvered weapons. No, the best way had always been to destroy the Cards from the inside out.

But he was here now, watching me with narrowed, bright eyes as I shivered out of the ocean. His silver-gray hair was a bit longer than its usual buzz cut, but otherwise, he looked unchanged. I couldn't see my face at all in his carved features. Not really.

He wore cargo pants tucked into high boots. Beneath his faded navy jacket, he had two guns holstered to his belt. Where the Cards had been sophisticated and nearly regimented in their black uniforms, Alaric was haphazard. I tried to imagine him in a clean, tailored King's jacket, but I failed. Yet he was more warrior than any Card I'd ever met. He could even give Laykin a run for his money.

The thought of my missing friend had my silver sputtering again, though weaker now that I'd nearly drained myself dry in the ocean.

"What-what are you doing here?" I blurted between my cold, stiff lips, not because I was surprised to see him, really, but because he'd been waiting for me. We needed to talk, but I wasn't sure how much he knew. Did he know he could be my father? And what had Tayna told him? Would Alaric hate me for it? And when did I start caring what Alaric thought of me? Just because he might be my father didn't change the fact that he was an absolute brute.

I crossed my arms in front of my chest and scowled.

Alaric just quirked an eyebrow. "You look like hell."

His eyes drifted to the diamond necklace I wore, then to the tattoos on my shoulder, and the new ink Gideon had added just below the Queen of Hearts tattoo. *His* mark.

But Alaric didn't say anything. He shrugged out of his jacket and handed it to me. I narrowed my eyes at him, then snatched the jacket and pulled it on, doubling the fabric in front to shield myself from the wind. Still, I was quaking.

"Once you have yourself a shower, we can have a conversation, Lissa."

Not Queen. Not this time.

Lissa.

I think it was the first time he'd said my name, which only had me snapping, "So Madam Cartenoth was telling the truth, then?"

He ran his tongue over his teeth, his nostrils flaring like he had a bad taste in his mouth.

"Fucking perfect." I shook my head and stalked around him. I'd shed enough tears today. I'd felt enough panic. Now the anger was settling in, and I needed to focus on finding my friends. I didn't have time for whatever Alaric wanted to say. It didn't matter. He didn't matter.

Tayna watched me from the docks as I stalked through the sand and back toward the ship. My muscles cramped from the breeze against my salt-wet skin. The moisture dried to a fine crust of sand and salt that pulled and cracked as I moved.

"What happened? Are you okay?" Tayna asked as I marched myself up the wooden stairs.

I couldn't talk anymore. Every time we talked, it only seemed to make the ache in my chest grow.

He ran to catch up to me, grabbing at my shoulder, but I shrugged him off.

"Stop it, Lissa," Tayna reached for me again as I shoved his hands away.

Banu had left the entrance open for us, and I stalked into the corridor.

"Lissa—"

"I'm going to find Enver and Laykin."

"We. *We*, Liss."

I turned on him, and he nearly walked into me. His momentum carried him until I was glaring up at his insistent, golden eyes.

"Let me in, Liss." He was resolute.

I took the measure of him, my tongue ran along my bottom lip, and I tasted the salt from the ocean. "I want to go to the Veiled."

Pure horror lit his expression.

"Lissa—"

But I broke free of his grasp and started walking again. "You know this is the only option," I said over my shoulder. "If anyone has any answers, it'll be Olita Ravidian."

He was chasing me again. "You have no idea what you're asking. My mother... she—"

"You already searched the forest around the farm for Enver and Laykin, right?"

"Of course. Alaric promised to have a team scouting the area, looking for any sign of them until we returned."

"And you found nothing while you were there?"

Tayna sighed. "Not even a tire track. I think it's likely they never even made it to the base of the trail."

"Then we can't just head back to the community, keep combing the mountain, and hope for the best, Tayna. They aren't there."

"Lissa!" He grabbed my arm as I ascended the ladder to the upper floor, where the medical room was located. "At least let's go back to the Whigs to regroup—"

"For what?" I demanded. "Alaric can take Phenola and Karadin back if they want to leave. There's no use in hiking all the way back there just to turn around and head back into the city."

"My mother—she isn't a kind woman. She could very well put a bullet in my head without thinking twice about it. And you, well, I have no doubt she would love to get her hands on you."

"Great. She can hands me all she wants if she has information about Enver and Laykin and where to find them."

I slipped free of his grip again and hauled myself up the rungs of the ladder. I felt more like myself now that I'd released some silver, and I was clear on my decision. This was our only reasonable option, even if Tayna didn't like it.

He swore from behind me. The metal sang as my boots hit the rungs.

Tayna's response echoed after me as he easily kept up. "It could be a suicide mission, Lissa. For us both. My mother and I didn't exactly part on the best of terms."

"I'm not asking your permission, Tayna." I waited for him at the top of the landing. He pulled himself up from the ladder, standing to his full height until my chin tilted back to meet his gaze. "But I would like you to come with me. Olita isn't likely to hurt me because of my silver, and if she tries, well, I have my silver. You know this makes sense."

I knew the reputation of the Veiled matriarch. I'd seen the scorched patches of earth and the bodies in the streets from the fights that had ended with other gang members dead. Their bodies were nothing but charred husks thanks to the silvered explosives the Veiled favored. Bombs first, then guns, were their favorite way to deal with threats. All of it silvered. Members of the Veiled even donned the color as their uniform. Deep gray with shimmering undertones that sparkled in the sun. Those who ranked highest in her order wore well-fashioned suits of the material and chrome masks that covered most of their faces. I'd never seen them, but I'd heard the rumors. They were her Phantoms. Some of them even favored metallic fangs for their front canines, a quick and easy way to dose up on silver. They were the creatures of the night made flesh, and they only left the Veiled fortress when there was death to deal. Lots of it.

I waited for Tayna's answer, holding my breath, wishing things between us could just be easy again.

"Even if this makes sense, we should take a pause. We should think this through."

I turned from him again to keep moving. Before I could even take a step up the next rung of the ladder, he grasped me, pressing me against the cool metal of the ship's hallway. "Wait."

His voice was low.

And I did. It was hard to resist being close to him. I wanted it so badly, but somehow no longer knew how.

His chest met mine as he exhaled. His warm breath fanned across my face. The leather straps he wore across his chest to holster his gun caressed across my collarbone. His torso was still bare. The hard lines of his abs were exposed between the burned shreds of his shirt as my fingers pressed against his skin.

He took a step back as I laced the touch with the smallest spark of my silver. There was a fucking dare in his gaze, not even a breath of surprise against the pain. It was as if he wanted the burn and expected me to lash out.

"We're wasting time." I shoved him again, ignoring the emotion pooling in my belly. I snaked out from his grip and stalked down the hall again. "I'm not going to change my mind about this."

How many times had I asked myself who I was over the last week? How many times had I wondered who I'd become? And maybe I didn't have all the answers yet, but at least I knew I was the type of person who would go to the ends of the earth for her friends.

I would find them, even if it meant putting myself at risk at the Veiled.

"And what's your plan, exactly?" Tayna's large strides had him easily keeping up, but he didn't reach for me again as we reached the hallway landing of the hospital wing. "You're expecting to leave Phenola, Karadin, and the baby behind with the Tanks? You think Banu will continue to waste his precious resources on us?"

A deep chuckle sounded at the end of the hallway. "We're not so destitute, Tayna." Banu's rich voice rang from the shadows at the end of the walk. His hulking form came into view a few seconds later, bathed in the white light that reflected off the stainless-steel walls. It shone in his cunning eyes. "You think you can convince Olita to tell you her secrets?"

I wondered how long he'd been listening to our conversation. These halls tended to echo, and I was well aware that the leader of the Tanks used it to his advantage.

"You said yourself, your Silvers left clues heading East," I called back to him. "What other option do we have?"

Tayna cut in. "Olita will not help our cause. She'll manipulate us and then stab us in the back, most likely to get her hands on Lissa's silver."

I glared at him. "I'm not so easily manipulated."

"The baby and your friends are welcome here as long as they need shelter," Banu said. "If they want to return to your community, we can help arrange that, too."

"What's your price?" I countered.

"No price. Kavi and Valenia were my friends, like your Enver was close to you. If you find them and can convince Olita to work with you and give you whatever she knows, that is payment enough. Someone has to start standing up for the people in this city, and I'm trusting you to do what you can to fight for our Silvers, Lissa Metarro."

His clever eyes watched me as he held the door of the medical wing open for us. The way the light caught his eyes, he almost looked Silvered himself. But I realized it was a watery look, more hardened determination than a show of any hidden power. Banu's scouts in the city hadn't found his missing Silver friends. I was his last hope.

"I'll find them," I promised.

And he nodded. "Then my resources are yours."

"We'll take what you can spare for food to get us through a few days of travel," Tayna said.

"So you'll come with me, then? You're in?" I asked skeptically.

He turned that golden gaze on me. That spark I'd seen back in the halls as he'd pressed into me returned, if only for the briefest of moments. "When will you learn?" he asked. "With you, I'll always be in."

My gut twisted tighter and hope flared between us.

It was a start.

16

Lissa

Phenola surprised me with her reaction to my explanation of Enver and Laykin, the missing Silvers, and of my plan to negotiate an audience with Olita Ravidian and the Veiled.

Karadin was stoic and tight-lipped. She thought the idea was reckless and dangerous.

But Phenola nodded. "I need to speak with you, Lissa. Alone."

"I know what I'm doing—"

"I know your mind is made up about this trip. I have no intention of trying to convince you to stay despite what I think about the risk." She eyed me meaningfully. "But if you are planning to face Olita, then there are still some facts you need to understand."

"More secrets?"

"More like truths lost to history." Her gaze found Tayna's then. But he looked at me like he was just as unsure.

"The room," Phenola said again.

And the others complied, leaving us to our conversation.

Phenola waited until the door had closed. Calli let out the softest of coos as she napped in Phenola's arms. She had a thick cream blanket covering her legs and torso. The baby's small head peeked up from the warmth.

"Why has so much of the past been hidden? Will it ever be done?" I crossed my arms, waiting for her to speak.

She sighed. "Bat loved her secrets."

"What does this have to do with Madam Cartenoth?"

"More than either of us realizes, I think. She didn't just collect trinkets and relics from the past, Lissa. She collected certain items, certain texts, too, certain valuable texts, if you will. She kept a hidden compartment in her room. One book, in particular, she valued above the others. I planned to finally read it after she died. But, well, there wasn't exactly the opportunity with... everything. I'm sure looters have gotten to the shop at this point. But with our luck, that baseboard is still intact, and the book is still hidden. I don't know what it says, Lissa. Bat just called it 'a book to start wars.' There are truths in it that have been lost to our city for decades. Bat wouldn't have been so secretive with it otherwise."

"Is that how she knew about my mother and the Cards?" I asked.

Phenola shook her head. "I don't know. I don't even know how helpful this book will be. But it may give you something of a bargaining chip other than your silver in your meeting with Olita. I wouldn't share that you have it with anyone besides Tayna. But information can be as good as silver in this city, and I want to help you however I can."

"You've known longer than most that this city needs to change." I thought back on our conversation months ago when Phenola had admitted there was a rebel group willing to challenge the gangs. I was still a Queen then. Kenji was alive. I'd thought Tayna was dead. At the time, I'd thought she was crazy, throwing her support behind a fool's mission. Maybe it still was a fool's mission. Was it worth Kenji's life to take down the Cards? Was it worth Gideon's life to find my freedom?

In whatever way I could, I wouldn't waste this chance I'd been given.

I would protect my friends with my life.

I would do whatever it took to find Enver and Laykin.

"I'll find the book," I promised Phenola.

Her eyes shone with unshed tears as she, no doubt, thought of Kenji and his sacrifice, too. She squeezed my hand. An absolution.

She hadn't once blamed me for his death.

In the days since Gideon had pressed that gun into his gut and fired, she hadn't once turned her gaze on me with accusation and betrayal. Phenola had never diluted herself into thinking their mission with the Whigs was safe. She'd been practical about the risks, and Kenji made his choice.

But who was to say what price was worth the change?

Would we all die by the time this revolution in the city was fought?

"I don't have any more promises I can give you," I said, wishing I could guarantee Calli's safety in this ruin of a city. I wished I could do something that would make Kenji's death worth it.

And I would try.

But even with my Silver, I wasn't sure I could succeed.

"Kenji would be really proud of you, Lissa."

Tears flecked in my lashes, blurring my vision. "He wouldn't even be thinking about me right now." I shook my head. "He'd be too busy fawning over Calli."

She laughed then, watery and sincere. "He really would. He'd only give her to me so she could eat."

"He'd be fussing over you two so much that Banu might kick him off the ship before Karadin could kill him."

"He'd take the lecture and smile!"

"He'd take it for you."

Her smile wavered then as the reality and the tears set back in.

"He did," Phenola nodded. "He did it all for us."

My answering nod was all I could offer in return.

"Will you stay here?" I asked, unsure if she was ready to go to the farm and the Whigs without Kenji. After I thought Tayna was dead,

I'd had no desire to return to our loft for years. Even the thought of that empty space made me feel sick.

But Phenola sighed. "I'm ready to get off this ship. Calli will need to see some sunlight soon."

The thought of the sprawling farm and the fresh summer days did sound like a dream right now after our time on this metal ship.

"Then Tayna and I will see you there. Banu has promised whatever you need for rations. Oh, and Alaric's here. He came back with Tayna. He'll help on the hike with an extra pair of hands. And you can take the walkies back with you just in case."

"Be safe." Phenola gave my hand a final squeeze. "And Lissa"—she eyed me meaningfully then—"don't let your grief make you forget who you are."

Her words sank into that twisted uncertainty living in my gut.

But I leaned into her, embracing her shoulders and nodding while keeping space for the sleeping Calliope between us. "I'll see you soon."

Before she could see the doubt in my eyes, I left.

It was Alaric waiting for me outside the medical wing. His arms were crossed, his gaze tilted to the floor, and a flask hung limply from his wrist. His eyes were unfocused, distant. For a moment, I wasn't even sure if he realized I was there.

But then he spoke. "And here I thought you were just confused. I didn't realize you were a fool, too."

He took another long swing from the flask, a dribble leaking down his chin.

I scoffed, moving to push around him, but he stepped in front of me. The clear challenge of it was written on his face. He'd let me go on the beach, but now we'd have it out. I knew he was just waiting, waiting for me to push him with my silver.

I squared my shoulders, standing a little straighter. "I don't have time for this. If you won't give me answers, then I'm going to get them for myself."

"Olita will have a field day with that."

"Meaning?"

"Meaning, you have to learn the rules if you want to play the game. And you don't know shit."

I gritted my teeth. This would not be a productive conversation.

"Lovely. More cryptic bullshit."

Alaric was in my face before I even realized he'd moved. His teeth were bared, and for the first time, I felt a spike of fear. But I held my ground, even as he spat, "You want some truths? Alright, here you go. Your mother manipulated me. She and Ishmael thought they could use people and that it didn't mean anything. But it meant something *to me.*"

Ishmael.

Madam Cartenoth's words rang in my brain. *The King and the Queen made a princess.* But if my mother was a Card, then she must have been like me. She must not have been willing.

"My mother hated the Cards. She—"

Alaric laughed. It was a deep and cruel sound from the very center of his chest. "Hated? Your mother was in love with Ishmael. She wasn't just a Queen. She was *his* Queen. She was the original. And it was all she wanted. More, more, more just like her. It didn't matter what it cost the rest of us."

It was all I could do to shake my head even as he kept ranting. Even as I knew he wasn't the first to say this to me. But it didn't make any sense.

"I don't know if you're mine. But if you are, it doesn't really matter because it was all wrapped up in their fucked-up little experiments. We were all little pawns in their game. And they may be dead, but we're all still just playing right along with their rules."

"Experiments?"

"Your mother wanted to replicate her genetics. She wanted to create more Silvers like her. She and Ishmael wanted to create a whole empire of magical little offspring. They were playing gods, and well, look how it ended. The fates said no. So don't mess with it, girl. Just leave it alone. Walk away."

I scoffed, looking him up and down. "Like you?"

The broken warrior.

He'd been running from whatever had happened for decades. That much was clear. He was pathetic. "I hope you're not my father. Because I don't want the blood of such a coward."

I shoved past him.

And this time, he didn't follow me.

17

Lissa

Tayna and I barely spoke in the truck.

My hope had given way to worry as we left the ship. It wasn't for myself but for my friends who were out in this city somewhere and needed my help. All I wanted to do was find them.

Occasionally, I would catch Tayna glancing my way before his eyes would flit back to the road again. The scar over his eye was pinched as his eyes narrowed on the oncoming city stretched before us. He was worried, too.

This time, I hadn't insisted on driving.

He knew the way, after all.

But we'd said enough to agree that we would sleep just outside the city for the night after looking for the book at Tea and Trinkets.

It would take us just a few hours of travel to reach the Veiled thanks to the Humvee, but with the sun already peaking toward the afternoon, we'd wait to approach the Veiled until the morning.

I'd almost insisted we go tonight. We wasted precious hours in the city as it was, even with the promise of Madam Cartenoth's book of secrets. If Enver and Laykin were in trouble, well, hours could be the decider. Worse than that. I knew too well that bad things only took seconds.

Tayna didn't glance my way again. Instead, his hand found mine, twisting into my fingers and holding tightly. The gesture made my chest squeeze, even as I exhaled at the feel of him.

A thread pulled taut between us. When he'd held me on the docks, I'd felt more like myself than I had since the cliffs. Was that what I wanted? To be my old self? I'd give anything to be in a world where Kenji was still here, but I wouldn't give anything to be the girl trapped in that mansion again, even wrapped in my grief and uncertainty as I was now.

There was no going back.

I felt it in my soul, in the way my silver tugged and pulsed beneath my skin.

I was becoming something new. There was a call in my bones I couldn't ignore. And I didn't understand it, but it was fueling me forward.

I looked back out at the waning sunshine, fading beneath the ocean waves behind the Humvee. It was a dreary sort of sunset, the kind that promised rolling fog and mist-flecked air. Summers were volatile like that. The clouds liked to drift low near the sea, keeping the weather mild and the sun at bay.

We crested the hill from the ocean to the ruins of the city. In front of us, I could see the tree where we'd sat eating soggy french fries and dreaming about a future spun from the books we read. Two children who had nothing to cling to except for dreams and books.

I glanced at Tayna, and he was already watching me through the twilight.

It was a brief connection, but there was a shared promise in it. Despite everything, we still held the same dream of a better life. I still wanted to believe it could exist.

Tayna turned the Humvee into the market square. The gnarled tree loomed before the ocean. It gave way to the crumbling buildings and people who looked just as broken. The evening cast silhouettes against the debris along the road. The sun painted the shadows of the people just as the artists had graffitied pictures across the walls of this city. Swirling neon designs flickered against the headlights, their colors starkly contrasting with the evening's gloom.

Faces loomed with shocked expressions against the glare of our headlights. The Cards had long used the Humvees to enter the city. No doubt the roads had been quiet of vehicles like this in the weeks since Gideon's death.

"We're drawing too much attention," I muttered to Tayna, noticing a group of Fortas watching us with narrowed eyes from the entrance of the club.

"I know. But we don't have another option." Tayna murmured, "We can't exactly park and walk from here."

He was right of course. My silver eyes would attract enough attention all on their own. The truck was safer in that regard.

Tayna's hand returned to the wheel, flexing tightly, and my gaze tracked to the guns he had strapped across his chest. I had mine tucked into the backpack at my feet. I'd kept the one he'd given me on the beach hidden in my bag. Tayna wore his weapons like they were extensions of his arms. His skin was nearly as tanned from the summer sun as the body-cross leather holsters.

I didn't like guns. I hadn't wanted to touch one after leveling that pistol at Gideon's chest. But I couldn't deny I felt safer knowing it was close. Just in case. If I'd had a gun down in the cells that day, maybe Kenji would still be alive.

Once we turned off the main road toward the back entrance of Tea and Trinkets, the streets were quieter. A few stragglers, mostly drunks or Silver addicts, slumped against alley walls here or there. But the wary eyes that watched us faded into hazy, heavy-lidded flinches.

"You can park there," I told Tayna, pointing at a spot between the fences that provided even more concealment. Kenji had parked there on the night he'd taken me to Tea and Trinkets and revealed his relationship with Phenola.

We moved quickly to the shop once the truck was parked. The muscle memory of our time living together on the streets had me ducking beneath Tayna's shadow and keeping close to his heels in time with his steps.

A man walking by happened to glance down the alley. He seemed just as startled as we were to make eye contact with another person and hurried on his way.

Phenola had been right. The back door of Tea and Trinkets was open. The lock on the screen door was torn away. There was a boot mark on the interior wood door, with splintered fractures hanging limply. Looters hadn't wasted any time helping themselves to the shop once Phenola and Madam Cartenoth were gone.

My first step inside crunched with all the broken glass littered around the place. Most of it was from the front window, which had been completely scraped from the frame. But some were from the priceless relics that had called this shop home. The looters had apparently found more pleasure in destroying than stealing them.

The damage made the grief swell from my chest to my throat. I pushed my silver down.

Control.

I tried to remind myself they were just things, just items.

But this shop had been a refuge for me since I was a girl. There wasn't any tea left on the shelves. Hell, the shelves had been pulled from the walls altogether. There wasn't the floral smell of Madam Cartenoth's soap wafting around the space. Now it was just the stench of rat piss. And there wasn't any light or life left. Its soul had been gutted, leaving only stray trails of moonlight from the destroyed window.

Near the window, I spotted a rainbow-colored thing made of wood with a large red slat that got progressively smaller, changing colors until it ended at a small purple tile. A wooden dowel was attached to the contraption with a string. The dowel was missing now, but I remembered this toy. It was a small piano, something made for a child in the time before the war. I used my finger to caress the keys, unable to replicate the clanging sound I remembered all those years ago. Madam Cartenoth had threatened to make me buy it if I continued playing it. Why had she kept it, then?

"Lissa," Tayna hissed, beckoning me toward the back house.

I sighed, setting the toy back down on the ground. It wasn't like we could take it. What would be the point? I was sure the looters thought the same. So it would remain in this shop, a small constant that somehow brought me comfort.

I followed Tayna, carefully dodging debris as I made my way behind the counter and through the back door into the living area.

It was nearly pitch black in the space, so I used my silver, casting a white glow across the room that emanated from my fingers like a flashlight.

Even this space had been picked through, not that there was much to steal to begin with. But the fridge hung open, the silver powering it long spent. The cupboards were empty and thrown wide. The small table and mismatched chairs were knocked to their sides.

"We'll be lucky if they haven't found this book," Tayna mumbled.

In the small bedroom, the sheets had been stripped, leaving a stained mattress. I was surprised it hadn't been taken, too. I'd been afraid to walk into this room again. The last time I was here, I'd held Madam Cartenoth's hand as she died, then emerged to find Dia waiting to drag me back to the Cards. But I was surprised by how much peace I felt in this space.

It was dusty and dingy and no longer livable by any means with the vermin that had taken over just as quickly as the looters, but there was no grief here. Not in this room. Instead, it felt like a place to remember an old friend, and it made my lips quirk into a smile to remember her blunt insults and scoffing demands that I be more than a Queen or a street rat. Somehow, I'd gotten to a place where I didn't know what I was. But I was still certain she would be pleased.

Was I a Whig, then? Or an entirely new kind of rebel?

Tayna dropped to his knees and began feeling around the slats of wood flooring for any raised edges.

I found a lamp on the bedside table and touched it gently until the bulb flared to light, casting a yellow glow.

"You're getting good at control," Tayna said, nodding at my hands.

The light caught against his scar. A painful reminder of the first time I'd lost control of my silver in the market. "It took me too long."

He stood, but I turned away, scanning my side of the bed for any loose pieces. The corners of the wood dug under my nails as I tested if they were secured.

"You know I would never blame you—"

His words cut off as one of the slats along the baseboard broke free with a clatter. I swore as the wood tore into my fingers.

Tayna knelt in front of me, grabbing my wrist before I could even inspect the small cuts myself.

"Ow!" I grumbled as he moved my hand to the light.

"They're just splinters." He grinned.

I silently cursed his dimples as I allowed him to carefully pull out the small slivers of wood that had wedged their way under the skin of my pointer and middle fingers. I could have done it myself. I didn't need him to coddle me. But I settled for scowling as he focused his attention on his task.

His hands were gentle, his touch warm.

"There," he said after a moment, his voice low.

But when I tried to pull my hand back, he held my wrist firm.

His eyes found mine, and my breath stopped, aware of the energy shift. His grin had turned to a sparkling heat, his tongue tracing along his bottom lip.

Oh.

He brought my fingers to his mouth, licking them from knuckles to nails. He sucked the blood from them until the wounds healed, watching me as he did.

My lips parted as I tried to remember to breathe. It was all I could do just to watch him. His expression was pure ecstasy as he savored me.

My heart ricocheted. My skin felt heated, and my pulse pounded in my throat. His mouth did weird things to my stomach. But he was also taking silver. Tayna was tasting my blood as if it were the most natural thing in the world, as if he'd been doing it for years.

So I shoved him hard enough that he dropped his hold. Gritting my teeth, I growled, "Don't do that!"

Tayna looked like a man who'd suddenly discovered a game he very much liked. He smirked, standing from his knees to hover over me, where I still crouched on the floor. "You taste delicious, Lissa. Last time, I was unconscious and didn't get to enjoy it."

I balked at his audacity, at the sheer nerve of him, and yes, at the effect his words seemed to have on my senses.

"You'll make yourself sick," I snapped. "You can't mix silver."

"Whose silver do you think I've been taking?" He eyed me meaningfully. "Karadin's been giving me small vials from her supply.

And I'd been stocking that supply since the cliffs.

I sucked my teeth, swallowing down my frustration mixed with... something else.

"Get your book," he said, his teasing still evident in the words as he nodded his head at the slight opening that had appeared in the wall next to the bed, just like Phenola had said it would.

Right.

I could see the pages of a small, leather-bound journal. With one final glare thrown at Tayna, I crawled to the hole and slid the journal from the nook, ignoring the heat that had me pressing my thighs together as I sat back to wipe away the dust and inspect the cover.

There was nothing.

It was just a simple brown leather binding kept closed by a string wrapped tightly around a small disk on the front cover.

"What does it say?" he asked.

I shook my head. "The cover's blank."

He offered me his hand, pulling me to stand before I could loosen the strap and look at the contents inside. "We should go. You can inspect it in the truck, but we've already stayed here long enough."

He was right, of course.

I dusted off my pants before turning back to him, straightening my shoulders until I was at my full height. He might still tower over me, but at least he'd know I wasn't going to balk in front of him. Ever.

"If you taste my blood again without my permission, Tayna, I swear to you, you'll never taste another part of me again. Do you understand?"

He chuckled, running his tongue along his upper canine as if he could still taste me there. "So... you're saying there's a chance?" He leaned in closer to me.

And I let him. I allowed our eyes to meet, and in his, I found hope. He wanted me to engage with him. He wanted me to play.

So I quirked a brow at him. "Not on your life." Pushing his chest, I stalked around him toward the Humvee.

In truth, I'd been tempted to taste him back.

I was so caught up in the moment that I didn't check my surroundings as I walked out of the shop.

Mistake.

Something rammed into my back so hard I pitched forward into the misty muck of the alley as a gunshot went off behind me. It was all I could do to keep the journal pressed against my chest as my shoulder smacked into the pavement and pain cracked along my skull.

18

Lissa

A cackling laugh split the air.

My cheek slid along the asphalt and grime. It wasn't the first time I'd tasted the dirt of these city streets. It was disgusting. Blood and moldy grit filled my mouth. I tried to spit as pain ratcheted over my body. I couldn't tell where I was hurt.

But it was Tayna's body curled around mine.

He'd pushed me?

He'd shoved me down into the alley.

Was there a gunshot?

"Are you okay?" Tayna's lips grazed along my ear, his words close and clipped.

"That's a fancy truck you got there!" A raspy voice with a lilting accent called from behind us.

My brain began to register what had happened.

We'd been spotted, and Tayna had tackled me rather than see me shot.

I spun in his grasp, reaching for his face, but he pressed quickly from my body with an, "I'm good," before he turned to face the man who'd spoken to us.

"No use letting the Cards' misfortune go to waste," Tayna said, raising his hands so the man knew he wasn't going for his guns. I was unarmed. My gun was still in my backpack in the truck. But, well, I didn't need a gun right now. I *was* a weapon.

I shielded my eyes so they wouldn't see my silver gaze as I looked up to find three men sauntering toward us. The one at the front had a red bandanna tied around his upper arm. The others had theirs folded across their brows. Fortas then.

They were a newer gang, established over the past few years. At first, Gideon hadn't taken them seriously. They were more nuisance than any concern to the powers in this city. Even now, they were barely organized. Their ranks thrived on chaos and anarchy more than on vying for any sort of control.

"Eh." The man at the front gave Tayna another once-over. He was shorter but thickly built with a thin mustache and an X tattooed beneath his eye. "I hate to tell you, my friend, but I think this is where you find the same misfortune as the Cards. But don't worry. I also won't allow it to go to waste. And I won't waste your pretty friend, either."

His gaze slid to me in a way that communicated exactly what he meant, and it had nothing to do with my silver. Disgust and anger coiled through my veins at the way his eyes slithered over my skin. He grinned with rotten teeth.

So I dropped my arm. I let him see my eyes as the rage bubbled from the pit of my belly. Fuck if it didn't feel good.

And through the muck and grime on my face, with my silver buzzing in my veins like it was purring, I smiled back at him.

"And here we thought we were lucky because we found a truck, chicos." The man's mustache curled as his smile grew. He thought he'd won some great prize tonight.

He tossed the gun between his palms as if testing its weight, then leveled it at Tayna's chest.

Of course, he thought the man was the threat. He saw Tayna's build and Tayna's guns and assumed I was a helpless Silver.

Good.

The electricity coiled through my veins.

It felt good, that power.

"It's funny," I said, rising to my feet, aware that the muck smeared across my face probably made my eyes look alien against the moonlight. The man hesitated at my words, his finger on the trigger. "That you think this was luck."

The man quirked an eyebrow.

And the burly one next to the mustache man said, "Well, what is it then, plateadito?"

I shrugged and then released my silver, letting it stream from my fingers to the pavement like lightning crackling along the earth. Sparks of asphalt sputtered into the air. "Karma." I grinned.

This was just the release I needed.

"La reina de plata!" one of the men behind the mustache bellowed.

And I couldn't deny that I liked the fear in his voice as I stepped closer to the men, careful that my sparks of silver arched away from Tayna as I moved.

Once they realized I was approaching, my steps forward became their steps backward. The mustached man fired, but the bullet ricocheted off my silver in a spray of electricity.

I'd always fought to keep myself under control. I never wanted people to fear me. I never wanted to hurt anyone. And while that might still be true for most, these men didn't deserve my pity or my control.

The third man ran—simply sprinted down the alley back where he'd come from toward the main road. The one who'd called me "la reina de plata" looked like he might follow. The mustached man holding the gun shook as he tried to hold it level at my chest.

"Lissa," Tayna snapped behind me. I heard his rifle cock.

I ignored him, balling my fists instead to snuff out my silver as I grabbed the barrel of the gun. "Try it."

The gun clicked as the Forta pulled the trigger.

But no shot was fired.

I smiled.

I'd sent just enough silver into the barrel to stop the pin. Alaric hadn't just shown me how to fire a gun. He'd also taught me how guns worked.

I yanked the weapon from the mustached man before he could attempt to fire a second time. It was surprisingly easy, and the gun went clattering to the sludge of the street.

My silver balled at my fingertips as I considered what to do to the man. Men had controlled me for so long. They'd lied to me, stolen from me, and cheated me. All because they were bigger and stronger, and I was helpless, unable to control my silver.

This man would have killed Tayna. He would have drained me dry. Maybe worse, he would have violated me in all the ways possible, body and blood.

But I wasn't helpless anymore.

I'd never be owned by a man again.

The Forta in front of me was cowering in his terror. I could see the sparks of my silver flaring and reflecting in his blown pupils.

What was it Gideon had said all those nights ago at the bonfire? *You read your books and eat your pastries and judge me all you want, little Queen.*

But I wasn't judging him anymore. Now, I understood what it meant to make the hard decisions to keep my friends safe.

The sparks lit the path in front of me.

It was so easy.

"Lissa!" Tayna's voice was sharp.

Sharp enough that it cut through the haze of my silver.

I hesitated, pausing as I watched Tayna's expression harden, his jaw setting.

Was he afraid?

Of me?

No, it was something else.

Not afraid, but he'd seen the certainty in my eyes.

He realized I was no longer the girl who hesitated in the face of danger.

I leaned closer to the mustache man until I could see the pock marks running underneath his stubble.

My silver glowed hot between us.

"Run," I whispered, relishing his fear for a few moments longer.

And he did.

I watched him go. I watched him sprint like his life depended on it.

Had I made a mistake letting him leave?

Only a few minutes ago, he'd sauntered into this alley and fired at me as if his bullets gave him the checkmate. He didn't realize he was a pawn playing against a Queen. Was this enough of a lesson that he and his friends would think twice next time a girl was minding her own business in a darkened alley?

I wasn't sure.

After swooping to pick up the pistol from the ground, I turned to Tayna. The lines between his brows were deep, and his nostrils flared.

"What the fucking hell was that, Lissa?" he demanded.

"That was me, doing what I had to do to protect us." I shrugged, lifting my fingers as the silver extinguished from my palms.

"That was reckless." He grabbed the gun from my hands, put the safety on, and tucked it into his pocket. "What were you thinking? That stunt with the gun?"

"I was thinking"—I glared up at him—"that those pricks were about to shoot us and steal our Humvee."

"If I hadn't said your name, would you have killed that guy?"

"How is this any different from those cars at the ocean?" I demanded.

"It's different because of that look in your eyes that said you enjoyed it this time. Would you have killed him?"

"What does it matter?" I asked, even as I weighed his words. "You've killed lots of people."

"Not like that. You've always maintained that's *not* who you are."

"What if I don't want to be that person anymore, huh? What if I don't want to be that scared little Queen who cowers behind the men in her life?"

Tayna scoffed. "Come on, Lissa. You've always been strong."

"And now I'm showing it."

"Lissa..." His face relaxed, the tension leaving only to be replaced by pity as if the words hadn't really been as strong and as sure as I'd meant them.

And wasn't that what I was doing? Challenging him to see if he would reject this new violence in me the way I'd been trying to pretend it didn't exist?

He reached for me, but I skirted out of his touch. "No. No, Tayna. I don't want your pity, and I don't want your comfort. I can protect myself, and I'm going to do that now. I'm going to protect myself, and I'm going to protect my friends. And if that means I have to kill some-one. Well, I won't hesitate when it matters. Not again."

19

The Phantom

I preferred my rooms to be dark, even when I was alone.

The darkness had always called to me.

My raven sat perched next to me as I scrawled on the small pad of parchment that would attach to the bird's leg.

Only the flicker of silver candlelight allowed me to see the ink as I practically stabbed my pen into the paper.

Not yet. Hold until my order.

The idiots were growing restless. Patience was an art form, a skill. One that most people, men especially, did not possess. Just because the game was in motion didn't mean rushing to make all the moves at once. It was decidedly the opposite. One move at a time, teasing out the tell that would give the plays away.

They didn't need to understand.

They simply needed to obey.

Just as I finished securing the paper to my bird's leg, there was a quiet knock on the door.

I ran my tongue along my silver-pointed canine. "Come in."

There was a pause for a moment, and I wondered if she'd heard me. My voice was a low growl. I'd grown to appreciate the silence as much as the darkness.

The heavy wood door creaked open after a moment, and a petite woman with jet-black curls slipped into my room. Her silver eyes were wide and uncertain as she glanced around the space. One of the new ones, then.

She gasped when she saw me. Her chest rose and fell as she took me in from my black boots to the tip of my silver mask. The chrome suit I wore strained against my muscular frame. I'd worked hard to maintain my honed physique. My father had insisted on routine, and training had been a part of my daily ritual for as long as I could remember.

To the girl's credit, she didn't flinch from me. She instead clasped her hands behind her back and did her best to look me in the eye. Her rapid blinking was the only cue to her nerves, even as she met my gaze beneath the mask.

"You requested a Silver?" she said, her voice light and airy in the space.

Rather than respond, I approached her. Slowly. It was always so much more satisfying when I made it last.

She watched me the whole way, with each of my steps, until she was staring up at me with those wide, silver eyes.

"They didn't explain—"

I pressed a finger against her lips, effectively cutting off her words, and then I leaned down to breathe her in, inhaling as I ran the edge of my mask along her collarbone.

She gasped, and when I straightened, she was reaching for my mask.

I grabbed her wrists with enough force that I saw a flash of fear in her wide, innocent eyes, pinning them back to her sides. Tugging on them for good measure as I pressed them against her thighs, I looked at her again.

"Got it," she breathed, clutching her hands behind her back once again. "No touching the mask."

"Good." I grinned. Obedient little thing.

Yes, she would do just fine.

This time, when I dipped back down to her neck, I pulled her in close, until her body was fully flush against my frame.

To my surprise, she kept her hands behind her back, falling into me as I gripped her. Pliant and submissive then. Typically, I liked my women with a bit more fight, but she would do nicely for a night.

Keeping her securely against me with one hand wrapped around her back, I lifted the mask just enough to expose my silvered canines. I ran my tongue along the curve in her throat, and then I sank my teeth into the soft flesh of her neck.

She let out a startled yelp, and I felt her body tense around me.

On instinct, her hands released from behind her back to grip my shoulders. I couldn't tell if she was pushing me away or pulling me in. Some of them liked the pain.

The first taste of her silver had me near feral with the need. I'd gone too long today. It was well into the night, and my last dose had been—when? This morning?

I pulled at the puncture wounds. Her silver was a balm to my aching chest.

God, it felt good.

Few things felt this good.

I ran my length along her belly, and she gasped. Was it lust? Or fear? More than likely, a bit of both. It only spurred me to bite deeper, to draw more of that delicious silver blood into my mouth as I drew her close, my face buried against her neck.

"Oh god," she gasped.

And this time, I knew it was from pleasure.

She liked this.

She pressed her chest against me, her body rolling as she began to moan.

I could bend her over this desk right now, bury myself inside her.

But I shoved her away, pressing the mask back into place as I licked her blood from my teeth.

She was gasping, her breasts heaving between the low cut of her dress. "Don't stop," she panted with need, no longer timid but breathless. Small silver lines of blood trickled from the healing puncture wounds on her neck.

I was hard.

Fuck, I was so hard it hurt as my cock strained against my pants.

But I turned away from her.

It would be so easy to push up her dress and bury myself deep. She was wet for it. She'd scream for me.

But I could not afford distractions right now.

And I was so close to the real prize I craved.

"Get out." The words were barely a whisper.

Her mouth popped open in shock.

But I whirled on her when she didn't immediately obey my command, and whatever she saw in my expression had her scrambling for the door.

Soon.

Soon, I would have both silver and pleasure.

But now was not the time to get lost in dalliances. Now was the time for patience. And I had work to do.

20

Lissa

The journal's cover was smeared with black goo when I picked it up from the asphalt. I wiped it off on my pants the best I could, but they were covered in the gunk too. I'd only brought one change of clothes in my backpack. Maybe I'd get lucky as we drove on the outskirts of town, and there would be a stream somewhere I could wash them.

Wishful thinking.

I could feel the sludge drying in my hair, too, and cracking along the side of my face. I brushed away the dried bits as best I could.

"We should go before mustache man decides to bring back his friends," I said over my shoulder, wondering again if I'd made the right decision by letting him live.

"I'm right behind you," Tayna said just before I felt him at my back. He wasn't touching me, but he was close enough that I could feel the heat of him, the way he blocked the cool breeze of the night from reaching me.

I knew what he was doing. It was the same thing he'd done when he pushed me to the ground. He was using his body as a shield. He was taking the bullet in the back, if need be, rather than see me hurt.

It was ridiculous, really. I would have a better chance of healing from a bullet wound than he would. With my silver, I'd also have a better chance of responding to an attacker. But I didn't say anything because he'd always protected me. And, well, because a deeper part of me liked the feel of him so close. My spine tingled with that awareness of him, and I had a moment of insanity as I imagined pushing myself back against him, allowing him to cocoon me in his warmth. He would, too. He probably wouldn't say anything at all if I curled myself into him. He'd simply respond, pressing his body flush with mine until I asked for more.

More.

Because simply being close to him was never enough.

The leftover adrenaline from the night, paired with the way he'd sucked my fingers in Madam Cartenoth's shop, had my body feeling clammy.

My silver and my hormones were volatile, it seemed.

"Are you cold?" Tayna asked. His breath was so close to my ear that I felt the warm tendrils of it caressing along my hairline.

"Fine."

But I was walking faster, as if I could outrun this sudden flood of emotion, as if I could outpace Tayna and clear my head. I needed to focus on this book and on Enver and Laykin, not the way Tayna had pressed his fingers into his mouth with desire so plain across his face.

Of course, the mere seconds of silent reprieve in the truck were all I got before he was climbing into the driver's seat, giving me a funny look, and locking the doors before turning on the ignition.

"Are you sure you're good?" he pressed. "What happened back there... what those men said. It was vile, Lissa."

But that wasn't it.

God, that wasn't it.

Again, I thought of that night in our loft that first time when my body had taken control of my mind, and I'd finally kissed Tayna after months and months and months of talking myself around of the desire.

But I wasn't a teenager anymore. I was a grown woman, and I could control my emotions. I could control myself. I could think logically, and I could think rationally about this situation.

"I'm fine," I said again, aware my voice bobbed on the words in time to the pulsing of my heart.

Thankfully, this time, Tayna didn't press. His eyes narrowed, but he nodded and pulled the truck from the alley.

Back on the road, the Humvee's headlights were the only source of light as we drove from the city center. I wiped at the edges of the journal with the corner of my still-clean shirt. I didn't dare open it and smear the pages, but the waiting had my knee shaking with nervous energy, wishing I could look inside. I could use the distraction.

My gaze tracked to Tayna's face, lit by the white glow of the Humvee.

He was focused on the road. The scar that cut over his brow and into his eye was stark against his tanned skin. His hair had grown since we'd left the Card's compound, and a lock curled across his forehead.

He took up so much space that his body folded awkwardly into the seat. One arm leaned against the driver's side door, the other slung across the wheel. The cut of his triceps peaked out from beneath his white shirt. The fabric dipped in at his waist, catching on the ridges of his abdomen.

"You keep looking at me like that, and I'm going to stop this truck," Tayna said, not taking his eyes off the road. "I'll finish what we started in Madam Cartenoth's shop."

That had my eyes widening as if he could read my mind, and I pressed myself into the seat. "It's just adrenaline left over from the fight," I murmured.

"Yeah." He ran a hand across his jaw as if smoothing out some tension of his own. "I know what that feels like."

"I'm still mad at you for taking my silver," I grumbled.

"Only mad?" There was humor again in his gaze.

"Don't push your luck." I intended for the words to be snapped, but now a grin tugged at the corners of my lips, too.

So I looked away, back down at the journal where the dirt and grime of the streets were drying, until I could wipe away the biggest flakes along the edges, carefully undoing the tie and cracking open the pages.

It was yellowed with age and smelled musty like it'd been sitting in that alcove for years. But some of the pages had bold black writing. Carefully thumbing to the beginning, I held it closer to my face so I could read the words against the dim light of the Humvee's interior.

But there weren't any words.

The pages were filled with numbers.

Scrawls of numbers.

Formulas.

A chart that looked like a 3D model of some geometric shape.

Another that showed a pattern of interlocking octagons.

I thumbed through the pages.

All of them in the same fashion.

Some pages were marked with an X. Some pages had arrows pointing to yet more pages. Some were simply filled with numbers and notes scrawled next to them that didn't make any sense.

Biogens interact at temperature spike.

Hormonal links strongest after puberty.

Epigenetics or mutation key for expression?

"What is it?" Tayna asked, glancing over at the book but unable to read the words through the dim light of the cabin.

I studied another page. This one was scrawled with an image of a central point with two orbits circling. Smaller, opaque dots had been filled in like a constellation in space. I held the book to the side to get a better view of the image.

"It's some kind of science, but I can't make sense of it."

I read books about faraway lands and adventures and mythical places. I'd never been adept at other subjects. My mother had taught me all she could. She'd sat at the table, making me practice addition and multiplication and algebraic formulas until my head hurt. But she'd died when I was ten. My brain could only retain so much science and math at that age. By the time I'd been on the streets with Tayna, books were more about an escape than an education. They taught me to dream and hope and believe, which were arguably more important skills for a child in my position than physics. But still, I was no help in this situation when faced with complex formulas and scientific theories.

Tayna glanced over at the pages. "It just looks like scribbles to me."

"I thought you were the rich fancy one? Your parents didn't have genius tutors on staff?"

He side-eyed me. "My brother was always my mother's golden child. He was the one poised for greatness. After Gideon killed him, well, I didn't stick around long enough for the tutors to be fired, but I can assure you, they wouldn't have been kept on the payroll for my sake."

I imagined Tayna as a young child, the loss of his older brother and his father crashing down on him in one day. Yet instead of crumbling underneath the grief of it all, he had seen through the bloodshed for what it was: power struggles among Silver addicts. And he'd run rather than join the gangs, taking his brother's place in the family line. I had a deep respect for that eleven-year-old boy. It was amazing he'd lasted a week out there after forgoing all the finery for a life on the streets.

It was amazing that both of us had survived.

Street rats.

Remnants of our parents' choices left to forge a new path in a ruined place.

We were doing that, weren't we?

And not just me and Tayna. But Phenola and Enver and Laykin... and Kenji and Gideon. We were all just playing our parts in a game that those who came before us had started. I hadn't wanted to play before. But I was learning the moves now. After everything, maybe I could learn enough to actually make a difference. Perhaps winning meant ending the game once and for all so kids like us, Silvers especially, no longer had to live in fear.

21

Lissa

Tayna pulled the Humvee into the dirt along the side of the road. We were surrounded by a flat expanse of desert with mountains rising in the distance, framed by thousands of stars.

A small reservoir just off the road that had me itching from the dirt on my skin, desperate to wash away the black goo.

I left the strange journal tucked between the seats. No one was around this far out of the city. Most people didn't have access to a vehicle, and it was only ruins between this stretch and the Veiled. In the distance, large windmills turned slowly against the moonlight. Some were toppled on their sides. Giant turbines that had once powered the city the way silver did now. How strange to think that a hundred years ago, people would capture the wind and turn it into energy.

I made a beeline to the water, wanting nothing more than to feel clean, but Tayna cleared his throat behind me. The dirt seemed to fissure along my crusted skin as I paused, rubbing it across my face and feeling it flake off, gathering beneath my nails.

"Do you want me to go with you or—"

Or…

The word hung there, as unfinished as everything between us.

But I shook my head. "I've got it. I just need a few minutes."

Maybe in addition to scrubbing the dirt from my skin, I could scrub the sudden desire from my brain.

Cold water.

Cold, clean water would do me good.

"Right." Tayna nodded, his neck stiff. "I'll set up for bed, then."

Was he thinking about the reservoir at the farm? Of course, he was thinking about those moments when we'd almost, almost gone all the way within the warm cocoon of that spring. And I'd wanted him so badly then. It had felt so good and so right as his fingers had trailed along my skin, washing me clean while he'd massaged my shoulders until I pressed back against him.

I gritted my teeth against the onslaught of memory.

Too many fucking memories.

I stalked alone to the shallow bed of water in the dark.

I cursed, peeling off my shirt and sports bra.

It might be summer, but that didn't stop the ocean air from wafting over my skin.

This water was decidedly not akin to a hot springs. It was frozen and murky, and who knew how long it'd been sitting still without rain. But I dunked my shirt beneath the surface nonetheless, shivering against the night air. I used the fabric to scrub at my skin. Even as I shook with cold, the relief of wiping the dirt from my cheek and neck felt too good to stop. I groaned, even as my teeth clattered.

"You alright out there?" Tayna called.

I choked on the sound in my throat. "F-fine!"

Goose bumps pebbled over my skin, the hair prickling as it stood on end. At least the sharp bite of the cold was a distraction. It was definitely a balm to my overheated skin.

We'd been tucked into that truck together for too long.

And now we'd be tucked inside it together all night.

My plan had been to put the shirt back on once I'd cleaned myself and dunked it back into the reservoir, but it was a losing battle. My hands shivered violently, and the fabric stuck to my skin to the point that I would more than likely stretch it out irreparably by the time I got it over my head.

So I settled for my sports bra. It wasn't like Tayna hadn't seen all of me anyway. Even though somehow, now, it felt different.

When he'd returned to the Tanks, something had changed between us. The fear that something could have happened to him, paired with the brutal reality of losing Laykin and Enver, made me realize how misplaced my anger had been. In my sadness, I'd pushed him away when, really, he was the person I needed close most of all.

And I was done pretending that wasn't true.

The grief was still there. Maybe it always would be. With Gideon, I'd mourned Tayna. With Tayna, on the farm, I'd mourned the relationship Gideon and I could have had. And now that Gideon was dead, I was mourning the loss of the man himself. It seemed like a vicious, cruel cycle from the universe.

But grief was far from the only thing I felt now. There was desire and trust, too, and they all existed together in a way that somehow, with him, didn't feel so hard to carry. It was always that way with him, and I didn't want to feel so alone.

I trudged back to the truck, wet and shivering, to find Tayna leaning against the side waiting for me. His tanned skin reflected against the moonlight, and I imagined tracing my fingers over the ridges along his arms. Even his forearms were corded with muscle. My eyes tracked to his shoulder, where I could see the edges of his heart tattoo, purple against the midnight of the sky. I'd never actually thanked him for coming to the Cards to get me. Everything had happened so fast over the past couple of weeks.

His golden eyes burned as I studied him. That look said he wanted to study me, too, wanted to explore all the pieces of me that he hadn't yet seen.

And would I let him? After everything, would I allow him to know me in that way?

He uncrossed his arms, his fingers coming out to brush across my bottom lip. It was the smallest of touches, a whisper of skin that felt as light as the breeze.

"Your lips are blue," he murmured, but his gaze stayed on my face, not trailing lower to the exposed skin along my midriff.

Being out here in the dark, in the middle of nowhere, felt like some kind of fever dream. As if in this cocoon of stars and quiet, we could pretend just for a moment that we were still those street rats learning to navigate our feelings for one another for the first time.

Tayna said, "We should talk."

And the spell of his heated gaze and this night was broken.

I shivered against the breeze and wished that instead of speaking, he'd pull me into his arms, tuck me in his warm embrace, and allow me to forget our reality for just a moment.

I could have forgotten for a night.

"Okay," I sighed. "But I'm cold." I skirted around his imposing figure to slide into the back seat.

Tayna had already lowered the seat into a makeshift bed, laying out our bed rolls and sleeping bags in a neat row, side by side. The gesture made my heart squeeze, and I gratefully crawled inside, cocooning myself in the warmth.

Tayna crawled inside with me, closing the doors around us and maneuvering himself gracefully despite the limited space in the Humvee. My spine tingled with that awareness of him.

He reached into the front seat and turned on the ignition, flipping the vents to heat.

The soft light from the interior glowed white around us, just enough that I could make out the silhouette of his chiseled features as he settled next to me. He didn't get into his own sleeping bag, and my eyes were drawn to the way his shirt pulled against his chest as he propped his head on his hand and watched me.

"You're wasting silver," I murmured.

"We have plenty," he said. "And you're shaking so hard the whole truck is rattling."

"I'm fi—"

But he cut me off. "Stop saying that. You don't have to be fine all the time. I was worried about you tonight, Liss."

"I can handle myself."

"That isn't why I was worried." His low voice danced in the space between us as the heat twisted its way into my scalp and down my neck from the vents.

I knew that wasn't what he'd meant.

"You couldn't be my protector forever, Tayna. Eventually, I had to learn how to protect myself."

"Back there—" He sighed. The sleeping bag rustled as he shifted on top of it. "You're better than that, Lissa."

"I didn't kill him," I grumbled, moving to shift away.

He grabbed the sleeping bag surprisingly quickly, sliding me across the back seat and pulling me even closer. I gasped as the space between our mouths became inches.

I should pull away.

But I didn't.

"Don't be like them, Liss," he breathed. His gaze lowered to my mouth as he spoke, and I resisted the urge to bite my bottom lip. "I know you've been hurt by this city. But don't let it turn you into one of them."

"One of who?" My voice was barely more than a whisper, aware he was mere inches away.

"People like my mother."

I did try to pull away then, but he held me tight enough that my breath caught from surprise. My gaze snapped back to his. My chest constricted. The heat flared to life inside me like it'd never truly gone away. The cool water had done nothing to soothe the ache I felt deep in my belly.

"I'm not going to try to convince you to go back to the Whigs. Just don't forget who you are. My mother will try to make you forget. But she can't have you. She can't have you."

"Tayna—" I hadn't even realized my hands had snaked free of the sleeping bag until they traced up the back of Tayna's neck. My fingers were frozen against his skin, but he shuddered for a different reason entirely. His body trembled, and he turned his head, his hair falling into his face as he kissed along my wrists.

"She can't have you," he said between those soft kisses that made me melt beneath him. "She can't have you because you're mine."

With my hands still around the back of his neck, he rolled on top of me. Even through the sleeping bag, I could feel his hard length press against my lower stomach as his lips moved from my wrist to the line of my jaw and my chin before he sealed his mouth against mine in a searing kiss.

I moaned into his mouth. All the pent-up frustration and desire that had been permeating through the truck now found an outlet in this one sudden kiss. It was as if I'd jumped from the precipice, submitting to the torrent of emotions and lust.

I was pinned beneath him as his tongue pressed between my lips and teeth, exploring my mouth as I ran my fingers into his hair.

"We're meant to be like this," he said on a breath before claiming my mouth again. "We're meant to be together, you and me. Don't forget it again, Liss. I can't take not being close to you."

His deft fingers found the zipper of my sleeping bag and made quick work of sliding it down. He lifted himself just enough to push the heavy down aside.

A brief waft of air caressed my skin before his body pressed into me. His hands were tracing down, down along my hips.

"I'm still—*ah*—mad at you for taking silver," I said against his mouth, even as his fingers slipped behind to grab my ass, pressing me more firmly against his erection.

"Feel free to take it out on me." His smile was a wicked promise as he rolled his hips into me again until my head was falling back against the seat of the truck.

"You know what I'm angry about?" he asked, pausing as he looked down at my body.

"What could you possibly be ang—"

He pushed up my sports bra, exposing my breasts to his hypnotized gaze. His iris looked almost iridescent like mine against the white glow of the Humvee's interior.

"I'm angry," he said, palming at my breasts until I was panting, "at all of these layers still in my way."

And with that, he was pulling the sports bra over my head, tossing it aside before quickly sweeping his shirt over his head in a similar motion.

My hands raked over his chest, my nails digging into the ridges I found in my path, before I was grabbing at his belt, flipping open the buckle, and sliding it free of his waist.

"I want to take you slow," Tayna groaned as I undid the buttons until I could reach my hand beneath his briefs and grip his length in my palm. At the first stroke of my fingers wrapped tightly around his cock, thoughts of slow dissipated from his mind. He was kissing me again, drawing our bodies close as I pumped him in my fist. "But I'm not waiting to fuck you again. His voice was low. "Do you want me to fuck you, Liss?"

I nodded against his mouth, stroking him harder.

"Say it," he growled against my lips.

"Yes," I breathed.

"No." He grabbed my chin, and I paused. "Say it all. Tell me what you want."

I hesitated. It had always been a game with Gideon. When I'd wanted him, he'd never required me to say it. In fact, part of the thrill had been in the chase and the challenge. But the way Tayna insisted on my words now made me wet and needy in a whole new, desperate way.

So I looked into his eyes as I said, "I want you to fuck me, Tayna."

He groaned, low and deep as he grinned and kissed me again. "That's right, Liss. God, I can't wait to be inside you." His hands traced to the waistband of my shorts, and he slid them over my ass as far as he could pull them before pressing himself down my body, trailing kisses across my bare skin, until he knelt at the apex of my thighs. "I'm going to fuck you, Liss. But I'm going to taste you first. Your blood was hardly enough."

He yanked my shorts down until I kicked out them off, and then he spread my thighs wide. He pinned my knees apart and buried himself between my legs. He didn't start slow. He didn't trail gentle kissing on my thighs. No, he absolutely devoured me.

My back arched up as my hands scrambled to grab the seat overhead for purchase as he sucked and licked at my clit just as he'd done to my fingers.

I was shaking. God, I was utterly quaking beneath him, but he didn't let up. He didn't show me even the hint of mercy as he kept my legs pinned as wide as they would go. And just when I thought I couldn't possibly take any more, he buried two fingers inside me.

"Tayna, I can't," I panted. "I can't."

He ran his teeth along my clit just hard enough to have me gasping as he said, "Take it, Liss. I want you right on the edge for me."

I shook my head.

He paused, pulling back from my body just enough that I knew he meant it.

"Don't stop." My words were a groan of desire. "Please don't stop."

He pressed two fingers back inside me but didn't touch my clit again. He found a rhythm like that, those digits stroking in a deep wave. "When you come, I want you pulsing on my cock, understood?"

I moaned.

"Understood?" Tayna paused his movements.

"Yes!" I cried, sobbing around the pleasure of it all.

And then his mouth was on me again, and god I was going to come. He pressed one hand against my lower belly as he sucked at my clit. His other hand focused on toying with my entrance until I was utterly convulsing beneath him with the need to come.

"Tayna!" His name was a plea.

"You have no idea how long I've waited to hear you scream my name like that." But his pace slowed. "Scream as loud as you like, Liss. No one can hear you but me."

"Please," I panted as he slid his tongue along my center one final time before pulling back.

His belt buckle rattled as he slid off his pants, including his briefs.

He hovered above me, pressing himself against the ceiling of the Humvee, and I drank in the sight of his body, silhouetted against the soft interior glow. It was like he was glowing with silver, his skin glistening with a sheen of sweat that only highlighted his muscled frame.

Now the interior of the truck was plenty warm.

My skin was burning.

He didn't have to hold my legs open anymore. I was desperate for him. My body unfolded beneath him as he moved to hover over me, our bare skin aligning in the dark.

"Say it again," he breathed above me, reaching down to stroke his cock, lining himself up at my entrance.

"Please." I obeyed like the feral thing he'd made me.

Every inch of my body was aware that he hadn't let me come yet. The draft from the vents had my skin buzzing. He held himself a breath away from making contact, his hard length poised at my entrance. I needed to feel the press of him—of all of him—as deeply as possible.

"Full sentences, Liss."

"Please fuck me, Tayna," I said without hesitation. "Please, please fuck me."

I rolled my hips just enough that the tip of his cock ran along my wet center, and we both groaned.

Even still, he kept his control. His eyes were on me, tracing the lines of my brow, my cheeks, my nose, my mouth, marking every inflection of my face as he sank inside me, slow inch by slow inch.

My hips swiveled as he got deeper, adjusting to the stretch, loving that I could feel him like this finally. He felt even better than I knew he would.

I'd spent more time than I wanted to admit fantasizing about him, but the reality was all-consuming. It wasn't just sex. It was a soul-deep connection that had always been there between us. I needed him in a way I'd never needed anyone in my life before. He was the steady presence that kept me grounded even when everything in this city felt chaotic and changing.

He was home.

And I sighed with the utter relief of it as he bottomed out inside me as deeply as he could possibly go.

He held himself like that, as if he was as taken by the moment as I was.

"This is—" he watched me through the darkness, and it was all I could do to nod. Because it was. It was everything.

He pressed his forehead into mine. His hand stroked gently down my face as I adjusted to the fullness of him, to the utter reality of this moment. And I wanted to stay like this forever. I refused, just for a moment, to worry about everything outside of this truck. There was only Tayna and me and this night.

He kissed me with the first thrust of his hips. His tongue dancing inside my mouth in the same rhythm as his cock inside my core. I groaned into his mouth, and he drank the sound as he did it again and again.

He had me too close to the edge. My body was already primed for the orgasm he'd denied me with his tongue and his damn fingers. But god, I didn't want this to be over so quickly.

I threw my head back and fought to suppress my orgasm.

Not yet.

God, not yet.

Not when we'd just started.

"Take it, Liss," he breathed. "I love how wild you are beneath me."

My hands fisted into the sleeping bag. "I'm going to come, Tayna," I moaned.

It only drove him harder. "Not yet, baby." He dragged his teeth along my jaw as I shuddered and spasmed around him. "I want you to come with me. Can you do that? Will you come with me?"

Sweat was breaking out over my skin. It was overwhelming pleasure.

It was all I could do to nod.

"That's my girl," he growled against my skin, licking and kissing a path along my neck as he continued to drive into me, rolling his hips so each thrust had me gasping and fighting my release. "Hold it, baby, hold it. I'm so far from done fucking you."

My hands moved to his hair, dragging his mouth back to mine in a crushing kiss. My fingers fisted in his hair, not caring that I was pulling tight enough to hurt. It only spurred him on more. Our chests rose and fell against one another, both of us holding onto our release, both of us not ready for this pleasure to end, even as my body begged for what it so desperately needed.

"So, so good, Lissa," Tayna groaned between kisses.

"I'm—" I choked on the words.

But he knew, pressed against my cheek, and nodded. "I'm right there, too, baby." His strokes became harder. "I'm right there with you."

And I knew there was no holding back the orgasm anymore.

"Come with me, Liss."

And I did.

I shattered.

This wasn't just a pleasure that had been withheld at this moment. This was a pleasure I felt like I'd waited an entire lifetime to feel. This was safety and protection and, yes, even trust that I'd thought could never be mine when I'd thought Tayna had died. It all culminated in this moment as we spiraled into our climaxes together.

It was pure ecstasy.

For a few moments, neither of us spoke, still caught up in the high.

Our bodies were slick against one another. Bare skin on bare skin.

As sensitive as I was after my orgasm, I shuddered as his breath caused his chest to caress against mine with each inhale.

My fingers traced across the planes of his shoulders.

His hands wound into my hair as he dipped his forehead against my shoulder, catching his breath.

"Fu-fuck." Tayna shuddered, still fully pressed inside me.

I, for one, was already wondering how long until we could do that again.

But the haze of desire was also beginning to lift.

Tayna slid from my body with another sigh of pleasure.

I groaned in protest at the sudden emptiness.

What time was it? How long until sunrise?

He brushed a soft kiss over my lips. "Come here."

And despite myself, I melted into him.

In the morning. In the morning, I would remember my grief and fear and uncertainty because right now, as Tayna cocooned himself around me, there was a blissful moment of pure and utter peace.

22

Lissa

The Humvee was cramped, and the sleeping bag left a lot to be desired in terms of padding. Eventually, we had to turn off the truck for the night, and the cold crept in. Tayna and I zipped our sleeping bags together for warmth, huddling skin to skin. My clothes were still damp, and his were scattered around the back seat where we'd created our makeshift bed.

Despite it all, I slept better than I had in weeks, curled up against his chest as his fingers grazed down my back in long, tender strokes. It reminded me of all those nights in our loft, huddled together. Of course, we'd been clothed then, but the nostalgia pulsed with recognition in my chest. My whole body seemed to exhale, and when I blinked open my eyes, the hazy rays of lavender morning were peeking through the foggy windows. Our shared breaths had clouded the glass, but I could make out the silhouette of the mountains in the distance. One of the remaining functioning turbines reflected the light as it rotated lazily, as if it still wasn't ready to start the day, either.

I burrowed myself deeper into the sleeping bags and deeper into Tayna's chest. One of his arms was slung low across my waist. The other was propped under my head like a makeshift pillow. My neck felt stiff. I could already tell there would be aches and pains from this cramped truck.

I squinted, searching for my canteen. I needed water. But it was in the front seat, and I couldn't yet inspire myself to move. Not when I could feel Tayna's length pressed against my backside in a way that had me arching into him ever so slightly. I imagined him lengthening in my palm if I reached beneath the sleeping bag.

Even though the thought turned me on, I hesitated. In the dark night, I could pretend it was all a fever dream. It was intoxicating and thrilling. Sex with him was something I'd wanted for a long time, and damn if it hadn't exceeded my expectations. But something inside me still felt erratic and raw.

He'd seen it last night when I'd almost killed those men outside Tea and Trinkets.

And in the light of day, the fear and uncertainty about Enver and Laykin and the Veiled wormed its way back under my skin. The thought had me pushing my silver down, taking steadying breaths.

And then I saw it.

A shadow flitted across the window.

Not a turbine. Not the mountains. Not anything that could be mistaken for the trick of the light.

It was the flash of movement just beyond the glass.

I sat up.

"Tayna." His name echoed the dread flitting up my spine just as a *thwunk* vibrated the truck as something landed on the roof.

And just like that, he was awake, jolting with the noise. "What the—"

Another thwack against the roof, and my arms flew over my head as I crouched down against the floor on instinct.

There was someone—or multiple someones—outside our Humvee.

And by the sounds of it, they were trying to get in.

Or maybe they had no idea we were in here. Maybe they thought the truck had been abandoned. Maybe they hadn't tried the door yet because they weren't sure if they'd find something valuable inside or rotting corpses.

Tayna seemed to have the same thoughts because, in the next second, he grabbed his rifle and crouched down, bracing his shoulder between the side of the truck and the front seat with his leg propped against the opposite door as he leveled the gun at the window.

"Stay down," he ordered me.

And I scrambled to obey while I grabbed my shirt and slipped it over my head. At least then I wouldn't die completely exposed. Not that corpses cared who saw their flesh.

My silver pulsed beneath my skin in my panic, but it wouldn't do any good. I couldn't use it unless I wanted to electrocute the whole vehicle. The only other weapon I had was my pistol, which was shoved inside my backpack in the passenger seat.

Another *thunk* on the roof and then... something flapping?

What in the hell?

I sat up, my eyes meeting Tayna's as we both seemed to realize the same thing at once.

I swiped a hand over the window nearest me, clearing the fog.

The sun was bright but not so blinding that I couldn't see the barren stretch of desert, yellowed against the morning sun.

Not even a tumbleweed to be seen near the truck.

I looked up, craning my neck to see the roof.

It was a bad angle, but I could see... nothing.

Tayna pushed open the opposite door, crouching low and leading with his rifle. His powerful body moved with the grace of a predator as he unfolded his large frame from the truck while pointing the gun up.

But he lowered the weapon as soon as he scanned the roof with the barrel. Then he was blinking against the sun as he gazed into the sky. His shoulders dropped as he exhaled.

It wasn't a sigh of relief, but a sound of deep foreboding.

"What is it?" I asked as I stumbled from the truck next to him, not nearly as graceful or stealthy as he'd been.

I followed his gaze into the sky, where two birds swooped overhead. The large creatures had rust-colored wings and proud speckled chests. They blocked the sun as they flew, circling higher as if we were the prey.

"Are they vultures?" I wondered aloud, still squinting at the sky.

I'd never seen birds like that before. They looked like they were considering swooping at us, talons first. One let out a screeching cry that echoed through the warming morning air.

"No," he sighed. "They're messenger hawks from the Veiled. My mother raises them on the property. She keeps them like pets."

A pit formed in my stomach, not because the birds scared me—which they did—but because those birds meant we were being watched. How long had they been circling us in this desert?

It was at least long enough. Long enough that Olita knew we were coming.

There would be no surprising the matriarch of the Veiled, then. But would she greet us as friend or foe?

We watched the hawks against the brilliant blue of the sky until they broke from their circle and disappeared against the mountains.

23

Lissa

"Do we just walk up and knock?" I asked Tayna, staring at the expansive wooden door stretched in front of us. It was part of an elaborate wall system. The only break in sight was a massive oak-paneled door, supported with dark iron rods slashing through the center in an intricate filigree pattern that didn't so much look welcoming as it did exclusive.

"Not unless you want to be shot." Tayna shielded his eyes against the morning sun as he took in the lookout posts.

It was hot this far from the city. The ocean mist and wrapping vines had long ago given way to cacti and dried-out-looking bushes. A hawk soared overhead in the cloudless sky, seemingly circling our location as if we were the only living things it had spotted in days. They knew we were here.

Gideon hadn't been lying when he said the Veiled was grand. It wasn't just a mansion but a fortress tucked behind a massive cream-colored concrete wall that stretched well above even Tayna's towering frame. It was ornately decorated with swirls of adobe trim sashaying along the top, jutting to spiked pillars at equal intervals.

Slim chance of climbing.

I scanned the barren desert around us. Nothing but rock baked into rust by the sun and a few crispy-looking weeds. "Not many places out here for me to dispel silver, I take it."

It hit me then that I'd never been this far from the ocean before.

"We won't be here long enough for that to be an issue," Tayna grumbled. "We should get back in the truck."

"Any chance you just happen to remember some kind of convenient hidden passageway or tunnel that gets us into this place?"

Tayna sighed. "I don't remember much. Except that in all the times I tried to find a way out, there wasn't one. I waited four months, memorizing the supply truck schedule before I actually ran away."

He must have been terrified. Just eleven and all on his own. Yet the terrors and the unknowns in the city had been worth the risk to him. He'd decided to leave rather than stay in this fortress of luxury.

"Uh-huh," Tayna said, watching me sidelong. "It really was that bad."

I grimaced. But we were here. And I wouldn't leave unless I was sure Olita had given us whatever information she could about Enver and Laykin and the missing Silvers. Standing in front of this compound, I felt an inexplicable pull. I'd felt it since making the decision to come to the Veiled. I wasn't sure what I would find behind these walls, but something deep in my gut urged me forward. It was a compulsion I couldn't shake. "Do you think we can use the Humvee to barrel through the door? Or I could use my silver?"

"No, Liss, I think there's a good chance they'll—"

A bullet pinged off the hood of the truck, and I dropped, gripping the door with all my might on instinct.

Tayna crouched next to me, wrapping an arm around me as he tucked us behind the Humvee's protective frame.

My breath shook as Tayna held me. It was all I could do to keep my silver back as the shots continued ringing.

"Is there a secret code word or something?" I hissed, thinking of Banu and the Tanks.

"Or something," Tayna grumbled, still waiting.

The lookouts would have been able to see the Humvee coming for miles in this empty desert.

So why had they waited so long to start shooting?

I got my answer only a few moments later as another round of bullets pinged like deadly rain over the dirt, and a groaning sound echoed from the wall.

I covered my ears. The spray of bullets kicked up dust around the truck, making me cough as I tried to see through the haze. The desert was suddenly a chaotic mess of stomping footsteps and hazy figures.

"Don't use your Silver!" Tayna yelled right before rough hands grabbed me. "Just do what they say!"

Through the fog, the outline of a man came into focus. He wore a silver mask that glinted against the dust.

A Phantom.

He was tall and athletic, dark against the dust, and shrouded in the dirt.

But I knew that frame.

I had traced that body with my lips on more than one occasion.

I had memorized those lines.

Gideon.

My body felt frozen. My pulse pounded in my throat as I took in the silhouette of the man I thought I'd never see again. How was he here? How was this possible? My heart spasmed even as my silver sparked, my body unsure where the sudden rush of emotions would land.

But the dust continued to clear, and more men came into focus behind the figure at the center. They were all clad in identical silver suits, with glittering silver masks covering their faces. And they were marching toward us.

Not Gideon.

Just one of Olita's men.

Of course, not Gideon.

One of the Phantoms at the sides of the group broke off, charging Tayna, pulling the guns from his chest, and wrenching his hands behind his back. I was given the same rough treatment from the man at the center of the group. He gripped my shoulder before jerking me around. Gloved hands gripped me tightly but methodically. The movements were mechanical. I folded against his frame, his body tight against mine as my breathing ratcheted up. The dust clung to the insides of my nostrils.

Not Gideon.

And the sadness became anger. It became a swirling in my chest that suddenly made it very difficult not to burn all of the Phantoms holding us. Each time their masks caught the light through the dust, I flinched.

But I trusted Tayna.

In this, I trusted him.

Still, I struggled against the man as he worked quickly to bind my wrists, and I fought to regain some semblance of control.

"What the fuck?" I demanded as my shoulders were strained until I thought they might pop from the sockets.

"Walk," the suit-clad behemoth ordered me in a low, strange growl as he shoved me forward.

I strained to see him again, to confirm that, no, I'd never met him before. Tall, broad-shouldered and—I faltered again—dark eyes. Almost black. It wasn't just his mask reflecting the light but his irises, too.

There wasn't time to study his features further as I was forced forward, walking through the dirt and spent bullets into the Veiled's fortress.

Unease settled over me. Or maybe unease was the wrong word. It was a foreboding feeling. Something deep within me recognized this moment in a way I hadn't expected.

I was keenly aware of the man at my back, with one hand wrapped around my shoulder as he guided me forward.

My entire body tensed at the feel of him.

I glanced over my shoulder to find Tayna. He would ground me in this chaos, but I was shoved again by the dark-eyed Phantom holding me before I could see him through the haze.

"All right, all right," I said, keeping a tight leash on my silver as I was marched through the doors.

I felt like I was walking into a dream.

The dust hadn't carried beyond the walls, and suddenly, I could breathe. The fresh air was so stark that I began coughing.

Once I regained control, I found myself in a tropical oasis of a courtyard. It was a complete contrast to the desert and dust just on the other side. Grass was planted in neatly tufted patches with palm trees sprouting in the centers and white flowers dotting the bases. Serene and rhythmic splashing came from a large turquoise fountain in the center. Cream-colored stepping stones created a walkway, which we followed into a series of open corridors with wooden banisters and adobe-tiled ceilings.

The heat beat against my dust-covered skin as I took in the opulent surroundings.

No one aside from the Phantoms was in the courtyard that I could see. Not even a gardener. But this was hardly a natural desert oasis. The upkeep for grandeur such as this must be astronomical. And maybe that was the point. It was impossible to walk through this entryway, smell the gardenias wafting through the air, and not think about the power and wealth it must require to keep this single courtyard so pristine, let alone the entire fortress.

The place seemed even more expansive than when we'd taken it in from the outside, but I had no doubt all of it was just as finely maintained. It was a maze of interconnected corridors, and I quickly lost track of the turns we took, too busy trying to take in the details.

Would these twists and turns feel familiar to Tayna?

I craned my neck to try to see him again, but the black-eyed man was at my back, pressing against my shoulder until I stumbled through an entrance that didn't lead to another open hallway but an entryway to a grand room.

He smelled like leather and smoke.

I glanced down at the gloved hand he kept curled around my shoulder. No hint of skin or tattoos.

The tiles gave way to plush rugs under my boots, and the smell of musky incense hung in the air. The space was darker than the corridors outside, but filigree lanterns hung from the ceiling, all with brightly colored glass that reflected the light into intricate patterns and colors against the walls.

The room beyond the entryway didn't feel like a space to greet a couple of rebels who had found their way to the Veiled, but rather a space where one might worship long-forgotten gods.

It was bright and airy and clean. The back wall was entirely glass, allowing an expansive view of the mountains beyond, framed by wooden filigree room dividers that drew the eye toward the center. A woman in a white pantsuit stood at a podium. Enver would have died at seeing her expensive-looking outfit. And the reminder of my lost friend was enough to bring me back to my mission. I wasn't here to ogle the finery. I was here for answers.

The woman's back was to me as if she, too, were seeing the mountain view for the very first time. I supposed it was satisfying to know that the effect of the view and the finery never fully faded. Or maybe it was her thoughts that had her so entranced. Her dark hair was swept into a chignon at the nape of her neck. She seemed almost delicate, with her pinned-back shoulders and slim stature, but when she turned at the commotion in the room, her expression had me stopping in my tracks and contemplating retreat.

It wasn't malice or intelligence or dominance or even condescension that had me wanting to take a step back, though those were all present in some swirling combination of her severe expression. No, it was her eyes. Her golden eyes glittered with feral delight. Eyes that were so familiar to me yet suddenly felt so wrong.

And then her gaze swept from me to Tayna, and her expression fell to distaste.

"And so the prodigal son returns." She said it almost as if they were in on a joke together, her words smooth and resonating. She folded her hands in front of her as her lips thinned, quietly exuding the power she wielded in this room, in this entire fortress.

"Mother." Tayna nodded his head in deference, and I saw some of the boy he used to be. He didn't back down from Olita's harsh expression, but I caught a flicker of… was it fear in his gaze? It was gone as soon as I'd seen it. His eyes went as cold and distant as his mother's as he returned her gaze. But it was that brief look, more than anything, that made me question my decision to come here.

"It's been, what, over a decade?" She stepped toward us, where her Phantoms still kept us closely guarded in the center of the room. "I'd assumed you were dead."

That got Tayna's attention. Some of the life returned to his features. "You expect me to believe you don't know exactly what I've been doing?"

Olita shrugged. "I don't bother myself with things that are worthless to me."

I ran my tongue along my dry and dusty lips as I glanced back at Tayna, wanting to defend him but also aware it was smart to first take the measure of this woman. She wore her bored composure like a shield, throwing jabbing parries with those cruel words directed at her son. He'd warned me his mother was a harsh woman. I'd known Olita's reputation, yet I hadn't expected this reunion to be marked by such malice.

I could easily burn through the bindings at my wrist. Just as easily as I could burn the Phantoms in this room.

But Tayna's returned glance my way told me all I needed to know. This wasn't a battle he wanted me to fight for him. This confrontation was his, and he stood straight even as his mother drew closer.

"Careful, Mother, or you'll ruin this happy reunion."

"Yes." She sighed deeply, seeming more put out than happy. "And what has you traveling all the way out here, risking your hard-earned rebel reputation, to entertain an audience with me?"

"I'm sure you're aware of everything happening in the city."

Olita quirked a brow. "Everything?"

Tayna kept his expression neutral. "We want to trade information. We'll tell you what we know, what we've seen, if you'll do the same."

"Of course." Olita seemed genuinely disappointed. "Trading secrets. What a tiresome game. I expected you to be more prepared."

"You were always the general, Mother. I was never even a soldier."

Olita ran a hand along the dark-eyed Phantom's shoulder as she passed him to stand in front of us. She was taller than me by an inch or two, especially in her pumps, but Tayna still stood a head taller than her. Yet her regal presence made up for her stature.

"You're filthy." She took me in and then her son.

"Your Phantoms weren't exactly welcoming." Tayna eyed the masked men. "And we've had a long few days."

"So it would seem. Something obviously made you desperate enough to come here."

"It was my idea."

Olita turned her harsh expression on me. But the distaste softened into curiosity as she took me in.

"And who are you to convince my son to return to me?"

This morning, after we'd seen the hawks, Tayna and I had discussed lying. On the drive to the Veiled, we'd talked in circles about how we would play this conversation. In meeting Olita, who would we be?

We'd settled on the truth. Because she was right, I was desperate. And maybe I was a fool to think my silver was enough to protect us in the face of this empire she'd built with men around us who looked like they could snap my bones with one hand. That foreboding settled in my belly again as I watched her, but I pushed my shoulders back. Let her see my silver eyes through the dirt and know that even in my desperation, I was not entirely powerless.

"I'm not here to reunite you and your son. That's his business. I'm here because I think you have information."

"A risky move for a Silver." Olita eyed me. "You're putting a lot of trust in me that I won't take you prisoner and drain you at my leisure."

I was doing no such thing. Yes, she was my one hope for information about Enver and Laykin, but if she wouldn't give it and decided to be cruel instead, well, then she would discover that I'd recently found my cruelty, too. And it came with a bite that was far more electric, shall I say, than my bark.

Tayna hadn't agreed to that part of the plan, but he hadn't needed to. I would do what needed to be done if it came to violence. Olita seemed to be a similar sort of creature, and in that, I could respect her.

"What is this information you seek?" Olita asked.

"Silvers are going missing," I said. "My friend and her guard have gone missing."

"And you think I—what?" Olita's lips twisted, her golden eyes flashing with condescending amusement. "Stole them in the night?"

"You did just threaten to drain me at your leisure," I pointed out.

"Not my style." Olita shrugged. "But then again..." She turned her back to me and began walking toward the large window. "You're used to Gideon's style of leadership, aren't you?"

I swallowed, waiting for her to say more. This was a risk we'd taken. We didn't know how much Olita knew about me. Of course, Tayna and I imagined she would have heard about Gideon's Queen, who could spark. But how much did she know about Tayna and me? How much did she know about the Whigs? How much did she know about the fall of the Cards?

As if sensing my questions, she tossed a feline smirk over her shoulder. "Oh, I know it all, Lissa Metarro. You look just like your mother."

And with that, the doors behind us swung open.

The floor seemed to shift beneath me as I burned through the bindings at my wrists.

The danger suddenly felt clear.

The threat was so transparent in Olita's confident expression.

This was a mistake.

I whirled on the dark-eyed Phantom, whose hands were clasped behind his back. His posture was relaxed even as I sparked, and it made me hesitate.

It was only a moment.

My Silver sputtered as our eyes truly met for the first time, and that bone-deep recognition hit me again.

You.

The word echoed in my mind as if called in some primal, intrinsic way. I couldn't see his face beneath the mask, yet I *knew* him.

But then an airy voice was calling my name. "Lissa! Oh, Lissa!"

Delicate arms embraced me.

And Enver was laughing into my hair, her familiar floral scent enveloping me. "You're here! I can't believe you're here. You found me!"

And my world, once again, tilted on its axis as nothing I was seeing made any sense at all. I sank to the floor, and Enver, clutched in my arms, came with me as we held on to each other as if that could keep everything from feeling so damn fragile.

24

Lissa

"You're covered in dust!" Enver said, once she finally pried herself from my arms. She wore a cream-colored linen dress that almost perfectly matched her white-blond hair, which was clean and styled in loose waves down her back. Her cheeks were flushed with the warmth of summer, and her silver eyes were radiant.

She looked... happy.

"You're okay," I breathed her in.

She nodded, ignoring Olita and her Phantoms as we stayed on the floor, like two school children playing while their parents watched.

She gripped my cheeks in her palms. "I'm okay," she promised. "We got lost. After we split up, we couldn't find the point where Tayna told us to wait. And the radios weren't working, so we went back into the city for the night."

"You should have waited for us!"

"We were running out of water, and we didn't know how long you'd be. Phenola—oh!"

"She's fine," I said quickly, sensing her line of thought. "She's fine, and the baby is perfect. It's a girl. She's—her name's Calliope."

"Calliope!" Enver pressed her hands together, bringing them to her lips to revel in the joy and relief. "Oh, I can't wait to meet her."

"How did you get here?" I insisted, lowering my voice, trying to pick up on any hint of distress from Enver. "Did they force you? Where's Laykin?"

"He's here!" she said quickly. "He's safe, too. We're both safe. And no one forced us, Lissa. Olita has graciously taken us in. We've been treated like guests. Laykin's been volunteering during the rotations. Otherwise, he'd be here, too. Just wait until you see this place! It's absolutely incredible. Like five times the size of the Cards compound, and even more grand. There's so much color and life here. And there are dinner parties every night!"

I glanced up at the dark-eyed Phantom who continued to watch me with a narrowed expression beneath his mask. His eyes were dark as he studied me like I wanted to study him. Color. Right.

I pushed myself to stand and offered Enver a hand up.

"And are the other Silvers here?" I asked Olita. "Do you have them, too?"

"I don't make it a habit of kidnapping Silvers off the streets. That was Gideon's style, not mine." Olita waved me off. "You should both shower before dinner. We can talk more then."

"We don't plan on staying." Tayna took a step toward his mother.

But she held up a hand, and he froze, almost as if he was afraid his mother would spark like I did. But he'd never looked at me like that.

"I'm offering you a warm meal and a soft bed." Olita's lips thinned at the insult of his denial.

"Our friend just had a child. We're anxious to get home," I explained.

"Yes." Olita's eyes narrowed as she watched her son. "Home. I've heard of your ragtag band causing havoc throughout the city. You presume yourself to be rebels. Going to take down the Cards and establish a new world order?"

"It's already happening," Tayna snapped, and I could tell he regretted the words as soon as he said them. Too much. He'd said too much.

But it was Enver who cut in. "Please stay." She grabbed my hand.

"Enver..." I watched Olita warily. We hadn't come to make ourselves at home. We'd come here to rescue my friends and then leave. As beautiful as this place was, something was also decidedly off, and it wasn't just Olita's stoic, harsh demeanor. An uneasy energy pulsed in the air that had me tamping down on my silver. I was already weighing the room to gauge the reaction to the fact that I'd burned through my bindings. If the Phantoms were surprised or threatened, they hid it well beneath their masks.

I glanced again at the dark-eyed Phantom in the corner of the room, wanting so badly to piece together his features beneath the mask. He watched me back, his gaze steady, making the hair rise along the back of my neck. He took up just as much space as Olita in this room, the combination nearly suffocating.

I thought of what Olita had said just before Enver had pushed through the doors.

You look just like your mother.

Olita had known my mother. Or at least, she'd known of her. And we'd found Enver and Laykin. They were safe. What was more, it didn't seem like the Phantoms were eager for our blood. Sure, it hadn't been the most welcoming reception, but we'd expected as much. And now that we were here, we might as well take advantage of Olita's offer. What could it hurt to spend one night here? Just one night. Enough time to have dinner with Olita and see what other secrets she might reveal.

I thought of the journal tucked in the Humvee. Maybe she knew who wrote it. Maybe she would understand the scientific text. But I didn't trust her, and I didn't believe her when she said she didn't know about the other missing Silvers. I'd given Banu my word that I would do whatever I could to find his friends.

Tayna met my eyes where we stood between his mother and her Phantoms. He wanted to leave. His expression was hard.

One night. Only a night.

He gave the barest shake of his head. I tasted the iron and salt on my tongue from the dust as I held his gaze, insistent.

One night.

I knew I was asking him to trust me in this.

Tayna ran his tongue across his teeth.

His jaw was tight as he said, "Dinner and a bed would be lovely, Mother." Then added, his voice dripping with barely constrained derision, "And it would be just great if you would untie me, thanks."

"Seems like something Lissa is particularly good at." Olita deadpanned while I kept my expression neutral.

"I only spark when threatened," I said.

Olita flashed me her perfectly white teeth as she said, "I might not be a Silver, but you and I are not so different. So let's agree to keep our hands to ourselves, and we won't have any problems. Agreed?"

I nodded, fully aware that this was the first promise I'd made to the matriarch of the Veiled.

25

Lissa

Two Phantoms silently led us down one of the open-air corridors to our rooms. The dark-eyed one had stayed behind, and I couldn't help but look back at him as we'd left. That feeling of eerie familiarity had lingered. I wanted to see his face.

The sun was out in full force overhead. The heat crept in even under the shade where we walked, making sweat bead along my hairline, mixing with the dust on my skin.

This fortress, I learned, had once been a large resort property, which made sense, given the scale. They ushered us to two rooms next to each other at the back of the property, with views of the palm trees and grass giving way to the mountains in the distance.

The expansive, grand rooms were full of light, with beige linen accented against dark wood furniture and real potted trees. I hadn't been sure what sort of accommodations we should expect after Olita's stony introduction, but this room was the height of luxury. What's more, I noticed that our rooms felt separate from the rest of the property. The halls were quiet, and it didn't seem like people actually lived in this section. It also didn't escape me that two more

Phantoms were patrolling at the end of the corridor. I couldn't help but wonder if they were always stationed there or if this was a new development, given our arrival.

We weren't prisoners, then, but we weren't trusted either.

Which was fair enough.

As soon as the Phantoms left us alone, Tayna knocked on my door.

"We shouldn't be separated," he said, the scar across his eye deep against his drawn brow.

"Agreed." I hadn't wanted to be alone in this room, either, appearances be damned.

Tayna immediately closed the windows once he was inside, while I took in the space, which was all airy fabric and bronze fixtures. There was even a canopy draping from the ceiling and cascading over the elegant king-sized bed.

Suddenly, staying here for a night didn't seem like the worst option.

"You should shower." Tayna nodded toward the bathroom as he searched under the couch as if looking for radios hidden throughout the room.

He turned back to me once he seemed satisfied.

"Your mother's an asshole." I crossed my arms over my chest.

Tayna sighed and grabbed me by the arm, dragging me into the ornate bathroom. I had just enough time to appreciate the green tiled walls and copper bathtub before he turned on the gold-handled faucet and pulled me close until we were almost nose to nose.

My stomach clenched.

For a moment, I thought he was going to kiss me.

For a moment, I wanted him to kiss me. I wanted him to ground me away from this place and that Phantom who'd made me feel entirely off-center.

I focused my thoughts instead on remembering the feel of Tayna's lips. He'd cocooned me in the darkness of the Humvee while his hips aligned with mine, and everything felt right. The way we'd explored one another hadn't been timid or hesitant, but it had been patient and slow. He'd taken his time with me. His kisses consumed me in their languid discovery, in their soft comfort, and their intimate familiarity.

The space between us didn't have enough air, and his warm golden eyes caught mine, such a contrast to my silver gaze.

"We should always assume Olita is listening," Tayna murmured, just enough to be heard above the water.

"Right." I cleared my throat, but the word hitched despite my best efforts.

And of course, Tayna caught it. "What are you thinking?"

I shook my head. "Nothing."

I forced a steady inhale and exhale as his hands traced my shoulders. We were here to find the missing Silvers. We were here for answers. Yet, if I was being honest with myself, I'd wanted to stay for myself, too. I wasn't sure yet what to make of the Veiled. It hadn't been at all like I'd expected. It was so much brighter than the city, despite Olita's rough introduction.

"Tell me," Tayna murmured, placing his hands on either side of the wall beside my head, caging me against his body.

I didn't know how to untangle my thoughts. My emotions had been so confused and unclear since the cliffs. Was this what people meant when they said grief was a cycle? Was it normal for it to not only feel like you lost someone but also like you lost yourself?

Maybe I needed to stop thinking so damn much.

"We can leave anytime you want." Tayna's breath was hot against my lips.

"No," I said quickly. That's not what I wanted. I searched for the words, some way to express this need in me, making me feel so certain there was something important in this place, something driving me to stay. "I—"

There was a soft knock on the door, and Tayna's gaze snapped up.

"Don't move," he growled down at me before demanding. "Who is it?"

"Oh, um, I brought you clothes!" Enver called back.

I exhaled, the tension in the room breaking. Tayna balled his fist against the wall next to my head. I kept my gaze on him as I skirted out from under him to open the door. My lips pursed against my uneven breathing. But I'd been hoping Enver would come.

"Come in." I opened the door and practically dragged her inside, tossing the clothes on the entryway table before pulling her into the bathroom. "Tell us everything."

"Why is the water on?" She looked from me to Tayna as if trying to figure out if we were together again. But then she noticed our dirty clothes, and her eyes narrowed even further. "Are you two—"

"Enver! Not important right now," I snapped before she could say more.

But that only made her grin. "This reminds me of when you and Kenji caught Laykin and me that time at the compound. Remember? And Laykin was so salty about it. But Kenji couldn't stop laughing."

"This isn't anything like that!" I insisted but still found myself smiling at the memory, too. That *had* been a good day.

Enver wrapped her arms around me, holding me despite the dirt. "I missed you so much, Liss."

"I thought something really bad happened to you," I mumbled into her mane of hair.

"Olita's been really good to us. The people here, they don't treat Silvers like weapons. It's different, in a good way."

She seemed genuinely happy in this place, which was maybe more unsettling than if she'd been taken against her will. Sure, Enver had always been one to enjoy the finer things, but she seemed so sure that the Veiled and Olita could be trusted, and I didn't yet understand why.

"And don't worry," Enver continued. "We hid the Humvees before we went into town. Laykin can tell you how to find them. We knew a bunch of Humvees would draw attention. Plus, we didn't want to risk all the supplies."

"You can both show us when we leave tomorrow," I said, pulling back to meet her silver gaze.

But she wouldn't meet my eyes. Not really.

"Enver…" I growled her name, sensing there was more she wasn't saying.

She finally shrugged. "Tomorrow is just so quick. You haven't even seen this place yet."

"I lived here for the first eleven years of my life," Tayna grumbled. "I can assure you, all we're missing by leaving is whatever game my mother is playing these days."

"She was really horrible to you, Tayna," Enver conceded. "I've never seen her so… stern. But she doesn't hate you. You have to know she's just hurt that you left. In fact, when she found out Laykin and I were friends with you, she just wanted to know if you were alive. She was concerned about you."

Tayna's jaw tensed, but he didn't argue with her even though I could tell he wanted to. Instead, he just said, "What else did you tell her?"

"Nothing about the Whigs!" Enver insisted. "Promise! We told her what happened to Gideon and the Cards. She already seemed to know that anyway. And we told her we were supposed to meet you but got lost. That's it, really." She paused to mull it over. "Oh, and well, she wanted to know about our lives at the compound. She wanted to know what sort of job Laykin had and how much silver I was required to give, and how Gideon gave orders, stuff like that. Mostly just because we said we wanted to help out at the Veiled. She took us in, so we wanted to thank her in some way for her hospitality."

This place was definitely hospitable. I looked around again at the room, and Enver followed my gaze.

"Isn't it just so luxurious? Laykin and I have one together closer to the main ballroom."

"And why didn't my mother put us in those living quarters? Why are we out in the west wing?"

Enver shrugged. "She probably just wanted to give you some privacy since she knows you don't want to be here, Tay."

Tayna snorted.

"You said Laykin is helping with rotations?" I cut in. "How are you helping around this place? What are you giving her?"

"Nothing more than I was giving Gideon. And I don't mind the draws. They don't just have a clinic here, Lissa. They have a whole hospital building."

"And what about the other Silvers?"

Enver just lifted a shoulder again. "They're nice."

"Okay, what else, though, Enver? I can see there's more."

But she just shook her head, laughing lightly and shaking her head at me. "That's it, Liss. You'll see. This place is so much better than the Cards. Gideon was all militaristic this and business that. But the Veiled is actually thriving, Lissa. You haven't even seen the whole fortress. There's a Zen garden and an art studio and two swimming pools and so many games. And the people are beautiful! And fun! People have so much fun here. I've been learning this game with a racket. It's called tennis. I'm not very good yet, but a woman's giving me lessons."

I wasn't sure what I'd expected Enver to tell me, but I hadn't expected her to be so excited about this place. She might not have told Olita all of our secrets. She'd kept us safe. But it seemed my friend was also now keeping some secrets for Olita. I could see it in the way she wouldn't quite meet my eyes, though I wasn't sure what she was hiding.

And maybe I was too skeptical because of everything Tayna had told me. Maybe it was that I was still thinking about Banu and his missing friends. Maybe it was the way that dark-eyed Phantom had looked at me when we'd arrived. It was like he knew me, too. And his eyes... those eyes were...

I shook my head.

Maybe I was being ridiculous. I'd learned to trust my gut, yes. My days as a street rat had taught me that, if nothing else. But Olita didn't seem like she was particularly interested in harming us. She'd offered us a room and dinner, and Enver would tell me if there was truly danger lurking in this place. We'd made the right decision to stay. It was only a night. It would give me time to see this fortress for myself.

Maybe I could sneak off and explore the grounds. I wanted to confirm in whatever way I could that Banu's missing Silvers weren't being held against their will somewhere. I owed that to him.

"You both should get cleaned up," Enver said. "You'll feel better once you're clean and have a hot meal. Just wait until you see the food, too!"

I forced a smile. "You're right. I'm overdue for a shower and something to eat."

"And Laykin will be so happy to see you!" Enver shimmied her shoulders. "I brought you something fun to wear tonight. You're welcome!" she sang as she left the room. "See you in a few hours!"

Silence fell as soon as she'd gone.

Tayna was still leaning against the bathroom wall. I was still considering Enver's strange confidence in this place.

"We'll stay long enough to get any information we can, and then we'll leave," I said finally.

"Agreed." He pushed from the wall. "I don't know why my mother is allowing us to stay, but I can absolutely guarantee you it isn't because she has some guilt over our relationship or because she misses me in any way."

I nodded thoughtfully. "But there has to be a reason."

"We'll get what information we can tonight. In the meantime... if I remember right, we were about to shower."

We?

I let Tayna catch me in his arms and take me to the bathroom. My entire body lit under his touch, even as my mind was still on the Veiled.

I knew he was right.

Staying at the Veiled was a risk.

But something about the danger only made me more certain that I should remain.

26

Lissa

The dress Enver left was obscene.

I wasn't one to be a prude, but the scraps of turquoise fabric could hardly be called a dress. It was wispy and sheer, really more like undergarments than a dress for dinner. My entire midsection was exposed, and she'd left a jeweled belt that was more decorative than helpful. xThe color was in direct contrast to the rust and beige of this property, and I wondered if Enver had known that. It would be like her to know just how to stand out in a crowd.

I'd been wearing cargo pants and T-shirts for so long now, as drab and dull as I'd felt. Putting on the dress was like armor. I thought of the masks the Phantoms wore. I didn't feel more like myself in this dress, but it was a shield of sorts, and there was power in it.

I left the diamond necklace Gideon had given me around my neck. It didn't really go with the ensemble. The paved square diamonds were too sleek for this unconventional and free-spirited outfit. But, well, I hadn't taken it off since that day on the cliffs, and I couldn't bring myself to part with it now. It was the final thread of Gideon I had left.

"I would have pulled the trigger," I said to my reflection in the mirror.

The woman staring back at me looked more sad than sure. I'd rimmed my eyes with black and kept my lips neutral. It made me feel more like an Egyptian princess than a queen, but well, beneath it all, I was the same scared street rat.

But I could do this. It was one night. A single night to face Olita and get the answers I'd come for. Then we would leave.

My fingers drifted lightly across the diamond necklace a final time.

As I emerged from the bathroom, Tayna's eyes widened, then he looked away from me with a low curse.

Yes, this was definitely a different sort of attire.

"I'll take that as approval," I said, smoothing down the front of the skirt.

"Well, you'll outpace my mother for elegance, which will have her steaming at the dinner table."

I lightly cleared my throat. "I'm not asking what your mother will think."

His eyes darkened. "You're really trying your damnedest to miss this dinner, aren't you?"

He stood. His fingers skated around the bare skin of my waist as he pulled me close.

I swallowed down the "yes." I wanted to slip onto his lap and let him see just how high the slits of this dress could rise up my thighs.

He looked good, too. Better than good. He'd shaved until just a hint of stubble was left on his square jaw, and his skin was golden against the afternoon light. He wore a breezy white linen shirt paired with neatly pressed khaki slacks. The light fabrics made sense for this more arid climate, and I imagined the people who lived here would be dressed similarly.

Except the Phantoms, that was. I thought of the black-eyed man from earlier with his dark silver suit and shining mask. He might be clean-cut and crisp, but his energy was unpredictable and dark. He'd reminded me so much of Gideon. Then again, I'd imagined Gideon so many times since he'd died. It was no wonder I was looking for him here, too.

He was nowhere.

And the Veiled would be the last place he'd be, even if he were somewhere.

Tayna ran his fingers lightly down my arms. "Be careful tonight, Liss." I caught his grassy, earthen scent. He was still a farm boy, even if we were hours from the Whigs. "My mother knew exactly what she was doing when she mentioned you look like your mother. She's not offering you her secrets out of the kindness of her heart."

"I know." I let my eyes track up his torso to meet his golden gaze. It broke my heart over the past few weeks not to be this close to him. All of the missing. All of the emptiness. It had nearly broken me. I'd missed trusting Tayna. I'd missed talking to him. I'd missed feeling his arms around me. And now? Well, now I'd allowed myself to relish in his touch. We were... good. But did that mean the broken pieces of my heart were no longer scattered somewhere out over those cliffs? As much as I wished I could furiously gather the pieces of myself, a part of me still felt separate. I was different. There was before the cliffs, and there was now.

He seemed to sense my hesitation and took a step back, turning to his bag, which rested in one of the chairs near the window. After a few minutes of searching, he removed a small vial. It caught chrome in the light.

Silver.

"Tayna—" I started, but he was already downing the liquid.

This, more than anything, ripped at my insides.

He was different, too.

"It's okay, Liss." He swiped his wrist across his mouth, tossing the bottle back into the bag. "It's just a little. Just in case."

And hadn't I been the one who'd always told him he was overreacting? Hadn't I been the one when we were kids to slip silver into his water when he was sick? Hadn't I been the one to tell him repeatedly that he was nothing like these addict parents he'd described?

"We should go," I said, still fighting the urge to object, to scream...

to what? It wasn't fair of me to tell him he couldn't protect himself, especially not at the Veiled and not when he'd agreed to stay for me.

So I threaded my fingers through his.

On the way to the dining hall, a figure emerged at the other end of the open-air corridor. His gait was self-assured and sophisticated. The silver suit he wore was perfectly tailored over his pale complexion. His blond locks were slicked back, which only heightened the blue of his eyes.

"Laykin!" The relief tore through me, and I sprinted to him, throwing myself into his bulky arms.

We didn't hug. Not normally. Laykin wasn't really the hugging type, but I wrapped my arms around his neck and squeezed. I'd been so worried that I'd lost him just like I'd lost Kenji.

To my surprise, Laykin gripped me back. "Hey, Queenie," he breathed in his deep timbre.

The nickname Kenji gave me made tears prick in the corners of my eyes. "I thought something really bad had happened to you."

"We're okay." He sighed. "Better than okay, actually. It's been really good here."

"So we heard." I pulled back to study him, still feeling skeptical. Yes, Olita's reception this afternoon with Tayna had been horrible. But seeing Enver and Laykin so settled, it was hard to say the leader of the Veiled was living up to her scary reputation. "She's already got you in a suit."

The creases on his forehead were deeper than the last time I'd seen him. Stress? Or grief? But he looked just as built as I remembered. If anything, the suit only made him look larger.

Laykin tugged at the lapels of his jacket, as if proud of the getup. "I've been helping around here. It's nice to be useful after everything that happened with the Cards."

I understood the need to stay busy, but I found myself looking around the corridor as if maybe we were being watched.

There was no one except Tayna, who'd narrowed his eyes and crossed his arms. He was practically puffing out his chest at Laykin. The two had formed an alliance, but I would hardly call them friends. Tayna had shot Laykin, after all, when he'd found us on a scout. And Laykin had held on to his loyalty to Gideon until the very end.

"You had Lissa worried," Tayna said. "We risked coming here to find you and Enver."

"And here we are." Laykin met him with a proud posture of his own.

"Let's go." I rolled my eyes, wrapping my arm through Laykin's before they started throwing punches in the hallway.

The sun set in the distance, dipping beneath the mountains and casting watercolors in the sky. And I had a dinner that needed my focus. Silvers were still missing. And there were still secrets from my past. I deserved to know about my mother, and Olita Ravidian might be the only person left on this planet who could give me the answers I so desperately sought.

So I smiled. I smiled my brightest smile.

And I prepared to play the game of gangs.

27

Lissa

I heard the music, the dull rumble of laughter, and the clatter of glasses before we'd even rounded the corner. Tayna kept close to my back, my arm brushing lightly against the fabric of his shirt as we walked.

"Some things never change," he grumbled.

"She had parties like this when you were a boy?"

"Every night. Of course, I wasn't allowed to attend them. But sometimes I snuck in just to watch before my brother caught me and dragged me back to my rooms. He was always my mother's pet."

"You'll have to show me your old room. I'd like to see where you grew up."

Tayna scoffed. "It's hardly worth remembering. Trust me."

But I reached for him, letting go of Laykin to squeeze his hand in mine. A lock of hair swept over his forehead as the scar across his eye softened when he met my gaze.

The room was lit with warm candlelight against the purples of the evening.

The floor-to-ceiling wooden doors of the dining room were

thrown wide. Trails of people came and went, and I marveled at the richly colored outfits worn by all. From the deepest jewel tones to the pastels of summer, all the garments and people wearing them were elegant. It was such a sharp contrast to the city. Even the Cards, who had been the most powerful gang, had maintained simplicity and order in all they did. This was a decadence I'd never seen.

Ornate carved beams divided the room into two, with a second floor overlooking a large dining room table. It was all warmth, from the terra-cotta walls to the dangling filigree light fixtures, to the U-shaped marble dining table against the far side of the room.

In the center was dancing and an orchestra. People swayed together rhythmically in precisely coordinated patterns. Faces close. Hands clasped. Arms raised. The light fabrics of gauzy skirts swirled with practiced steps. I wondered if this dancing was the ballroom waltzes Jane Austen had described so vividly. The only dancing I'd ever seen had been at the bonfires or the clubs. And that was not elegant. That was bodies tangling for a semblance of release. This dancing was practiced, and the beauty came from the containment— held breaths that never strayed close enough.

"Do you know how to do that?" I asked, mesmerized by the sweeping steps.

"I'll teach you," Laykin offered. "It's not hard to learn."

For a coordinated fighter like Laykin, probably not. But me?

Tayna only glared at him.

But something else in the room caught my attention. Plants were stretching and reaching from all corners of the space. I ran my fingers over the silken leaf of a particularly full fiddle leaf fern.

"I like that you like the plants more than you like the dancing," Tayna said, a teasing lilt tracing his words.

"My mother had a plant like this when I was a child."

A fern this large, well, it could be as old as thirty or forty years. Older than me. Old enough that my mother could have planted it. The thought was a silly thread of hope. But Olita's words sat heavily with me. She'd known my mother. Had my mother come here, too? Had she admired these plants? Or... had she planted them herself?

"Be careful letting my mother get inside your head," Tayna murmured, his lips brushing along the shell of my ear as he spoke close to me. "Like she already has with Laykin and Enver."

I nodded. I noticed it, too, how easily and quickly they trusted Olita and the people in this place. Was it the promise of an easy, better life that had convinced them? Or something else? I looked around like I might find the answer in this space.

Instead, I felt a strange sense of déjà vu, thinking about standing where my mother might have stood decades earlier, maybe seeking some of the same answers about the world. The questions weighed heavily on my chest. If I accepted that she'd once been a member of the Cards, did that mean Ishmael kept her prisoner like Gideon kept me? Were we destined to now repeat history? Would I run like she had only to eventually be caught and killed?

Laykin led us to the back of the room, around the throngs of people who didn't pause in their dancing and laughing and eating to pay us any attention at all. My eyes met Olita's, and she rose from her place at the center of the table.

A few of her Phantoms stood around her, not seated at the table with her. But the black-eyed Phantom was noticeably absent from the room. His dark presence wasn't reaching out to me through the warm candlelight.

Enver sat next to Olita, and my heart lifted again at the sight of her. She mouthed, "Hot," to me, looking me up and down and nodding. I failed at hiding my smirk, shaking my head at her brashness.

"Now I can see what Gideon saw in you." Olita also took me in with a sweep of her sharp eyes. "Much better without all of that dirt on your face." But then she narrowed her expression at my throat. "And what an interesting piece you're wearing. Rare."

My fingers grazed across the diamond-paved necklace.

"My mother has an eye for the finer things," Tayna groused.

Olita hardly spared her son a glance. Her gaze was still trained on my throat. "It's real?"

I shrugged, dropping my hand. "As far as I know. It was a gift."

Olita only pursed her lips.

"We appreciate your hospitality." I kept my grin tight, raising my voice so she could hear me above the strings that drew out an uplifting melody. "The suites you've provided us for the night are more than we need."

"So I heard." Now, Olita did shoot her son a narrow-eyed glance. "Apparently, two weren't necessary."

"We got used to sharing space on the streets," I interjected before Tayna could open his mouth. I could see his pupils flare with derision. He was going to lose his patience with her before we'd even sat down for the meal, and then we might not get any answers at all.

"Is that what you're calling it these days?" Olita scoffed, rolling her eyes over to Enver, who blushed. "Sharing space?"

"I wouldn't know, mistress." Enver shook her head, as demure and placating as she was at the Cards. I resisted the urge to raise a brow at her.

This time, Tayna beat me to the response as he settled into a seat across from Olita. "It's interesting that you're suddenly concerned with my space, Mother. You've given me so much of it over the years."

Olita's dark-painted lips met her wineglass, taking a deep drink as she studied him. "I don't save space for useless things."

Tayna's chair creaked as he clenched, but before he could say anything, Olita gestured at one of her Phantoms. "Make sure we aren't interrupted. And tell the kitchen I'm ready for my meal."

The Phantom nodded slowly—dipping his head so low it was nearly a bow—before stepping swiftly to his task.

The dancing around us continued. Enver and Laykin sat on either side of Olita like honored guests. Tayna and I took seats on the opposite side. The five of us were the only ones occupying the enormous table. It seemed there was a barrier around us, some sort of invisible line where the others in this dining room would not cross.

As I settled into my seat, I looked back over at the crowd of people beyond the table. There had to be a few hundred people between the split floors of this space. Still, none of them were looking at Tayna or me. And I realized as I took in the room, I didn't see one silver gaze among the crowd. Granted, the flickering candlelight didn't provide the best lighting to study the people around me, but there wasn't a single hint of silver in any of the eyes I could see throughout the room. Not one.

I nearly jumped as Olita began speaking. "You won't find your mother in that crowd."

"My mother is dead." I turned to her, my back now to the room. I remembered Tayna's warning and wouldn't be baited by my mother's death.

"Yes." Olita's eyes narrowed as she studied me. "A pity she never reached her full potential."

She wore white silk tonight, the cap sleeves of her gown breaking way to form a cape that trailed over her chair like the glittering sand along the beaches below the cliffs. If I thought I'd ever looked like a queen wearing the fur-lined cloak Gideon gave his Silvers, I paled in comparison to Olita's stoic radiance.

I met Olita's gaze, not flinching from her unblinking assessment.

I didn't like this woman. I didn't like how she seemed to enjoy toying with us and, most of all, toying with her son. I could respect that she'd taken care of Enver and Laykin, but there was something deeply unsettling about her demeanor, aside from her coldness. I couldn't put my finger on it. It was such a contrast to the oasis and life of luxury she presented around us. It all felt like a contradiction, like the heated air around me might suddenly begin to boil before I could run. Silver sparked along my fingers, and I balled my fist against the table. It coiled beneath my skin, primed with my trepidation.

"There she is." Olita's golden gaze flashed with triumph. "So much like your mother."

"It sounds like you mean that as a compliment." I shoved my hands under the table, angry that she seemingly got the reaction she'd hoped for. "But how does that make any sense if she was a Queen for your enemy?"

"She never told you any of it then?" Olita shook her head. "No, of course she didn't. You were denied your destiny at every turn."

"My destin—"

Plates of salad were presented in front of us as if in a synchronized dance. The waitstaff, all dressed in cream linen, floated into the room like curtains billowing in the wind, and were gone just as quickly.

I was hungry, my mouth immediately watering at the plate in front of me. Tayna and I had been surviving on stale bread, dried fruit, and nuts over the past two days.

Another sweep of servers, and we had water and wine as well.

I glanced at Tayna like all of this might be some kind of test. There was a reason Gideon hadn't allowed his Silvers to drink alcohol. What if Olita had laced our wine with Silver that would make me sick? That would nullify my silver, the best protection we had here. But Tayna picked up his wineglass and took a long, large swig.

Olita picked up the wineglass in front of me and took a small sip before setting it back down and picking up her own glass. She didn't look angered by my distrust. No, instead she seemed almost pleased. As if my trust had been the game, and I had won by refusing it.

She mulled the wine over in her mouth before swallowing. "Your mother and I were the closest of friends. Practically family."

I paused with my fork halfway to my salad, my silver suddenly feeling volatile again. The last thing I needed was to melt the silverware. I let it clatter to the plate. Enver paused mid-chew, looking between Olita and me, as if she thought I might launch myself across the table at the woman for even suggesting such a thing.

But I wasn't angry.

I was confused.

And I was so tired of feeling confused.

Just when I thought I was beginning to grasp the tendrils of my past, they were rearranged.

"If you were such good friends, then why didn't I ever meet you?" My words were clipped with derision.

Olita didn't take the bait of my tone. Instead, she picked up a green bean on the end of her fork and bit delicately. She chewed slowly before swallowing. "Gideon told you nothing either, then?"

"Quit playing games, Mother," Tayna spat.

She just took another long, slow bite of her salad before she said, "How do you think I've lived this long?"

"And what is it you want?" I asked, catching the hint that her answers wouldn't come for free. Tayna had warned me this would be the case. She gave me just enough to keep me listening, but this woman would hold her secrets close to her chest like playing cards in a poker game.

"I'm not looking to drain you dry, Lissa. And I have too much respect for the memory of your mother to treat you like a child. She clearly raised you well. You're a smart girl—"

"She must really want something if she's doling out this many compliments," Tayna gave me a sidelong glance.

"It was a mistake allowing you to join us at this table, my son," Olita sighed, swirling her wine. "You never could appreciate the strategy of a good bargain. Such things are for queens."

And for once, I didn't object to being called a queen. If that was what I would need to be to learn the secrets this woman kept, then so be it. "And what is it you want?"

Olita rested her elbow on the arm of her chair, running the rim of her wineglass lightly over her burgundy-painted lips while she studied me. "I want your friendship, Lissa."

"My friendship?" I cocked an eyebrow.

"My son may have built himself a little cadre of rebels, but you and I both know you weren't meant for that simple life. You were meant for something much, much bigger, and I can help you fulfill that potential. Become a member of the Veiled. Be my ally, just like your mother was my ally. You can train. You can study. You can help me revitalize this city. That's what you truly want, isn't it? It's what your mother and I wanted, too. Hell, you can even visit my son and his merry little band of misfits whenever you want. Have your freedom but work with me here. Look around. You can clearly see what I'm capable of creating. You and I want the same things."

Tayna had the good sense not to speak for me, but I could see his jaw clench, his shoulders tense.

I studied Olita, trying to understand her angle. "And how much silver would you require each week in return?"

"None."

Tayna snorted, taking another swallow of wine.

"If you choose to donate, that's your decision, and I'm sure it would go a long way to maintaining life at the Veiled. But I will not force you. That's not part of this request. Silvers here are treated with autonomy and respect. My request is simply your friendship, that you find a place for yourself with the Veiled."

I looked again at Enver. She'd told me this was the case, that Olita treated her Silvers differently.

If I was being honest, her offer was tempting. It sounded too good to be true, and I parced through her words for the catch but came up empty.

Still, my intuition prickled along my skin, warning me that there was more to this bargain than I was currently seeing. Yes, Olita was horrible to Tayna. And no, I didn't trust her. But I also desperately wanted to know what she was playing at. As it was, it felt like staring at a blurry image and only seeing pieces of the true shape.

But I couldn't make out the full picture.

Maybe this feeling was simply my own paranoia after the way Gideon and so many others had treated me for years. Olita may very well be offering me a different opportunity.

But no, I remembered Tayna's words not to trust her.

And something had caused my mother to turn her back on this woman.

That was the point I needed to remember most.

Even if my mother had once been friends with Olita, even if she'd been in love with Ishmael, in the end, she'd left. My mother had left the gangs behind. She'd died rather than return.

But could I leave now without any of the answers she held?

"I need some time to think," I said to Olita.

"Of course." Our salad plates were cleared and replaced with steaming plates of chicken, broccoli, and potatoes smothered in a decadent gravy. She gestured to Enver. "Let Enver show you the Veiled. You'd be foolish to make an agreement without experiencing life here. I think you will find it's far from the prison you're afraid it is."

"There's even a library here that you'll love." Enver's eyes sparkled with her encouragement. I knew she wanted me to stay. "I can give you the full tour tomorrow!"

I swallowed down a bite of chicken, needing to eat despite the uncertainty in the pit of my belly.

"That would be nice," I said, looking at Tayna who was helping himself to the bottle on the table and topping off his wineglass. His other arm was crossed across his chest as he drank.

I hardly tasted the rest of my food. Conversation passed between the table, mostly it was Enver making conversation about the wonders of the Veiled. Her voice sounded like it was coming from underwater as I contended with the decision in front of me.

I wasn't afraid of this game.

I wanted in.

But I didn't trust Olita.

And she was asking for my trust in exchange for her secrets. Not my life. Not my captivity. Not my silver. My trust.

Why?

Sure, my silver was different. Yes, having me as an ally would, no doubt, afford some sort of protection to the Veiled. But to what end?

Once our final plates were cleared, an upbeat melody began bouncing its way across the space. A cheer broke out as arms linked and people began spinning around the room.

Enver gasped and stood from the table, grabbing Laykin as she exclaimed, "This one's my favorite! We can't miss it, Layk!"

Olita smiled, settling deeper into her chair with her wine in her hand. "This was Tayna's favorite as a boy, too."

Tayna snorted, and I realized his eyes had become unfocused as he shook his head at the spectacle.

"You're drunk," I hissed at him under my breath, leaning into him so no one could overhear our conversation.

"I hate this song," he clenched his jaw.

And I looked back over my shoulder at the dancing, smiling crowd as they spun in fast circles around the space.

Tayna reached for the wine bottle, as if to top off his glass. Hadn't it been full just a moment ago? I put a hand on his arm.

He shrugged me off.

"How else... do you expect me... to survive this fucking night." His words were slow and tripping. He reached for his glass, but I caught his wrist, just as my eyes caught the glint of a silver mask from the corner of the room.

I froze.

And though I couldn't see those black eyes, I knew. It was the Phantom from earlier. It was the Phantom with eyes like the night sky. Black and blue and so horribly familiar.

He stood tall in the shadows, but he wasn't watching the orchestra. No, he was watching me. And somehow, somehow, I knew beneath that mask he was smiling.

"I'm going to bed," Tayna grumbled, stumbling to stand as I stood at the same time to brace him. I felt delicate next to him. My fingers barely circled half of his upper arm. What good would I be in keeping him upright? Yes, I needed to get him to bed before he said something he'd regret. Or worse, something that would cause Olita to snap and send us packing.

"Leaving so soon?" Olita quirked a brow.

"It's been a long day," I said, my voice carrying as the final note of the loud melody wrapped its way around my center, and the crowd of people began to cheer. It felt strange, this joy in a place full of secrets, just outside a city that was so ruined.

Tayna swiped a new bottle of wine from the table and took a swig. "The sooner we leave this place, the better, dearest Mother. We should leave tonight, Liss."

"We'll leave once you've slept." I tried to grab from the bottle, but his reach was too broad as he held it out. I shoved at him. "Come on."

"Thank you for dinner, Olita."

I wanted to get Tayna out of here, and I wanted to be alone with my thoughts. There was too much in this place that had my head spinning, and I hadn't even had a fourth of the amount of alcohol Tayna had consumed.

"Such a nice dinner, Mother," Tayna bowed dramatically. "You've really outdone yourself trying to woo Lissa."

Olita just swirled her wine and watched him from where she remained seated in the center of the table. The orchestra began playing a new song behind us. This one was slower, the music full of long, romantic chords.

I glanced at the corner of the room where the dark-eyed Phantom continued to watch me.

"Let's go, Tayna," I said.

"Oh right, right," he bellowed while I pushed him to the door. "Let's not embarrass Mother. She hates when I embarrass her. I'm such an embarrassment. Not like her chosen special son. News flash, Mother, Gavril is dead! Gavril is dead. Your disappointment is the only one you've got left."

Olita said nothing, watching her son with silent derision.

Even as we stumbled our way through the people and toward the door, no one so much as glanced in our direction. It was as if we were the street rats scurrying among the finest of the city.

I pushed Tayna into the hallway, finally breathing a sigh of relief as the music began to fade behind us.

"You can't trust her, Liss." Tayna sauntered down the hall ahead of me, still clutching the neck of the wine bottle. "And you sure as shit can't make that deal with her."

"Let's just get to the room," I said, glancing around to make sure there wasn't anyone in the corridor who could overhear our conversation. Now that night had fallen, lamps lit the hallway, casting an orange glow against the adobe.

"This isn't as fun as that night we drank tequila." Tayna sighed, hanging his head as he slumped step after step.

"No," I agreed. "No, it's not."

And then, he was pressing into me, my back folding against the wall as he cocooned me in a way that reminded me of our first kiss and that night in his room at the farm.

"Do you understand?" he whispered near my lips. The gold of his eyes caught in the light with such earnestness that it twisted my chest. His eyes were so similar to his mother's, yet they couldn't be more different. Where Olita's shone with contempt, Tayna's shone with a hope that made it hard to look away. "Now that you've met her. Do you see why I kept it from you?"

I swallowed against the lump in my throat at his question, unable to look away from him, as I only nodded. I did understand, but that didn't mean I would leave.

Now was not the time to have that conversation.

His lips brushed so gently against mine as he breathed a deep sigh of relief. "Thank you."

He pressed away from me, the wine in the bottle sloshing as he nodded, and I fell into step beside him, our arms brushing and his hand twining into mine, as we returned to our rooms.

28

Lissa

Tayna set the wine bottle on the side table before sprawling onto the center of the mattress.

I sighed, grabbed my sleep clothes, and went to the bathroom to change.

By the time I returned, he was snoring softly, asleep and curled up beneath the covers. He'd managed to kick off his boots, which were scattered at the foot of the bed.

I should have felt exhausted, too. It had been a long day. But I wasn't tired.

After grabbing the wine bottle, I turned off the light and stepped from the room, taking a swig as I pressed my back against the adobe wall. It was selfish of me to insist we stay here when it clearly weighed heavily on Tayna. We should leave. It would be smart to leave in the morning.

The cool stucco surface prickled against my back as I closed my eyes and breathed.

My mind spun around Olita's proposition. Not that I considered joining the Veiled. I couldn't possibly join the Veiled. Especially not when I'd only just fully escaped Gideon and the Cards. I had no desire to become another pawn. Ever.

But Olita hadn't asked me to be her pawn. If anything, it seemed like she desperately wanted my trust. And Olita knew things. She had information about my mother and my past that she was keeping close to the vest unless I made that deal with her.

I missed Gideon.

Shit.

That pang hit closer than it should have.

He would know what to do. He would know how to play this game with Olita. He would know the rules. I was learning as I played, but not fast enough. I needed to figure out a way to avoid her deal while still getting the information I wanted.

I took another swing of wine.

And then I heard something.

It was a strange, erratic noise coming from somewhere deep within the walls.

Clack, clack, clack.

I looked to see if someone was tapping along the corridor at either end. But I was alone.

For as many people as there had been in the dining hall, not a soul could be seen in this corridor. Not even the Phantoms from earlier stood watch at the end that I could see.

Still, the noise continued.

Clack, clack, clack.

The hair rose along the nape of my neck as I pressed away from the wall, taking tentative steps until I could peek around the corner where the corridor opened to the outside. The night sky stretched above, dotted with thousands upon thousands of stars.

A building in the distance caught my eye.

It was located on the other side of the fortress, yet I could see it stretching into the sky, at least ten stories tall. And there were lights on, though I couldn't see what was inside. Still, it was clearly occupied.

It was a strange-looking building, like it had been added later to this place and wasn't part of the original infrastructure. It was more fortress than oasis, though the warm lights inside didn't suggest it was a prison. If anything, it looked like a place where Olita herself might take up residence. It looked secure. I imagined her occupying the top level with a suite of rooms like Gideon had at the Cards.

Yet Olita made it clear she was not Gideon.

So what was this structure then?

Unease crept up my spine. It was an eerie apprehension I couldn't explain.

I was suddenly very aware that I was outside my rooms. Alone. At night.

Was someone watching me?

The hair at the nape of my neck prickled with the awareness of eyes.

But I could see nothing through the dark.

And then a woman screamed.

It was shrill, echoing through the halls just on the other side of where I stood.

The wine bottle slipped from my fingers at the sudden sound, shattering along the pavement beneath my feet.

My silver sparked as I took off running in the direction of the cry.

Someone was in trouble.

I rounded the corner, the electricity at my fingers stark against the dim light of the corridors.

A woman was pinned against the wall by a man in a silver suit.

A Phantom.

She struggled against him, her long hair wild around him.

She was crying.

But he had her by the shoulder. His hips pressed into her, pinning her in place as he forced himself on her.

I thought about the men in the alley outside Madam Cartenoth's shop. I never should have let them go. I shouldn't have let them walk away only to hurt someone else.

I wouldn't make the same mistake again.

"Hey!" I called loudly and raised my arms. My silver sparked, just as a hand clamped over my wrist. Gloved fingers gripped me tightly despite my abilities, and I gasped, whirling as the glow of electricity glinted against the silver mask.

The dark-eyed Phantom clutched me, holding me steadily in place even as my silver sparked. He loomed like a shadow over me, like the mere presence of him would blanket my silver.

"She—" I gasped.

"Look," he told me, the word low and resonant. It was a command that called to something deeper in me. My stomach clenched.

I turned back to the corridor, where the man and the woman were still entwined in their embrace. The woman watched me with wide, fearful eyes. Not fear of the man. No, she buried herself deeper into his arms.

Fear of me.

I gaped as I took them in, unable to look away as the reality of the situation became so clear in front of me.

The man wasn't hurting her at all.

It wasn't an attack.

It had been an intimate game.

I felt the Phantom watching me at my back as the realization sank in.

Humiliation and regret washed through me, snuffing out the silver at my fingers. My stomach roiled.

I would have hurt that man. I would have thrown him from the woman with my abilities. A second longer and I would have lashed out.

I would have killed him.

My chest felt tight.

"Go," the dark-eyed Phantom at my back said to them.

The couple nodded weakly. The man gripped the woman's hand, pulling her against him as they moved with quick steps out of the corridor.

I watched them leave, realizing that I'd been so sure the Veiled and its secrets were the things to fear. But they had every right to fear me too, didn't they?

Something in me stilled. The control that had felt so tenuous since the cliffs was hot in my belly. Tayna was right that I'd never wanted to use my abilities to hurt people. I'd always hated the idea of being a weapon. But now it felt like the violence was rising in me all on its own.

I turned to face the Phantom, to explain myself, to—

He was gone.

The hallway beyond me was dark.

I looked around as if I might just be missing him in the space.

But I was alone.

My hands shook, and my thoughts were jumbled.

My quick steps carried me to the end of the hall, back out into the open-air courtyard, still searching for the shadow of a man.

"Hello?" I called tentatively, as if I could summon him back and explain myself. But what was there to say? He'd seen exactly what I'd been about to do.

And he hadn't chastised me.

He hadn't punished me or dragged me to face Olita.

He'd simply told me to look and then left.

I released a breath, running a hand through my hair as if that would help ground me after this night. I pressed myself against the wall, trying to steady my nerves.

That couple's face, their fear... I'd almost made a horrible mistake.

I forced the silver back, cursing the abilities that made me so volatile and dangerous.

But the way the Phantom had grabbed me and held me, he hadn't seemed afraid of me at all.

Had his gloves protected him from my burns, or had he simply taken the heat? And why had his touch felt so steadying? He'd grounded me with a single word and then disappeared without an explanation.

Who was he?

With a final glance over my shoulder, I ducked back to my rooms, realizing that as unsettled as the Veiled made me feel, and as much as Tayna did not want to stay, I couldn't leave.

I should.

I should go back to the farm and forget about Olita's offer and the dark-eyed Phantom.

But just as I felt there was something about my silver changing, something in me was changing, too. It wasn't just the silver coiling in my veins but a desire I didn't yet understand. Part of me was drawn to this place. I wanted to understand. The Phantom had gripped me and whispered for me to look.

There were so many things in this place I hadn't yet seen.

And I wanted to stay.

I wanted to see.

29

Lissa

"And what is the point of this again?" I asked as I missed the bright lime-colored ball with my racket. Again.

"It's a game, Lissa!" Enver said from across the court, her voice like music against the morning breeze. "It's fun!"

I retrieved the ball, my jog clumsy. I was already sweating. My hair stuck to my forehead, where it was falling out of my ponytail. I lobbed the ball back in her direction.

It hit the net and bounced back toward me like it was mocking me.

Fun. Right.

I'd left Tayna in bed this morning when I woke with the dawn. My anxiety had pulled me from my restless sleep, which was just as well. Last night had left me unsettled.

I'd wanted to find the dark-eyed Phantom.

Instead, I'd found Enver in the dining hall eating breakfast, and she'd dragged me to the courts to teach me this racket-wielding humiliation she called tennis.

It was so... cheery.

I hadn't told her what had happened last night, that I'd almost lost control. I felt ashamed. And yet, it hadn't felt like the Phantom had wanted to embarrass me.

It felt like he'd wanted me to understand something. Not the couple. Not their intimacy.

But something deeper, like there was a bigger point I was missing from that moment.

My curiosity about the building from the previous night also niggled at the back of my mind.

I'd inspected it in the morning light. It somehow stood out less in the daytime, even though it was separate from the rest of the property. It was painted in the same adobe style as the corridors. Foliage was planted like art around the perimeter, mostly large succulents and palms that could withstand the heat. It must hold hundreds of people if it was, in fact, a place where people lived. But it was quiet. Quiet, except for the Phantoms looming on guard outside the entrance. I wouldn't be able to gain access to the building without permission.

"If your goal is to convince me how great the Veiled is, this... game... is not helping your cause." I lobbed the ball again. I was distracted.

I barely made it over the net, but I made it over, which was an improvement. Before I could even celebrate, Enver sent it back with an easy stroke to the corner of the court. I set up my backhand, swung, and missed the ball entirely. Nothing but wind met the strings.

Enver just laughed. "It takes practice! You're doing great."

I should be learning as much as I could about this fortress. I should be looking for the Phantom. I should be reading from the journal I'd found at Madam Cartenoth's shop and trying to figure out its secrets. Those were worthwhile uses of my time. Tennis, decidedly, was not.

"Can we take a break?" I asked, my shoulder sagging and racket dragging on the ground.

I needed water.

Enver bounded up to me. She wore a bright blue pair of shorts and a white shirt. She'd tied a breezy scarf around her neck, maybe to catch the sweat, but she was barely out of breath, her skin glowing against the sun.

She'd let me borrow a similarly bright and cheery outfit, which included a white spandex skirt and a pink—*pink*—T-shirt that hugged my body and ended at my waist. I'd never felt so much like a street rat pretending to be a princess in my life. But Enver embodied the lifestyle. I couldn't argue with her that the tennis and the parties and the finery suited her. We'd always been opposites in that way. It was one of the main reasons it had taken us so long to become friends. We saw the world differently.

I drank deeply from the bottle of water she handed me.

"Okay, so maybe not so much tennis," Enver chuckled, her silver eyes sparkling. "But you'll love the library. Trust me."

"I thought you were going to give me a tour?" I asked, steering the conversation toward things that would actually be useful.

"Well, you've already seen my room and the dining hall and meeting center, where I found you with Olita. And now the tennis courts. I can show you the library this afternoon if you want?"

"What about that tall building at the back of the property? The one that's out on its own?"

"Oh." Enver shrugged. "That's just the hospital. No reason to go there unless you're sick, so keep drinking that water. Don't want you passing out in this sun!"

"Ten floors for a hospital?" I eyed her skeptically, remembering that there weren't any Silvers at dinner last night except the two of us.

"Olita really believes in taking care of people. It's the most important thing to her."

"People? Or Silvers?" I asked pointedly.

Enver just shook her head. "You're only saying that because you're used to Gideon and the Cards. Didn't you see last night how happy everyone is here? How incredible and beautiful it all is? Olita has created something special. She was being sincere last night, too, when she said she wouldn't force—"

"Lissa!"

The frantic sound of my name behind me had me whirling.

Tayna was haphazard, his eyes wild as he saw me. "Lissa!"

"What's happening?" I asked, meeting him at the side of the courts as he grabbed my arms and my face, checking me. "Tayna?"

He wore a white shirt that clung to his broad chest and the khaki pants from last night. They were rumpled from sleep. He looked like he hadn't brushed his hair.

His eyes were like a blazing inferno, swirling with manic energy.

All I could think of was the way he'd run for me at the docks when he told me Enver and Laykin were missing.

My stomach sank.

What now?

But instead, he held me. His eyes traced across my face, the panic cooling.

"Fuck, Liss, I woke up, and you were gone." His jaw was clenched. His scar pulled tight across his face. "There's a broken wine bottle in the hallway."

My shoulders sagged with relief that there wasn't more bad news. I couldn't handle more bad news. "I'm fine, Tayna. It's fine," I breathed. "I just dropped it last night."

I didn't know how to tell him the rest.

Instead, I added, "Enver wanted to teach me tennis this morning."

He pressed his forehead into mine, the relief flooding him as he held me and didn't let go. He shook his head, closing his eyes as he took me in. "Fuck. This place. My mind went to the worst-case scenario." And then he lowered his voice to a breath. "I can't stay in this place."

Enver pursed her lips but didn't speak next to us.

I put my hands on either side of Tayna's face. "I'm okay. I'm sorry. Everything's okay."

"We should leave," Tayna said. "Now."

"Tayna…"

"Listen to me, Lissa." Tayna's voice was low. "What else do you possibly need to know about this place?" He looked over at Enver. "And if you were smart, you and Laykin would come with us."

Enver was fidgeting with the racket in her hand. "I'll let you two talk." She gave me a small grin before excusing herself from the courts.

"Talk?" Tayna let out the breath of an incredulous laugh. "We've done enough talking. We found Enver and Laykin. We need to go back to the Whigs. Last night..." He shook his head.

I sighed. "Let's not do this here. Like you said, there are eyes everywhere." I glanced over my shoulder as I took his hand, leading him back to our room.

I hadn't found the dark-eyed Phantom this morning, but I still had the distinct feeling of being watched.

Through the corridor, I glimpsed the hospital building looming in the distance.

"We can talk as we pack," Tayna said as we made our way to our rooms.

He pushed open the door.

He was still on edge as he began pacing the room.

"Tayna..."

"No, Liss," he shook his head, not looking at me as he started gathering his things.

My voice was thin as I said, "I understand if you can't stay here, Tayna. I understand why you feel like you can't stay. I know there's a past here that isn't comfortable for you. But I can't leave. I just can't. Not yet."

That had him freezing. His fist, clutched around a shirt, hovered just over his backpack.

I could tell he'd taken silver this morning before coming to find me. He had that manic energy I'd come to know so well in the years I'd spent at the Cards.

"Tayna, please." His name felt raw against my tongue.

I thought about telling him everything from last night, but that would only make him want to leave more. If he knew how volatile I felt in this place, he'd insist we go. He wouldn't understand that it was the exact reason I felt compelled to stay.

His rigid body vibrated with unspent energy. I could see the tension in the lines of his shoulders. The way he was hunched on the floor reminded me of a caged animal about to break from its chains. He was suffocating in this place, and it had only been a day.

Finally, he spoke. "All this place has to offer are ghosts from our past. There's nothing left here. For either of us."

"It's more than that for me, Tayna."

"No!" he growled. Each word was a punch. "No, Liss, what you need is to let it go."

"Let it go?" I marched at him, my anger spiking. He stood. His full height loomed over me as I got in his face. "This is my chance for answers. This is my *one* chance, Tayna. You owe me that!"

"Are the answers worth your life, Liss? Huh? Because my mother won't stop at your loyalty. She's playing a pretty game with you right now, but she will suck the life out of you." He laughed incredulously. "Sure, she won't take your silver blood. Not by force, at least. But she'll manipulate you until she's drained you dry one way or another. It's what she does."

"I won't let her manipulate me like that."

"You already are!" He snapped. And then he stepped back. Took a breath. Steadied himself as he raked a hand across his face. "Don't you see what's happening? She's already winning by getting you to stay."

"You don't think I can play this game?"

"I think it was a mistake coming here."

A lump rose in my throat, thick and cloying. I thought about the way his hips had rolled into me in the darkness of that Humvee, the closeness I'd felt with my whole being. But now we felt worlds apart again. How could I make him understand?

Still, I said the words I had to. The ones that felt right in my heart. "I'm not leaving."

He glared at me, his jaw tense. His eyes blazed with an intensity that only made my silver burn to rise and meet him.

I was not backing down. I was not changing my mind.

He turned from me. His powerful shoulders tensed near his ears as he began shoving his clothes into his bag again.

The silence hung as heavy as the sun outside as I stood there watching him.

Leaving again.

This always happened. This always happened with us when it seemed like we were so close... to something.

Not a single part of me could walk away with him, though. Something in my gut was screaming at me to stay. It wasn't just about the information Olita knew about my mother. It was the other Silvers who were noticeably absent at dinner last night. It was that hospital building looming just beyond the grandeur. It was that Phantom and his dark eyes that beckoned me with their familiarity. There was something here, something important that I needed to understand. I could feel it in every fiber of my being.

I had to stay. For the first time since the cliffs, I felt like I knew what I was doing, even as I knew it was reckless.

With a heavy exhale, I turned to leave the room. I couldn't stand here and watch him walk away. Not again.

"No." The single word was a command.

When I looked back, he was shaking his head. I wasn't sure if the word was for me or for him. He threw the T-shirt down on the ground.

"No," he said again. It carried in the quiet room. "You know what —" His eyes met mine again, hot and demanding. "I'm tired of you pushing me away, Liss. You're always trying to push me away, and I'm not fucking going anywhere."

"Me?!" I demanded. "I'm not pushing—"

He threw the backpack on the ground and stalked toward me.

I didn't have time to decide whether I was going to meet him with my silver or back up against the wall. He was on me. His mouth collided with mine. His tongue swept into my mouth. His hands fisted into my hair. He lifted me into his arms, my legs twining around his waist on instinct.

We were still on opposite sides of this. I knew it.

And kissed him back anyway.

"I'm not going anywhere," he said roughly against my mouth. "Got it?"

It felt like my chest was cracking open. His body pressed into mine, and I came alive as he kissed me. It was always like this. Ever since I was that girl in our loft who couldn't breathe at the thought of being so close to him. Now his mouth stole my breath, plundered my soul, and made quick work of untwisting my heart with his heat.

I was lost in the feel of him. It was too good. It was too right. Even as a logical part of my brain said "wait," my body and my heart screamed "yes." And I was so tired of thinking. I was so tired of turning over the uncertainty, of questioning myself. I was trusting my instincts. And this felt right.

So I let go as he carried me to the bed and lowered us onto the plush mattress.

My fingers played under his shirt, and he cursed on a gasp as my nails dragged up the ridges of his torso.

He broke the kiss only so I could drag the shirt over his head before he was on me once again. He rolled his hips into me as I scrambled to feel every piece of him. My needy soul found such relief in the sensations of pleasure he was offering.

"Don't shut me out," he murmured between kisses. "I can't take it anymore."

I dug my nails into his skin in answer, pulling him closer, kissing him deeper. Our tongues danced as he groaned into my mouth and lit my body on fire as I felt the rumble of it against my chest.

He wasn't close enough. Kissing him like this felt like releasing my silver. All of my pent-up frustration simply let go as our bodies found that familiar, primal rhythm.

I needed this.

After last night, this was what I needed to feel like myself again.

My fingers pressed between our bodies, fumbling for the buttons of his pants.

He grabbed my wrist with one quick hand, stopping me. His gaze was strained as he looked at me, his eyes sparking with desire, but also something deeper. "Don't make that deal with her, Liss. I'll stay. I'll stay here with you and help you get your answers. But promise me you won't agree to be hers. *Promise* me."

I met his earnest gaze and nodded, our breath mingling in the small space between our mouths. I wanted to taste him again. I wanted his tongue in my mouth while he thrust his cock inside me. But I forced myself to speak because he needed my words more at this moment. "I promise."

And I meant it.

I just hoped I could keep it.

For a brief moment, I imagined the couple from last night, primal in their game, the Phantom's hand closing on my wrist.

Look.

The word stirred deep in my core.

But I focused on Tayna.

He pressed his forehead into mine, rocking into me as the tension in his body released. "Fuck. Good," he breathed. "Good."

Instead of kissing me again, he tugged at the bottom hem of my shirt until I sat up, allowing him to pull it over my head. I wasn't wearing a bra, and his gaze went from one peaked nipple to the next as he bit his lower lip and took me in. His sleep-tousled hair fell into his forehead as his golden eyes tracked over my body. I flushed beneath his awestruck expression.

As if he couldn't wait any longer, his head dipped between my breasts, kissing my sternum gently as his hands began exploring, massaging as I arched into him.

I needed more.

I craved this distraction and release.

"Tayna—" His name was a plea on my lips as his mouth traced lower along my stomach, and I scrambled for purchase along the sheets.

He was a sight as he traced down my body until he ran his teeth along the hem of my pants, and I shivered with desire. He pulled the covers down with him so I could see him kneeling between my legs, hooking his fingers into the elastic of my skort, sliding it down, down, down until I was entirely exposed in front of him.

"Mmm," he sighed, tossing the clothing aside as his heated eyes met mine. "I can already smell you, how turned on you are right now. Fuck, it's sweet."

As if compelled, he ran a finger over my entrance and groaned.

"So wet," he murmured. "Tasting you again is all I've thought about, Liss."

"Then taste me." I felt wanton and wild beneath his gaze, like if he didn't touch me, I might lose control. And not of my silver, of myself. I was lost to the wanting, hadn't wanted to admit how coiled in anticipation I'd been.

He complied, pushing my legs wide but keeping his hands pressed just above my knees and his mouth hovering just above my clit so I could feel the light fans of his breath against my heated skin, the hint of what was to come, but nothing more.

I squirmed beneath him.

"Stop it." He chuckled. And the puffs of his laughs didn't help matters. "Stop it, Lissa. Let me look at you. You're so fucking perfect. I want to savor every part of this."

I didn't want him to savor me.

I wanted him to consume me.

I let my knees fall apart fully as I threaded my fingers into his hair, gently massaging along his scalp, loving the feel of the thick strands cascading between my knuckles, basking in the sight of him between my legs.

I felt the stubble of his cheek against my outer folds before I felt the first swipe of his tongue directly along the center of my clit.

"Oh my god." My head kicked back at the sudden sensation, and the hand that had been so gentle in his hair turned into a tight fist as I tried to contain the rush of pleasure through my veins.

He laughed and did it again.

And then he increased the tempo of his strokes until I was choking on the sounds of pleasure and desire coming from my chest. When he added a finger, I couldn't stop the roll of my hips that had me grinding into his face, seeking more. I wanted more. More than his finger.

He didn't let up, not for a second, even as I writhed. The sensations overtook my body.

"I—I need—"

He added another finger, stroking deep inside me, and my words turned into a loud moan.

"What do you need, Liss?" he asked, only stopping to pant out those words before he was sucking on my clit again, rolling it gently between his teeth before flicking his tongue over the most sensitive part of me.

"More," I choked on the word.

His strokes became frenzied and pulsing. I wasn't sure anymore which waves were him or my own body cresting toward the edge.

He used his free hand to press me open wider, my hips sinking deeper into the bed as he rolled his tongue straight across my center.

"I'm going to come," I panted.

His groan of approval vibrated through my body, but he slowed, teasing out my pleasure and savoring me.

He added a third finger inside me, and I had to grip the sheets as my silver sparked.

He chuckled as I writhed.

"Tayna!" My every sense was on fire.

And when he flicked his tongue across my clit again, I unraveled. The orgasm shattered through me as my back arched, and I tried to remember how to breathe as the pleasure coursed through my veins down to the tips of my fingers.

Tayna didn't stop licking me, touching me, pressing into me, even as I shattered beneath him. His hand on my pelvis was the only thing keeping me from bucking against the mattress. And god, I felt like I was high. My body continued with tiny, fluttering pulses as the orgasm waned but didn't fully release.

I was still hot. My body was still seeking.

My eyes drifted open, shuddering pleasure still cresting through my core, as I smelled something musky and charred.

I jolted upright.

The smoke wafted through the air.

I'd burned the sheets.

I'd lost control.

"Did I hurt you?" I checked my palms. No silver sparked.

I sat up and gripped the side of Tayna's face. "Did I burn you?"

Tayna's hair was mussed, and his smile was lopsided as he grinned up at me. "So good I made you spark, huh?"

I grabbed for a pillow and smooshed it into his face. "Oh, please."

His laugh was muffled against the down.

"I could have really hurt you!"

He shoved the pillow away and launched himself on top of me, pinning me to the pillowy mattress.

He tried to kiss me, but I turned my head to make sure I wasn't about to singe anything else in this place, especially Tayna.

I thought of the couple last night and felt sick.

There was something wrong with me.

He gripped my chin, dragging my gaze back to him. "You didn't burn me," he said. "Come on, Liss, promise. It was just a little zap while you were writhing in pleasure."

I sighed, rolling my eyes and considering reaching for another pillow.

He pinned my wrist above my head as if anticipating the move, and then murmured against my lips, "And I'm just getting started. You and I have a lot of time to make up for."

He rolled his pants-covered hips into me, settling between my legs, and the friction was delicious against my already sensitive skin. Our gazes locked as his lips skimmed across mine, and he watched me with such intensity that I found myself growing wet beneath him once again.

This felt good. I wanted to stay like this with him forever. But for how close we felt, the peace only lasted as long as I could forget everything else happening around us.

But I could forget for a while longer.

In this room, it was easy to pretend things were simple.

He kissed me deeply, his tongue moving between my lips to taste me in the same way he'd tasted my core. He was consuming me, breathing me in. The mellow earthiness of his scent filled my senses, and I lost myself in the feel of his body. My fingers trailed to explore along the bare skin of his torso. Our kissing was lazy and melodic.

I sighed into his mouth as his fingers began to play over my sides, around my hips until he was squeezing my backside. His hands slipped between my body and the mattress to cup me closer to him. My hips rounded into his pelvis, and I could feel how well we fit together. I needed to feel it all.

There was a knock on the door.

We ignored it.

I pressed my chest against Tayna's hard pecs, my nipples sliding against him in a way that had me biting back a groan, even as he kissed me deeply. It was a kiss that promised a deeper sort of connection to come.

The knock came again.

I had no sense of time, of how long we'd been in this bed. There was only Tayna's mouth on mine, and the certainty I didn't want to stop.

"Lissa?"

It was Enver's muffled voice on the other side of the door.

"Shhh," Tayna whispered against my lips. I could feel his grin tracing my mouth as he reached a hand between our bodies and hooked two fingers inside me to the knuckle. I bit my lip against the moan bubbling in my throat.

I held my breath as he began working them inside me, watching my face as I struggled to stay silent.

"Tell her we're still talking," he murmured.

I choked on the words but managed to call, "I'll meet you later, Enver! Everything's fine!" The last word ticked up in a near squeak as Tayna caressed the pad of his thumb down the center of me.

"Oh, okay. Um, you missed lunch!" she called.

"I didn't," Tayna murmured against my ear as he continued toying with my clit, making me gasp.

My mouth fell open, and he just managed to cover it with his free hand, muffling the sounds of my moaning as he increased the pace with his fingers.

"I can't wait to be inside you," he said, dipping his head to capture one of my nipples lightly between his teeth.

"Um, if you're staying until later, does that mean you're staying? For a while, at least?"

Fuck. Enver was still at the damn door.

But I wasn't ready to give up on this forgetting yet. I needed more.

Tayna ran his teeth along my breast, and I arched into him.

He lifted his head long enough to murmur, "Tell her to go away." But he didn't pause in pumping his fingers in and out of my soaked core.

"Yes!" I gasped. "Yes! Staying." I swallowed the groan as Tayna moved to my other breast. "For—" I fought for the words. "At least a few days?" The strain in my words made it sound like some odd sort of question. That was a problem to sort in another time.

This was so wrong, but I also couldn't stop. I needed Tayna's hands on me. I was too afraid that if he stopped, I would remember all the reasons I had not to do this. I wanted him rougher.

"Um, okay! That's great news, Liss, really." Enver called. "I'll see you at dinner then!"

After a few steady moments of silence in which the only sound was Tayna's fingers sliding in and out of my body while he sucked and nipped at my skin, I couldn't take it anymore. I shoved at his shoulders. And when that didn't work, I shoved him again with a jolt of my silver until he wrenched himself from my body with an, "Ow!"

But I pounced on him until he was falling back onto the mattress, and I was fumbling with his buttons, yanking at the zipper, and finally, finally pulling the pants from his body.

He was hard. His thick length curved up toward his belly button. I thought about licking him, considered running my tongue from the base to the tip. But that could come later. I'd do it all later. Right now, I was desperate to feel him inside me.

His gaze was full of fiery lust as he watched me crawl on top of him and gripped my hips as I positioned myself over him. He held me, guiding me onto his length.

I licked my bottom lip as I reached down to stroke him, lining up the head of his cock with my entrance.

"Wait." The word was low in his throat.

"What?" I felt breathless with the suggestion, panicky that he would deny me now.

But he said instead, "Kiss me while you sink onto me, Liss. I want to feel your tongue in my mouth while I fill you."

I shuddered at his filthy words as I leaned over him. His cock rested at my entrance, the head already slick with my desire. My chest molded against his, our lips just a breath apart.

"Like this?" I asked.

And he grinned in that way that was so full it made the scar over his eyes stretch and my heart squeeze with pleasure.

"Like this," he said, wrapping me in his arms as he claimed my mouth at the same time he pushed his length to the hilt in a smooth roll of his hips that had me crying out against his lips. He held me firmly as I adjusted to the feel of him. My body so ready for this, yet he was so thick inside me.

He groaned deep in his chest as he ran his teeth along my bottom lip before consuming me again with his kiss, still holding me tightly in his arms.

I clenched around his length, and he pressed his hips up until I could feel him hit the deepest parts of me in a claiming that had me gasping, even as his tongue swept between my lips.

"Fuck." His fingers threaded into my hair as he grasped me tightly. "It's too good." Those were the only words he said between panting breaths before he was kissing me again, holding me melded against his body as he began to rock his hips.

I whimpered in pleasure at the first thrusts of his cock. It was so deep, just like I needed.

"You like that?" he asked, finding a steady rhythm for our bodies as I nodded and moaned.

"Harder," I breathed.

I dug my fingers into the mattress on either side of Tayna's head and pressed myself back against him until I felt the friction I craved, until he was fully inside me, and I could roll my hips around, feeling every glorious inch of him. Until I was gasping and building toward another orgasm.

Having him like this, claiming him for myself, it felt like a well breaking open, my heart finding a release it so desperately craved. This was for me. This was mine. He was mine for as long as I could have him.

"God, Liss." He tipped his head back, his golden eyes shining as he watched me rock my hips.

I sat back, letting him take in the show of my curves as I swiveled on top of him, grinding into him in a way that had me panting. I loved the way he watched me. It made me feel beautiful and wild. And I found myself smiling at the wonder on his face. I traced the scar over his eye with my thumb as he gripped my hips and groaned.

"More." His words were sudden as he lifted, taking me with him as he rolled on top of me, only withdrawing for the briefest of moments. Our bodies melded together as he thrust into me.

And then he was truly fucking me. It was passionate and unrestrained. My fingers clutched for purchase at his sides as my legs hooked around his backside, loving that I could feel every inch of his length as he ground into me. I ran my nails across his back roughly until he was arching against me, but he didn't slow.

One of his hands snaked behind my neck, holding me in place so he could continue kissing me deeply while his other hand found my knee, hooking it higher so he could press into me even deeper.

It was too much. The sensation building in the pit of my belly had me panting. And I never, ever wanted it to stop. But I was reaching my breaking point. Sweat beaded in my hairline, our bodies slick as we moved together in a primal dance unique to us.

I broke the kiss long enough to say, "I'm going to come."

His eyes were hot with my words as he met my gaze, our noses brushing as our hips continued that delirious push and pull that had him grinding against my clit with each stroke.

"I want to feel you, Liss," Tayna said, his voice low and rough with his lust. "I want to feel every second of you unraveling around me."

"God, Tayna," I panted, and he didn't slow. He didn't stop.

He took me straight to the edge, then he said, "Now let me see it."

My gaze met his as the orgasm crashed through me. Even as my back arched and I moaned with my release, his eyes stayed locked on mine. Even as he continued thrusting inside me, he held me open, demanding every ounce of pleasure I had to offer.

He followed me over the edge. His grip tightened on me as he, too, let go.

As our cries of ecstasy faded and the only sound left in the room was our panting, he pressed his forehead to mine, threading his fingers into my sweat-drenched hair. His lips brushed gently over my cheek as we struggled to catch our breath.

He didn't pull out, not yet. And I could still feel every spasm of his cock and every squeeze of my core around him as the orgasm continued to subside.

"You're perfect," he murmured, trailing his lips softly over my cheeks, caressing me with his fingers. "I could stay like this forever."

My hands stroked down his back, and he shuddered against me.

"In this place?" I asked, coming back down to earth and realizing we were still very much far from home.

He laughed softly. "Definitely not. But when we get back to the farm, we're not leaving our bed for a week."

Our bed.

"I'm in this with you, Liss," he added. "Until the end. I want you in it, too."

And I nodded, taken by the sincerity in his words.

"Kiss me?" I tilted my chin up to meet his lips, and he obliged, a low rumble in his chest, even as he started growing hard inside me again.

"We could stay like this for at least today, right?"

I laughed. "For at least another little while."

And for a little while longer, I let myself forget everything outside this room, including the dark-eyed Phantom.

30

Lissa

Olita wasn't at dinner that night.

Or the next.

And neither were any Silvers aside from Enver, who seemed to be a constant presence at this place. She was my tour guide, ushering me around as if showing me the luxuries of the Veiled could convince me to give up my life. It wasn't the luxuries that had kept me here the extra days. It was the certainty in my gut that there was something about this place I needed to understand. I found myself looking for the dark-eyed Phantom in the corners where we walked. I felt eyes on me but never connected with any in the shadows.

When Enver wasn't dragging me to see the vegetable gardens or the swimming pools or the relaxation rooms, Tayna and I were coming up with a plan to get into the hospital. Not only was I sure it was where Olita and her Silvers kept residence, but also that it was the key to the secrets of this place.

Of course, Olita closely guarded her secrets like she closely guarded her Silvers.

"You never went inside?" I asked Tanya, watching from where we perched near one of the walls by our room, where we could clearly see the hospital entrance.

"I dunno, I was a kid. I don't remember."

"But that's where your mother lives? Did your father live there with her, too?"

"I don't remember, Liss. I don't remember going to their rooms."

Something about that statement felt so wrong.

I tried to hide the pity I felt in the pit of my stomach at his admission. It was sad and something I couldn't understand, feeling so detached from a parent.

As a child, I probably spent more nights sleeping in my mother's room than I did my own. She was my everything. And yes, she'd been killed early enough in my life that I knew what it felt like to be left out to sea. But Tayna had never felt the safety of his parents' love enough not to feel out to sea. I wanted to reach for him. I wanted to take away that vast loneliness, but I also knew Tayna didn't want my pity.

So I swallowed it back and said, "And what about the Silvers? Do you remember the Silvers?"

He raised an eyebrow at me, tiring of my inquisition. This wasn't the first time I'd attempted to pry memories from him. But he didn't have many beyond his tutoring and his time in his room with his books and his mother's dismissive gestures at the dinner table.

"I had a Silver nanny for a while. I remember that. She was young, and I thought she was pretty. And then I walked in on her and Gavril wrestling..." He glanced suggestively at me. "Naked."

I cringed. "Oh god! I bet he felt terrible!"

But Tayna laughed. "Gavril? I don't think he ever felt guilty about anything. No, he just glared at me and kept going."

"How old were you?"

"Eight or nine."

"Oh." The silence stretched between us.

I looked at the sky. Only a few wispy clouds interrupted the blue. The sun made my skin feel tight, but in the shade, it was manageable.

Finally, I sighed. "I think we've gotten the rotations down."

As we watched, two Phantoms approached the building but didn't go inside. Instead, they nodded to the others before taking their place on either side of the doors.

"Six rotations. Four hours each. And my guess is one completes a rotation around the perimeter on the hour every hour," Tayna replied. "Does that mean we're done staring at this building for the day?"

Something traced up my thigh, bunching my linen skirt from behind as it crept higher. I lost myself for a moment in the thrill of it until a finger hooked around my underwear.

I smacked at Tayna's hand. "You're unbelievable!"

But I was grinning. And he didn't remove his hand.

It had been that way for the past two days. Yes, we'd been looking for answers. But we'd also been... distracted. And we'd already been distracted twice today. No matter how many times he made me unravel with pleasure, I still found myself wanting more. I couldn't seem to get enough.

Maybe it was the luxury of this place or maybe it was that behind these walls, the city and the heartache beyond faded somehow. But I couldn't deny that I was losing myself to this time with Tayna.

It felt too good, even as I knew it couldn't last.

Tayna used the finger hooked in my panties to beckon me closer, and I found myself sinking into him. His broad frame cocooned me even as the hawk appeared, swooping overhead against the sun.

"Oh shit," I grumbled, realizing the sun was starting to wane from the midpoint of the sky. "I promised Enver I'd meet her. It's library day."

Tayna's fingers paused, but he didn't pull away from me. Instead, he gazed down at me wickedly. His fiery gaze daring me to tell him to stop.

"Tayna," I groaned. "I have to—"

He sank a finger inside me and I folded against him, my forehead pressing against his shoulder as my mouth parted.

"Okay, go," he murmured against my ear as he slowly—so goddamn slowly—removed his finger.

I was flushed as I stumbled back a step from him. I could feel the heat in my cheeks.

We were both losing focus.

Meanwhile, my time to understand this place and make a choice was running out.

I was wasting time. I was pretending like the light was the truth of this place. It felt too good, even as I knew it was wrong.

"I'll see you in a bit." I forced myself to take a few steps back, creating more distance between our bodies.

"Have fun." Tayna turned, resting his elbows against the wall as he smirked, putting his finger into his mouth and licking it clean, savoring my taste.

I had to clench my jaw to keep it from falling open. I was all too aware of the mocking heat between my legs.

I cleared my throat, feeling steadier on my feet. "Try not to get caught snooping around this place, ya?"

"Street rat, remember?"

And he looked nothing like a street rat. More like a street lion with a grin that was more feral than friendly. I finally forced myself to turn away and head down the halls to meet my friend.

Enver was lovely in flowing emerald pants and a white blouse that cut low in the front. All of it breezy and light for the summer heat, which felt like it'd gotten even harsher in the past few days. My skin prickled beneath the rays.

I wore a simple, gauzy dress that had been part of the options left for me in our room. And I needed a shower after Tayna and I had spent a large portion of our day wrapped in each other. But there hadn't been time between the sex and then more sex and finally managing to drag ourselves from bed to scout the hospital building.

God, sex with Tayna made my chest ache.

It was different than with Gideon. I could admit that. It had been so entirely different. With Gideon, there was always a game. There was a push and pull. Pleasure and pain. Lust and love and hate and all the blurred lines in between.

But with Tayna, the way he'd taken me, it was sure and secure.

Being with him felt safe.

"You're glowing." Enver grinned.

And I couldn't even hide it. I was.

"Well, thank god for that." She sighed. "I hated the way you two were so distant at the compound. And then I know Olita and Tayna have a strained relationship, so that can't be easy."

"He doesn't like to talk about her," I admitted.

"Maybe we could encourage them to talk? Like to each other?" She nudged me with her arm.

Enver saw the good in people. I'd give her that. She believed in Olita just like she'd believed in Gideon.

"Yeah, maybe," I said skeptically. "I've noticed Olita hasn't been at dinner for the past couple of nights."

The dark-eyed Phantom hadn't been there either. But I kept that one to myself.

Enver shrugged. "She's busy. Not everyone attends the dinners in the hall every night." She hooked her arm casually through mine as we walked down the open-air corridors. The heat reached us even in the shade. It made my skin slick where my arm met Enver's, but she didn't seem to mind.

"And what about the Silvers?" I tried to ask it casually, but Enver's steps noticeably slowed as she weighed her words.

Finally, she said with a small shrug, "Everyone's welcome."

"Come on, Enver." I paused, tugging her to a stop with me. The hint of sky I could see beyond the adobe was the purest blue. "I haven't seen any other Silvers at this place besides you. That isn't an accident."

Enver sucked her teeth as she looked around the corridor.

There was no one around.

Still, her response was measured. "Olita has kept everyone at the Veiled safe all these years because she's so secretive, you know. I don't ever want to lie to you, Lissa, but I gave her my word when I came here that I would respect her rules."

"And what are her rules?" I pressed.

She gave me a side-eyed look. After another moment, she said, "Of course there are other Silvers here. You'll meet them if you decide to stay, and you'll love them. I've only been here a short time, but they already feel like sisters in so many ways."

Sisters? She hadn't been here that long. What could these women and Olita possibly offer that would have Enver so enamored with them and this place?

"You're that happy here?"

"I am." And even if she hadn't said anything, her soft smile made me believe her words were true. It was so bright and full of a promise she'd been missing at the compound. "And just look at you." She nudged me again. "Only a few days here, and you're all glowy, too. Is this place really that bad?"

She wasn't wrong.

And I had a moment of guilt for feeling so happy.

But no, I deserved some semblance of happiness. Didn't I?

I knew it wouldn't last. I knew eventually my time would come to an end, and I would owe Olita a decision. Choices would need to be made. But right now, right now I just wanted to enjoy this moment, especially with Tayna.

"Yeah, well..." I tugged her back down the corridor, our arms still twined. "If I had known how good he was with his tongue, I never would have kept him away."

She cackled in a way that was surprisingly un-Enver-like. Then we were both laughing as we walked arm in arm down the open halls.

There was no one else around, and the soft summer breeze tickled across my collarbone as Enver led me through the maze of this place. I felt good for the first time in months. Yet I found myself glancing over my shoulder as if the hair rising on the back of my neck wasn't from the breeze at all. But rather, the prickle of eyes.

A hawk swooped low in the sky.

I scanned the hallways again.

But there was no one.

"That Phantom that's always with Olita," I hedged, "do you know who he is?"

I'd lost sight of the bird again between buildings, but still had the sense we were being watched.

"Phantom?" Enver shrugged, leading me around a tall fountain in the center of one of the open spaces between the halls. The cool mist caressed my skin. "There's usually always at least two with her, if not more. Laykin's determined to officially join their ranks. Can't you just see him all straight backed in one of those creepy masks?" She shivered dramatically.

I honestly could see Laykin among those men. He had the build and demeanor for it. He would fit in well with the Phantoms and their brutal reputation.

"But this one is different." I couldn't let it go. "He seems familiar."

"I don't even know how you can tell them apart. I can hardly even recognize Layk when he's on duty."

"And you're okay with that? You're okay with him being one of Olita's Phantoms?"

"It's not any different from one of Gideon's Jacks, really."

"You know she has a brutal reputation in the city. Her Phantoms are known for having sharp metal canines. And they kill without mercy. They'll drag a Silver from the streets and drain them dry."

"Those are wild rumors, Lissa!" Enver countered, "I've never even seen any of the Phantoms leave the fortress. And even if it's true, the Cards weren't any less brutal."

I could tell I'd hit a nerve with my pressing. But she was right. The Cards had been just as bloodthirsty throughout the years. The difference was that I'd never thought it was okay. Enver had managed to make peace with it. And didn't she have the right to choose her life just as I wanted to choose mine?

After we walked in silence for a few minutes, she asked, "So will you leave then?"

And I sighed, contemplating the question. I wasn't ready to leave, not yet. Not only because I'd learned nothing, but because a part of me actually liked it here. I liked how Tayna and I were together here.

But I couldn't stay like this. Tayna wouldn't stay. And Olita wouldn't allow us to remain without agreeing to her terms. Her price felt too steep. Yet I didn't know how to simply walk away.

I thought of the book we'd found at Tea and Trinkets. I thought of Alaric's cryptic words about my mother's betrayal. I thought of Madam Cartenoth revealing my mother had been aligned with the man she'd claimed to hate above all else. What had happened all those years ago? And why did it feel so important? Maybe it wasn't. Perhaps I was a silly girl trying to make sense out of things that should stay buried, just as Alaric had suggested. Did it really matter at the end of the day where I came from? Would it change anything if I knew why my silver was unique? Maybe it wouldn't, but it mattered to me. It felt important. Like perhaps it would make the weight of my decisions in this war feel less heavy if I knew why my mother had decided to hurt the people around her all those years ago.

"Well, if answers about your own history can't convince you to stay, then maybe answers about the history of most of the world will," Enver said, her tone going light as she stopped in front of an intricately carved double door. The dark wood had been etched with a swirling kaleidoscope pattern that extended into the archway above.

Enver pushed open the doors, and I had the distinct and immediate thought she was right. This must be the history of the world. And it could most definitely make me want to stay.

It wasn't a library.

It was a cathedral. Two stories, floor to ceiling, with stack after stack, row after row of books.

I didn't even know so many books could still exist in the world, let alone in a single collection. This, *this* had to be one of the wonders of our ruined world.

Stained glass windows reflected colored light across the floors and ceilings, casting a rich rainbow of crimson and emerald and sapphire color against the mahogany bookshelves. It sparkled against the spines as if beckoning us closer.

And I obliged.

"You can read whatever you want." Enver spun into the room as she fed off my excited wonder. "The only rule is the books must stay in this room."

"And that you keep your voice down to respect those reading," Olita said, surprising us both as she came around the corner from one of the shelves. She wore thin-framed glasses on the tip of her straight nose and held a thick volume in her hands that looked old, but I couldn't see the title on the page.

"Right." Enver lightened her words. "Sorry."

Olita ignored her platitudes and turned to me instead. "Looking for anything in particular? Maybe the histories?" She eyed me above her glasses, and I felt the weight of her gaze, the need to stand slightly straighter.

"I prefer the classics," I hedged. I absolutely wanted to comb through this library for anything about the history of the Silvers. I was sure Olita knew exactly which books would give me the secrets I so desperately sought. But she wouldn't simply hand them over. That was all part of the deal she wanted me to make.

"Why don't you let me show you?"

I had a feeling this chance encounter wasn't at all about books.

Enver took the cue. "I'll be in the romances if you need me!"

Olita just kept that pleasant grin plastered to her face as she watched Enver go. "That one aims to please, doesn't she? I'm surprised my son isn't fawning over a girl like that, if I'm honest."

I wasn't sure if she was insulting me or complimenting me with that statement. But I said, "Tayna has always preferred the classics, too."

And Olita's grin widened as she turned and began walking through the stacks. Her strides were graceful but unhurried. I took that as my cue to follow.

"The shelves are organized by fiction and non-fiction and then genre," Olita explained as she walked. "You'll find labels between the shelves."

"Where did these come from?" I was still absorbing all that I was seeing. Thousands of books lined the shelves, tens of thousands. I resisted the urge to run my fingers down the wall of them closest to me.

Olita just smiled that tight-lipped grin of hers as she said simply, "A friend."

Right. That only made me feel like she'd stolen them. Or she'd killed someone and then stolen them.

But she surprised me by continuing. "My husband was the reader. I was the scientist."

"It's unexpected then that he didn't teach Tayna to read." The thought slipped from my lips before I could catch it. But Tayna had only known basic letters and words when we'd met. I'd taught him to read when we'd found each other on the streets. He'd been a quick study, yes, but it was clear no one had taken the time to teach him.

Olita's feline gaze snapped to me, and I resisted the instinct to flinch. Her eyes really were so reflective of Tayna's gaze. "We had other priorities in those years. Like protecting this community from those who would have preferred us dead."

I knew the stories. The Cards and the Veiled had a bloody history. Especially after the Veiled killed Ishmael. Then the fighting truly began. And Gideon had ended it by killing Olita's husband and eldest son. The price of war. And I couldn't help but wonder if Olita thought her family was worth the sacrifice to keep her precious community. Did she love her Phantoms more than her blood?

"You're wasting time reading books like these." Olita gestured to the shelves as we arrived in a back corner of the library. I saw titles both familiar and unfamiliar. Hundreds of books to discover. And I couldn't resist the intake of breath at the stories contained on these shelves. Stories that were otherwise lost. "Just like you're wasting your time loving my son."

Now my gaze snapped to Olita as if she'd slapped me from my trance. Is this why she'd wanted to talk to me? To convince me to end things with Tayna? It made sense. If Tayna wasn't a factor, I could admit that the draw to stay at the Veiled would be much stronger.

"You don't know Tayna at all," I said.

"And you don't understand this world. Take your place at the Veiled and let me teach you."

Right. Her offer.

"And if I ally with you, will you pledge to ally with the Whigs, too?"

"The Whigs have nothing to offer."

"Isn't peace enough?"

"There will never be peace in this city."

"Not if things continue the way they have. That's true. You could end the fighting right now, and you know it. Especially with the Cards disbanded."

Olita chuckled as if I were a naive little girl. "Dia is looting his way through the city as we speak, rebuilding the ranks. He'll, no doubt, worm out enough fools to start something, cause destruction, and then get them all killed eventually."

"He wouldn't stand a chance if we stood together against him."

"Ah, so you're asking me to fight then? To risk more of my people's lives. All for this supposed peace? I have peace. Right here."

I was getting nowhere.

I turned back to the books and selected a title I'd heard mentioned, though I'd never actually seen a copy: *Dracula* by Bram Stoker.

Olita laughed. "I could have guessed you had a taste for the dark side."

I hesitated in my selection, but then clutched the book. Let her take from it what she would. I did have a taste for the dark side. And just like her, I would protect the people I loved. If she wanted my loyalty, she'd have to give me something more in return, something that would actually help this city beyond answers about my past.

As we emerged from the shelves, I glanced over my shoulder a final time, meeting the dark eyes through the cracks in the books that I'd felt watching us all along.

Lissa

After our conversation in the stacks, Olita left me to my reading, and Enver settled in across from me. We sat like that for some time, but I was hardly concentrating on the book. I knew the Phantom still watched me from somewhere within the shelves.

And there was that noise again, that steady *clack, clack, clack* from somewhere far away.

I wasn't scared by the Phantom's presence. Maybe I should be. I hadn't seen him since that first night in the cooridor, but I'd felt him watching me. And I was just as curious about him.

I shook my head.

He wasn't Gideon.

Of course, that was ridiculous.

But it wasn't just the familiarity that drew me to him. There was something else I hadn't yet been able to name.

The *clack, clack, clack* sound came again.

"What is that?" I finally asked Enver.

"Hmm?" she asked over the edge of her book. The cover showed a muscular man embracing a woman whose light-pink dress was caught in the wind as they stood at the bow of a great ship.

"That noise," I prompted. "I keep hearing it."

She shook her head. "I don't hear anything, Liss."

It had stopped with her words. The silence of the space hung as if suspended in time. The afternoon light reflecting through the stained-glass windows, the dust in the air like glitter, was the only movement I could see.

I snapped my book closed and set it on the side table next to the chaise I'd settled into at the center of one of the stacks.

"I'll be back."

That pull in my gut had become a tighter knot, and I couldn't ignore it anymore.

"Are you okay?" She sat up a little straighter, but I waved her off.

"Just going to look for a different book."

That was a lie.

I'd read just about three pages of *Dracula* before staring off into space. I could leave. I could say goodbye to Enver and go back to Tayna. I could fold myself in his arms and get lost in the feel of him sliding in and out of me again like he had this morning. I could forget Olita and Gideon and the Phantom. We could leave this place and go back to the Whigs. I could build a life there entirely separate from whatever secrets this place held.

And maybe that would be okay for a while.

Maybe there would be comfort in it for a time.

But I knew eventually this nagging in my heart would only grow stronger. The pull for something else was an electric pulse of its own in my veins, and it was only getting worse since coming here.

So instead of going back to the room, I twisted deeper into the shelves, making my way past the fiction section Olita had shown me earlier and to a darker, dimmer place where the books seemed older and the colors from the stained glass couldn't reach.

I found him there, waiting as if he'd known I'd seek him out.

He stood tall against the stacks, his suit perfectly fitted to show off his toned physique. Barely a hint of skin was visible between the mask, the high-collared shirt he wore beneath the jacket, and his gloves, but I didn't need to see skin to know he was a predator.

I kept myself on the opposite side of the shelves from him, taking him in as I demanded, "Who are you?"

His eyes were shining bright despite the dim room. He was pleased. And I glanced over my shoulder as if this might have been some trap. I'd made the decision to come find him, but it felt like he'd lured me to this moment. He'd made his presence known at every turn, and now, I could no longer ignore it.

"Just a ghost." His words were a low, rumbling whisper. Despite the control in his voice, this man felt entirely unpredictable.

"Did Olita tell you to watch me?"

His eyes flashed with a darkness that made my stomach clench. I recognized that feeling. I got it when I used my silver. It was a subtle thrill in my bones.

I swallowed it down.

"Are you watching me to make sure I don't see what's really going on in this place?" I pressed.

It wasn't just dinner parties and dancing and tennis courts and warm days in the sun. I knew that.

His voice was a growl. "No, Lissa."

The words only confirmed what I already knew.

My silver crackled at my fingers, not from fear but as if summoned, pulling from my veins.

I swallowed it down.

"Are you always holding yourself back like that?" He asked it like he wasn't asking about my silver at all.

"Yes," I admitted.

I realized that wasn't something I'd ever said to anyone before.

No one had ever asked.

"Why?" His fingers traced along the books as he took a step toward me.

"Why?" I took one back. Wasn't it obvious? "Because I don't want to hurt people."

He'd seen what almost happened in the corridor a few nights ago. He'd been the one to stop me.

"Maybe you'll hurt people more by trying to pretend you're something that you're not."

His dark words wormed their way to the very center of me, exposing me in a way I hadn't been ready for when coming back here to find him. I thought I'd be the one asking the questions. Instead, he was laying bare all my fears.

"I just want to control it," I swallowed. "I'm getting better at controlling it."

He caught the lie. "It looks to me like it's controlling you."

He scanned his head along the shelves, tossing his neck from side to side as he took another casual step in my direction.

Slow. Measured in his steps.

And yet...

This time, I didn't retreat.

My heart spiked in my throat as he got closer still, until I was looking up at him through my lashes. He was just close enough that I could catch his leather and smoke scent, like he might spend a lot of time among these books himself.

I'd been close to him before but had yet to face him like this, had yet to see him fully take me in the way I'd known he'd been watching me.

I wanted to take him in like he was doing to me, but there was no hope of reading his secrets with the mask in place. His eyes were the only clue to his intentions, and they traveled back up to my face. Slowly.

He finally asked, "Do you like that I watch you?"

The question felt like a challenge.

"Of course not—"

He stepped into me, and my words faltered.

Awareness prickled along my skin as I stepped back on instinct now, only for my back to graze against the shelves.

He'd backed me into a corner, and I hadn't even realized it.

I held my silver. There was a game in his expression. Something in me stirred. I felt like I was on the edge of a cliff, wondering what it would feel like to jump.

My eyes tracked along the mouth opening of his mask. Did he wear one of those silver canines? It was too dimly lit this deeply in the shelves for me to make it out if he did.

He seemed to be grinning still as he leaned in to murmur, "Liar."

His voice was a rich rasp. Each word was spoken like a rumbling purr, as if he were forcing the sound from his chest.

"You're not Gideon." I couldn't help the tremor in my words. It was a stupid thing to say, as if this pull to him was only because he reminded me of Gideon. He wasn't Gideon. And yet... he was so familiar.

"Gideon." He scoffed at his name like it was a curse. "Gideon was never patient. Not like I am."

He traced along the books at the side of my head as if he was imagining tracing along my skin but was holding back from touching me. Restraining himself.

Why?

My heart pulsed faster.

This Phantom was like a spider, coiled to lunge, and my entire body recognized the tension. It wasn't only my nervous system recognizing danger. The twist in my gut was something darker coming to life in the very center of me, something I'd been trying to ignore since the cliffs.

My eyes tracked to his mouth again.

"Patient?" The word was as shaky as my breath. My silver sparked against my palms as I balled my hands into fists. "What are you waiting for?"

Part of me felt like I'd been waiting for this moment, too.

He leaned in again, his breath tracking across my cheek.

He wasn't touching me, but it somehow felt like he was consuming me.

I could see his demon smile, stretched tight beneath the mask. The hint of a silver canine peeked over his lip, confirming my suspicions.

His presence paralyzed me. My silver sparked at my fingers, glowing in the space between us, but he was overwhelming in his proximity. Even with my silver, he made me feel helpless so close to his body.

"I'm not waiting anymore." His voice was so low I almost missed the words. "We're playing the game, you and I."

He pressed away from me then, grinnng. He tucked his hands behind his back as he stepped away, increased the space between us with measured strides.

I felt unsteady, disoriented by the sudden distance between us.

My silver fizzled as he continued taking steps back, and I had the unexpected, irrational desire to reach for him.

I didn't want him to disappear again.

I braced myself against the shelves as I watched him, my mind reeling as I tried to take in what had just happened. I'd thought coming back here that I would have the control, but he'd completely and utterly commanded me without even touching me.

He smiled like he knew, before fading into the shadows of the stacks, his eyes still locked on mine.

An arm caught me around the waist, and I released a yelp of surprise as I was pulled sideways along the shelves. A body pinned me. Lips connected with my skin, trailing along my jaw and to my mouth. A soft male groan vibrated against my chest.

"You've been gone for too long," Tayna said against my lips, dipping in for another consuming kiss.

My stomach twisted, like I'd been yanked from some deeper understanding just before the moment of realization.

My thoughts collided, too fast to follow.

"Tayna!"

His kisses stole my breath as I was trying to catch it.

I pulled back, but the Phantom was gone from where he'd been standing between the shelves only a moment before.

"How did you find me?" I asked him on an exhale.

"Enver said you wandered off this way. This place is a maze." He was grinning at me and biting his bottom lip as he tucked the strands of my hair behind my ear and pressed another soft kiss against my lips. "I can't stop thinking about you, about the taste of you. It wasn't enough this morning."

I should tell him about the Phantom and about my conversation with Olita. And I would. I would tell him everything... I would. He was kissing me again, his fingers trailing down my body.

"You're wet, aren't you?" he breathed.

And I had a sudden jolt of panic. How did he know?

But then I remembered earlier, when he'd touched me before I'd met with Enver, his fingers sliding along my center, and I choked out a "Yes."

"I want you," he said against my mouth.

I caressed along the edges of his face, centering myself. He was here. Of course, that was the familiar flutter deep in my belly.

"Take me back to our room then."

He gripped my waist and pressed into me. "Grip the shelves above your head."

His fingers were already finding the hem of my dress, bunching up the sides over my hips.

He was serious.

My blood heated.

The Phantom lingered somewhere between these shelves.

And he was watching.

"Wait."

This was all happening too quickly.

"I don't want to," he breathed.

"We can't, Tayna." I tried to turn in his grasp, to press him back, but it became a moan as he trailed his hands along my backside instead, squeezing my flesh under my dress. I could feel him hard through his pants, and despite myself, I wanted to rub along his length.

"Someone will hear us," I said on a gasp as his fingers slipped between my cheeks to run through the wetness he found at my center.

"No one is back here," he murmured between kisses.

But I knew that wasn't true.

"Enver—"

I choked on the words as his fingers pressed deeper.

"Guess you should be quiet then," he murmured in my ear, pumping his fingers. I did grasp the bookshelf then, scrambling for purchase as he worked me with his hand.

I felt dizzy.

We had to stop.

We—

"Tayna!" I gasped, trying to keep my voice low, a last desperate attempt to contain myself.

I was losing control.

And most disorienting of all, part of me liked the sensation.

I wasn't sure how much of this was desire and how much was something darker coming to life inside me.

Tayna's answer was a soft chuckle as his fingers slipped from my body to unbutton his pants.

I took the reprieve to scan the shelves again.

No eyes watched me through the pages.

But he was still close.

I knew he was still nearby.

Tayna lined the head of his cock to my entrance. I cupped a hand over my mouth to muffle the sounds I made as he pressed slowly inside me.

My eyes rolled back as I arched into him, unable to deny this feeling, unable to deny that it was heightened knowing there were dark eyes watching me through the shelves.

I bit my lip to keep from crying out as he began to thrust inside me. So deep. He was so deep. I pressed back into him, gripping the shelves tighter.

His breath was at my ear, and his rich, earthy scent invaded my every sense. Even as he was achoring me with his hand on my hip, I was spinning. I felt disconnected from myself, and there was only this feeling, this release. He worked my body into a fever pitch that had me choking on the moans and cries of the pleasure he was wringing from me.

"So good, Liss," he murmured against my ear.

And it *was* good.

But when I closed my eyes, I saw a silver mask.

I scrambled for something, anything to cling to.

His palm pressed against my mouth, and I let out the smallest whimper in answer as he quickened his pace. My body was pulled as tight as a bowstring.

This was wrong.

But I didn't want to stop.

"I'm gonna come, Liss," he growled, reaching around to press into my clit, which was all it took. I unraveled. The orgasm hit me right as I heard his intake of breath. The feel of him losing control just as I was only heightened the pleasure. I let go to the wave of it, unable to stop the sob of release as it slipped from between my lips.

It was the hardest I'd ever come.

The world went black around me for a breath.

I clung to Tayna as if he could ground me in what had just happened.

If he hadn't been clutching me, I would have crumpled to the floor.

Goose bumps pebbled my skin as Tayna trailed his fingers along my shoulders to my back and up my neck. He seemed to sense the way my knees were buckling because he caught me around the waist as he slowly pulled out, cradling me against his body as he trailed kisses along my shoulder blades where his fingers had just been.

He held me, and I clung to him, desperately trying to ground myself.

I couldn't catch my breath.

My vision was slowly righting itself.

"I love you, Liss," Tayna breathed against my ear. "I've always loved you. Wherever you are is home."

I exhaled.

I thought I might pass out.

His words weren't unexpected, yet I felt out to sea, unable to cling to that declaration as I tried to make sense of everything that just happened.

"I—"

It was all I could do to breathe. Maybe I *was* out of control.

"You don't have to say anything," he caught me in a kiss. "I just—I couldn't take not saying it."

I pressed my palm against his cheek, resting my forehead against his chest.

"I can't lose you," I said to him, feeling like I might start crying.

"Hey," he caught my face in his hands, crouching gently to meet my gaze. His gleamed with such earnestness that it broke me. "You won't ever lose me."

No, but I realized, somewhere in this place, I may have lost myself. And I didn't want to go back.

32

Lissa

The Phantom watched me the next night at dinner, his eyes tracking me as I danced with Enver. Her steps were graceful while mine were... unpracticed. Her word, not mine. I would have said my steps were clumsy and severely lacking coordination. Still, he watched me. And I was all the more clumsy as I thought about what he'd witnessed between the books yesterday.

I forced my focus back to the steps.

And forced my gaze back to the boy with chestnut hair and bronze skin and sparkling eyes who loved me. He'd always loved me. Hadn't I known that? Vocalizing it should have been as easy as breathing because it simply... was. But I hadn't said it back. And he hadn't forced the issue. He hadn't even seemed to notice that I hadn't responded, only kissed him and allowed that to be enough.

It made me feel sick.

Because of course I loved him back.

But saying it would mean giving myself to him in a way that I wasn't sure I could. Not now.

One, two, three.

Front, side, back.

Clasp hands. And turn.

I moved, all while feeling disconnected from myself. I felt unmoored. Not even Tayna's presence was enough to anchor me tonight.

Olita was at dinner, sipping wine from her table at the head of the room.

She watched me, too.

She watched me like she was watching the time run out like I used to watch the hourglass in Madam Cartenoth's shop. The little grains of sand slipped so quickly through the funnel that I hardly noticed the time passing until it was gone. How much time would Olita allow me before demanding my answer?

And what was my answer?

I didn't have one.

Maybe that was why I hadn't answered Tayna, either.

He met me in the center of the dance floor, looking surprisingly sure of himself. His steps were steady as he followed the music, not tripping once, even as he caught me by the waist.

My silver sparked, sharp and unexpected.

I yanked my hand away. "I'm sorry!"

He hissed and shook it out, but then smiled. "Still sparking around me?" His tone was amused as we split apart in time to the song, guys on one side and women on the other.

I almost forgot the curtsy, missing the beat but catching it as I rose.

"Maybe that's enough dancing for one night?" he asked, offering me his hand as if wondering if I was safe.

I forced my silver back, slipping my fingers into his outstretched palm.

"Should we eat?" He watched me, too, as if sensing that something wasn't quite right.

Despite my mood, the dining hall that night felt somehow livelier. The music seemed louder. The dancing felt more sensual. The wine was flowing freely. It was as if the Veiled had exhaled, and an electricity in the air compelled us all.

The air around us felt intoxicating, not helping the sensation that I was floating in some strange dream that had somehow gotten twisted.

Enver was on the dance floor, too, with Laykin. And even Laykin seemed more at ease than his usual stiff-backed self as he spun her around the room. She was laughing in that brilliant, captivating way of hers, and he did not look away.

My gaze wandered back to the Phantom, feeling a small spark of my silver threaten as I met his gaze. I'd need to find a way to release it soon. I was volatile.

I cleared my throat, realizing I hadn't answered Tayna's question about dinner. "Yes." I forced a smile. "Let's eat."

Olita had already finished her plate but was waiting for us, the house staff standing at attention with our salads on the table. I tried to make eye contact with them, but none looked my way. They stared straight ahead, a clear indicator that I would get no answers from them. Apparently, Olita's people were loyal no matter their position in this fortress. She had allowed us inside this place. She showed me what life was like, but I didn't get to become a true part of this world until I gave her my loyalty.

I settled into my seat, feeling the Phantom's eyes tracking me. Burning warmth seeped into my cheeks at his gaze.

With the way we were arranged, Olita at the head of the table and Tayna and I seated next to each other, it felt like that first night again pressed under her scrutiny. Not so much a dinner as it was a trial, and Olita was judge and jury.

Unlike the last time, Tayna avoided the wine. And any conversation with his mother. But before we'd left to come to dinner, he'd downed another small vial of silver before taking my hand and leading us outside.

Seated in front of Olita as we ate our perfectly prepared food, she seemed primed for a discussion I was not ready to have. If I told her I wasn't interested in the deal, I believed she'd let us walk out the doors and back to our Humvee. But we'd never be welcome inside these walls again.

The Humvee. I'd nearly forgotten about the truck and the strange book I'd found at Tea and Trinkets. I'd been distracted here. Too distracted.

The food was ash in my mouth.

I needed to focus.

The room was a cacophony of music and laughter and the clanking of dishes and the clink of wine glasses.

Tayna put a hand on my thigh.

"Sorry, what?" I asked, realizing someone had asked me a question.

"I was asking about your mother's tutelage." Olita's voice was light. She leaned back in her chair, a glass of red wine poised between her fingers. "Did she teach you science?"

I cleared my throat. "We spent a lot of time in her gardens."

My voice felt distant in my ears.

I looked at Tayna, feeling like I'd missed the conversation. "Why would she teach me science?"

"Because she was the best one I've known." Olita shrugged, clearly baiting me with the information.

And I was like a fish on the hook. "My mother was a scientist?"

"Oh yes." She swirled her wine and took a sip. "She was obsessed with discovering the origins of the Silver, understanding the genetic makeup that led to your evolution. That's what she believed, at least, that the scientists who created the Silvers had unlocked the next phase of human capability."

"And what did she find?" I pressed. The beat of the music was like a heartbeat in the room. I could feel it rattling through my chair as I caught glimpses of flowing fabrics and smiling faces between the lattice windows.

But Olita only sipped more wine. That was as much as she was willing to divulge for now.

So I changed tactics. "Did she ever visit this place?"

Talking about my mother gave me a tether, and I clung to it.

"You know my terms, Lissa." Olita sighed.

"I know, I just—"

"She lived here for years before you were born."

"She lived here?" I suddenly felt the rush of feeling so close to her in a way I hadn't in years. Were there things still here that belonged to her? Did she sit in the library and read books with Olita like I had read with Enver? Where was her room?

I had to hold myself back from vocalizing the rush of questions. I pressed my palms together in my lap to keep my silver from sparking.

Clack, clack, clack.

That noise.

My eyes tracked to the Phantom, our gazes snagging against the flickering silver firelight.

Clack, clack, clack.

I could barely hear it above the muffled music, but it was like a heartbeat of its own, always calling to me in this place.

"What is that?" I turned back to the table, meeting Olita's gaze from where she still watched me, leaning back in her chair so her golden eyes were shrouded against its high-backed frame.

Tayna leaned into me. "It's an old place, Liss. Strange sounds are normal."

"Most likely the plumbing." Olita exhaled, growing bored with me, yet again.

But the way she said it, so dismissive, it felt like a lie.

"And what about your Silvers? Where are they? I haven't seen any others except Enver."

Olita set down her wine and leaned into me. "That's because you are only permitted to see what I allow. My Silvers prefer their privacy, as do my people. We've survived this long because of it. So until I know I can trust you, you are only allowed into a tiny fraction of my empire, girl. Do not think you can exploit my generosity and manipulate me into giving you more." She pressed from the table, her long red nails digging into the wood. "You may finish and then enjoy your evening. Your bad decisions are your own." She looked down her nose at her son.

Tayna stared right back but didn't speak. He kept his hand on my thigh, and I resisted the urge to look again at the Phantom leaning in the shadows.

"Time is running out, Lissa," Olita said over her shoulder as she left the table. "I want an answer. My generosity only goes so far unreturned, and you're pushing the limit."

Olita's Phantoms, including the dark-eyed one, followed her back into the dining room until it was only Tayna and me left sitting. Even the waitstaff had cleared the remaining plates and disappeared into the shadows.

My thoughts were a jumbled mess. My gaze found Tayna's, and I could tell he wanted to leave. He was ready to put this place behind us. He'd been patient with me, just as Olita had, everyone expecting a decision that I didn't feel ready to make.

We should leave.

I knew we should leave.

After what had happened in the library...

For some reason, at that moment, I imagined Gideon sitting on my other side. His dark presence suddenly so close that I glanced over my shoulder. There was only the dimly lit room and revelers beyond.

If you want change, you have to be willing to sacrifice, little Queen. His deep, melodic voice was just out of reach in my memory.

But what about sacrificing myself?

Self is the easiest of sacrifices.

And I saw him then, throwing himself over those cliffs so I didn't have to live with the reality of pulling that trigger. Yes, he'd been willing to sacrifice.

My silver churned beneath my skin.

Tayna's words cut into my fantasy. He seemed to sense my growing unease. "We should head back to our room."

Yes, yes, we should.

I needed some space to clear my thoughts.

And I needed to figure out how to release some of my silver before I completely lost control.

33

Lissa

We found Enver among the crowd, and she immediately gripped my hands, sweeping me in a circle that had my hair flying around my face and my vision blurring.

"Enver!" I tried to halt the movement, the room a swirl of colors.

Tayna caught me by the waist as Enver released me, and I stumbled as the people around me came back into focus.

"Dance with me!" Enver sang, grabbing Laykin's hand and raising their joined grip so she could spin beneath his arm.

"I think you've had too much wine." I kept the words light with a smile, but I wanted to leave this dining hall.

She shrugged and kept on spinning in Laykin's grasp. Even he was smiling, effortless and content. Would I feel the same way if I decided to stay at the Veiled? I tried to picture myself building a life among these people and found myself scanning the room again for signs of the dark-eyed Phantom.

He wasn't in the shadows anymore, at least that I could see.

But it was hard to make out the faces.

I'd always avoided crowds. As a Silver who grew up on the streets, crowds meant trouble. But at the Veiled, I might as well have been one of the Phantoms. Some of the people in the room had noticeably turned from us rather than look at me.

And some of the Phantoms, I realized, had even joined Laykin in the dancing. They'd forgone their masks but kept their silver suits. A black-haired man with porcelain skin grinned as he spun a woman across the floor, and I caught a flash of his silver tooth. He wore the canine like a crest, a symbol of pride.

Laykin saw me watching and leaned in. "Olita has a strict consent rule among the silvers. The teeth are more for show. Unless you're into that sort of thing, that is." He gave me a sideways glance as he held Enver as if he knew exactly what I was into.

"Consent, huh?" I murmured, thinking of the way the black-eyed Phantom had pinned me against the shelves yesterday afternoon. Something told me he wouldn't require my consent before sinking that tooth into my flesh.

And I supposed Laykin's implication was right. Gideon hadn't either. Not always. But he'd demanded my desire, and my body had folded to him easily every time, even when I wished it wouldn't.

Tayna traced a hand down my arm. "We should go. You look tired."

I nodded distantly, shoving back the complex knot in my belly. It made the silver jolt beneath my veins.

God, I'd need to find a release.

Soon.

How many days had it been?

Four or five?

Too many.

Especially when my silver had been so volatile since the cliffs.

"Stop hogging the new girl, will you, Tay?"

I couldn't help the gasp of surprise that slipped through my lips at the voice so close. None of the Veiled had even approached us, let alone talked to us. I noticed a few wary glances tossed our way as I turned.

It was the dark-haired porcelain-skinned Phantom I'd noticed earlier. His canine flashed as he grinned at me. He wasn't wearing his mask.

Tayna's eyes narrowed at the man, who was tall and slender in his fitted suit. He'd unbuttoned the top few buttons of the black shirt he wore underneath, exposing his flawless skin.

"Darian?" Tayna was hesitant as he said the name, like he couldn't quite believe it.

But the man's smile widened, which only sharpened his angular features and made the silver canine look longer.

And then they were hugging, Darian fist pumping Tayna's back lightly as he embraced him.

"A Phantom then?" Tayna looked Darian up and down as they parted. "I expected you'd be long gone from this city by now, traveling the world."

"Traveling's still ultimately the goal, but for now, Olita pays me well enough to convince me to stay."

I was stuck looking between the two men, feeling confused by this apparent reunion of childhood friends. Tayna hadn't mentioned a friend. The life he'd described had been a lonely one, full of strict rules and expectations that he not be seen or heard. The thought hadn't occurred to me that there would be other children at the Veiled. I hadn't seen any children since we'd arrived here.

I hadn't seen any children.

Or any Silvers besides Enver.

The thought hung there, incomplete and nagging.

"And your mother?" Tayna asked.

"She's been looking forward to seeing you, too, but work is keeping her busy these days. I rarely see her myself. I'm sure you can appreciate that."

"We can't, actually," I said, facing Darian fully. "All I've seen are tennis courts and libraries and parties. But something tells me that's not the craziness keeping your mother busy, is it?"

Darian watched me as if he were waiting for me to spark. Not because he was afraid, but because he wanted the show. After a few moments, he quirked a brow as if in challenge. "No, it's not."

I waited for him to give me anything else.

Of course, he didn't. Instead, he scooped my hand into his and planted a gentle kiss on the back of my palm as he bowed his head to me. I pulled my fingers back before I did, in fact, spark.

"We haven't had the pleasure yet. Orders and all. But I've been anxious to meet the rebel queen everyone's been buzzing about. I heard you put on quite the show your first night here."

I swallowed at the memory of the couple in the halls. I still hadn't told Tayna what had happened.

I looked around the room as if I might have become the center of gossip and somehow missed it. But no, no one looked our way. No one whispered nearby.

I scrambled for words, to explain.

My silver sparked.

Tayna noticed and took a step just slightly in front of me.

Another song started up around us, the music sweeping and quick in its steps. This one involved clapping, which the dancers took up in a rhythmic pattern. Even some of those who were talking in groups like ours tapped along to the beat.

"And what about you?" Darian asked Tayna over the music. "You left in the night, what was it, thirteen... fourteen years ago? Didn't even tell me before you fled. I never expected to see your face, let alone see your face back here."

"It was..." Tayna kept his expression blank, but I saw he was searching for the words. "I was just a kid."

"And that scar?" Darian gestured to it with his chin before looking at me.

My chest constricted, and my eyes narrowed. Was Darian intentionally trying to provoke me?

Tayna reached for me, but I shook my head. I was too close to the edge to be touched right now.

He instead turned back to Darian. "It was a small price for life on the streets."

I realized he didn't fully trust Darian either.

"We should get back to our rooms," Tayna said. "It was good to see you, Darian."

Darian looked down at me, and I realized how tall he was. He was about the same height as Tayna, and his posture was perfect. He was still smiling, but something about his expression was cold. "Yes, well, I should get back to my wife."

His eyes met the lithe woman he'd been dancing with earlier. She didn't so much as glance our way as she moved with sophisticated grace through the steps of the new dance.

Wife.

The outdated word clanged in my mind.

But there wasn't time to process what it told me about the Veiled. I needed to leave this room full of people. I needed to find a place to release some silver.

Enver sashayed toward me, her steps light even as they swayed. "Do you know that Phantom?" she asked.

The music and the laughter and the people and the grandeur and the secrets, all of it felt like suddenly too much.

My silver sparked at my fingers.

"Lissa?" Enver reached for me tentatively.

But I skirted her outstretched hand before she could touch me. "I just need to..."

And I felt it there, swelling just under the surface of my skin.

It had been held there too long. And I was too caught up in the pieces of this place that felt like they were right in front of me, yet just out of reach.

I met Olita's stare through the ballroom.

Her golden eyes pierced mine through the crowds, filtering past dancers and flowing fabrics.

My head was screaming.

And then I felt it more than I heard it.

That *clack, clack, clack.*

God, was that in my head? Maybe that noise was my soul screaming at me to run, run, *run* from this place.

"I'll meet you at the rooms," I said to Tayna as I turned, breaking Olita's stare to walk quickly outside.

"I'll come—"

"No!" I didn't wait to see if he followed me as I ran. He couldn't help me in this. I'd only be more dangerous and volatile with him near, trying desperately to keep myself contained.

The Phantom had been right about my control.

I didn't have a plan.

Where could I possibly go in this fortress to let go of the energy pulsing beneath my veins without collapsing an entire building? The water had always been my refuge. The ocean or a lake could ground me. But here? Everything was too close, too enclosed.

Shadows from the lanterns in the corridor flickered across my path, and then a larger shadow stepped in front of me. The light reflected off his silver mask as he gripped my shoulders to steady me.

Just in time, I recoiled, barely managing to avoid running into him, to put my hands out to brace myself, to burn him with the silver crackling along my exposed skin.

"I—"

I let go of the breath I'd been holding.

"You look like you need a drink." There was the lilt of laugher in the low words.

Was he mocking me?

"What I need right now is control," I snapped.

He took the measure of me. "That is the opposite of what you need." But he seemed to understand as his eyes watched my hands, sparking against my fists. "Come with me," he said before turning on his heels.

His strides were long and quick to the point where I was running to keep up with him, and I was grateful. When my silver got like this, it was tenuous at best and explosive at worst. I shouldn't have allowed it to get this bad. I should have known. I should have spoken to Olita about it. But I'd been so distracted by this place. I'd allowed myself to get distracted until I'd forgotten myself.

Stupid.

Following the Phantom down the twisting dark corridors without a clue where we were heading also seemed foolish. But what choice did I have? The silver was a tightly coiled knot in my chest, fighting to worm its way to the surface, and if I didn't release it soon, it would consume me. And then I'd become that silver little bomb of nightmares, hurting whoever happened to be in my path.

We broke beyond the corridors, the night sky extending overhead. The hospital building lay in the distance.

He was taking me to the hospital building.

He was taking me inside.

Part of me wanted to stop right then. My instincts told me to dig my heels in and not move.

As much as I wanted to see inside that building, I didn't trust this Phantom. If it was that difficult to get inside, who was to say he would ever let me walk out again?

But he was also taking a risk. I was clearly volatile, and he was taking me into a building that housed Olita's most precious secrets. So I followed, even as my silver spiked as we approached the doors.

To the guards at the door, he said nothing. They scrambled to remove themselves from his path as he keyed in a code and shoved open the door.

I stayed at his heels as I took in the room.

The air was surprisingly cool. A breeze wafted across my face, leveling my senses. Relief shuddered down my spine.

It was the newest building I'd ever been in. I'd lived in mansions and visited warehouses. I even thought of the Tank's ship then. Of Madam Cartenoth's shop. Of the home I'd grown up in with my mother. Of the bar where Tayna had worked when we were street rats. All of them old and worn.

This building was a stark contrast. It was shining and clean. White floors without a scuff to be seen. Bright white light illuminated everything around me. Shining glass walls separated the entryway from the elevators that looked like rippling coastal water.

It even smelled new, like a fresh electric current, metallic but oddly satisfying.

I didn't know what I'd expected to find. Of course, all the Silvers and hospital staff wouldn't simply be gathered on the first floor waiting. But there wasn't a single other person in sight. In fact, it looked like no one had ever set foot in this place for all its perfection.

The Phantom looked at home in this place as he pressed a button with a down arrow, and the doors of the elevator opened.

There'd been an elevator at the warehouse that Tayna and I had called home, but it hadn't been operational. We wouldn't have dared try it even if it were.

My breath hitched at the metal box. My silver sparked as the Phantom stepped inside. I pursed my lips against the vibrations under my skin. The nerves were not helping my limited control. I felt myself beginning to tremor from the feel of it.

I shook my head and took a step back.

I couldn't get in that thing.

Not only was I scared of the giant metal box suspended in midair, but I was also terrified of being in that box with the Phantom when I could lose myself at any moment.

My gaze swept the entryway. "Aren't there stairs?"

I was balling my fists so tightly I felt the skin breaking beneath my palms.

The Phantom put a hand on the door, keeping it from sliding closed. "Get in, Lissa," he snapped, his words a gravelly command.

His eyes were black as night beneath the mask and steady.

But I shook my head, stepping back, my silver sparking.

And before I could even smell the smoke, the Phantom had grabbed me and pulled me inside, pressing me against the wall as the doors slid closed behind me.

I wasn't too far gone that I didn't clock the numbers next to the door. One through twelve. But the Phantom had selected one at the bottom of the list, labeled "B3."

The elevator was smooth as it began its descent, and I swallowed the small yelp of surprise. The Phantom merely stood straight, pressing a hand down his suit jacket and turning to face the doors. My skin felt alive where he'd touched me, the silver flaring as I struggled to even my breathing.

"I could hurt you," I said softly. He had the right to know how close to the edge I was right now. Didn't he understand the danger he was in being this close to me?

He didn't turn to me, but from his profile, I thought I saw his brow quirk in the slightest tic beneath the mask. "*I* could hurt *you*," he growled so low I almost didn't catch the words, spoken like a threat.

He didn't understand. "My silver—"

In a flash of movement, he was stripping his jacket, revealing the black button-down beneath and pressing into me, pinning me against the corner of the small box taking us down and down.

I tried to make myself small, curling in on myself to avoid touching him, but he pried my arms from my side, pressing my balled fists squarely against his chest.

"Stop!" I begged, even as I heard the silver burn, even as I saw his shirt begin to singe.

Tears pricked my eyes as I lost my control and felt the silver slip free from my palms, into his chest.

"Please!"

I couldn't stop it. My silver released. And I couldn't hold it back. I was completely losing control.

He was too close, everything about him overwhelming as I lost myself to the moment.

But then the elevator doors opened.

The Phantom stepped back.

His singed shirt hung limply over his shoulders, strips burned out from the front.

But he wasn't bleeding. He didn't appear to be injured.

My limbs were shaking. Tears had spilled over my cheeks. My chest was tight as I tried to control my breathing, to control my silver, even as I was aware I'd failed.

Or... had I?

I'd lost control. I knew I had, but he wasn't burned.

"I don't understand," I choked out the words.

"You will." His grip tightened.

And then he was pulling me from the elevator into a dark corridor.

34

Lissa

The hallway was a stark difference from the room we'd left above. The musky scent of mildew hit me. Light illuminated at our feet as we walked, casting a faint glow against the stone walls.

I felt slightly more in control of myself now that I'd released some of my silver... into the Phantom's chest. I hadn't imagined that. His shirt was tattered in the front. I watched his broad back, his muscled shoulders visible through the taut fabric as he moved. The hint of his black hair curled around the nape of his neck, covering the skin there as he walked. I wondered if he had tattoos. Gideon had intricate black markings twisted up his arms and around his chest.

This man was not Gideon.

No, he was something even darker if that was somehow possible.

It radiated from him, a danger that made all my senses scream.

He felt untethered in a way Gideon was controlled.

And now I'd followed him down into some dark corridor. But I'd been a desperate idiot. My silver had been on the brink of unleashing on this place. The one time I'd lost control like that in public, I thought I'd killed Tayna. And I had killed others that day. I thought of the Card who'd grabbed me and sneered at me on the dirty city streets. Then I thought of his lifeless face, burned and muddy as I'd blinked open my eyes to find disaster.

I shook away the memory, shivering slightly at the spark of silver, muted but still alive beneath my skin.

The Phantom kept hold of my wrist, pulling me along without a look over his shoulder even as I sparked.

Just as I was about to jerk against his grasp and demand an answer about where we were going, the hallway turned. Lights flickered on at our approach, and we stepped into a large, cavernous room. A softly glowing pool stretched, inset at the center.

In my awe, I stumbled, not realizing steps were taking us down to the water. The Phantom caught me by the shoulders. My adrenaline spiked. My eyes leveled with the tatters along the front of his shirt, singed away from my touch.

This close, it confirmed what I'd already seen. The skin was unburned. But... it wasn't unblemished. Not tattoos but raised ridges along his chest, the skin looked as if it had been melted and then frozen back in place.

My fingers hovered as if drawn to the injuries.

"I—" The words wouldn't come, but I was compelled to touch his skin.

Before my fingers could make contact, he grabbed my wrists abruptly.

"Get in the water, Lissa," he growled.

The Phantom's silver mask reflected the light in a rippling wave that reminded me of the exposed skin on his chest. I felt a deep ache at the wounds that must have caused such damage. It must have been silver. It could only have been silver to cause something so horrible.

He released me, and I steadied myself, taking in the room.

"What is this place?" I asked, holding the railing that would take me into the depths.

"Your mother had this pool designed for this very purpose. It was built on top of a well with grounding coils beneath that will channel your silver into the depths of the earth below. It's safe."

"Oh." It was all I could manage beneath the swell of emotion that rose from my chest, spurring me to slip off my shoes and take the first step into the pool despite my distrust of the man now at my back.

The water was warm, perfectly comfortable as I sank farther, the light fabric of the dress I'd worn floating up my legs as I drifted deeper. I imagined the water was my mother wrapping her arms around me in a steady embrace. It didn't make me feel safer. It reminded me that I was deeply alone.

My mother.

My mother created this place where I now stood.

But she could not protect me from what I was becoming, a woman who was losing control of herself and the abilities that coursed beneath her skin.

I released a breath, sinking deeper until part of my chest was covered. The water was thicker and more buoyant than a typical bath. It was salt water, so viscous that I was sure I could float on the surface with little effort. I licked my lips against the mist of it in the air and tasted it on my tongue.

It felt good. It always felt good when I let go like this.

As the silver began to ebb, I looked around the room as if there might be more clues about my mother's presence, but there was nothing. No trinkets. No plants. No echoes of who she'd been aside from this pool, designed for Silvers like us.

The Phantom stood above me, watching me lazily. The white scars across his chest didn't hide the muscle. If anything, they only made the corded ridges beneath his tattered shirt more stark, more undeniable.

My vulnerability crept into the space where the silver leaked from my veins.

I was alone.

I was alone in a hidden part of the compound with a man I did not know, who made my skin buzz with awareness and my senses spike with adrenaline. A man who did not feel safe. A man who had yet to even show me his face.

My eyes tracked subtly to the hallway beyond where the Phantom stood. If I needed to outrun him, could I make it up the elevator before he caught me?

No. There was no way.

He would be on me before the elevator doors even clicked open.

If I screamed, would anyone hear me?

"They wouldn't," the Phantom's deep tenor said above me as if reading my thoughts, his voice echoing lightly around the room.

He'd moved closer while I'd been contemplating an escape.

Slowly, so slowly, my eyes tracked up to meet his masked face where he stood at the edge of the pool. My breathing caught in my chest.

He liked that I was afraid.

I coiled the silver back into myself, suddenly aware I might need it for a fight.

"Tayna would find me."

"And would you like that?" I felt caught in his gaze, like a fly spun in the spiderweb, only waiting for him to consume me.

He didn't move.

He didn't come closer, but I took a step back in the pool. My silver was almost depleted, but not entirely. Even then, what could my silver do to protect me against this man if my touch hadn't burned him at all? He didn't seem affected by me in the least.

For the first time in a long time, I felt powerless.

"I love Tayna," I said, swallowing against the fear but failing to keep the tremor from my words.

The Phantom laughed, low and rasping and horrible.

"I'm leaving," I said, my steps sluggish, pulled against the salt water as I waded back toward the stairs. But the Phantom stopped my exit. He moved so quickly, meeting me at the edge. He stepped into the water, forcing me back into the pool.

"What are you doing?" I demanded, backing up farther, glancing over my shoulder.

I could swim. I could pull myself up onto the ledge and run.

But where the water came up to my ribs, it barely skimmed his stomach. He was at an advantage over me in every way. I had a sudden flash of him pushing my head under the surface. He hadn't shown me violence like that. Not yet. But I knew, intrinsically, that he would make such brutality seem simple.

"Tell me you love him again," the Phantom said, his words dark and toying. "Convince me."

"Stop." I didn't want to play this game. Not like this. This had nothing to do with Tayna.

And maybe that was part of the problem.

This wasn't about Tayna.

This was about me, and as much as Tayna was my protector, in the end, he couldn't save me from this. Even with my silver contained, I still didn't feel in control.

I continued backing up until my shoulders hit the lip of the pool, the pebbled surface rough against my skin.

"Say it," the Phantom demanded in a low hiss.

That dark uncertainty coiled in my belly.

I had the urge to run just to see what this Phantom would do if I tried.

"I love him," I breathed. The words were stunted on my tongue.

I *did* love him. Tayna, more than anyone else, deserved my love. But I felt my heart squeeze as I said the words, willing them to be true.

The Phantom only shook his head.

"I love him," I said again, forcing conviction into each word. He was just getting into my head. He was playing a sick game by making me say it, making me convince him like this. As if he was owed my sincerity. "I've always loved him."

But the Phantom kept moving closer.

"I love him." It sounded more desperate now, louder and pleading even as I felt the words fall short. "I—"

The Phantom pinned me against the side of the pool, his body enveloping around mine as his arms stretched wide to either side of me. The spider was savoring his meal.

"I—" I tried again but stopped as his dark gaze met mine, full of wicked humor and pitiless certainty.

He didn't press his body into mine, instead keeping me caged by the threat of him. But he was close, so dangerously close.

A tear tracked through the salt water on my face.

The Phantom caught it with his gloved hand, rubbing it between leather-covered fingers.

I opened my mouth again to object, to insist, to—

The Phantom caught my jaw in one gloved hand, halting the words in my throat.

And I didn't struggle.

Even as I knew I should.

My silver should be sparking.

It wasn't.

His dark eyes studied my face as he held me.

"I liked watching you in the library," he breathed.

I swallowed.

I'd known he'd been watching. He'd seen me unravel in every way possible, and now he was stealing the final threads.

Something dark coiled in my belly.

"I think you liked it too."

I jerked from his grasp then, and he let me.

Still he continued, "I think you need more than soft touches and innocent rendezvous."

"No," I shook my head.

"I think you came as hard as you did because you knew I was watching."

I continued shaking my head.

It felt like a hollow denial.

He hadn't hurt me. Not physically. But he invaded me in deeper ways, exposing parts of me I didn't want to see.

Still, he kept me caged between his arms, even as I refused to look at him. "I think you'd like to be my little pet, Lissa, dragged into the darkness with me. You are not meant to be a creature of the light. No matter how much you want to be."

"You're wrong," I insisted, even as that pull in my veins unfurled at his wicked words.

The Phantom bent close to my ear. My breath caught in my chest as I thought of that silver canine he wore. Would he bite me? Was this some sort of payment for helping me and bringing me down here?

My body shivered against the thought.

I would fight.

But instead, he spoke. His words were dark and damning. "Are you turned on right now?"

I shoved him, hard, lashing out with everything I had left.

He only laughed, merciless and deep, as he released me.

I scrambled at the edge, clawing my way over the side of the pool and onto the stone. My knee scraped against the rough surface, but I barely felt the pain.

I didn't look back as I ran from the room, but still, I caught his final words as they echoed around the space. "I'm going to enjoy seeing how far you can run, Lissa, before you realize this is who you were always meant to be."

35

Lissa

Tayna was awake and pacing the room when I burst inside, turning to scramble with the lock on the door as if the Phantom might have followed me back through the halls. My feet were bare, my steps leaving dirty puddles on the tile floor.

My pulse was racing, my silver sputtering erratically at my fingers for all the small sparks I had left.

"Lissa?" Tayna stalked toward me. "Where were you?"

His voice was panicked as he reached for me.

But I skirted his grip. "No!" I put my hands out reflexively, as if that would help. "My silver—" And thankfully, he paused. "Just let me get it under control."

I was shaking. My body was shaking. My nervous system was completely out of sorts. We needed to leave. We needed to leave now.

The Phantom's words trailed me.

What if it was already too late?

"What the fuck happened?" Tayna demanded, his hands hovering like all he wanted to do was reach for me. "Why are you wet?"

But what was I supposed to say?

"One of the Phantoms…"

"Which one?" He was already looking at the door. I knew he'd hunt the man down. But after everything that had happened tonight, I just wanted to leave this place. We had to leave. I couldn't stay here anymore. That Phantom was my ghost, and he was haunting me.

…This is who you were always meant to be.

I shook my head against the doubt that began to creep in again.

I just needed to get control of myself.

He'd manipulated me. He'd twisted my thoughts and self-doubt until he'd made me believe I didn't know myself. But I did. I did know myself.

I thought of the cars on the beach and the burned woman dragging herself through the sand because of my silver. I thought of the men outside Madam Cartenoth's shop that I had almost killed for threatening me. And I thought of Tayna, who deserved my love more than anyone, and still, I'd hesitated.

My silver sparked, and I flinched as the electric current shocked me back to the moment.

"Lissa… fuck." Tayna's voice anchored me and, god, I needed the anchor. "Who did this to you?"

How could I tell him I'd done this to myself?

I choked on the words. "One of the Phantoms. The one who's always with Olita. He has these eyes—"

"What eyes?"

"They're… they remind me of Gideon. He has these black eyes but sometimes they shine blue. Gideon's used to do that, and I just thought—"

"Black eyes?"

"Yes."

"He has black eyes?"

"Well, kind of… Tayna, I know it's not Gideon. I know he isn't Gideon, and that it's impossible that—"

But Tayna was stalking around the side of the room, going for his bag, beginning to shove clothes into his pack before my mind could even catch up with what was happening.

"What are you doing?" He wasn't helping the fear that was still spiking my silver.

"Pack your things, Lissa," he directed, only looking up to pull a worn hoodie over his head. "We're leaving. *Now.*"

"What?"

Yes, I wanted to leave. I knew we had to leave, but his sudden panic, before I'd even explained myself, didn't make any sense. None of what had happened tonight made any sense. I was confused. My mind was confused. My body was...

Fuck.

"Lissa." He said my name like a command. "Pack your things. I will explain on the road."

Something in what I'd said had made Tayna just as afraid as I was now. He'd asked about the Phantom's eyes. And—

"Do you know him?" I asked, approaching where he had turned to shove my things into my bag for me since I was too stunned to be useful.

He pulled out a sweater and handed it to me. "Put this on."

And I did, even as I was still shaking.

"Who is he?" I pressed again.

"I'll explain everything, Liss, I promise. But right now, we *have* to go. We never should have come here. If I had known, we never would have—" He shook his head, letting out a deep exhale. "Can I touch you?"

I glanced down at my fingers, still feeling unsteady, but at least I wasn't sparking anymore. So I nodded, and he took my hand, hooking his fingers around mine. Slinging my pack over my shoulder, I let him lead me into the corridor.

"What about Laykin and Enver?" I hissed, trying to keep up with his brisk pace.

"They've made their choices."

"Tayna," I balked at his callous dismissal. "They're my friends!"

I didn't leave them at the Cards, and I wasn't about to leave them now.

Tayna sighed, pausing and turning back to me. "Lissa, you don't understand. That Phantom—"

We heard the heels clicking down the hallway before we saw the shadows closing in on either side of us.

Phantoms.

Tayna whirled, pulling me behind his body as if he could shield me from his mother and the Phantom who walked beside her. Everything that had happened tonight, everything that happened between us at that pool, was a turning point I was only beginning to understand.

"You," Tayna snarled at the Phantom. His voice was low and dangerous, even as we were the prey and the hunters closed in on us from all sides. I knew then that we would fight. We would fight our way out of this. Together.

I would leave this place with Tayna. I would get as far away from the Veiled as I could, and things would make sense again. I could fix all of this.

I could fix myself.

Olita cocked her head but held her ground as she stopped in front of us. She ran her tongue over her teeth. She had deep burgundy lips and black-rimmed eyes even at this late hour, and her white suit was neatly pressed as if she hadn't been getting ready for bed at all. She folded her hands across her body, standing like she was a giant towering over her son.

"Come now, Tayna," Olita said. "Is that how you greet your brother after all these years?"

"Your—" I looked at the Phantom, then back at Olita.

But Tayna was already lunging forward, even as the Phantoms on either side of him rushed in to hold him back. He broke free of their grasp with surprising force, barreling toward the dark-eyed Phantom standing tall in the center of the corridor. His hands were clasped behind his back, and he was watching me. His body was positioned to face me fully as if he couldn't care less what was happening with Tayna.

Even as Tayna rushed him, even as I yelled his name to stop him, even as Tayna's fist connected with the man's mask, the Phantom didn't falter from watching me. It was the force of the blow that finally had him staggering. The mask flew from his face as he hit the ground, catching himself with his gloved hands.

The first thing I saw was his silver canine as he laughed. He licked at the blood that trickled from his lip at a split from Tayna's hand.

The second thing I saw was the scars.

Half of his face was riddled with raised, crisscrossed scars. It looked like a bolt of lightning had struck him, sending tendrils from his forehead to his cheek. The splinters of it reached as far as his neck before tapering beneath his shirt to create the ripples I'd seen earlier.

His dark hair was pushed back, having been tucked beneath the mask, revealing his olive skin. He had a straight, narrow nose and prominent jaw. And the way he laughed, his shoulders shook with it as he tilted his head, preparing for another blow, yet not putting up a fight in return.

"Tayna, stop!" I screamed, finding my voice amid the chaos.

He looked so familiar... yet... yet...

He very clearly wasn't Gideon.

Tayna's brother.

My heart lurched as my silver jolted, and I threw out my hands between the two men. "Stop!"

Tayna barely managed to hold himself back before connecting with the electricity bubbling from my fingertips.

"What are you doing, Lissa?" he demanded. "Get out of the way."

Tayna was panting heavily, not taking his eyes from the man on the ground as the other Phantoms closed in around him, pulling him back.

Olita had stepped to the side of the fray, watching her sons with a raised eyebrow.

I didn't move.

"Who are you?" I demanded over my shoulder, once it was clear Tayna had regained some semblance of control.

My silver sparked.

"Answer me!" I demanded.

The black-eyed Phantom stood, dusting off his jacket and grinning. "Good to see you, too, Brother." His voice was the low rumble I'd come to know in the days I'd been at the Veiled. He licked at his bloodied lip.

Red blood.

"We're leaving," Tayna spat at him.

"And miss all the fun?" His black eyes sparked. "We're just getting started."

36

Lissa

"I thought your brother was dead?" My words were strained. "I thought your brother was killed in the fighting over thirteen years ago?"

"So did I." Tayna turned to his mother and then back to the black-eyed Phantom, who was still smirking, which only made the scars on his face deepen.

His eyes shone as they met mine, and I had to look away. The familiarity of them still had me reeling. Now, without the mask, the similarities were even more striking. The recognition felt like a knife to my heart.

The swelling and cuts from Tayna's blows were already healing as the Phantom stood to his full height in front of me, and silver sparked at my fingers just by the look on his face. He was so smug, so pleased with this turn of events.

I realized he wanted me to see him fully.

He wanted me to know the face behind the mask.

"How did you survive, Gavril?" Tayna asked the man, positioning himself just slightly in front of me. The angle of his body meant he could easily intercept if Gavril tried to reach for me.

Gavril shrugged nonchalantly, his fingers curling toward the scars on his face as if to say that it wasn't entirely smooth sailing.

Gavril.

I took in the name as I took in the man standing before me. There was something more boyish about him than I'd ever seen with Gideon. Maybe that wasn't the right word... playful? He smiled easily, whereas Gideon had reserved his smiles for me on special occasions. Smirks, sure, but this open laughter? It made the blacks of his eyes sparkle, his canines flashing silver with the promise of mischief.

"But he—you—I thought you were..."

The words died on my lips. Because the hope had been silly, and voicing it felt even more foolish.

"You wanted me to be my brother." Gavril traced his tongue over his canine as if tasting the word.

"Tayna..." I shook my head. All of the pieces coming together in my mind. "Your..."

Gavril dipped his head in a nod of confirmation.

Olita cut in, "Gideon and Gavril are twins. Fraternal but, well, you're clearly picking up on the family resemblance. They both took after their father more than me. Tayna's father's genes were weaker." She shrugged and waved, as if that explained why Tayna looked more like her.

"You're brothers." I felt like I needed to sit down. My fingers flailed as if searching for something to brace myself against the tidal wave of truth.

"Half brothers," Tayna growled.

"That's how Gideon recognized you that day on the cliffs?"

"Gideon and I never met. I had no idea he was my brother, but I recognized his eyes. I didn't want to believe it. Those black eyes. I'll never forget those black fucking eyes." He looked into Gavril's now, glaring like he might punch him again.

"And you—" I took a step toward Gavril, but Tayna reached a hand across my chest to stop me from getting any closer to him. "No!"

I snapped, my silver sparking as I pushed away his arm. "You didn't die that day."

My voice cracked on the words. If Gavril was here and alive, then it meant Gideon really was dead. He was gone. Gavril saw the thoughts flickering across my face as I blinked away tears.

He noticed my pain, and ran his tongue along that canine, before gesturing a hand across his face. "I became a Phantom."

The scar across Tayna's eye was a small scratch compared to the mottled skin along the right side of Gavril's face. Gideon must have done something truly terrible to cause injuries this lasting, even with the help of silver.

"This is why you wanted my loyalty?" I turned on Olita. "This is the secret you've been keeping? But why keep Gavril a secret?"

"My son is the key to a better world, and Gideon already tried to kill him once," Olita explained. "They were two sides to the same coin. With Gavril gone, Gideon had free rein to control this city—to control you. We were hoping we'd get the chance to speak to you and explain. We are not your enemies. There's a reason your mother trusted me, Lissa, and if you choose to trust me too, I will tell you everything. There's so much to tell you."

"The key to a better world?"

But Olita just pursed her lips. She'd said all she would say until I agreed to join her ranks at the Veiled.

I glanced back at Tayna, who looked like he wanted to reach for me and yank me from this place. His hands were balled into fists, and he was watching Gavril like he was waiting for the man to attack. I was wary, too, especially after everything that had already happened tonight. But I also knew there was so much Tayna didn't know, either.

I couldn't accept a lifetime of unanswered questions. I was in this game now. I would play this game. I would see this through. I couldn't turn back now when I was so close to the answers I so desperately wanted.

"Lissa—" Tayna seemed to sense the decision swirling to the surface within me. "Lissa, we need to leave."

"Why?" I asked, finally turning to him.

"You know why. She isn't asking for a day or a week or a month. She's asking for your loyalty. Permanently."

I turned back to Olita. "And will you force me to stay at the Veiled?"

"You're free to leave at your leisure."

"And you'll agree to negotiate an alliance with the Whigs? We want to form a council of representatives who will speak on behalf of the gangs and this city."

Olita quirked an eyebrow. "To what end?"

Her question threw me. "What do you mean, to what end?"

"What's the purpose of this council?"

"To stop the fighting in the city. To allow for growth and opportunities. To help people feel safe in their homes. To see kids educated and not starved in the streets."

Olita smirked. "You're thinking too small."

"It's not impossible," I countered. "I've read about it in dozens of books. It's worked before."

"Mmm," Olita mused. "Did it now? I think the crumbling city beyond my walls would suggest otherwise."

"Then what do you want for this city if not to rebuild it?"

"We must begin anew. We must start fresh and think of progress. There is no use in going backward."

"The Whigs want progress and peace. Those are my terms. You agree to this alliance, and I'll consider your offer. Now that the Cards are gone, you don't have anything to prove to anyone, Olita. The Veiled is the strongest gang in the city, and signaling your willingness to cooperate with the other factions would go a long way toward peace."

"I will not agree to your make-believe peace." Olita waved me off. "But I will agree that I will not attack the Whigs unless they come for me or provoke my people first."

I looked at Gavril, that feral glint in his eye. I remembered his words when we were in the pool.

I'm going to enjoy seeing how far you can run, Lissa.

I thought of that day on the beach at the Cards' compound. Gideon had dared me to run, and I had sprinted. I'd known he would give chase. I wanted him to give chase. It was different with Gavril. He was a more feral darkness that spoke of a danger I didn't yet understand.

"And if I don't accept your deal?" I asked Olita. "What then?"

Her lip curled. "I have no use in my ranks for those I can't trust."

"And you'll let us leave?"

Her eyes narrowed as she considered. We knew her secrets. We knew Gavril was still alive.

The Phantoms around us waited. I balled my fists against the silver threatening at my fingers in anticipation of her words.

I would fight.

I would unleash every bit of the silver in my blood if she tried to force us to stay.

Finally, she spoke. "As I said, I have no use for disloyal rebels." Olita turned on her heels, and over her shoulder, she said. "Now get out."

The relief nearly clouded my vision.

Leave. We could leave. And that would give me time to think. It would be the space I needed to feel like myself again, to remember who I was and what I believed.

Tayna grabbed my hand.

Gavril watched the gesture with that keen amusement pulling his scars taut. Even with his injuries, he was a striking man, just like his brother. But there was a mania there that also had me taking a step back. It made me not want to turn my back on him, not want to expose myself to him in any way.

"The Phantoms will see you out," he growled.

"We know the way," Tayna countered quickly, pulling me toward the corridor.

I felt relieved at the idea of walking away from this place with its manipulations and its games and its secrets. Tonight had been enough for me to know it was the right decision.

Still my eyes tracked a final time to Gavril.

I felt the pull in my belly one more time.

Leaving.

Yes, we were leaving.

We had to leave.

But the Phantoms blocked our path, and we halted abruptly at their closeness.

"One final piece of business," Olita sighed, and I froze. "You *have* benefited from my hospitality for nearly a week, and I've gotten nothing in return. Maybe another trade is fair since you're leaving without agreeing to my deal?"

Of course, she wouldn't let it be that easy.

"What do you want?" I turned slowly toward her again. Dread crept along my spine.

My eyes went to the Phantom—to Gavril—his midnight gaze still gleaming wickedly at the game.

Maybe there was no walking out of the Veiled.

"That necklace you keep tucked beneath your clothing. The diamond one? It's a pretty trinket, isn't it?" Olita mused, caressing a finger beneath her lip.

My hand fluttered to the paved diamonds beneath my shirt. "It was a gift."

"And now it can be your gift to me for my hospitality." Olita's red lips widened with delight at this bargain.

I looked at Tayna and then back at Olita.

There was a choice here, a dangerous choice.

Gavril slipped his mask casually back into place. The gesture had the hair rising along my skin as if a chill had suddenly picked up along the night air.

Could I channel enough silver to escape?

But what did the necklace matter? Gideon was gone. Olita was right. It was just a trinket, really. Precious gems held no value in our world. It was simply a thing of beauty. And if it would get us out of here without incident, it was worth it, right?

But it was the only thing I had left from him.

"If you want silver, I'll give you silver," I offered.

Olita's eyes narrowed at me. The silence hung thick between us as she weighed my offer.

And then her lips twisted. "No. I think I'd like the necklace."

I swallowed and resisted the urge to take a step back. There wasn't anywhere to go.

"Why, if it's useless to you?" I pressed. "It's just a relic."

"Then give it to me." Her words were light, but something underneath made me pause. Something made me think there was another secret here.

"And if I don't?"

"Don't make this difficult, Lissa." Olita sighed. "Just hand it over and be on your way."

"No." The word was out before I'd even really thought it through. But I knew in my bones, I wouldn't hand it over to her. My intuition was screaming at me.

Olita took my measure.

Her grin curled into something calculating.

"Fine," she said simply.

A thread snapped in the air at the word, all the tension snapping with it.

Olita flicked her wrist, and her Phantoms closed in.

And I made my choice.

Not to run.

To fight.

To let go of the power I'd been so carefully trying to control within myself.

That fast, I was unleashed. I had just enough time to drop Tayna's hand before my silver was crackling. Reaching my arms out, I hit the circle of Phantoms surrounding us, throwing them back as if a bolt of lightning had struck the center of our group. It was all I had left. Every measly ounce of electricity I hadn't already drained in the pools.

A few of the Phantoms hit the walls of the corridor. Olita and Gavril remained standing. But barely.

My eyes connected with Gavril's for the briefest moment, just long enough to see his were shining with the gleam of excitement before I grabbed Tayna's hand and yelled, "Run!"

37

Lissa

The Phantoms gave chase.

I caught only the glint of their silver masks when I dared to toss a wild look over my shoulder. We sprinted through the corridors. My sense of direction was entirely skewed, but I trusted where Tayna led me. He'd spent the last week studying the hallways, and he remembered—maybe on instinct—how to navigate them.

"We'll never make it out of the gate!" I yelled, thinking of the way we'd come into this place, of the high fence that only opened if Olita allowed it to open.

"Just trust me," Tayna yelled back, not turning around but pulling me tighter as we ran out into the gardens, the starry night stretching before us. Only moonlight lit the path in front of us. My chest began to burn from the exertion. The breeze dried the sweat along my brow. I could feel my heart beating erratically in my throat as the adrenaline pushed me forward, forward, forward.

"Stay with me, Lissa!" Tayna called. "We're going to climb."

I saw then what he was planning. A tree was planted next to one of the walls. But they were nearly six feet tall. We would have to jump down on the other side into the caked desert clay. There was no way I could make that jump.

"We can do it!" he insisted. "Just trust me, Liss. Trust me!"

And then he was shoving me at the branches, pushing me up as I gripped the trunk and climbed. My boots scraped along the bark, but I made quick work of scaling the tree. As soon as I found my balance at the top, I spun to grab for Tayna.

The Phantoms were just breaking through the courtyard. They were gray wraiths in the night, only shifting shadows through the corridors as they spilled into the garden like smoke.

Gavril was at the front of them. His black eyes were focused entirely on me as he realized we were scaling the wall and sprinted for us. His eyes still shone with dark glee.

Tayna gripped my hand. It was the leverage he needed to scale the wall. I clenched my teeth and grunted as he found purchase on the stump beside me. I glanced over the wall, seeing only darkness below.

It was too dark.

Just a stretch of black dirt, hidden by the shadows of the wall.

Fear spiked in my belly, made hot by the adrenaline in my veins.

"We can't," I breathed. "We can't!"

But Tayna was already lowering himself. "I'll catch you. Lissa. Just jump! Follow behind me!"

And then he was gone, over the side of the wall.

"Tayna!" I screamed.

And I hesitated.

It was a breath.

A final, uncertain second at the Veiled as all the secrets behind these walls slipped through my fingers.

And Gavril's hand closed around my ankle.

Our eyes met. And in that space between moments, I imagined allowing him to drag me from this tree. I pictured him yanking my ankle and pulling me into his dark embrace.

I shouldn't want that.

A part of me did.

But I found the will to kick out at him, "Let me go!" I twisted in the branches, scrambling away from the man who dragged the darkness from my veins and liked what he saw.

"I wouldn't." He grinned, holding on tightly. "Even if that's what you really wanted."

A crazed look glazed over his eyes.

I couldn't hear Tayna below. I didn't know if he'd landed safely on the other side of the wall. I didn't know if he was okay. I didn't know if the Phantoms had already opened the gate to snatch him back in the same way Gavril gripped me now.

All I knew was this moment and the struggle, as I kicked out at Gavril, barely clinging to the branch of the tree that was my salvation. Even as it scratched along my arms and my cheek and my chest, I held fast.

I couldn't let him have me.

Even if a small part of me wanted it. I needed to know I could still choose something else.

And I realized what I had to do.

I let go.

I let go, flinging myself forward. My silver sparked to life beneath the night sky, and I pressed hard against Gavril's chest.

He didn't make a sound as he was thrown from my body with the help of my silver.

The knob of a branch scraped up my spine in a long and fiery gash that had me crying out in pain.

I barely managed to regain my footing, clambering back to the wall, gripping the edge. Without looking back, I threw my legs over the side and gave myself over to the fall.

The ground came too fast.

Strong, sturdy arms caught me, and we tumbled into the dirt.

Tayna cried out as we hit the sand in a pile of limbs.

"Tayna?" His name was a desperate plea on my lips.

He grunted but didn't respond.

"Are you hurt?" I felt for his face in the night.

"Nothing silver won't fix," he groaned. "We have to get to the truck."

The gate hadn't opened next to us.

The quiet scared me most of all, like a held breath around us.

I wasn't sure how much silver I'd hit Gavril with, but it hadn't been enough to kill him. I didn't think, at least. My silver hadn't seemed to affect him at all in the pool. But I could at least hope the jolts I'd doled out tonight would slow him down long enough so that we could escape.

It seemed unlikely.

I helped Tayna stand, his body tensing with each movement.

"Can you even walk?" I hissed.

"It's my ankle." His words were strained, and he leaned on me heavily as he took a step. "And probably a few ribs. I fell on my side."

"Okay. Okay." I braced myself under his arm, but he was so much bigger than I was. I made a sorry excuse for a crutch. "It's going to hurt, but we have to move, Tayna."

We were sitting ducks.

There was no way we'd outpace the Phantoms.

Tayna exhaled sharply as we began walking, staggering through the night.

I expected the gates to open. I expected the Phantoms to stream into the desert and drag us back behind the walls of the Veiled. But the compound had gone eerily silent. Everything was still except for Tayna and me as we shuffled our way to the Humvee.

And then a hawk screamed overhead.

Not just any hawk. It was Gavril's creature. I knew it in my bones. It soared above, circling and circling, but never coming closer.

"What is he doing?" I huffed with each step.

"Taunting us," Tayna groaned. "They're letting us go, but this isn't over."

"You were right," I said. "It was a mistake coming here."

"I swear I didn't know he was alive, Liss. I swear I didn't know."

The hawk followed us all the way to the truck, keeping its

distance overhead. By the time we reached the Humvee, my skin was covered in a fine layer of sweat and dust.

Tayna slumped against the frame as I dug around in his pack for the keys.

"I'm driving," I grumbled.

He cracked a grin, his head tilted back as he caught his breath. "Yes, ma'am."

I gave the hawk overhead one last look before climbing into the truck. Once Tayna and I were inside, I locked the doors and skidded in the dirt as I pulled away from the Veiled.

PART III

THE MATCH

38

Lissa

We drove through the remainder of the night until the first glow along the horizon illuminated the open expanse of road before us. The city was a cloudy blue cutout in front of us, shrouded in the haze of ocean mist.

No one had followed us that I could see. My eyes tracked the rearview mirror maybe more than I watched the road in front of us. Not even the hawk trailed us anymore, yet I felt like I couldn't catch my breath.

I felt like I hadn't fully left.

"Lissa—" Tayna reached for me, but I shook my head.

He paused, brow furrowed. He continued to sweat despite the air blowing throughout the truck. He needed silver, but we'd have to stop for me to give him any, and right now, the safest option was to continue into the city.

He tried again. "You have every right to be angry with me. I—"

"I'm not angry with you."

The words hung there like echoes of the night we'd just endured had imprinted their way onto my soul. I felt like crying at the darkness that seemed to cling to my skin even now, far away from the Phantom's black gaze.

I toyed absently with the diamond-paved necklace.

The Veiled had left my mind tangled. There were too many secrets to unravel. My thoughts were skipping from Gavril to my mother to the necklace still hanging at my nape. Olita had wanted it more than she wanted my Silver blood, which had to mean something.

She'd been interested in it the moment she'd seen it at dinner that first night. But it wasn't until tonight that I realized there was a deeper reason.

She'd risked many lives to demand I hand it over. I could have easily killed her Phantoms with my silver. She hadn't attempted to keep me prisoner. She hadn't been interested in my blood. No, in the end, she'd wanted jewelry.

"You look like you're angry," Tayna said, his voice dry. He needed water. We both needed water.

I *was* angry.

I was furious.

It was bubbling deep in my gut, and if I hadn't been so exhausted, it would have sparked at my fingertips. As it was, the rage I felt only made my body and mind feel that much more fragile.

The anger was for myself.

How could I be mad at Tayna when I'd kept the secret that had led us to this night?

I hadn't told Tayna about the Phantom. He'd been watching me since the first day we'd arrived at the Veiled. He'd taunted me, watched me, and spun his web until I'd ended up in that pool with him, pinned against the wall and wondering if he was about to sink his teeth into my neck. And worst of all, part of me had wanted it.

If I'd told Tayna about Gavril's attention after that first day, maybe things would have turned out differently.

So why hadn't I told Tayna?

That was the deeper fear, the deeper anger with myself.

"I understand why you didn't tell me about Gideon," I said finally.

"I wasn't hiding it from you," he said.

"I know."

"You know?"

"Or, well, I understand." I couldn't bring myself to look at him. "Sometimes there are truths our minds don't want to untangle. And if we voice them, it makes them real."

The pit in my stomach seemed to expand at my words. I was excusing Tayna, but I was also trying to defend myself.

Now Tayna did take my hand, and it felt good. His hand engulfed mine even as I kept it on the steering wheel. It was warm and solid and steady. He was all those things for me. But I wasn't sure I could be those things for him.

We'd left the Veiled, but a part of me still felt tethered in that place.

"We should find a place to stop," I said as we entered the outskirts of the city.

"It's a risk to be seen." Tayna removed his hand from mine to grip the door as an anchor, pulling himself upright and wincing at the movement. He tracked our surroundings, searching for signs of the gangs or anything out of the ordinary.

"We don't have much of a choice," I insisted. "We don't have any food or water, and we need to take care of the worst of your injuries."

"You're right. But I don't like it."

I didn't like it either. My hands were tight against the steering wheel. The morning mist from the ocean, so close now, curled around the truck as we drove. I looked for an inn. It couldn't be one of the run-down ones on the central strip. It had to be fancy enough to have running water and a decent bed.

The first one I spotted was more of a brothel than a hotel. Typical. As we passed, the women came into view. They were all thin—too thin—tossing their hair and bending to snuff out their cigarettes with seductive rolls of their hips.

The man standing with them sneered at us as we drove by.

I lowered the sunshade, not wanting the silver in my eyes to glint through the windows of the Humvee. The last thing we needed was popped tires and more trouble.

Especially when my silver was tapped.

The city itself was dim in the faded light of morning. Even in the summer, the marine layer from the ocean crept across the buildings. It was a drab cloud that made everything all the more gray. Gray walls, gray streets, gray people.

The Humvee drew attention, just as it had when we'd arrived in the city on our way to the Veiled. Other vehicles were on the roads, to be sure—mostly beat-up old tankers. A group of Fortas passed us in some kind of late-model Cadillac, flashing their silver grills in well-worn sneers. Theirs weren't as sophisticated as the Phantoms' canines but maybe even more menacing in their rough-hewn shapes.

I shivered.

The streets had never felt safe, but somehow, without the Cards, the roads felt wilder than before, even in the dawn. Men drank in the streets, laughing and calling to one another. They donned leather jackets, but I couldn't tell which gang they belonged to. Only a few short weeks ago, I would have said they were Cards. But now... They swaggered like they owned these streets. Without Gideon, was it anyone's for the taking? And what of the market? Had it survived like normal, without the Cards protecting the stalls and vendors?

The dread turned my stomach. I hadn't thought about what would happen to the people at all. I'd thought the Cards falling would be a good thing for everyone. I thought it would mean we'd be one step closer to peace. But from the looks of the city, it had only spelled more havoc, more chaos.

Tayna rested a hand on my leg. "We'll make it better. We don't need the Veiled."

I only nodded absently and turned back to the road. I had to believe that was true. Otherwise, what had all of this been for? I wouldn't let Kenji's death be in vain. I wouldn't let Calliope grow up in this city like those girls on the streets.

And Gideon... would building a better city make his death feel justified, too?

I held that thought, now a comfort somehow along with the ache, as we pulled into the small parking lot of a motel.

It was a rickety building, with rows of rooms stacked in two stories facing the water. It would have been nice once, a beachfront property where I imagined families might gather after a long day at the ocean. Now, the metal of the roof was rusted along the edges. The once crisp white paint peeled. But I liked this spot because we could pull up close, and the rooms all faced out, which meant we could keep an eye on the Humvee.

"We don't have any money," Tayna pointed out as he gripped his ribs and tried to lift himself from the seat.

"I got it." I put a hand on his shoulder. "Just stay here."

"No fucking way." He pushed at my hand.

"Tayna—" I gave him a sidelong glance.

"You're not going in there alone."

"You're not exactly going to be useful right now if anything bad happens."

He just scowled at me.

"Plus," I said, grabbing my bag from the back. "You're not going to like what I'm going to trade to get us a room."

That made his scowl deepen. "Excuse me?"

I held up my wrist.

And he exhaled thinly, falling back into his seat against the pain in his ribs. "Goddammit, Lissa. If you're not back in five minutes, I'm coming in there."

"Better start moving now, then." I jumped from the truck and eyed him. "In your state, it'll take you five minutes just to get out of the truck."

I closed the door and slipped inside the hotel lobby before I could hear his retort.

There was a woman at the counter, middle-aged and weathered. She didn't look up when I entered, and I didn't think it was because she hadn't heard me. She was unbothered and likely used to people who didn't want to interact with her much anyway.

I approached the counter and cleared my throat.

"Thirty for the night." Her voice was a dull monotone.

"I'm hoping for a different option," I said.

"We're not a by-the-hour kind of place, girl. We—" She paused when she finally looked up at me, seeing the silver in my eyes and the dirt on my face. The way she looked at me made me feel like a street rat again. She wasn't judging. She was wary, her eyes narrowed as if seeing right through me. Suddenly, I wanted to sprint back to the truck and hide.

But I wasn't that scared mouse anymore, so I straightened, meeting the woman's gaze, letting her see the silver in my eyes.

"I'll give you a vial," I said, my voice even and sure. "We need a place for the day. We'll be gone by morning. That's worth a lot more than thirty coin. In fact, I think a vial might be enough for a permanent residence in this place."

"You're not just asking for a room, girl. I imagine you'll also expect my silence then?" The woman's nose wrinkled at her pinched expression.

"That, and for someone who can keep an eye on our vehicle. Like I said, we'll be gone by morning. And we don't want trouble."

"Something tells me you're the trouble."

"I—"

But she waved off the defense I'd been about to give. "I know who you are. Used to see you going into Tea and Trinkets on market day with your fancy cloak. A lot less dirt on your face then. You brought fish and bread for Madam Cartenoth."

I nodded, feeling my chest tighten at the reminder.

"She was a good woman."

"She was," I agreed.

"Take the room. And keep your blood. My brother'll keep an eye on your Humvee." She pulled a key from a drawer and pointed it at me with a severe look that deepened the lines on her face. "Gone by morning, understood? There's only so much trouble I can take in a month, and lord knows this has been a month for us. Maybe you most of all."

I swallowed and accepted the key.

"Upper floor. Back corner. Nicest room we have. Don't expect that mansion you're used to. But it's clean. And don't worry about your truck. No one messes with my brother around these parts. He owns the bar across the street, too. And the gangs like to drink more than they like to destroy shit. Once y'all have some rest, go see him. Tell him Antonia sent you over. They'll give you something to fill your belly."

I thought about insisting on some form of payment, but I could tell this woman—Antonia—wouldn't accept it even if I pressed, so I took the key and thanked her again, with a final promise we'd be gone by morning.

39

Lissa

Getting Tayna into the room on the second floor at the end of the hall was enough for one day, even without the hell we'd endured last night. We were both exhausted. Plus, sitting in the truck for that long stretch of time had only made his ankle swell larger, and the bruise across his ribs deepen. I'd taken one look at the purple flesh and known the priority was to get him inside.

He needed silver.

The room was clean, just like the woman at the front desk—Antonia—had promised. It was simple. A big enough bed covered in a blue patchwork quilt sat in the center. A picture of the ocean hung on the wall against a window that looked out onto the city.

I dropped our bags near the door, trying to track in as little dust as possible. Tayna slunk slowly down the wall opposite the bags.

"Getting you back on your feet will be a nightmare," I said as he sprawled his legs out in front of him.

I busied myself with digging his pocketknife out of the front pouch of his bag.

"Come here." He tilted his chin up, beckoning me to him.

My stomach twisted with the guilt still warring in me. I couldn't simply fall back into his arms, not after everything that had happened at the Veiled.

"Tayna—"

He quirked a brow, the dimples pulling at the scar across his eye. "Come *here*, Liss."

So I did. But when I moved to sit beside him, he stopped me. "Pants off first."

I hesitated. "We shouldn't."

There was nothing I wanted more than to fall into his arms. Being close with Tayna was the best way I knew to feel grounded. Yet I felt so confused about the feelings in me that the Phantom had made impossible for me to deny, even if I wanted to.

"What?" His gaze narrowed on me as if now seeing a deeper hesitation in me. "What is it?"

I suddenly felt like I might cry. It was a rush of emotions grounded in things I didn't understand.

"Come here," Tayna reached for me.

And when I shook my head, he slid along the wall to grasp my wrist, pulling me into him.

"Come here," he said again, holding me tightly.

I buried myself in his chest, murmuring against his skin. "I'm hurting you."

"No, you're not," he said into my hair. "You need me."

I nodded against him. I *did* need him.

But I was no longer sure that was enough.

"I think something's wrong with me," I admitted, my voice shaking.

"Hey," he gripped my hair and pulled me to look at him. He was so good that it made my heart ache. "Nothing is wrong with you. Did Gavril say something to you? My mother?"

I think you'd like to be my little pet, Lissa, dragged into the darkness with me.

I shook my head to clear the memory as I croaked, "I don't feel like myself."

Tayna clutched me, held me assuredly. "This is what they do, Liss. They are master manipulators. But we got out. We're gone."

It didn't feel like we were out. It felt like Gavril and Olita had let us go knowing we couldn't truly escape their games.

Tayna kissed me. It was a gentle caress, a comfort and a request. He was warm against me as I allowed myself to fold into him.

"I don't want to hurt you," I said against his mouth.

I wasn't talking about his broken ribs.

But he only deepened the kiss, pulling my legs to hook around him until I was straddling him as he tried to erase my uneasy thoughts with his mouth.

I braced my hand on the wall near his head so my full weight wasn't pressing into his hips. I could feel his length grazing along the underside of my pants. He was hard, and I shuddered with the sudden desire. After everything that had happened in the past twelve hours, it felt too good to stop. I wanted him close.

Still, we should stop.

He gently pried the knife from my fingers, flicking it open.

And I forgot why we should stop.

He was warm and sturdy beneath me. My hands traced gently beneath his shirt, along his stomach, careful to avoid his ribs. This was real. The two of us together, this was real and solid and safe.

The truth was, I was afraid. The night from the Veiled had left me with the unshakable certainty that the Phantom wasn't done with this game. But what scared me the most was that I wasn't done with the game, either. He was right. A part of me craved the darkness, and I needed Tayna to snuff it out.

"Take off your shirt," he murmured against my mouth. "I can't do it myself."

I obliged, pulling the fabric over my head and unclasping my bra until I was bare in front of him, only wearing my cotton underwear.

He didn't waste time running his hands over my skin, massaging my breasts until my head tipped back. His fingers danced over every inch of me until he finally, finally reached my center and pushed my panties aside. I was wet. I could feel how wet he'd made me.

He groaned low in his chest, pressing a finger inside me while his thumb circled my clit.

And only then did I feel the soft sting right above my left breast. It was just enough to make me gasp, my eyes falling to Tayna's enraptured expression as he tossed the knife aside, all while running that finger in and out of my core.

He watched me as he lowered his mouth to the small slice in my flesh. His eyes fixed to mine with rapt attention, and I leaned in, offering myself to him.

Tayna continued touching me, his hands running along my shoulder blades in gentle caresses as he pressed his mouth against the cut, his tongue licking over the small nick where my blood welled. It stung at first, but then he was caressing my skin with his tongue, sucking gently at the flesh and groaning. My hands twisted through his hair as I resisted the urge to writhe against his pelvis, trying desperately to hold myself still as he worked me.

It all felt deliciously good. And I had an instant where I wondered if this was what it would feel like if Gavril bit me with that silver canine—if I would lean into that pain, too.

I flinched. Not at the pain from the cut but at the sudden thought. It clawed up my throat, making me clench around Tayna's fingers.

He'd gotten into my head like Tayna said.

That was all.

I didn't want him. Of course I didn't.

I—

What I needed was more of Tayna.

His damn finger wasn't enough, even as he worked me into a frenzy. Wetness pooled at my center and goose bumps pebbled on my skin where his fingers played over my most sensitive places.

After a final flick of his tongue, he lifted his head. My mouth was waiting for him, and he captured it greedily. I pressed into him, this time more forcefully, as if the pressure of our bodies could clear my unwanted thoughts.

I groaned against him, knowing the silver was already working to heal the worst of his injuries.

I needed more.

I needed him to make me forget.

"Can you lift your arms?" I asked, fumbling with the edges of his shirt.

"Give me another minute." He laughed, his nose running along my cheek as he peppered kisses along my jaw, removing his finger just enough to circle my entrance.

"Am I hurting you?" I was breathless, and I didn't want to stop. I was afraid if I stopped, I would think of the silver mask at the edge of my vision.

"It's better. It's already better."

And then my mouth was on him, our tongues meeting as our hands explored. He moved his hand from my core, and the emptiness made me feel hollow. I wanted him inside of me. I needed the warmth of him. I needed him to make me cum, to drown me in a pleasure that would erase the darkness that coiled in the pit of my gut.

"I want you to fuck me," I said against his mouth.

"God yes," he groaned against my lips.

"I can't wait anymore."

It felt like I was still running, running from the Veiled and those moments at the pool that had made me feel like I was no longer myself.

With Tayna, with Tayna I was myself. Hadn't that always been how it had felt between us?

"I need you," I gasped.

He finally pulled his shirt over his head, and I could see the bruises along his ribs had already faded to yellow-green blotches.

"You have me," he said as I reached for his pants. "You've always had me." I gripped the length of him as he kicked his head back. The rest of his words were a low rumble in his chest. "Everything I do is for you, you know that. I love you, Liss, so damn much."

And it made me want to cry because I loved him, too, but my love didn't feel safe and secure and pure like his felt for me. Mine felt like it was made for breaking. And maybe he couldn't hold me together anymore.

Would he still love me if he saw the confused mess my mind had become?

He lifted me from the floor and carried me into the bathroom.

It was a closet of a bathroom. A toilet just inside the door, a single sink with a tiny vanity mirror on the wall and the shower taking up the final half of the space. Tayna flicked on the water and, before it was even warm, he carried me under the spray.

He pressed my back against the wall, gripping my thighs as he lined himself up at my entrance and slid inside. We both cried out at the primal feel of him bottoming out in me.

This, *this* is what I needed.

One of my hands gripped his bicep while the other scrambled for purchase against the tiled wall.

He didn't waste time, pumping his hips as the steam from the shower filled the room. We were pent up, breathing heavily, desperate for one another. I couldn't get enough of his body, of the man he had become, of the way he knew all the right ways to touch me.

I needed to come, but also desperately didn't want this to end. I wanted it to be him and me like this forever. I wanted to forget the outside world. I wanted to forget Olita and the secrets she promised in exchange for my soul. I wanted to forget Gavril and the way he'd taunted the darkness in me.

"Make me come, Tayna," I groaned, moving to reach between our bodies where I could press a finger against my clit.

But he shook his head, grabbing my wrist, water spraying across our skin as he pressed my arm against the tile.

"Not yet."

But it wasn't enough.

The pleasure wasn't enough, even as he held me at the edge.

I bit my bottom lip as he thrust up until I felt my eyes rolling back, my head leaning against the tile. His fingers kneaded into my backside where he held me, pinned against the wall. I was entirely his for the taking.

His head dipped, licking the water droplets from my skin.

"Tayna." His name was a plea. Because I needed more. I needed—

My breath hitched as he suddenly lowered me to the floor, withdrawing from me for only a moment before turning me to face the wall, the spray from the shower hitting my shoulder blades before he was encasing me with his large frame.

"Spread your legs," he said against my ear. "Wider. Ass up."

And then he sank into me from behind. "Just like that," he exhaled, quickening his pace.

I scrambled for purchase along the wall, trying to find anything to cling to.

"Harder," I begged as he held my hips, pumping into me.

My cheek pressed into the cool tile, my hands splayed on either side of me. And still I found myself grasping for something I couldn't quite name.

"More," I demanded.

And he delivered.

He reached around to press into my clit, as I greedily rubbed myself against him, desperate for the sensation.

"I'm right there with you, Liss."

But I was thinking about the Phantom. I was imagining him catching my waist in the pool before I could run away. I would struggle. But he wouln't let me leave, feral in his desire. In my mind, he was sinking that silver canine into my neck as he pushed my dress up and drove into me.

The wicked image sent me over the edge. The orgasm shattered through my body, leaving me crying out in pleasure at the overwhelming sensation as I felt him tense and then follow in his release.

Tayna.

It was Tayna.

He continued his slow pump inside me until every ounce of pleasure was wrung from my body.

I stayed pressed against the wall, shivering against the pleasure.

I'd wanted sex to make everything better.

But my mind... my mind still felt like it was searching.

I spun in Tayna's embrace, gripping him tightly, wanting so desperately to feel the same safety and grounding he'd always made me feel before.

He kissed along my shoulders. The water ran down his hair, into his eyelashes, and over his lips as he whispered, "I love you."

And I pressed my lips against his bare chest, burying myself into him as I echoed the words. "I love you, too, Tayna. I love you so much."

Thankfully, with the shower, he couldn't see the tears mixing in with the droplets on my face.

40

Lissa

By the time I woke up, evening was falling.

As much as I didn't want to move, we needed to find food. And then we needed to leave. Life on the farm was calling. Only a few days, and we would be back to that peaceful existence with Grant and Rixa and, yes, even Alaric. I couldn't wait to see Calliope and Phenola again, too. I imagined Dan and Ann standing guard at her crib. That was all I needed to get my mind straight. Home was calling.

I would feel better at the farm.

I would forget thoughts of Gavril and feel like myself again.

It would be me and Tayna.

I curled against Tayna's sleeping frame, cocooning myself within his warmth and running my lips along his neck, just above his collarbone.

He let out a soft hum of approval, his hands coming around to pull me closer into his chest.

"We need to get up." My voice was low, still clogged with sleep.

His chin brushed up and down against my head where he cradled me to his chest, but he didn't move. Instead, he wrapped his leg around mine and relaxed back into the pillows.

My stomach growled so loudly I was sure he could feel it against his belly, too. He chuckled softly. "I know, I know," he said, still not opening his eyes. "Food."

"And we need to check on the truck," I said, beginning to peel myself from his body.

"When we get back to the farm, we aren't moving for a week," Tayna grumbled, also pulling himself from the bed.

My heart twisted.

Everything would feel right when we were home.

Sleeping had helped.

I felt better.

We dressed, brushed our teeth, and attended to our needs in the bathroom. It'd been more than five years since we shared a small space like this, yet my body fell into a natural pattern around him. It was effortless, moving and trading space together.

I unclasped the necklace from around my neck, even as it felt wrong to take it off. I wanted to keep it on. I wanted to keep it close. But instead of wearing it, I tucked it carefully into my pocket. If it truly had more value than I realized, it wasn't good to flaunt it in the city, especially not when we were trying to keep a low profile.

Tayna stood in front of me, taking a wide stance so he was more at eye level with me and pulling my hoodie over my head, down my forehead until it was nearly covering my eyes.

"Just like old days," he said.

"Yes, except you're about a foot wider."

"You callin' me fat?" he teased.

"You know what I'm calling you," I said, trailing my hands down the ridges of his biceps.

"I like how you've changed, too." His eyes fell to my chest and then to the curves of my hips.

"Stop looking at me like that." I flattened my palms against his chest, gently pressing him back. "We can't stay in this room anymore."

He grabbed my hands, quickly pulling me in for a peck on the lips before releasing me. "Let's go," he said, his voice low and his golden eyes hot as he threaded his fingers through mine and pulled me to the door.

My chest twisted with his earnestness as I fell into step beside him.

It was a beautiful summer evening. The gloominess of the day had given way to a watercolor sunset. The majesty of the ocean against the colors of the sky made the contrast of the ruined city behind me even more striking. If only I could have seen it at its height, when the city was thriving and the dock in the distance wasn't crumbling.

The Tank's ship and a few fishing boats were the lone vessels for as far as the eye could see. It was a quiet, peaceful evening, but night-time was when the city came alive.

"Humvee's still here," Tayna said, looking over the railing of our room. "Looks like no one's messed with it. The woman's brother must really not be someone you want to fuck with in this city."

Just across the way was the bar Antonia had mentioned, and I could see people—mostly men— milling around out front. I pulled my hood further down my forehead.

"Maybe we should wait until it's darker," he murmured, and I imagined how my silver eyes must be glinting against the golden rays of the setting sun.

"We need to get on the road," I insisted, anxious to get back to the farm. I didn't want to stay in this city any longer than we had to. Just enough to eat. We'd taken our belongings from the room, intending to return the keys before we left. "And what are they going to do anyway? I can easily take anyone who tries to mess with us."

"You do have a point." Tayna side-eyed me. "A quick bite then."

He kept my hand tucked in his, walking just ahead of me, his body shielding mine as we made our way into the bar.

It was loud, some kind of old-school rock playing over the speakers. Pool tables were scattered throughout, and the bar lined the entire right wall. It was a decent-sized place, but it was definitely at capacity with the number of people already inside.

Crowds were good, though. We were less likely to attract attention.

Plumes of cigarette smoke wafted around us as Tayna pulled us to one of the back tables. I tried to avoid choking on the air, grateful to see the booth Tayna found was away from the worst of it. He slid in beside me, not on the opposite side of the table, pocketing me into the seat.

"If anything, I should be the one guarding you," I grumbled.

But he smirked, crossing his arms on the table. "Not how this works, Liss, even with your fancy silver."

"What'll it be?" a man asked, coming to our table.

"Evening," Tayna grinned. "Antonia sent us. She said you'd—"

The man's gaze cut to me, then over his shoulder at the rest of the bar. "Good you kept a low profile," he said. "It's active in the city tonight. Dia's been stirring up trouble."

"What kind of trouble?" Tayna leaned in, lowering his voice like the man, who must be the brother. He was stocky, but he didn't look particularly dangerous. His dark hair was balding on the sides, and his beard curled in different directions, just like his hair, giving him a haphazard look. I wondered what he'd done to earn his reputation around the city.

The man glanced over his shoulder, then back to us. "My sister promised you a meal, but I require payment for trading my secrets, whether she likes it or not."

The man was eyeing me now, and I knew he didn't want coin.

We'd prepared for this. Tayna and I had replenished the vials he'd brought with him before we'd left the room. I now had four small containers filled with my silver blood. I was going to leave one on the desk for Antonio when we left the hotel, but well, her brother could have it if it meant information. I produced one, pinched it between my fingers, and slid it discreetly across the table.

The man pocketed it quickly.

"I'll be back with your beers, and we have fried fish and slaw tonight. We can talk while you eat. If I stay here too long, it'll raise suspicion." The man looked over his shoulder again at the crowd. Indeed, a few people were throwing glances our way. But then he was gone.

"Hopefully, we didn't just lose a vial of silver," Tayna muttered.

"Something feels off, Tayna. Whatever this trouble is with Dia, it has everyone twitchy."

"Agreed." Tayna scanned the bar. "We'll eat, hear whatever information he has to offer, and then get out of this place. Plus"—his hand traced my thigh under the table—"I want that week in bed with you all to myself."

"Only a week?" I grinned. "Why not a month?"

"How about a lifetime?"

My gaze snapped to him.

"Don't look so horrified." He laughed. "We can make it official whenever you want. But I'm in this for the long haul with you, Liss. This is forever." He squeezed my thigh, and I swallowed against the rush of emotion.

Of course that was what I wanted, too.

Yes.

That was the right answer, right? I could picture building a life with him on the farm. I could picture that quiet, peaceful existence... couldn't I?

I *did* want Tayna. But I didn't know how to have him while letting go of the rest. The Veiled and Gavril had left me uncertain of everything.

But what if that uncertainty was because I wasn't meant to live the rest of my life on a farm in a quiet life, feeling okay about the fact that I knew so little about my silver and where I came from.

It didn't feel like enough.

Even if it meant I got to keep Tayna.

Before I could figure out a response, the bar owner returned with our beers.

"The food will be up next," he said.

"And our conversation?" Tayna stopped him.

"Right." The man glanced over his shoulder before sliding into the booth across from us, folding his hands on the table. "Let's make this quick." He leaned close enough that I could see the dirt under his fingernails even in the dim light. "Dia's been recruiting. I'd venture to say with even more success than Gideon was having at the end there. The man's a brute."

I tried to hide my flinch at that part. "We know."

"Bet you do." He raised an eyebrow at me, glancing at my shoulder to where the tattoo was hidden beneath my sleeves. "Apparently, he's allied with the Fortas. The Tanks are even giving in to discussions. And there's rumors of some new rebel group that's been popping up around town."

Tayna opened his mouth, but the man cut him off.

"You can keep your secrets there. I know what you're going to say, and I won't press. That wasn't part of our deal. But you should know, Dia likes the bloodshed. It's different from with Gideon. He's meaner. Rowdier. There's tension all over this city. Fights have been spilling into the bar. I've had to drag two bodies out at the end of the night just in the past month."

My appetite soured even as a man dropped off the food at our table.

The steaming fish and coleslaw actually looked pretty good, but I found myself forcing down a bite as my nerves spiked.

"Anyway, that's what I've got. The bloody business with the Cards wasn't the end. It was the beginning of the bloodshed. So far, the Veiled and Olita's Phantoms have been holed up at their compound. They're staying out of the fighting for now. Probably waiting and watching as the remaining gangs kill each other off. But my money's on Dia, snake in the grass that man. Mark my words."

"And that's all you know?" Tayna pressed. "We gave you a full fucking vial of silver. Anything else going around about the rebels?"

"Only that Dia's been hunting for them. And he'll find 'em too." The man eyed us meaningfully. "It's only a matter of time."

I took a long pull of my beer.

Tayna took a long look at the man. "And are there rumors about the location of this group?"

The man shrugged. "North's all I've heard. Past the Card's compound."

Tayna nodded, giving no sign to confirm or deny the location. The Whigs worked hard to spread that rumor, to send Gideon on a wild goose chase beyond the city. As long as Dia continued with the same search pattern, we'd be safe.

We finished our food but left most of the beer untouched. We had a long road ahead, after all. The bar owner had agreed to fill up our canteens with water and gave us a hunk of cheese and some oranges, which were all he could offer us in the way of sustenance for the road. When Tayna reminded him, again, that we'd given him an entire vial of silver, he'd thrown in some kind of hard bread, too. It would be enough.

One more night and we'd be home.

With full bellies and as many secrets as this place could offer, we stood, weeding through the crowd that had clamored inside.

A hand grabbed me before I could reach the door, yanking me backward. My grip on Tayna jerked free as I lost him in the crowd.

"Lissa?" Shocked surprise twisted my name from a smooth female voice.

"Samiya?" I asked, just as surprised to see Banu's right hand in this place.

"You're back? You're in the city?"

I tried to keep my head low with the crowd of people around us. "We're just passing through. We're on our way out now."

"And what of the Veiled? What of Kavi and Valenia?" The missing Silver women from the Tanks. "Did you find them?"

I shook my head. "I'm so sorry, Samiya. I was planning to send a message to Banu once we were back with the Whigs. We didn't find anything at the Veiled."

Her lips thinned. "There's no hope then."

I wanted to reach for her hand, but I didn't think that was a gesture the warrior woman would appreciate, so I said, "If I hear anything, I promise I'll send word. I'll do whatever I can to help you find them."

"Lissa." Tayna grabbed my arm, scanning the room.

"We have to go," I said to Samiya. "But please tell Banu... tell him we..."

What could I possibly say? What did I have to show for my trek into the Veiled? Nothing. Nothing I could offer her would make any difference or make her people any safer. If anything, what we'd learned from the Veiled is that Olita would not help. She and Gavril were satisfied to remain isolated behind their stucco walls while the city fell to gang wars and bloodshed.

Samiya's pursed lips turned into a sneer when she realized I had nothing to say. "Only our allies when it benefits you, then?"

"Of course not!" I insisted. "We'll fight with you. We'll stand with you. Whatever it takes."

And I meant it. I didn't want to abandon this fight.

"You say that as you're what? Running back to your peaceful little farm and leaving us all here?"

"We won't."

I said the words, but wasn't that exactly what Tayna and I planned to do? We were leaving this city to spend our time lounging in bed together, hiding away on the farm? All while this city and our allies needed us.

The woman was only confirming the feeling I'd had worming into my gut since I'd decided to go to the Veiled. I was not meant to be someone who ran from this game.

"We'll talk to Alaric and—"

"It doesn't matter." She scoffed, her eyes taking the measure of me and finding me lacking. "Banu may believe in you and your special silver, but I'm not impressed. So run, Malkia. Try to run. See how long that lasts. Dia will find you. Rumor is he's already close. Rumor is he'll have that place burning by the end of the month. Hell, Lissa, half of this bar is already allied with him. Banu even took a meeting. So go. Run. See how well that works out for the two of you."

And with that, she pushed through the crowd, leaving me to

contend with the weight of my foolishness. Tayna and I might be together, but that simple life was still an impossible dream. Not because of the threat of Dia, but because my heart would not be content with the quiet.

41

Lissa

Tayna and I spent the ride to the base of the hill, where we'd begin hiking, discussing the options for the Whigs. Flee or stay. Fight or run.

Samiya's words repeated over and over in my mind.

Dia will find you.

Rumor is he's already close.

Rumor is he'll have that place burning by the end of the month.

My fingers toyed over the diamond necklace in my pocket, unable to shake the nagging at the back of my mind that told me I was never meant for running. I would not hide in the shadows, but I would protect the Whigs. The first step was to make sure the community was safe, and then I would have to make a more difficult decision about my role in this city.

One thing was clear: My mother had made mistakes. But she'd also seen something I was only just beginning to understand. And because of those truths, she'd had friends that she'd let down and promises she hadn't kept. Maybe lies were pieces of life we had to learn to accept. But maybe there was also a wisdom in her actions.

She'd run to protect herself, to protect me. That much I knew. And her past may have caught her in the end, but it had worked for a while, and I had nothing better to offer the Whigs. My silver could only hold off a gang of men for so long. I couldn't kill them all, nor did I want to be responsible for that level of bloodshed.

As Tayna parked the Humvee off the road, hidden beneath the brush, I said, "The Whigs should run."

He paused. The silence was heavy in the air around us as he weighed my words. His eyes narrowed on the hill as if he could see the farm in the distance through the dense forest.

"You're right," he said finally. "It's time."

The city had gotten too dangerous. The gangs were too close.

"Maybe Gideon's death was a mistake," I said, the admission fragile on my tongue. "Maybe we were safer with him alive."

"Don't say that." Tayna's voice turned sharp. "Don't you ever say that. I know exactly where your mind is going, and you're wrong. None of this is your fault. I wanted the Cards gone just as badly as you. All of the Whigs wanted to see the Cards fall. And now that they have, we have to contend with those repercussions. All of us."

"So we run?"

"We run," he agreed.

The silence felt heavy as we pulled our bags from the truck and ensured the Humvee was hidden.

I felt afraid but also clear.

And just like that, our dreams of days spent in bed became just that: A dream.

The dogs began barking as soon as we crested the final hill.

I sagged in relief at the sight of the peaceful houses and acres of tended land stretched out in front of us as we broke through the trees.

As soon as Ann and Dan realized who was walking toward the farm, their barks turned to whining. Dan trotted happily in our direction, but Ann made a beeline for Tayna, bounding onto her haunches and throwing her weight against him, nearly toppling him into the dirt and grass. He rested his forehead against hers as she whimpered and nuzzled at his chest.

"I missed you too, girl," he whispered.

Dan bounced beside me, and I tentatively reached down to rub his ear. "Don't ever do that to me." I jerked my chin in the direction of Ann. The giant dogs still made me wary, but Dan wasn't so bad. And he didn't seem to mind my company either. He just stared back up at me, his tongue lolling.

A few minutes after Dan and Ann sounded their alarm, people came into view. Grant and Alaric stepped out from the main house, with its white walls and blue shutters. Grant immediately collapsed his hands onto his knees as if crippled by relief at the sight of us. Meanwhile, Alaric took purposeful strides in our direction.

I resisted the urge to stop in my tracks.

The last time I'd spoken to the man who was most likely my father, it hadn't exactly been a pleasant conversation. The words we'd exchanged on the Tanks' ship left me feeling bitter and discarded. So I did the mature thing and ignored him, marching forward with my eyes on Grant. Dan stayed at my heels.

Alaric halted as if to say something, but then thought better of it and continued to Tayna.

As for me, I buried myself in Grant's arms. I was covered in sweat and grime from the hike, but it didn't matter. He hugged me back.

"Oh, darlin'," he sighed. "Let's get you some food, huh, and you can tell us everything."

I nodded into his shoulder, suddenly feeling like I might start crying.

Home.

This was home.

I allowed Grant to lead me inside, where his signature pot of stew steamed away in the kitchen. It was early yet for dinner, but some of the children sat in the living room, dotted among the blue furniture, reading. A few raced to greet us, gripping my hands, but Grant shooed them away.

"No books right now," he said. "You can talk to Lissa and Tayna later."

Some of the adults leaned against the counter, Clary among them, her red hair pulled in a low ponytail at the nape of her neck. She stood straighter as we walked into the kitchen. "You're back!"

"Just walked up from the hill." Tayna nodded.

"Where's Phenola?" I asked. "And Karadin?"

"We set them up in one of the houses at the edge of the field," Grant explained. "She and Calliope will be there now. They're settling in nicely to farm life. Phenola's a natural with the animals. Karadin's already got a clinic set up out of her room."

"Will you tell them we're back?" I asked Clary.

"Of course." She looked like she wanted to reach for us, to reach for Tayna, but didn't. She moved toward the door, then stopped. "You're safe?"

"Yes," Tayna told her. "But we'll need to talk to the council. After dinner, okay?"

"Okay." She left the room, the air thick with all the words we had to say. And Clary seemed to sense, as did the others, that something had changed.

It seemed an impossible task to tell them that we needed to leave. This was their home. It had always been their home.

I suddenly felt exhausted. It was the deep-in-my-bones exhaustion that I knew sleep wouldn't cure.

Alaric walked in behind me as Grant handed me a bowl of the stew.

He cleared his throat. "Lissa, I—"

The way he said my name, so earnest, made my chest tight.

"Food first, hun," Grant said softly. "She needs to eat, and then she might be ready to hear what you have to say."

"Fine," Alaric grumbled, settling for pouring himself a beer from a barreled tap on the counter.

Grant eyed him as if to say *I don't think a drink is going to help you.*

I didn't think I had the energy in me to fight him anymore anyway.

"There isn't really anything else to say." I shrugged. "I heard you on the ship."

"And you never thought to wonder where she gets her stubbornness?" Grant smirked over at Alaric, whose scowl only deepened.

"It's more that my past isn't the biggest priority right now." I swallowed down the lump in my throat, along with slow bites of food. I took in this place, the light spilling into the kitchen and the warm smells and comfort of the people around me. "The rumors in the town are that Dia is close to tracking us down." There was no use burying the lead. "We have to leave. We can't stay here."

Grant looked at Alaric, then back at me. "We've heard the rumors too. We have an emergency plan in place for a moment like this. We can camp in the hills, take supplies to survive, and hide out while a few people return in shifts to feed the livestock."

I'd thought about this. For the entire ride and the entire hike back to the farm, I'd thought about this.

"I'll make a deal with Olita. If I can convince her to offer the Whigs protection, we won't need months."

"Lissa, absolutely not," Tayna said immediately. "I thought we agreed on this. Gavril is insane. Those missing Silvers, the way they hid their people from us—we have no idea what's actually going on there."

I pulled the necklace from my pocket. "We can also bargain with this."

Grant's brow furrowed at the trinket. "Lissa, that's beautiful but—"

"Where the fuck did you get that?" Alaric demanded.

"Gideon gave it to me. Do you know why Olita was so set on having it that she had her Phantoms chase Tayna and me from the Veiled?"

Alaric sighed, leaning against the counter and rubbing his forehead. And then he took a long, long pull of his beer.

"Fuck, Queen—Lissa—dammit." He slammed his fist on the

counter, twisting to lean against the smooth surface as if in pain, his shoulders hunched in on themselves. "I don't even know where to start with this shit." He looked at Grant as if pleading with him for help.

But Grant just put up his hands. "I think the beginning is good."

"Fuck." Alaric stared down at the beer, took a breath, and then said, "Your mother..." He swallowed and shook his head. "Naveera. She belonged to Ishmael."

Belonged?

Alaric took another pull of his beer.

"She was his Queen. The first of the Queens. They... loved each other." Another swig. Then the words seemed to pour out of him. "Or, well, Ishmael loved her in whatever way Ishmael was capable of loving another human. He was a bastard and a controlling fucking bully, but Naveera was his weakness. And she was loyal to him. She was also obsessed with the secrets of the silver. She and Ishmael both believed that her abilities were some fucking special elite bullshit."

Grant put a hand on Alaric's arm that seemed to steady him.

He sighed. "They thought the silver, her abilities, were the next level of human evolution. They saw your mother as the key to unlocking humanity's fullest potential. Your mother was a scientist, did you know that?"

"Olita told me as much," I confirmed. "And I remember her having a lot of books that I didn't understand as a child. But..." I shook my head. "None of it makes sense."

He nodded. "I'm getting there. Your mother, she dedicated her life to studying and understanding the Silvers. Even before she was a Queen, she'd worked in a facility outside of the city, some kind of lab... She never gave many details. But she and Ishmael... fucking Ishmael... all this fucked up..."

Alaric again looked at Grant, who squeezed his arm in encouragement. It soothed Alaric, but he still said, "I think I need another drink."

"Lissa isn't going to judge you, Alaric," Grant said tenderly. "And she deserves to know where she came from."

Alaric took another deep breath, drinking the last of his beer, and then the words came. "Naveera and Ishmael wanted to create the next race of humanity. They wanted children together. They wanted their offspring to create a new monarchy, a new ruling class with these elite Silvers."

It wasn't about creating weapons.

It was about creating something bigger.

Alaric continued, "The thing was, genetics is about finding the perfect match. You have to have the right DNA to create the right sequence of chromosomes that will create the perfect karyotype—the perfect makeup of markers—that will result in these Silvers. Normally, it's just the genetic lottery, but Ishmael and Naveera wanted to force the evolution. The problem was, they weren't compatible. Your mother had the genes, of course, but Ishmael did not."

"And you...?" I asked.

Alaric sighed heavily, looking up at the ceiling and then nodding. "Olita... at the time, Olita was more powerful than even the Cards, and she controlled the majority of the Silver population. So Naveera and Ishmael made a deal. If Olita agreed to provide them with the other half of the DNA they needed, they would create two boys and two girls who would be perfectly genetically compatible to create a new generation of Silvers. Your mother and I would... create the girls. Olita and Ishmael would create the boys. Each would raise a pair. Together, the children would unite the city and begin a new age. But it wasn't..." Alaric was shaking his head again. "It was..."

"It's okay," Grant murmured.

And even I felt Alaric's pain, tears pricking at the back of my eyes as he spoke. The tightness in my chest only grew with his words. That was why Gavril had watched me at the Veiled. We'd been two creatures made for the same end, and he'd recognized me. And maybe he hadn't just felt familiar because he looked like Gideon. Maybe he felt familiar because I'd recognized him in some deep and primal way, too.

Alaric's words were strained with grief when he finally said, "It wasn't so simple. The boys came first. Two sons. Neither Silvers, but with the DNA sequencing that would be a perfect match."

"Gideon and Gavril," I breathed.

This wasn't random. None of this had been random.

"My mother is fucking insane," Tayna spat.

Alaric nodded. "But the girls were harder. It wasn't working. The compatibility. The chance. The risk. All of it was too great. But we spent years—nearly a decade. And there were so many pregnancies and so many losses. And I couldn't—" His voice broke, and even as he sputtered, clearing his throat, I could hear the raw pain in his words. "I couldn't do it."

I watched the memory break Alaric. I saw the agony etched into every line of his face as the loss flickered through his eyes like memories of each of those children.

"That was the journal." I realized, looking at Tayna. "The journal I found at Madam Cartenoth's shop was a record of these failed attempts." I thought of the dozens of entries. Page after page of notes and sequences and dates and tries. I thought of my mother, persevering through miscarriage after miscarriage. Some her own. Some those of Silvers who weren't given a true choice.

I couldn't imagine that suffering and loss. Especially not while sitting in this kitchen, the children of this farm just on the other side of the door, reading and learning together. They were so small and so fragile and so precious.

"Then how did I—what happened?" I managed to ask.

But Alaric just continued shaking his head.

"I ran," he finally admitted. "I'd had enough. It was too much. I destroyed as much of the work as I could, and then I ran, and I never looked back at that fucking place or those fucking people. Until rumors of you started swirling in the city. Until Tayna told me you were alive. Until you came to this fucking farm. I didn't want to believe you were my child. I'd run from it for so long. But fuck me if it isn't obvious. I wanted to play dumb, but it's so fucking obvious."

Tears spilled over my cheeks at his words. Hearing Alaric confirm them and accept me broke a piece in me. And maybe we weren't going to be the type to hug it out and spend hours gossiping about our lives, but this moment was enough for me. It was the confirmation of one secret about my past, at least.

"That necklace." Alaric pointed at the paved diamonds, which I'd laid out on the counter. "Those aren't diamonds. Ishmael had it made for your mother as a gift. Each stone holds a drop of her silver in the center. It's even more valuable than any precious stones. It's the code necessary to mimic the genetic sequence and create more Silvers like her. More Silvers like you, Lissa. And if Olita wants it, that means she's still experimenting. It means she's been holed up at the Veiled all this time, not licking her wounds in defeat, but planning her true takeover of this city. And it means we need to be prepared."

He was right.

And if Olita was still experimenting then it meant Gavril was right, too. Running away had never truly been an option. Not for me. Not when I might be the only person who could stop it.

42

Lissa

We met with the rest of the council after we'd eaten and showered. There wasn't time for rest. Not now. Clary had gathered them, and they were waiting to hear our plans for the farm.

I held Calliope, swaddled in my arms, with Phenola close beside me, as Tayna explained the plan. The small infant chewed on her fingers and burbled against my chest. The relief at seeing them had been enough to get me through this day. I wanted to hold them close for as long as I could.

Today, we would pack up our belongings. The children and their parents would go first. We'd have to leave in shifts. Between the Humvees and vehicles, we could take about thirty-eight people at a time, depending on the number of kids. Grant told us it would take a full day of travel to reach the camping point he and Alaric had scouted. Then a day for the trucks to return.

It was a risky plan. Even I could admit that. The roads were not safe. We'd learned that when we'd left the Cards. We'd need to pack as much food as we could, take as many of the livestock as possible, and salvage whatever crops were available. But it was summer. Most of the harvest was just beginning to blossom into the fruits and vegetables that sustained the community. It would all have to be abandoned.

The unease and uncertainty that had become a close friend pulsed low in my chest.

The first group would leave in an hour with Vinza and Phenola leading.

Once the council dispersed, I tucked Calliope back in Phenola's arms and followed Tayna to begin knocking on doors. Grant would oversee packing the food stores. Alaric would be on weapons and survival gear. Clary was organized the hiking parties. Phenola managed the livestock. Karadin was handling medical supplies.

Just over three hundred people were living on the farm, but the homes were spread out across the hills. Clary's family, for one, had lived in these fields for decades. Their house was on the other side of the planted rows, tucked back between the trees about a twenty-minute walk from the barn.

Maybe ten minutes into our trek through the woods, we heard it.

The dogs were barking in the distance.

And not warning yips.

They were alerting, loud and sharp and insistent.

Until the noise of their alarm was suddenly cut short. And a strange sort of silence hung in the air.

Tayna and I looked at each other.

Dread crept through my limbs.

And then we were sprinting, cutting through the stalks of wheat toward the main house. They raked at my arms and legs, but I barely felt the scratches.

Silver sparked at my fingers as we broke through the fields. Phenola stood on the front porch of her small cottage.

"Back inside!" I ordered quickly, and she obeyed as dark figures crested through the trees. Men in black. Dozens of them. They were dressed like the Cards, but Gideon wasn't leading this group. No, this was a different sort of gang. One that was more reckless and sinister.

Chaos spanned in front of me as I quickly clocked the scene.

Smoke was rising from one of the houses. Baskets of food were sprawled across the dirt where they'd fallen as people ran. Vinza was fighting a Card, landing a blow to his face. I saw a man dragging Rixa by her hair as she fought to stay upright. And that was where I started my sprint, not giving Tayna time to stop me.

The silver swelled in me, called to this fight.

With so many innocent Whigs dispersed, I'd have to use my abilities in more targeted, individual attacks.

And I didn't hesitate.

The man who held Rixa only glanced at me before my silver streamed from my fingers, the lightning of electricity throwing him backward as I barreled into him, until he sprawled in the field and didn't rise again.

It felt good, not wrong. I didn't hesitate. Not anymore. It was a release of the adrenaline I'd been bottling up inside.

"Are you hurt?" I asked Rixa, offering a hand to help her stand.

"Behind you!" she bellowed.

And I had just enough time to turn, catching a man's arm, burning his flesh before he could touch me. The man screamed in agony, falling to his knees as I refused to let go until I was sure he was singed to his bones. Even if he'd taken silver, it would require at least a few hours for his injuries to heal.

As soon as the man in front of me was down, I moved to the next, coming up behind one of the Cards who was laughing as he punched a man, a Whig I didn't know, repeatedly.

I shoved the Card roughly, giving the blow the bite of my silver so the Card was flying into the dirt.

Maybe I'd killed him.

I wanted to kill him.

I didn't pause to look.

"Lissa!" Tayna yelled for me over the fighting.

I looked up to see more men cresting the tree line.

There were too many.

And I knew why Tayna was trying to get my attention. We had to run. Our only option was to retreat.

A gun sounded, and I ducked on instinct, not knowing where the shot had come from.

Hands gripped my shoulders. My silver sparked, led by adrenaline, but the touch was familiar. Tayna. It was Tayna, and he shielded me in his embrace as more shots were fired, and we sprinted for cover.

As soon as we made it behind the trees, he was gripping my face. "Are you hurt?" His eyes were wild with panic.

"No," I breathed. "I'm okay."

But I didn't feel okay at all.

This couldn't be happening.

This couldn't...

"We have to go back out there and help them... We have to..."

I saw one of the men dragging a Silver boy away from the farm. He was one of the children I'd seen on my first day here, chasing butterflies through the field. He was often one of the children in the living room, reading.

Tayna tried to grab for me, but I wrenched free. "No!" I insisted. "We have to help them!"

"Lissa! They'll kill you!"

But I broke into a run, sprinting toward the boy, my silver already sparking.

It hit the Card squarely in the chest with such force that I knew I'd killed him. He crumpled to the ground. Not moving. His body lying at an unnatural angle.

I knelt and shielded the child. "Come here!"

His face was cut, silver blood streaked down his cheek, but the gash was already healing.

He started to cry.

"We're going to run to safety, okay?" I said. "Can I—"

Pain shattered through my shoulder.

The boy screamed, covering his head with his arm.

"Run!" I yelled at him as I looked down to find silver blood oozing from my arm. The pain had my vision blurring. I braced myself in the dirt as I tried to remember how to breathe. Each intake caused a stabbing sensation to ripple down my fingers and throughout my chest.

"Lissa!" Tayna screamed my name.

"Get the boy!" I tried to wheeze back. My voice was weak.

And then a blow knocked me into the dirt. A boot crushed the top of my chest as I scrambled to fight. But my silver sputtered, the pain taking all of my energy as I fought. I knew the bullet must still be lodged in my shoulder because it wasn't healing.

Dia loomed large above me against the afternoon sun.

"You." He grinned at me. "You're mine."

"F-fuck you," I bared my teeth at him as I struggled, but it was no use.

My silver was reduced to a spark.

He leveled a gun at my head. "Such a waste of silver," he sneered. "But you've always been more trouble than you're worth."

I turned my head to look at Tayna, knowing this was it. "I'm sorry," I wheezed at him in the distance. A tear leaked from the corner of my eye.

It was all I could offer.

I couldn't keep all my promises to him.

But hadn't I known I'd never be able to keep them?

The discharge of the gun rang in my ears. It was so close. And I felt the force slam into my body. Dirt sprayed into my nose and mouth.

I was choking.

The pain in my arm was so sharp.

But—

I hadn't been shot again.

It took me a moment to register what had happened.

A large body had blocked mine from the shot. A large body had taken the bullet instead, returning fire. The gun he'd fired at Dia now rolled from his hand into the grass.

Blood gurgled from Dia's mouth. He looked down at his chest. Even against his black clothes, I could see the dark stain of red spilling down his belly.

And as if he registered the wound in that moment too, he collapsed onto the dirt. His eyes were vacant and haunted with the realization of his own death.

Alaric rolled off me, where he'd pinned me with his body. A long groan left his lips.

"No, no, no." I moved to hover over him. There was so much blood on him I couldn't tell where he'd been hit.

"Lissa," he rasped as I yanked on the buttons of his shirt, trying to find the wound.

He'd blocked Dia's shot. He'd blocked the bullet from hitting me.

Tayna slid in the dirt beside me.

"He needs silver!" I screamed, hoping someone would hear, hoping someone would help.

I wiped at the wound in my arm, not even caring about the pain as I rubbed my silver against Alaric's lips.

He only choked up more blood. The red mixed with my blood as it dribbled down his chin.

"No," I said again. "No!"

"Bullet's... in there," Alaric managed to wheeze.

"Then we'll get it out." I began ripping at the fabric with my good hand, but he let out an agonized groan. "Tayna!"

My face was streaked with tears and blood.

And I realized Tayna was crying, too.

"No." The word fell from my lips in a long, pained moan.

I couldn't lose Alaric. Not now.

"It's o—kay," Alaric sputtered. "I was wrong, Queen. I was wrong."

"Please don't go." I gripped him desperately. "Please don't go before I get to have you as my dad."

His breathing became a hollowed spasm as I realized he was struggling to respond. The words were lost in the blood filling between his lips.

"We'll keep fighting," Tayna promised him next to me. "We'll remake this city. People will dream again. There will be more to life than gangs and silver. We'll make you proud. I promise we'll build it, and you'll be so, so proud."

And I realized the sounds of the hollowed spasms had stopped.

"I—" I sputtered. "I can—I can still bring him—back. I can bring —him back. Please, Tayna."

But a sound broke in front of us. It was a long howl of pain.

Not an animal.

Grant had come up from the forest where he must have been hiding with some of the others. Clary gripped him as Grant kept his eyes locked on Alaric as he stumbled in the dirt.

Alaric's eyes weren't tracking the sound at all.

He'd gone perfectly still.

Grant crawled to his husband, pressing his forehead into his shoulder as grief like I'd never heard filled the fields. Dan and Ann were with Grant, and they, too, joined in the cries. Their howls rose into the sky as if in a mournful prayer.

"We can—we can—" My words were lost to their pain.

The Cards were dispersing around us.

Now that Dia was dead, they were running. But the damage was done. Beyond the destroyed buildings and trampled fields, the farm was exposed. All those men running back to the city would know exactly where to find us.

"We can't stay here," Tayna said, even as Grant cradled Alaric gently in his lap, pulling his head into his chest. Even deep in his grief, Tayna was trying to give himself to others on this farm. I watched him swallow his tears. I watched him tuck the pain away into a deeper part of himself.

He stood, rolling his shoulders back.

"Tayna—" I reached for his hand. My fingers were streaked with red and silver blood. He pulled back from me, his eyes distant.

I felt the space between us as tears continued down my cheeks.

The Whigs, those still left, emerged from the ruins of the farm, coming to stand in the center of the field in a silent vigil for Alaric.

Through my blurred vision, I saw Phenola and Karadin, clutching each other.

This, *this* was what happened when we tried to run from the game.

This was what had happened to my mother. And now to Alaric.

"We have to leave this place," Tayna said, more loudly for those who had gathered around. "Pack what you can carry and start hiking. It's going to be long, and it's going to be hard, but we can do this. Make sure you have lots of water. More than you think you need."

Tayna wiped the tears from his face.

"Tayna—we can't—" My voice broke as I looked back at Grant in the dirt with his husband.

"We have to," he said.

And then, without another glance at Alaric or me, he walked away.

In the distance, past the smoke rising into the sky, I swore I saw a hawk swooping low before dipping below the trees.

43

Lissa

Grant stayed with Alaric, seated in the dirt and cradling his head in his lap, while Karadin pulled the bullet from my arm. It hadn't hit anything vital, which meant it didn't take as long to close.

Still, the wound wasn't all the way healed by the time I emerged back in front of the house. Grant still sat with Alaric, but someone had covered his body with a sheet.

Clary and some of the Whigs were digging a hole in the earth at the base of the large oak tree that shadowed the main house.

The sun cast long, golden rays against the fields as the afternoon waned.

We were dirty and tired and defeated.

The farm had been destroyed. It wasn't in the items but in the sanctuary of this place. The illusion was shattered.

"They would have burned it all to the ground if you hadn't been here," Clary said to me as I sat near the oak, watching them dig. "So many people would have died."

"It's because of me that they came here in the first place," I said, pulling at the tendrils of grass, wishing I could be digging instead. I wanted to help. And moving would give me an outlet for the anger and hurt. It was an endless well inside me.

"You know that's not true," Clary said, her eyes downcast as she focused her energy on her work, too. "They wanted Silvers. They saw the opportunity."

I thought about hunting down the Cards that had run after Dia was killed.

I could catch them.

I could kill them.

As much as I hated to admit it, Gavril had been right. I shouldn't hold myself back.

As it was, three of the Whig Silvers were missing. There were broken bones and scrapes among the remaining Whigs. I'd killed two of the Cards. Some of the men had dragged Dia off into the forest. The wolves would do the rest.

I wish he'd suffered more.

Alaric deserved more.

I wiped the tears and sweat from my face. Tayna paced in the distance, a rifle slung over his shoulder as he scanned the tree line, standing guard. I didn't think the Cards would return now that their leader had been killed. Not yet, at least. His pacing seemed like more of an agitated coping mechanism than anything else. He was restless and on edge. I knew he'd taken more silver after the attacks. He'd emerged from the house with the gun, and I'd just known. It was the look in his eyes. Gideon would sometimes get that manic look.

He had every right to do whatever he needed to do to cope. Alaric, after all, had been way more of a father to him than he'd ever been to me. I'd known Alaric was my father for only about a month. But Tayna had been with Alaric for nearly six years. They'd built this farm together with Grant.

Ann was close at Tayna's heels, stalking with him up and down the tree line as he paced. Dan, meanwhile, sat at a distance in the open space, looking out at the trees. He seemed to be waiting, as if expecting someone who would never return again.

That was how it felt, this grief. It was hollow and missing and empty. It was like trying to patch a million holes, yet never making a dent in the leak.

And it wasn't just for Alaric, though he had been at the center of this community. It was about the shattered illusion that anything safe remained in this world.

Clary was right. If I hadn't used my silver, it would have been a lot worse.

I'd avoided the suffering of others for so long. I'd been so afraid to use violence to protect those I loved. But now that it had come to that, I realized it wasn't frightening.

It liked it.

If this was how I could protect the people I cared about, I would do it. Again and again, I would do it.

The hole was a makeshift rectangle. The dirt was packed and rough this far from the fields, and Alaric was not a small man by any means. That thought only twisted my gut because the only thing left to do was to lay him there, cover the hole, and leave.

And that was it.

Gone.

A hand flashed in front of my face. "Let me help you up," Clary said, her eyes watery and her face slick with sweat. "It's time."

We wrapped Alaric in blankets and towels from the kitchen. It was the best we could do. Vinza and Clary picked wildflowers to tuck into the folds.

Alaric would have hated those. He would have thought it was a stupid and useless gesture but, well, that only made me feel like an asshole for thinking it. None of this was about Alaric, anymore.

Tayna stayed at the tree line.

Rixa tried to coax him into joining, but he'd shaken her off and continued his pacing.

I watched him in the distance now, wishing he would hold me, as Alaric was lifted, Grant still cradling his head. The Whigs all helped to keep his body level as he was gently placed in the grave.

Rixa and Vinza held Grant, who might not have stayed upright if it weren't for their support.

My arm finally felt okay enough that I helped to shovel until the final edges of the blanket were covered with soil.

Then I slipped from the group, wandering to Tayna.

"We shouldn't have stayed here this long," he said as I approached. "We're losing daylight."

"Hey." I reached for him, but he slipped from my grasp just as he'd done earlier, as if he couldn't stand to be touched.

I wouldn't be so easily swayed. "Tayna, look at me."

I grabbed for him again.

"Just leave it alone, Lissa," he snapped.

"Tayna." I pushed at him and was reminded of my first days on the farm, when Alaric had pushed me into training with him. He would have known exactly what to do with Tayna right now. So I pushed him again. "Look at me, Tay."

But instead, he kissed me, pressing his body into me so suddenly, forcing our mouths together, pulling me tightly against his chest. He gripped me to the point of pain. His lips were rough and desperate. My healing arm screamed.

I pried myself from his grasp, gripping his face.

I wanted to comfort him, but this wasn't comfort. This was desperation.

And I realized I didn't know how to be his anchor like he'd been mine.

And then he was crying, sinking to his knees in front of me and crying. He wrapped his arms around my thighs, burying his head into my belly until I could feel his tears soaking through my shirt.

I let out a breath I hadn't realized I was holding, tipping my head back to the sky, only to see that it was cast in a rainbow of pinks and oranges with the setting sun. The day was waning. This horrible fucking day would pass.

I threaded my fingers into Tayna's hair, running my nails through the thick chestnut strands, giving him time to grieve. We all needed time to grieve.

But there wasn't any time.

Now was the time to make hard choices to protect this community.

I may not be able to offer Tayna the same kind of grounding he'd giving me, but I could give him something else.

I just hoped, when all was said and done, he would understand.

44

Lissa

The council had decided to let everyone rest until daybreak. A watch rotation was scheduled through the night. The children were housed together in one of the back bunks with extra patrols.

Tayna wanted to spend the night at the tree line with the dogs, but I insisted he lay down, at least for a while.

Once we'd settled into the main house, he fell asleep quickly.

Just as I'd hoped he would as the silver wore off.

His heavy breaths filled the small space, his back facing me, curled in on himself. He hadn't held me, hadn't kissed me again. And I laid there, my eyes open and staring at the ceiling, until I was sure he wouldn't wake if I stirred.

Then, I gently unfolded myself from the sheets.

We'd packed our bags before getting into bed, including provisions, which meant there was nothing left for me to do but sling it over my shoulder as gently and as quietly as possible, before slipping from the room.

The house was still, though I wasn't sure anyone was sleeping particularly soundly tonight. Not after the day we'd had.

With the patrols manning the perimeter, I opted to slip out the side door and around the back. It would significantly increase my walking time, but it was important I made it out unnoticed.

I'd left a note for Tayna.

I begged him not to follow me.

I told him this was the only option to keep everyone safe.

I hadn't written that I'd loved him. It would have been unfair to say that, a contradiction of the choice I was making.

And this was the only path.

I knew that now.

It was always going to lead us apart. The quiet, peaceful life was not meant for me.

I saw that so clearly.

Alaric's sacrifice would mean nothing if we abandoned this place and instead spent our time hiding.

And the people who'd hurt us, well, they didn't deserve to keep ruling as they had for so long while we stayed in the shadows.

Dan whined softly at me as I broke out into the night.

"You can't come!" I hissed at him as he began loping next to me toward the trees. "Stay!"

But he just ran farther ahead as if this were all some kind of game, glancing back at me over his shoulder with his tongue lolling.

He was going to get me caught.

"Dan!" I hissed, my backpack bobbing at my shoulders as I darted past the guards on patrol and slipped into the forest. I lost sight of the dog as soon as I entered the cover of trees. The sun was just starting to lighten the horizon, and beneath the cover, it was still nearly black.

He blended into the pre-dawn darkness, shrouded by the brush.

I cursed but kept moving. If he wanted to get himself lost in these woods, then that was on him.

With a final glance over my shoulder, I made my way down the hill. The farm was quickly out of sight as I cut across to connect to the trail, sure of my footing as I made quick work descending toward where the Humvees were tucked out of sight of the road.

Was that how Dia had found us? Had the Cards spotted the vehicles somehow?

It occurred to me that maybe I would have walked all of this way, only to find them gone and stolen.

Not that it mattered. I couldn't go back. If the Humvees were gone, I'd go on foot. Though I'd only brought enough food and water for the daylong trip. But I could find my way. I'd been a street mouse once. I would become one again if it meant saving the people I cared about most in this world.

The sun began to peek through the trees by the time I made it down the hill.

As soon as I spotted the Humvees, I sagged in relief. Dan came bounding from the brush, hitting his head against my hand as if we were on some grand adventure.

"Dan!" The stupid dog had followed me all the way down the path. It was over a forty-minute walk downhill at the pace I'd been going, which meant it was well over three miles. There was no way I was dragging him back up. "You can't come with me!" I exclaimed, trying to shoo him away.

He sat in the dirt next to the passenger side of one of the trucks.

"No!" I insisted.

The way he stared up at me with an eyebrow cocked in certain judgment reminded me of Kenji and that night I had escaped from the Cards. Was that really only six months ago? My heart ached for the memory. How stupid and naive I'd been. Yet maybe I'd been better off as that girl.

The things Alaric had revealed about my mother flashed through my mind. I toyed with the diamond necklace I'd clasped around my neck before leaving the farm. Not diamonds. Each of the stones I thumbed contained a drop of my mother's blood.

A new race of elite humans.

If Gavril and Olita had their way, it seemed my mother would get her wish after all.

She might have loved me, but I refused to be a weapon in this game. No, I was so much more. And I still wasn't sure what had happened to make her run from Ishmael, but it didn't matter now. My choice was clear.

I wasn't a martyr.

No, I was a reckoning, and I chose this fate.

I slung my backpack into the back seat and then opened the passenger door.

"Fine," I said to Dan. "But if you end up as food for the Phantom's hawks, it's not my fault."

Dan seemed to roll his eyes at that as he jumped in the passenger seat and settled himself happily into the chair, leaning back with his tongue lolling and his eyes gleaming.

"And shut your mouth," I snapped. "Your breath smells like something dead."

He just licked his chops and continued huffing as I climbed into the driver's side and pulled out onto the road.

The sun was peeking over the horizon when I broke from the trees and onto the ocean-view path that led into the city. I took it in one final time, rolling down the windows and letting my hair billow in the wind.

Dan stuck his head out the window, too, and I let myself smile as the final ounces of my freedom faded with the waning darkness.

This was the choice I had to make, and I would not run from it.

Because now was not the time to burn the world.

Now was the time to smolder.

I would become the crackling ember, worming its way into the depths of this city, a small spark that no one would see coming. Not even him.

Until it was too late.

EPILOGUE

The Phantom

M other was pleased.

The plan was unfolding exactly as she'd hoped.

As if that wasn't good news enough, the doctor had confirmed three of the Silvers were with child. We hadn't seen that high of a rate yet. Even if we lost two, the odds were still in our favor of a healthy, live birth.

We were getting closer.

I could feel it in my bones.

This was destiny. *She* was my destiny. And she was so close to understanding everything,

The Phantoms standing guard at the door nodded to me as I approached and placed my palm on the scanner. The light flashed across my hand, turning green as the door clicked open.

The staircase descended into darkness, but small white lights lit along the floor as I stepped, an interesting little design Mother had installed some years back. It was old technology, powered by the sun instead of by silver. Humans were greedy, selfish creatures, but they were also clever when you backed them into a corner. The trick was to make them desperate enough to do whatever you asked.

Another door at the bottom of the staircase scanned my eyes, and I saw a flash of blue-black irises in the reflection as the laser tracked across my pupil. My eyes were one of the many traits I'd inherited from my father.

I'd never given the man much thought, really. He was a useless fool who'd had the right sequence of DNA. Beyond that, he was blubbering and stubborn, with no vision beyond collecting power.

The same could be said for my twin.

But Lissa, Lissa had surprised me. She reminded me of my mother in a lot of ways. She was naive. Untested. But I would change that.

A dark stone corridor stretched out before me, and archways that led to cavernous rooms jutted off on either side. Some of them were walled off with thick iron doors, and others were open and vacant.

I heard it then.

Clack, clack, clack.

It was loud down here, a booming echo of metal on metal that reverberated around the stone.

This was my playground. Mother once used it for her experiments when she needed to hide them from her husband after he grew suspicious of her intentions. Once he was out of the way, she built the hospital building to house her labs. She preferred the light. I craved the darkness.

My shoes clicked against the concrete floor, weathered and stained by water damage and, well, other kinds of damage over the years.

Clack, clack, clack.

The sound grated on my nerves, had me twisting my neck, the joints popping as I flexed my head left then right. I still wore my mask. As it was, I rarely removed it. I was not ashamed of my scars. On the contrary, I liked the way the taut skin stretched my grin. The white skin only heightened the contrast of my eyes.

What I didn't like was the attention the marks drew from passing gazes. I wanted to hide in the shadows, not become a spectacle for those at the Veiled. With my height and my stature, I stood out enough as it was. The mask allowed me a semblance of camouflage. The mask allowed me to move through my world as I pleased, just another face. Most at the Veiled weren't even aware I was the mother's son, and I preferred it that way, too.

They would know.

When the time was right, they would know.

I took a key from my pocket and slipped it into the padlock on the door, then pulled it open.

The clacking stopped.

Of course it did.

My neck still felt tight, a pressure building at the back of my head. I was growing impatient, restless. I craved a release. It was why I'd come down here, after all.

The room was dimly lit with only an overhead spotlight casting a white glow over a metal table bolted to the concrete in the center of the room.

The rows of instruments stretched around me on either side of the space—saws and knives and scalpels and wrenches. But there was also an assortment of medical equipment, including scissors and forceps, even heart rate monitors and shock pads. I'd learned exactly how to bring people to the edge only to pull them back.

The man strapped to the center of the table was naked. The silver I gave him regularly meant minimal scarring to his torso, but I'd cut away most of the tattoos that had been inked onto his flesh. That was one of my favorite games—to be the artist. But instead of painting his flesh, I was erasing it with precise cuts from my tools. It made him soft and new and mine to mold.

He didn't look at me as I entered the room. We'd been playing this game for weeks now, and I was starting to get bored. He barely even screamed anymore unless I got particularly nasty. He didn't talk either, but I attributed that more to the gag shoved in his mouth and secured around his head.

The only sound he made was the occasional pounding of the

metal cuffs around his wrists and ankles, which he beat in a steady rhythm against the table, hoping someone would hear and come rescue him.

No one would save him.

He was trapped in my web with all the other little insects in this place. He was mine to spin until I decided to finally rip off his head.

I'd cut him open dozens of times by now. I'd studied his insides, wondering if mine looked the same. I'd burned the same scars across the side of his face that he'd given to me, only to allow him to heal and do it again. I wanted to make sure he knew what it felt like, really remembered the sound of his cheek crackling in his ear as the skin melted away.

He'd grown thin. It hadn't taken long. The silver was its own sort of fuel, but the muscle he'd arrived with needed to be sustained with protein and fats and carbohydrates. None of which I'd given him. There was no use wasting precious resources beyond what was necessary. I liked watching him shrink. He was slowly shriveling in on himself. A wilted leaf that would unfurl with my games.

"Should we watch your heartbeat for a while today?" I mused, coming around to the side of the table, hovering over the top of him until I was staring into the blue-black eyes that were a reflection of my own. "Or maybe we should cut off that final tattoo on your shoulder. I've been saving that one for a special day. And I think it's a special day."

I pushed off the table, floating around the room as I chose my toys. A scalpel for carving, a torch for searing, and my favorite knife, a sharpened butcher's blade that I liked to have on hand in case I got the urge to stab something. Nothing was quite as satisfying as sinking a blade into the soft part of a stomach. If you hit it in just the right spot, it sank in like slicing through butter. I would hold my breath until it hit the spine.

I didn't like that he was ignoring me.

He stared up at the light like the spirits would float down and save him. I was the only spirit he needed to focus on right now. I was his god. I held his fate in my hands. And so, I grabbed a pair of pliers, too. We'd start with his fingernails today.

When I removed the first, his spine bowed off the table, and his neck strained. No sound escaped from his lips, but the sight of him writhing was enjoyable enough, so I took off another. And then a third. It was the fourth that finally drew a pained wheeze from his chest as he struggled to breathe.

The sound only ratcheted up my adrenaline, and I laughed as I took off the fifth. My god, did it bleed! My hands were slick with crimson. He choked on another breath, the sound so pathetic that I tossed the pliers aside, suddenly bored.

"Fine, fine," I sighed. "Have it your way."

To the main attraction, then. I reached for the torch, testing the flame with a few flicks of my finger. It was a smaller one, which allowed more precise burns. I didn't miss the flicker of fear across his face as the silver flame roared to life.

Yes.

The torch had the distinct smell of iron as it burned, and I inhaled the fumes deeply as I worked my way around the table and settled onto a rolling stool, crab-crawling my legs until I was settled right next to his arm, with the tattoo at eye level.

The door banged open, and the torch jerked in my arm, causing me to burn the flesh along the underside of his arm instead of the tattoo where I'd been aiming. He hissed low in pain, the exhale of breath the only thing that kept me from killing the Phantom standing in the door.

My nostrils flared as my eyes flicked up, not that he could see the annoyance from beneath my mask.

"You'd better have a really good reason for disrupting me," I seethed.

"I do, sir." The man grinned. He was one of the trusted ones who'd been by my mother's side for years. "Your mother sent word. The guards spotted a Humvee in the distance. It's heading this way."

She'd gotten my present then.

Standing, I set down the torch, my smile stretching until I could feel the scars taut along the left side of my face.

"It's your lucky day, Brother," I said. "Another more interesting toy has just arrived, and I'd much rather play with her."

Gideon bellowed, yelling deep from the pit of his stomach, thrashing wildly against the table. It was the first sound he'd made in weeks. And oh, *oh* it was so much sweeter than the burn.

"Don't worry." I patted his cheek as I moved toward the door. "When the time comes, you'll be key to making sure she understands."

His screams followed me out.

I was going to enjoy this game.

The waiting was over.

And this time, I wouldn't stay in the shadows. No, I would lure her into the darkness with me where she belonged.

END OF BOOK 2

ABOUT THE AUTHOR

Jess Stevens is a dark dystopian romance author living between Phoenix and Los Angeles.

Reckonings is the second book in the Silver Games series, which combines all of her favorite things: Women whose dreams shape the world. Men who would light the world on fire for said women. And fast-paced action that will keep you on your toes until the very end (toe-curling or otherwise).

When she's not writing, you can find Jess working in tech, getting out for a run, maybe baking some sourdough, and most definitely snuggling with her cocker spaniel pup.

For the latest updates, follow Jess on Tiktok or Instagram.

tiktok.com/@AuthorJessStevens

instagram.com/AuthorJessStevens